Charlotte Mary Yonge, Hentri Amédée L. L. Ideville

Memoirs of Marshal Bugeaud

from his private correspondence and original documents, 1784-1849 - Vol. 1

Charlotte Mary Yonge, Hentri Amédée L. L. Ideville

Memoirs of Marshal Bugeaud

from his private correspondence and original documents, 1784-1849 - Vol. 1

ISBN/EAN: 9783337378639

Printed in Europe, USA, Canada, Australia, Japan

Cover: Foto ©Andreas Hilbeck / pixelio.de

More available books at **www.hansebooks.com**

MEMOIRS

OF

MARSHAL BUGEAUD

FROM HIS PRIVATE CORRESPONDENCE AND ORIGINAL DOCUMENTS,

1784–1849.

BY

THE COUNT H. D'IDEVILLE,

Late Prefect of Algiers.

EDITED, FROM THE FRENCH,

BY

CHARLOTTE M. YONGE,

AUTHOR OF 'THE HEIR OF REDCLYFFE,' ETC.

IN TWO VOLUMES.

VOL. I.

LONDON:
HURST AND BLACKETT, PUBLISHERS,
13 GREAT MARLBOROUGH STREET.
1884.

LONDON:
PRINTED BY STRANGEWAYS AND SONS,
Tower Street, Upper St. Martin's Lane.

LONDON:
PRINTED BY STRANGEWAYS AND SONS,
Tower Street, Upper St. Martin's Lane.

EDITOR'S PREFACE.

THE original work of M. d'Ideville extends to three large volumes, and where the whole work is so interesting it has been a matter of considerable difficulty to reduce it in length without sacrificing important passages. As is well said by a writer in the *Quarterly Review*, No. 312, p. 452, from whose article we have been kindly permitted to quote, 'Marshal Bugeaud, Duke of Isly, was certainly a more remarkable man than nine out of ten who have been the idol of a biographer, and his career is fertile in episodes or incidents characteristic of the times, and throwing light on history.' The same article contains an extract from General Trochu's *L'Armée Française in* 1867, so interesting to Englishmen that it may well be added to the Marshal's life :—' There is a highly-interesting communication from him, based on his Peninsular experience, to General Trochu, in which he gives a vivid description of the contrasted bearing of British and French soldiers in the field. Arrived at a thousand yards from the English line, our soldiers began exchanging their ideas in agitation, and hastening their march so that the ranks began to waver. The English, silent, with grounded* arms, presented, in

---

* Probably 'ordered.'

their impassable immovability, the aspect of a long red wall; an imposing aspect that never failed to impress the novices. Soon, the distances becoming less, repeated cries of " Vive l'Empereur! En avant! A la baïonnette!" sounded from our ranks; the shakos were raised on the muzzles of the muskets, the march became a run, the ranks got mixed, the agitation became tumult; many fired as they marched. The English line, still silent and motionless, with arms still grounded, even when we were not more than 300 yards off, seemed not to be aware of the storm about to burst upon it. . . . .

' At this moment of painful expectation. the English wall moved. They were making ready. An indefinable impression fixed to the spot a good many of our soldiers, who began an uncertain fire. That of the enemy, concentrated and precise, was crushing. Decimated, we fell back, seeking to recover our equilibrium; and then three formidable hurrahs broke the silence of our adversaries. At the third they were on us, pressing our disorderly retreat.'

As the expedition of La Pérouse, alluded to in pages 2 and 5, took place in 1787, there seems some difficulty in the allusions to it. The Marshal's uncle must be the person named.

The war in Algiers and the colonisation, in which the Marshal was the central figure, have, we think, never been so fully set before the English reader in all their details, both of severity and excuses to be made for such severity, as in these volumes.

C. M. YONGE.

May, 1884.

THE AUTHOR'S PREFACE.

NEXT after the greatest military personage of the century, Napoleon I., the most perfect is Marshal Bugeaud. Our misfortunes and our faults have at the present time placed us in such a position among the powers of Europe, that it appears desirable to bring into notice the character of one of the most famous soldiers of France, who was also one of her best citizens.

The Marshal's family are justly proud of their hero, and have a good ground for comfort and pride in the thought that our foes themselves have a respectful remembrance of the victor of Isly, the conqueror and organizer of our possessions in Africa. In the month of September, 1870, a young Frenchman, severely wounded in action, was at death's door in the hospital at Haguenau. His mother was sent for in haste, and arrived in time to rescue her beloved from death. When the staff-officers learned that this noble woman, the widow of a general officer, was daughter to Marshal Bugeaud, they all bowed their heads. The Comtesse Feray tells us, ' It was a great pleasure to me to hear from the mouths of Prussian officers an enthusiastic recital of my father's campaigns, and to see the respect paid to his name. Most of his books, his instructions to the soldier, are translated into German, used in the military schools, and, must it be acknowledged, possibly more popular beyond the Rhine than in their own country.'

The work we have undertaken is not so much an individual creation as the orderly arrangement of precious documents, for which we are indebted to the family and friends of Marshal Bugeaud, especially his two daughters. For the purposes of our work, the Comtesse Feray has been good enough to put together her earliest recollections, and dictate to us invaluable notes full of living pictures of the scenes that cradled her infancy. Thanks to this filial piety we have been able in a sort of way to be witnesses of the Marshal's life during his earlier years, spent in such homely style at the ancient dwelling of the family, and to reproduce with exactitude this simple provincial home at the beginning of the Revolution, and follow step by step the soldier-hero through the episodes of his life.

The absorbing interest attaching to the remembrances of the Comtesse Feray, with their exquisite simplicity and devotion, is enhanced by the attractions of the Marshal's letters, a treasure affectionately preserved in the family, that we have the good fortune to be the first to reveal to the public, thanks to the kindness of M. Robert Gasson-Bugeaud d'Isly, the Marshal's eldest grandson. This correspondence, too often interrupted, will be united by descriptions and historical explanations that will enable us to fill up the too extensive gaps. In every line of these letters stands forth the whole character of the man. They display a powerful individuality, but always simple and loyal. Everywhere is he found the same, from the familiar letters where the young ' vélite' of the Guard tells his sisters about garrison miseries and adventures, to the stirring recitals he gives them of the battle of Austerlitz or the siege of Lerida. Afterwards there are the notes written to the Marshal's wife from a tent, on the eve of an engagement, in the wilds of Kabylia. In them the hero-father pours out his expressions of affection concerning his children and their future, not forgetting to add farming directions for Durantie, the oats to be sown in good season, and old trees to be grubbed before winter. His confidences to his son-in-law, his wife, or daughters, are sometimes very smart; men and events are judged by him with remarkable correctness and brevity. He paints a portrait in three lines, and his opinions given after 1848 about everyone of the African generals, most of whom were in the course of events called upon to undertake the government of the colony, will be read with active curiosity.

All the important events in which the Marshal was concerned, his first campaigns, his feats of arms, his sojourn at Blaye, his parliamentary contests, the difficulties of all kinds he had to surmount in Africa, his relations with the King and Ministers, his position in 1848, are illustrated by his private correspondence, by his daughter's notes, and the unpublished documents placed at our disposal.

HENRY D'IDEVILLE.

CONTENTS

OF

THE FIRST VOLUME.

CHAPTER I.

Birth of Thomas-Robert Bugeaud de la Piconnerie, October, 1784—His Family—Genealogy—The Marshal's Childhood—The Revolution—The Prison of Limoges—Death of the Marquise de la Piconnerie—The old Gentleman and his eldest Son—The Aunts and the Uncle—Escape from Limoges—The Château of La Durantie—Description of the old House—Rustic Education of Thomas Bugeaud—Wedding Dress—Severity of the Father—The Chase by Moonlight.

CHAPTER II.

Thomas Bugeaud applies for a place as a Clerk in the Ironworks of M. Festugières—His Enlistment—Barrack Life—Passion for Study—First Duel—Regrets for the Country—Laundresses' Ball at Fontainebleau—Education of a Soldier of Fortune—Letter of Trochu on the Marshal's Failings.

CHAPTER III.

Letters of Thomas Bugeaud to his Sister Phillis—His Friend Lamothe—He gains the Commandant's favour—Disgust at Army Life—Reviewed by the Emperor—Interview of Napoleon and Pope Pius VII.—The Coronation—March to Courbevoie—Almost sent to Italy—His wish to enter the Military School.

CHAPTER IV.

Leaving Courbevoie—Preparations of the Army of Invasion—Account of a Naval Combat—The English and Dutch—Failure of the Emperor's Plans.

CHAPTER V.

Letters of Thomas Bugeaud during the Campaign in Germany, 1805-Horrors of War — Arrival at Vienna — Description of the City and Suburbs — Hope of Peace—Account of the Battle of Austerlitz, Dec. 2, 1805 — Enthusiasm at the Victory—Interview of the two Emperors—Napoleon's Proclamation—First Promotion—Return to France—Fresh Start for Germany.

CHAPTER VI.

Campaign in Poland, 1806—Pursuit of the Russians—Action of Pultusk — Bugeaud wounded in the Leg— Made Lieutenant, December, 1806 —Stay at Warsaw—Polish Ladies—Return to France.

CHAPTER VII.

Thomas Bugeaud gets Six Months' Leave — He sends in his Resignation to the Minister, but his Sisters keep back his Letter— He is sent to Spain —Insurrection at Madrid—A Gallant Adventure—Siege and Capture of Saragossa—He is made Captain—Appreciation of the situation of the Army in Spain—Departure from Saragossa—Engagements of Maria and Balahite—His Promotion to the rank of Commandant.

CHAPTER VIII.

Siege of Lerida, 1810—Attitude of the Spaniards towards their Conquerors—Combats of Tivisa—Thomas Bugeaud despairs of Promotion—Aspirations for Return—The Ninth Light—Patriotic Silence about the Army in the North of Spain—Leaving Spain.

CHAPTER IX.

Napoleon I.'s Proclamation — His Abdication—Thomas Bugeaud made Colonel and sent to Orleans—A Legitimist Song of Colonel Bugeaud—His attitude during the Hundred Days—Appreciation of the Count de Chambord.

CHAPTER X.

Colonel Bugeaud with the Army of the Alps—Combat of St. Pierre d'Albigny, when he took Prisoners two French émigrés—Brilliant Combat of Conflans-l'Hopital—The Second Restoration—Colonel Bugeaud is reduced.

CHAPTER XXII.

THE BROSSARD TRIAL (1838-1839) . . . 270

Appreciation of the Treaty—The Jew, Ben Durand—Secret Article—Re-victualling Tlemcen—General de Brossard's Complicity—Court-Martial—Bugeaud's Deposition—Events of the Trial—De Brossard's Conviction—Revision—Acquittal—Correspondence with M. Boinvilliers—Letter to Gardère—Bugeaud Commanding on the Northern Frontier, 1839—Lille—Re-elected for Excideuil—Correspondence with the Duke of Orleans.

CHAPTER XXIII.

SYSTEM OF WAR IN AFRICA (1840) . . . 295

General Bugeaud in Parliament—Comments on the Treaty—The General's Avowal—Discussion of the Address—Paragraph on Algeria—Dangers of restricted Occupation—Absolute Dominion, Subjugation of the Country—System of War and Colonization—Change of Cabinet—Bugeaud's Inquiries of the Cabinet—Public Opinion selects General Bugeaud as Governor of Algeria.

CHAPTER XXIV.

POLITICAL ORATOR (1831–40) 306

Character of Bugeaud's Eloquence—Originality, Patriotism, and Good Sense — Poland — Colonisation of France — Agricultural Societies—Bugeaud, Protectionist — Wool — Importation of Horses — Cattle — The Roads of Excideuil—Hatred of the Opposition—Military Disorganization—No Universal Suffrage—Political Crimes—Amnesties—The Press.

CHAPTER XXV.

MILITARY ORATOR 325

Care for the Non-commissioned Officer—Defends Military Pay, 1831—Peck of Oats—Officers' Pay, 1835—Generals' Widows—Colonel Combes—Confirmation of rank under the Empire—Chamber of Peers—Generals as Deputies—The War of Ambuscades—The Good Soldier—Prophecy of the War of 1870—Fortifications of Paris—Pensions—Civil element in Committees.

CHAPTER XXVI.

GOVERNOR-GENERAL (1841) 342

Soult and Guizot Ministry—Marshal Valée's Retirement—Bugeaud's Appointment—Portrait by Guizot—Arrival at Algiers—Proclamations to the People and the Army—Sketch of Algiers by Veuillot—State of the Provinces—Strength of the Forces—Bugeaud's New System—His Lieutenants—Coming of the Duke d'Aumale—Correspondence with the Princes.

MEMOIRS

OF

MARSHAL BUGEAUD.

CHAPTER I.

BIRTH AND CHILDHOOD.

Birth of Thomas-Robert Bugeaud de la Piconnerie, October, 1784—His Family—
Genealogy—The Marshal's Childhood—The Revolution—The Prison of Limoges
—Death of the Marquise de La Piconnerie—The old Gentleman and his eldest
Son—The Aunts and the Uncle—Escape from Limoges—The Château of La
Durantie—Description of the old House—Rustic Education of Thomas Bugeaud
—Wedding Dress—Severity of the Father—The Chase by Moonlight.

BORN at Limoges, October 15, 1784; died at Paris,
June 10, 1849, Thomas-Robert Bugeaud de la
Piconnerie, Duke d'Isly, Marshal of France, was the
son of a gentleman of Périgord, Jean-Ambroise
Bugeaud, noble, Marquis de la Piconnerie, and of
Françoise de Sutton de Clonard, a member of an Irish
family which settled in France with James II. According to a letter addressed to the Editor of the
Tribune, in 1844, the Marshal ironically traced his
genealogy to a rather plebeian source. 'My grandfather,' he there says, ' was a smith; with his sturdy
arms, and by scorching his own eyes and hands, he
gained a fortune, that my father, an idle aristocrat,
employed in a spirited manner.' Two genuine

documents, the register of the Marshal's birth, and his father's marriage contract, establish his paternity with precision.

Of the marriage of Jean-Ambroise Bugeaud de la Piconnerie with Mdlle. de Clonard were born fourteen children, of whom seven lived :

1. Patrice de la Piconnerie.

2. Ambroise de la Piconnerie.

3. Thomassine de la Piconnerie, married the Vicomte d'Orthez.

4. Phillis de la Piconnerie, married M. de Puyssegenez. de Lignac.

5. Hélène de la Piconnerie, married M. Serinensan.

6. Antoinette de la Piconnerie, married M. de St. Germain.

7. Thomas-Robert Bugeaud de la Piconnerie, duke d'Isly.

Patrice Bugeaud, the eldest brother of the Marshal, had married Mdlle. Durand d'Auberoche, daughter of the Vicomte d'Auberoche, of a very ancient family of Périgord.

Ambroise de la Piconnerie, an officer like his elder brother Patrice, served in the army of the Princes during the emigration. He lost his life by shipwreck on the way to India with his regiment.

The Vicomte d'Orthez, husband of Thomassine, was descended in direct line from the Count d'Orthez, Governor of Bayonne, who refused to have the Protestants murdered on the occasion of the Saint Bartholomew.

A Sutton de Clonard, brother of Madame de la Piconnerie, the Marshal's mother, was lost with La Peyrouse, being second in command.

Lastly, Thomas Bugeaud, Marshal of France,

married in 1818 Mdlle. de Lafaye.* The Marshal left two daughters and a son; the elder married to M. Gasson; the younger married General Count Feray, who died in 1870. The Marshal's only son, Charles, Duke d'Isly, married Mdlle. C. de Saint Paul, and died childless in 1868. All the grandchildren of Marshal Bugeaud are authorised to bear his name.

Although several members of his family had emigrated in the years following 1789, the Marquis de la Piconnerie, after his release from the prison at Limoges, did not think of leaving France. The Marshal's childhood was far from being happy. His father, an old gentleman, harsh and selfish, ruined by the Revolution, had banished his daughters and little son to La Durantie, while he continued to reside at Limoges with his eldest son Patrice, upon whom he concentrated all his affection. The notes of the Comtesse Feray upon her father's childhood must be given without alteration :

My father was born at Limoges, in a hotel of the Rue de la Cruche-d'Or, in old Limoges, once the aristocratic quarter. A marble tablet marks the house, which is now turned into a shop.

He was the fourteenth child of the Marquis de la Piconnerie. Being intended for the Church, he entered into the world with the title of Monsieur l'Abbé. At six years old he was removed from his nurse's care, a fine child; his father ordered a handsome dress for him, and sent him to school, where he made rapid progress.

One year later, in 1791, all the circumstances of the family were changed; the Revolution had broken out; my grandfather, grandmother, and their youngest daughter, Antoinette, were in prison; their elder sons had emigrated. Thomassine, my eldest aunt, was married to the Count d'Orthez; and the younger children were left alone, and were obliged to work in order to support their imprisoned parents. Phillis, then aged sixteen, and her sister Hélène,

---

* Mme. La Maréchale Bugeaud, Duchesse d'Isly, Elizabeth Jouffre de Lafaye, was the daughter of Leonard Jouffre, Seigneur de Lafaye, and Catherine Aubarbier de Manègre. Her mother was of the Marquessac family, one of the oldest of the nobility of Périgord.

without a moment's hesitation, began to make shirts from morning till night. Their brother, who was not yet eight years old, cooked, ran errands, and took home the work when it was finished.

My aunt Phillis was frequently summoned to appear before the revolutionary tribunal, as her beauty had made an impression upon the monsters. Therefore she always took her little brother with her as a companion; and both of them showed so much quiet courage, that they managed to gain the respect of these men, and thus, thanks to them, the condemnation of their parents was delayed. However, notwithstanding their efforts, the sentence had been pronounced, and the day fixed for the execution of M. and Mdme. de la Piconnerie, when the news of Robespierre's death saved them from the scaffold.

When my grandmother was released from prison, she made her youngest son resume his studies. We have been told that a few days before the school prize-giving she had a vision at night. Her father and mother, the Count and Countess de Clonard, drew the curtains of her bed, took her by the hand, and said, 'Daughter, prepare to come and join us in heaven; you will die in four days' time.' The very hour was fixed. My grandmother, without any weakness, performed all her Christian duties, and, after having been a spectator of her little Thomas's success, went home, and died on the day and at the hour named by the phantoms.

My grandfather, whose fortune was but small, had been nearly ruined by the Revolution. He sent his daughters to the Château of La Durantie, and stayed at Limoges with his eldest son Patrice, the only one about whom he ever concerned himself. As for the youngest born, he never greatly cared for him. In times gone by, such was often the fate of younger sons.

My grandfather was a man with a terrible temper, and is still the theme of legend in that part of the country. Our country-folk are convinced that long after his death he walked the woods of Durantie by night, followed by a fierce pack of hounds and a troop of gentlemen. These honest folk declare that they can hear his voice roaring like thunder beneath the branches of the forest, and say that his great white horse, with fiery red eyes, can be seen from far by the light of the moon. It is to be hoped that our grandfather now rests in peace.

Patrice, like his father, was proud and violent; otherwise both of them had their amiable moments. Phillis, the eldest (unmarried) sister, was as beautiful as a statue, with an expression full of high spirit, yet of calmness. She would have been remarkable in the loftiest station, but her views were bounded by doing good, or by glorying in her brother Thomas, whom she had brought-up, and whom she almost worshipped.

Hélène, with lovely features and golden locks, had a feminine style of beauty; her ready and gracious intelligence adapted itself to all the circumstances and needs of life. The saying of her in the family was, ' Fit for the king's court or the poultry-court.'

Antoinette was small and plain, but very good. Her sparkling wit, her vivacity, and astonishing memory, were the delight of the family, and her death left a great gap among us.

Ambroise, a naval officer, whom his sisters often compared to my father, died at twenty-five in the expedition of La Peyrouse.*

The Château de la Durantie, near de la Nouaille, Dordogne, was in old times inhabited by my grandfather's brothers, priests or old bachelors, and his sisters, old spinsters, and nuns driven from the Convents of Périgueux and Limoges during the tempest of the Revolution.

My grandfather had twenty-three brothers and sisters. His mother, childless for five years, went on pilgrimage to the celebrated Virgin of Rocamadour in Lot. It is to be observed that her prayer was more than granted.

My father was attended to by no one at Limoges, for the Marquis and Patrice hardly ever spoke to him at all. He had been taken away from school after his mother's death, and was learning scarcely anything. He was lonely and felt forsaken by every one, but he endured his privations with resignation.

But one day, in despair at the state of isolation in which he was kept, he left a note for his father to say that he had gone to his sisters, obtained a bit of bread from the servants, and when evening came quitted Limoges. He walked all night, went the whole way on foot (eight-and-forty miles), reached La Durantie worn out, but overjoyed to see his sisters: he was then thirteen years old.

This poor habitation bore the name of the Château de la Durantie, no doubt traditionally, in remembrance of the old homes of the family. In remote ages there had been a feudal castle at La Piconnerie, a few hundred yards away from La Durantie, supposed to have been destroyed during the English invasion, but I am not sure enough of the fact to assert it. The only thing that I am certain of is, that it did exist; even in 1840 I saw a tower in the middle of the farm. The plan of this manor is among the documents in the possession of our cousin, the Marquis de la Piconnerie. The family had lived in the Château de la Gandumas,† and at

---

* See ante, p. 2.—ED.

† The Château de la Gandumas, which is still in existence, was the family property. It was there that the Marshal's grandfather had established some con-

La Durantie for infinite ages. After my grandfather it was only called Old Durantie. It was a long, narrow house, with an out-building attached to it, equally long and narrow, consisting of a ground-floor and loft. A building opposite completed a large square court, enclosed towards the road by a wooden paling.

The house was entered by a low door studded with great nails, leading into a vestibule paved with little pebbles. Opposite was the granary door, with a little hole for the cats in the bottom. Inside this door an almost perpendicular stair led to the wheat-store. On the right of the vestibule, another door opened into a great kitchen also pitched with pebbles; in the middle was a very large table with benches round it: on the wall to the right was a beautifully carved wooden cupboard, reaching to the ceiling, which had once contained the pewter vessels with the family arms. There was a soup stove in a corner; then some immense provision chests, black with age. The whole of one side of the old kitchen was taken up by a wide and deep fire-place. This was the foresters' favourite place, where they dried themselves of an evening by the flames of enormous faggots, with their dogs between their knees. A window looking on the court gave a view of anything that was going on. To the right of the vestibule was the parlour, or rather the common hall. This had what I cannot call a floor, but a sort of badly jointed planking. A sideboard took up the whole of one wall; and a glazed door opening to the garden made this room tolerably cheerful in summer. A window in front looked out on the court; at the back was a high chimney-piece with some pretence at panelling. As ornaments upon it in summer, great bunches of daffodils and honeysuckle were displayed in the old earthenware vases; in winter a row of enormous beetroots, some fine apples, and little sheaves of ears of curious sorts of corn. In the middle of the room stood a long thick table of wax-polished walnut, some chairs, and two arm-chairs of straw. These two arm-chairs represented all the comfort of the habitation.

To the right of the fireplace was the room of the head of the family; to the left a small door opening on a long and narrow corridor that led to three large rooms in the back building. The lower one was reached by a passage open to all the winds of heaven. It was the most elegant, there was a looking-glass above the chimney-piece; and the two grand old beds, hung with magnificent silk drapery, probably a remnant of the furniture

---

siderable iron-works, which are still in a state of activity. Thanks to this business the grandfather was able to bring up his twenty-three children. It was in allusion to him that Marshal Bugeaud said, 'My grandfather was a smith.'

from Limoges, were not in harmony with the rustic simplicity of the dwelling.

On the other side of the quadrangle a large building contained the cellar, the workshops of all sorts, and the corn-stores. The well, surrounded by a stone trough for watering the cattle, was opposite the house door. Lastly, the court was full of fowls, ducks, and turkeys, not forgetting the great manure-heap. And this was the dwelling where my father's youth was passed in company with his sisters.

Of his uncles, several had gone to America to seek their fortune, others had remained under the headship of the second brother, M. de la Durantie. Two or three sisters were married. Mdlles. de Saint Martin and des Places had remained in the nest, with nothing but their spinning-wheels to amuse them. At Durantie my father lived like Robinson Crusoe ; rising at dawn to go out to the chase, he came back at dinner-time in triumph, almost always bringing back some game, as an addition to the family fare, which, as usual, was chiefly composed of chestnuts. When resting he worked with his sisters, who taught him, poor girls, all that they recollected of their learning in the convent. They learnt Molière and Racine by heart together, and then acted the scenes, giving each other the cue. Forty years afterwards, my father and one of my aunts gave us a recitation of a dialogue of Molière, which they had repeated in their youth, and did not miss a single word. After lessons the little brother went off to fish, enlisting the little country boys of his own age in his wanderings. They all remained faithful to him, and most of them died as farmers upon the property. He did not trouble himself much about meals ; a fire of dead branches was soon lighted to cook chestnuts or potatoes from the fields, or he would seek the hospitality of the farmhouses, where the little master was universally known and beloved. My father has told me that he had no leather shoes ; wooden ones were very soon worn out in this active life, so he invented a way of making sandals out of cherry bark and string, which were a complete success. His sisters had no shoes, and spent months without going out.

My father was in great trouble at an invitation to a wedding at a house in the neighbourhood, where there were to be all the amusements of that good old time. It was impossible to attend in his dress of patched grey cloth. Just as, with swelling heart, he was about to send a refusal, he remembered he had seen, in an old chest in the loft, the dress that an ancestor had worn at the Court of Louis XV. With his sisters' help, he brushed the dust off the suit, and the dear girls soon contrived to attire their little brother. He had never seen himself so fine in his life, and off he went to the much-desired feast, where he danced three days with a success that made him very proud.

At La Durantie the quiet life of the girls and their little brother was only occasionally interrupted by the rare visits of my grandfather and uncle Patrice. Everything trembled before the lord and master. His children were never allowed to speak to him unless he interrogated them. One day my grandfather was giving an order to a servant about some farming matter. My father, then fifteen, thoughtlessly allowed himself to make a remark. The marquis in a fury lifted a great stick he had in his hand against the boy. My father, in a fright at his audacity, and foreseeing the results of the paternal anger, jumped out of his great wooden shoes and ran away to avoid the blow. My grandfather stumbled over his son's heavy foot-gear and the club gave the wall a violent blow.

My father had tears in his eyes when he told us of our grandfather's harshness. 'Never,' has he said, 'did he once give me a single caress, and I never remember his giving me a single kiss. I do delight to caress you, my dear children, and therefore I lavish upon you the tenderness that was so much missed by my loving heart.' Poor father!

After his mother's death the boy met with no affection save from his sisters, who loved him like mothers. However, he easily consoled himself, thanks to his passion for the chase and for life in the open air. One winter night, in beautiful moonlight, he was on the watch for a fox not far from the house, and seeing in the wood a whole flight of woodcocks waddling over the hardened snow he thought the sight so charming that he ran to the house, and, notwithstanding the cold, made his sisters get out of bed to partake of these sportsman's pleasures.

CHAPTER II.

PRIVATE SOLDIER (1804).

However, time went on. Thomas Bugeaud was nearly eighteen years old. Country life, sport, and study, were no longer enough for him. He felt the necessity of making a future. Considering that he had no patron to advance him in the world, and being unwilling to leave his own country, he applied for a clerk's desk to M. Festugières, who had married the elder sister of Mdlle. Elisabeth de Lafaye, who afterwards became his wife. M. Festugières was owner of some considerable ironworks in Périgord. He had a long interview with the young man, and told him : 'My boy, I do not want a gentleman as clerk, it is not a situation for you ; your ability should raise you into high rank in the army. Go into it since you are not well off.' Thomas, in despair, went home to embrace his sisters, started for Limoges, and in a couple of days his lot as a soldier was fixed.

The following letter was written by Thomas Bugeaud a short time before his enlistment. His hesitation shows how little taste he had for a wandering life of adventure :—

To Mdlle. Phillis Bugeaud de la Piconnerie, at Bordeaux.

La Durantie, May, 1804.

My Dear.—I did not answer your last letter immediately, because I was waiting for Patrice to ask his advice, and come to a decision one way or other. After we had both reached the conclusion that the best course to adopt for the present is what you have been kind enough to suggest, I ceased to hesitate.

I considered that, perhaps, in fourteen or fifteen months' time I might be obliged to go, and then so much time would be lost. If in three or four years I have no taste for a military career, I could take my discharge, and then be able to enter another profession. So, my dear Phillis, I have made my decision, and expect to go away about Easter. Will you be kind enough to send me the letter of introduction you promised, and also tell me all you think about my intention?

Though you say so, my dear, I do not think I can *walk alone*. I am not so conceited yet. You cannot know much of me if you think that I did not want your advice. No, my dear, I never meant to say so. I want it—a great deal of it. I only said that you could not make me see blue black, and black blue. Anyhow, you have always the same right over my heart and mind.

I am very sorry that I have not the means to come and see you before I go away. But you know, my dear, that I have hardly any money. I have already spent nearly all my year's allowance on the necessary outfit and in my illness. I am not quite well yet, and have returns of fever. I hope to be quite cured by the first fine weather, and to be able to start.

How I wish Bordeaux was on my road, or not far from it. How delighted I should be to go and wish you good-bye; but, alas! you are in the south and I am in the north.

However, I hope not to be parted from you for ever, and reckon upon presenting you in a few years with a brother worthy of you.

No doubt you think my writing very bad. Since I had the fever, I have quite lost the habit of writing, and must form my hand again.

Adieu, my love. Answer me at once. Kiss Helen and Edward, and give them a million compliments for me.

Do not omit to give my remembrances to my aunt* and cousins.

Your affectionate brother,

Thomas.

---

* Madame Mac-Karthy, sister of the Marquise Bugeaud de la Piconnerie.

It is to his elder sister Phillis, his faithful and devoted confidante, that the youngest son of the Marquis de la Piconnerie almost always addresses himself. There is nothing concealed from her; he tells her all his impressions, his most secret thoughts. all that he does ; and we know nothing more touching than this tender and filial attachment of the young brother to her who stood to him in the place of a mother, and in whose company were spent his early years in the old home of La Durantie. The sincere affection expressed by the young Bugeaud towards his sister Phillis never diminished. The Comtesse de Puyssegenetz all her life retained the ascendancy she had possessed over her brother during his infancy and youth. We have heard an affecting anecdote on this subject. A short time before his death, Marshal Bugeaud at a family dinner at La Durantie had a little discussion with his elder sister. Without intending it he had certainly vexed his dear sister a little, so that a little pearl of a tear appeared in her eye. Seeing this, the Marshal jumped up, and throwing himself on his sister's neck, himself burst into tears. 'Oh, my dear Phillis, oh, my well-beloved, can it really be I that have made you weep ? I shall never forgive myself.'

Thomas Bugeaud enlisted at Fontainebleau on the 29th of June, 1804, in the foot grenadiers of the Imperial Guard (corps of the vélites*), being nineteen years and some months of age. Appointment to the vélites of the guard was a little favour to the young Limousin recruit. The corps of vélites was com-

---

* 'The light-armed troops bearing the name of *velites*.'—*Smith, Dict. Greek and Roman Antiquities, Army*, p. 95.— ED.

posed of young soldiers of a little more education
than the rest, and the First Consul intended that it
should be a nursery for sub-officers.

The Comtesse Feray observes: 'Barrack-life was a time of
suffering to my father. The future did not look bright to him,
having neither friends nor money. He spent in study all the time
he had left from fatigues and drill. He even sold some of his bread
to buy books. He had not money enough to buy candles. When
his comrades were asleep, he read by the smoky barrack lights. He
was very often hungry, and in his dreams feasted upon the chestnuts
and mealy potatoes of old Durantie. As a recruit, he was very
badly treated by the veterans; his fine white hands, some marks of
the small-pox, his beardless chin, red hair, and especially his taste
for books, were the subjects for continual attack, while discipline
compelled him to be silent.

'At that time the soldiers had only one soup-bowl between six
men. It was set upon a form or table; the men made a ring round
it, and there was a rule by which they ate. Each in turn put in his
wooden spoon, and abstained while the others took their share. One
day my father, in his hunger, forgot the regulation, and when he
had swallowed one spoonful took another at once. On this one of
the " old grumblers" rushed at the glutton, and shouted at him in
a rage, " With your *thématiques* and *gérographie* you are only a
confounded greenhorn." Upon this he received the contents
of the bowl in his face. A duel ensued; the old grenadier was
killed; and from that day the young recruits, hitherto martyrs and
butts, were treated with much more respect in the regiment.*

'Although he was experiencing a time of peace, my father felt
little inclination for the profession of arms. He kept on writing to
his sisters, lamenting the poverty that had driven him from his
home. His greatest consolation was to go and sit at the foot of a
tree in the forest of Fontainebleau, and pour forth his tears. He
has told us: " I was one day in a miserable state, when a comrade
saw me. ' What are you about, you fool? Do not cry like a calf';
come to the laundresses' ball.' He dragged me along, and I was
still wretched when we went in. My comrade knew the ways of the

---

* This was the General's first duel. We are told that his second was during
the campaign in Austria, when a rough sergeant commanding the detachment
talked of offering insult to the daughters of a house where they had been hospitably
entertained. Corporal Bugeaud exclaimed against such dastardly conduct; a duel
was the instant result, and the sergeant killed on the spot. A third we shall have
to mention took place long after, in 1832, when the Deputy Dulong was killed.

place, he gave a nod to the prettiest girls; and then I was in the middle of them, and my melancholy soon put to flight in the whirl of a waltz. I was mad for dancing. The ball did me a great deal of good, and I did not go so often to pour out my sorrows to the wilds of the forest."'

The two following letters, written from Fontainebleau and Courbevoie by the young vélite of the guard to his sister Phillis, show that the hero was already meeting the miseries of his condition more patiently :—

Fontainebleau, 11 *Thermidor*, 1804.

My dear Phillis,—I was anxiously expecting your letter, and at last it has come. But for that I should not even now be reconciled to my profession; but now that you approve, I am content, and am vexed at nothing but the separation from you. I begin to have a better idea of the views of the government about our corps. Generals are often sent to see if we are doing well, and inspect our progress. Marshal Bessières reviewed us yesterday; he promised us masters, and it is almost certain that in a fortnight everything will be arranged. I am delighted at this. I have got back a great deal of my taste for study, and am really afraid, because drill and duty leave me so little time for learning. But in three or four months we shall know our drill, and then have much more time. A man could make very little progress with only the corps masters. There will be so many of us, that each one could hardly have a ten minutes' lesson, so that I intend to have a private master for each subject that I take up in public. That is the way to get distinction. I have but little hope of advance till M. Blondean gets a place. The first-come vélites have all the best of it; they have attracted the observation of the chiefs before us, and already some forty of them have been appointed instructors, and they will soon become sub-officers.

It is hard enough to become acquainted with the chiefs. They are afraid of making us jealous of one another by seeming to patronise any of us. Another thing is that there are only two of our officers whose society is in any way desirable; the others are good soldiers, but men of low birth and small means. However, I intend to do my best to do duty well with them, for a man must make himself known; without that he would always hang in a rut. I expect to make acquaintance with a young captain by means of the chase, for he is very fond of it. I have already got myself mentioned to him by a sergeant whom I know. I have spoken of myself as a great sportsman, and I hope that I shall soon go out with him. When we have been after game two or three times together, we shall be good friends.

It is still more difficult to make respectable acquaintance in the town. 'The soldier' is in very bad repute. There is great distrust of any one who wears uniform; and not remembering that the frock does not make the friar, people will hardly meet any of us in society, not even the superior officers. I have been told that there was only one vélite who mixed in good society at Fontainebleau, and that was because he had relations there. The chief cause of our banishment from honourable society is, that several vélites have insulted women, and otherwise misconducted themselves in many ways. And so we are reduced to the society of low women and barmaids. I hope you do not suppose I frequent it. When I have a spare moment I prefer to pass it in barracks, or in the room I have hired, in reading and learning English and geography. I have bought a dictionary from Paris. Even if I were disposed to dissipation, I have no time for it. We are obliged to be so very clean—both our arms and our persons—that we have to work without ceasing. We have at the outside an hour a-day, so you need not be afraid of the mother of all the vices. I never was more well-disposed, and in a corps of grenadiers I am behaving, perhaps, much better than I should in a hermitage. I go to mass on Sunday morning, and hear a sermon on that day, as much for pleasure as for piety. I sometimes say prayers, and have never been laughed at by my comrades for it. Several more do the same as I do, and the others do not deride them.

There are a great many of these young men who are not of good family, sons of peasants, artisans, &c.; there are also some of high birth, but in general this corps is not what is supposed. There is very little intimacy among the vélites; we meet and look at one another like strangers, and do not make up large parties. Each has two or three friends, with whom he goes out and shares his pleasures. We are not incited to expense, or asked to do evil.

The discipline is very strict and very harsh. There is an order against playing billiards; if a young man is known to have lost even so little money he is very sharply reprimanded. We have to be in by nine o'clock, and if late, are confined to barracks; if the offence is repeated, the guard-room.

Our chiefs all have very bad principles: they believe that after death there is an end of everything, that they are beasts like the rest: they believe in a Supreme Being, but suppose He is neutral. This is the language of all I have spoken to, and they introduced the subject. Unfortunately, there are only too many young men disposed to listen to them.

I hope, my dear, that I shall follow your wise counsels without difficulty, and that when Heaven grants me the favour of seeing you again, you will find me virtuous, and thankful for the great share you will have had in my good conduct, and the advice you have given me, and I hope will give me.

I have found X—— so little inclined to give me what he himself acknowledges my parents left me, that I have not ventured to ask him for any more. We have come to no arrangement. I sold him my linen, and the price, together with what he owed me, amounts to five hundred francs. I asked him to advance me the first six months of my allowance, and he refused, saying I was foolish; but he promised not to let me be in want, and to send me my allowance punctually. You may imagine that after paying for my journey, staying thirteen days in Paris at an hotel with M. Blondeau, buying several things I wanted, such as books, paper, nankeen breeches, dimity waistcoats, silver buckles, hat, uniform, and a lot of things necessary not to look like a beggar, I can have very little left; and I am afraid that X—— will not be in a hurry to send me any more. With the strictest economy, and spending nothing but what is necessary—like paying my masters—I shall find it difficult to wait two months. X—— thought that five hundred francs would be enough for my expenses, as having nothing to buy; he is very much mistaken. Besides that we have to pay something to the masters over us, there is a good deal to spend on our kit. We are allowed to make our uniform as handsome as we like. After duty is over, one can only go out in nankeen breeches, silk or fine cotton stockings, or with kerseymere pantaloons, and boots. It is only the rustics who go out differently dressed; and the way to gain notice is to show that one is not a man without means, and to be well appointed. M. Blondeau, who understands the case, strongly advised me to attend to this. I give you these particulars, so that you may not think I spend my money badly.

A thousand things to all, and my respects to my aunt. Adieu, my love; I am everything that a good brother should be to Hélène.

THOMAS BUGEAUD.
Vélite of the Grenadiers of the Guard.

Fontainebleau, 10 *Fructidor*, 1804.

*   *   *   *   *   *   *

The recommendation you mention might be of great service to me, though it is not often that this kind of patronage is successful, because all the men in power receive so many requests that they scarcely pay attention to them. However, those that come from a brother ought to be a little better received; so I beg of you not to neglect it. I should prefer the letter being addressed to General Bessières himself, as it is very difficult to present such a thing to a man of his rank. He knows me already, for he received me at Fontainebleau, the last time he went there with the Emperor.

If he is reminded of this, and would like to be of service to me, he can easily find me. I should be very glad to be in the theoretical class: those who have been taken into it are almost sure to be made sub-officers, as they are learning the duties. No one has been chosen who had no interest; ability and talents count for nothing. More than three-quarters of them are worth very little, while in our corps there are many educated young men to be found who are not the least thought of.

I have not lost hopes of getting into good society. I have made the acquaintance of the lady from whom I have hired a room. She is the wife of a printer; but in this part of the country women of that class have a much better tone than they have among us even in far higher rank. She has promised to introduce me to the sets that will be made up at the beginning of winter; she will get me invitations to balls and concerts; and when ι am there, I shall try gradually to form friendships, and, perhaps, shall manage to get myself a good ' bourgeois ' society.

* * * * * * *

Our commanding officer gave us a very agreeable surprise the other day. After drilling us about a great deal, he said he was so pleased with us that he would take us out for a march. And so we marched off, but had hardly gone a quarter of a mile, when we saw some baskets full of bread, bottles, cheese, and sausages. We jumped for joy at this sight, and when the commandant had made us pile arms, we formed groups, and made a capital breakfast. We toasted the commandant, our chiefs, and the glory of France. I went to him, and in the name of my comrades paid him a little compliment on the feast that he was giving us. He seemed pleased, and put into my hands a great Brie cheese and a hamper of Burgundy to share among us. When we had done eating we had a dance to beat of drum.

This, my dear Phillis, is the only pleasant moment I have had since I have been here. This little scene has given me a little taste for the army, and I felt almost for the first time a slight breath of ambition.

* * * * * * *

Adieu, my dear Phillis; do not make me languish any more. If you knew all the pleasure you give me you would make great haste to send an answer. I hope you do not want fresh assurances to believe that I feel like the most affectionate of brothers to you.

THOMAS BUGEAUD,
Vélite in the Grenadiers of the Guard.

The serious and candid side of this character is well displayed in these private confidences and by his bitter regrets at the difficulty of obtaining education. This desire to learn appears in all his letters. Indeed it was to himself the Marshal owed all he knew. During the troubled period of the Revolution and under the Directory it was almost impossible for a boy—for a young man without means, and living in the country, to obtain any thorough education. We have seen above that such an abode as La Durantie was little fitted to enlarge the circle of ideas and knowledge of the son of the Marquis de la Piconnerie. And so our homage is due to the perseverance and force of will of the young man from Périgord, ardently desirous to study, blushing for his ignorance, and attaining through his own exertions alone a very fair amount of information for a soldier of fortune. Afterwards he did a great deal to supply the want of early education ; and if he had not the ' culture that results from close study,' as General Trochu rather severely regrets, he made up for these imperfections by some very superior qualities.*

---

* General Trochu was aide-de-camp to Marshal Bugeaud in Algeria. He says in a letter doing honour to the Marshal's high qualities and his own sense of indebtedness to him : ' But he had not received the lessons of a well-arranged education, and had not the culture that results from close study. His merit was only the greater in having raised himself by his own efforts to the high position where we saw him.' In M. Trochu's works on the French Army, in 1879, full justice is done to the Marshal's high qualities. ' They (the Algerian generals) had the benefit of the lessons and example of a practised soldier, who was their inferior in education and culture of mind, but their superior in the scope of his natural ability, especially distinguished by the most uncommon good sense, and far above them in his experience of the great war—Marshal Bugeaud.'

CHAPTER III.

THE CORONATION (1804).

IN the letters which follow the young brother continues
to make a confidante of his beloved Phillis. His
whole character is revealed in these private outpourings; the little vélite is still somewhat shy and
haughty, and his taste for 'the military,' as he calls
it, diminishes every day instead of increasing. His
weariness and distaste for the regiment is more
evident, and is so strong that the enlisted volunteer
thinks of entering the Military School. But the cost
is considerable, the eldest brother, Patrice, rather
hard, and Thomas, alas! could not meet such heavy
expenses with the very small fortune left him by the
Marquis de la Piconnerie.

To MDLLE. PHILLIS DE LA PICONNERIE, at Bordeaux.

Since my last letter I have had several little adventures, both
good and bad. I remember you told me to try to approach my
chiefs. Well, my dear, I have done it, whether I would or no, and
that in a way that might have kept me still more aloof. I do not
know if I have told you that I had a friend of the name of Lamothe.
This friend had a dispute, and asked me to be his second. I could
not refuse, though there is a special order against fighting or being
a second. As we were on our way to the appointed place we were
arrested by the guard. Lamothe and his adversary were put in the
guard-room, and I was left at large till further orders. As soon as

the two combatants were together they had a desperate battle, and would no doubt have throttled each other had they not been parted. The commandant was very angry, and intended to punish them very severely; but as some one pointed out to him that Lamothe was not to blame, as he had been insulted, he suspended the punishment, and desired Lamothe and me to give our facts and reasons in writing. My friend was unable to write because he had sprained his wrist in the struggle, and so he asked me to do it for him; and so I made myself up into a Demosthenes to plead his defence and mine.

You know that among the blind the one-eyed is king. The chiefs who are good soldiers, who have obtained their position by bravery and nothing else, considered that what I said was splendid, and acquitted both of us. Since that time their manner to me is changed, and the commandant often speaks to me. Of late he addressed me in a very friendly way, asked me several questions as to my position, the way I was treated by the inferior chiefs, and a number of other things. I told him that I was very well satisfied, because it is a bad plan to complain. Then he said to me, ' You are one of my recruits, Monsieur de la Piconnerie. I presented you to General Bessières.' I did not fail to give him the credit, nor to manifest my gratitude. Then he tapped me on the shoulder, and repeatedly promised that he would not forget me. He also asked, ' You can write well, Monsieur de la Piconnerie?' ' Very little, commandant, but if my small talents could be of any use to you, I should be most happy to place them at your disposal.' He accepted this, and has employed me several times, and so I have had the pleasure of seeing his daughters, who are very ladylike.

You see, my dear Phillis, that I have reason to hope that I shall not be forgotten when there are places going among the vélites, for the commandant is all-powerful, and will be referred to in the selection of persons. I am very glad of this, though not ambitious. My love for soldiering, instead of increasing, diminishes every day, and I am come to hoping that I may not always remain a private soldier if only for the sake of being less unhappy. Perhaps at a future time I shall think differently; but it is such a hard case, one is such a slave, and under so many persons who generally abuse one, that a man has to be absolutely without feeling—like a bit of marble —if he is to be a soldier. I can tell you, my dear, that ' the military ' is a fine school for patience, and just the thing to form the character. I have a notion that when you see me again I shall be as gentle as a lamb.

Patrice is mistaken in saying that I am making progress in mathematics; I only told him that I was studying them. How could I get on when I have so little time to myself? Our labours are not lessened, and, I fancy, will not diminish till after the coronation of the Emperor, for as we are to go to Paris for it, the commandant has set his heart on making us drill as well as the oldest grenadiers.

As for English, I work very little at it. At last a master for drawing, grammar, and writing, has been given to us; but it is difficult to get on in these general schools, for the numbers are too great. We are more than three hundred in the drawing-class: so I have determined to engage the same master for my private lessons.

Adieu, my dear Phillis, believe me your affectionate brother,

THOMAS.

Fontainebleau, 1804.

For the last few days we have been journeying to Paris, and I am very much tired, for we carried our packs, and I had loaded myself very much, expecting to remain several days. But we were not even given time to rest. We arrived in the evening, next day were reviewed by the Emperor, and manœuvred a long time before His Majesty, who was said to be much pleased with us. Next day we went off again. I had hardly time to speak to M. Blondeau. He was very friendly, and by his advice and conversation gave me a little of the encouragement I stood in great need of. He promised to write to me as soon as he has succeeded, so that I may go to see him at Paris, where he expects to be very useful to me. I forgot in my last letter to give you the account you asked me for, and will do so now.

It is true that I am thinking of the Military School, because when once a man is there he is sure of getting out with the rank of sub-lieutenant, and can really learn there, for the authorities do not, as with us, attend only to making the lads go to drill, but also to giving them the knowledge necessary for making good officers—real soldiers, for an ignorant officer is unworthy of the name. It is true that in that school a most severe slavery has to be endured for a year or eighteen months, but I should be glad to part with my liberty for that time if I determine to follow the military profession. I stand well with my chiefs, and am as happy as possible, for a soldier. I am most kindly treated. But what vexes me is that they reckon too much upon my complaisance, and that there is not a moment when I am not overloaded with work; so that with all the racket of barracks I can scarcely secure a moment for my mathematical master. To make up for this I have been excused from guard-mounting and patrol duty, and am very glad of it. I have been appointed an instructor; and have to study the soldiers' schooling, and be present

at a two-hours' lesson. As I have begun so long after the others, I
must work hard to catch them up. I fully expect that for three
months I shall not be able to study some most essential things. The
names of my principal chiefs are Commandant Chéry, Adjutant-
Major Véjut, he is from Lyons, and the Commandant from near
Fontainebleau. The General commanding the corps is named Ulat.
Marshal Bessières is the General-in-Chief—at least I think so, for
he has often reviewed us.

Adieu, my dear; I kiss you.

Your brother,   THOMAS.

The following letter mentions some memorable
scenes at which Bugeaud was present :—

To MDLLE. PHILLIS DE LA PICONNERIE.

Fontainebleau, 25 Primaire, 1804.

My dear, I was expecting your letter with impatience, but not
grumbling : I will never come to that ; I am too sure of you to
fear anything. So it is no use to talk any more sentiment—we are
not obliged to pour it out in every letter ; let us keep to history,
and leave our hearts to take care of the rest, giving them *carte
blanche.*

I have seen a quantity of things that were new to me. The
Emperor came, as you know, to Fontainebleau to receive the Pope.
I had the pleasure of seeing him several times very close when he
went hunting. He even spoke to me, and asked me if there were
many vélites in a detached barrack he was passing. I answered
him, saluting. He acknowledged my salute, and passed on with the
speed of lightning. A few days afterwards he met the Pope, and
brought him back in his carriage. Every evening I went and
walked in the castle-yard to look at the Court equipages, and
though I have long been excused from guard-mounting, I asked to
go on, in hopes of being posted in the Emperor's or Empress's
ante-room. It was as I expected. I found myself on sentry at
the apartments of Madame Bonaparte. I saw her several times,
and had a quarter of an hour's talk with a lady of her suite, very
pretty and amiable.

The same day the Emperor went hunting. A stag was taken,
and the curée performed in the castle-yard in His Majesty's presence.
More than two hundred hounds threw themselves upon the poor
creature, and he was eaten up in a moment. You may imagine
whether I admired the sight ! We gave a grand banquet to our

brothers-in-arms who had come with the Emperor. Everything went off gaily, and more than one bottle of wine was emptied in drinking our healths. We went to Paris to be present at His Majesty's coronation; it lasted ten or twelve days. We had a great deal of trouble, and no pleasure at all. The weather was very bad, we were heavily loaded, and, to complete our misfortunes, we had to go beyond Paris, and occupy barracks four miles from the city. At every festival we remained the whole day under arms; it was very cold, and the mud abominable. At the end of the day we returned to our infernal barrack, and had to work like negroes to clean our arms and tidy ourselves for the next day. This, my dear, is the pleasure that I had. I got away one day to see M. Blondeau, and could only stop with him a moment, because he was very busy; he has not succeeded yet.

You cannot imagine the beauty and magnificence of the Pope's cortège and the Emperor's on the coronation day. The Pope went first on his way to Notre Dame. A number of very splendid carriages preceded and followed his, and it put all the others in the shade: it was drawn by eight most beautiful dappled grey horses, their manes covered with plumes that nodded over their heads, and the carriage was as fine as the team. A churchman marched a few paces in front, mounted upon a mule, and bearing a cross: he looked as if he was masquerading, and made the old soldiers, who do not believe in such things, laugh a great deal.

The Emperor passed a few minutes afterwards; he surpassed every one else. His cortège was of the same kind as the Pope's, but his carriage much handsomer; his eight dun horses seemed to make it fly majestically. It was all gold, and bore the imperial eagle and crown on the top. More than 80,000 soldiers in new clothing made a line as splendid as it was formidable. What I thought most beautiful was the illumination; everything was on fire, and the blazing lamps were cleverly arranged like trees and designs of every sort. Here was a firework, further on an enormous star, lighting a fountain that flowed with wine.

In a word everything looked heavenly. I should have thought myself in Olympus if I had not been sensible of the miseries of man. I caught a cold the first day of the festivities, and have had it ever since, so that I have endured a great deal, for I could not fall-out; and though it was deathly cold, we had to stick in the mud as upright as posts, and keep on presenting arms. Then there were six miles at least to walk before I could get to bed. I was even obliged to take a carriage back to Fontainebleau, or I could never have got there. To-day I have gone into hospital, where we are very comfortable, and I hope I shall soon be better. Ah, my dear Phillis, how often in these times of suffering did I think La Durantie, my dog, and gun, much better than this silly ambition, that makes a man leave his home to run after fortune through a thousand miseries. How glad I should be to be there with my sisters! At least they would be sorry for me, and make my illness bearable by their care; instead of which, I am here with strangers who do not even attend to me.

Soon there must be some corporals chosen among us—I hope to be one; that will be one step gained, and I shall be much better off, for corporal in the Guard ranks with sergeant-major in the Line.

There is an order against our having rooms in town, so I find it almost impossible to do anything till I can get some post that will give me a little room with another man. At this moment we are ten in a room, with only one little table, and as few have any taste for work, it is a witches' sabbath.

Adieu, my dear Phillis.

Your affectionate
THOMAS.

Now comes the first incident in the soldier's life, the transfer of the vélites of the guard from Fontainebleau to Courbevoie, and the disappointment at not having been chosen as one of the vélites incorporated in the army of Italy. This suburban garrison did not leave our Périgord man any very pleasing remembrances. For the first time he is oppressed and afflicted by disgust. 'If I ever come to have done with soldiering, I should be much better pleased to bury myself in the country, than to run after any more adventures. Perhaps the pathetic tone that I adopt makes you think I am weak, and can bear nothing, but if you knew how hard it is to be a soldier for a man who has any spirit, you would think differently.' He returns to his idea of entering the Military School, and meanwhile works at mathematics, and uses his small means in paying a master. The prudent Phillis must have been lecturing her dear brother, as we perceive by one of his letters.

These two letters are curious, and show the relaxation of morals at the time.

Fontainebleau, Pluviose, 1805.

My DEAR PHILLIS,—I have hardly time to read your letter; I devour it by bits, as I am making up my pack, putting on my sabre, and running to the beat of the drum. Just as I got it, we were told to be ready in an hour, to go to Paris, and on to Italy. We had not a minute, no time to put our things in security, satisfy our creditors, or get our clothes from the wash. We had to go at once, it was four in the afternoon, and to-morrow we have to be by two o'clock in the afternoon at Courbevoie, twenty leagues from Fontainebleau.

Courbevoie, Pluviose, 1805.

We arrived at the appointed time, and four hundred men among us were selected to go to Italy; I was one! but a second order came that only two hundred were to go, and I was not one of them, to my great regret. Those who go are incorporated with the old Grenadiers of the Guard, who are intended for the same destination, and we with those who remain, so that we are now admitted among His Majesty's guards. Thus vanishes my hope of promotion. Now that we are amalgamated with old soldiers, famous not for their science but for their services, their bravery and their exploits, who nearly all have the cross of merit, it is not to be presumed, and, indeed, it would be unjust, for novices with six months of service ever to command these conquerors of Europe; it is much that we are placed in their ranks. So I was very anxious to go to Italy with the brave fellows, who won their immortality there. I volunteered, but was refused, as I tried a little too late.

I hesitated at first because I had not a halfpenny, had left a few small debts at Fontainebleau, and my property was by no means secure. I also felt regret at leaving all means of instruction, but when I looked at the condition in which I should find myself at Courbevoie, I did all I could to get away, but to no good.

There were only two hundred men wanted, and all were glad to go. Just now I am in despair at having spoken too late, and am going to lead the most monotonous life here. Courbevoie is a large village, three miles from Paris, where there are no books to fall back upon, not a master of any kind, and too far from Paris to go and seek instruction in that home of the sciences. I am reduced to spend my days in going on guard, at the Tuileries, in eating and sleeping. There is nothing to do here, but the universal vice; you can fancy that, at this rate, I do not amuse myself much, and had rather be stupid in my room. Unprincipled young men are here in a haven of delight. There is hardly a grenadier of the guard who has not a mistress among the laundresses of Paris, who washes for him, feeds him, gives him on Sunday her week's earnings, and is only too happy if he will recompense her by a little fidelity.

It was quite a play, the night before the men marched for Italy, to see a whole company of women, well enough dressed, come to besiege the barrack, and wish their friends good-bye with tears in their eyes. There they were, hanging on their necks, and slipping their little savings of money into their pockets. I know a grenadier to whom a laundress gave fifteen louis for his journey.

Your loving brother,

THOMAS BUGEAUD

CHAPTER IV.

THE CAMP AT BOULOGNE (1805).

THE Consulate for life had lasted two years. General Bonaparte, who had become First Consul August 2, 1802 (the year X.), was proclaimed hereditary Emperor on May 18, 1804 (the year XII.), and the people ratified, by 3,572,239 assenting votes, the establishment of the new dynasty. Bugeaud, the vélite of the guards, was then twenty. His own station was changed very soon after he had seen his more fortunate companions depart for Italy. This year, 1804, the first of the Empire, was so much disturbed, so fruitful in occurrences, that half-a-century afterwards, the Marshal remembered these events which he had passed through, certainly as a very humble supernumerary, but his observant mind and good sense had formed a sober judgment on them.

It was during the summer of 1805 that the regiment to which Thomas Bugeaud belonged was selected for the camp at Boulogne. The First Consul's immense preparations, and the prodigious activity that he had displayed in his plans for the invasion of England, had been a little disturbed by the grave events of the year 1804, the royalist conspiracy of Georges Cadoudal and Moreau, and the proclamation of the Empire.

An activity, long kept secret, had been developed in our harbours and arsenals. To carry the expeditionary force into England, and attain the object dreamed of by the audacious genius of Napoleon, there was no need for lofty vessels, but for a myriad of gun-boats, flat barges, lighters, and pinnaces, propelled by sail and oar; all our ports, even our great inland cities, were put under requisition, and ship-yards established all over France. All the master's thoughts had to be swiftly executed. At Paris eighty gun-boats were built on the bank of the Seine, launched and taken to Havre, or sent to other divisions; they were equipped, armed, and sent along the coast towards the Straits of Calais. Squadrons of cavalry and light artillery on shore followed all their movements, ready to protect them against a hostile attack. From the Loire, the Gironde, the Charente, the Adour, all the harbours of the coast issued similar fleets. 1200 to 1300 vessels thus collected were to be concentrated at Boulogne, and the neighbouring ports, Wimereux, Etables, and Ambleteuse.

Thomas Bugeaud's pleasant vision of entering the Military School was soon to cease, at the will of the omnipotent Cæsar. Indeed, at this period it was perilous enough, or any way very useless, for the subjects of His Majesty, and especially for a vélite of the guard, to construct a plan, and build upon to-morrow. The regiment at Courbevoie received orders to march in twenty-four hours for Boulogne-sur-Mer.

A letter from Abbeville, dated 16 Messidor, 1805, was written during a halt. In the young soldier's hasty lines there is a sort of breath of patriotism: this is the first, 'We are going on a campaign, and at least the pains we suffer will be useful to the State.'

Is it not in this unconscious feeling of duty, and vision of distant glory, that we find the explanation of the admirable self-denial, discipline, and sublime heroism that Alfred de Vigny has summed up in his valuable work, *Grandeurs et Servitudes Militaires?*

To Molle. Phillis de la Piconnerie.

Abbeville, Wednesday, 16 *Messidor,* 1805.

You must have been astonished at my long silence, but, my dear, you will not blame me when your hear that before I answered you, I was waiting for certainty about a report of our moving, and that it has been realised. We started for Boulogne six days ago, and I did not know our actual destination till we came here. Uncertainty as to when we were going hindered me still further from writing to you. Here I am, my dear, every day trotting out very early, with my pack on my back, and getting to quarters very tired. I have already passed through the Isle of France, and almost all Picardy, a great province, and much resembling the Limousin in the nature of the soil, but it is better cultivated. The villages in it are horrible, the houses no better than our charcoal-burners' huts, and the inhabitants not a bit better-mannered than our boors of Limousins. Amiens, the capital, celebrated for the famous treaty, seemed to me common-place. It would not be worth mentioning without its cathedral, which is magnificent, and there are some pretty walks.

At last I am at Abbeville, pleasanter than Amiens. I am quartered upon a gardener, who seems to be a very good sort of man ; I have been over his garden, and so we talked of gardening. He told me several little things that I did not know, and I will give you one of his receipts that may be useful. If you have a number of lettuces, hearting at the same time, and wish to keep them in this pleasant condition for a long time, you must carefully pass a knife under the foot of the plant, and cut the great root that is its centre ; the other little roots will be enough to keep it alive, but they will not make sap enough to throw up the stalk.

I was working hard to get into the Military School, and now have to move. But I do not give up this design, as I can work for it, although at a distance. It is not like me to complain of this last event, as it is for active service. So I say no more, and, though the labour is increased, you shall never see me grumbling, since what I endure is of use to the State. It is only in garrison that a soldier can complain. I could easily get excused from going, in order to pursue my design, but I would not do the least thing tending that

way; it would have been cowardice, otherwise, except as regards
my plan, I am delighted to go campaigning. There is talk of an
expedition, and no doubt we shall take part in it; but politicians
think it is only to induce the English to make peace. What is
certain is, that half of the guard is on the way to the coast, and it is
stated that the other half, now on its way from Italy, will come and
join us. We have received canvas trousers and frocks for the
voyage. We shall be encamped at a short distance from Boulogne.
We have a sovereign who will not leave his troops idle, and he has
confidence in the vélites, for in this expedition we are more numerous
than the old grenadiers. As for me, I am quite sure, that, if there
is an action, we shall distinguish ourselves, for we are in the best
possible spirits, and all delighted to go. In general, in single
combat, that is in duels, we are braver than the old grenadiers of the
guard. At first they wanted to order us about, but they begin to
respect us. In fact, I believe that the Emperor thinks much more
of us than he does of them, and that one day or other the vélites
will form a separate body.

Adieu, my dear,

Your brother THOMAS.

The detachment to which Thomas Bugeaud belonged was ordered to proceed to the camp at
Wimereux, and he then wrote the following letter to
his sister, giving an account of several engagements
with the English vessels cruising off our coasts, in
order to distract our labours, and oppose the concentration of our little flotillas at Boulogne.

Wimereux, near Boulogne, 1805.

I arrived, my dear Phillis, at the camp of Wimereux, near
Boulogne, in very good health, and was very much interested in examining all these things, new to me: a very large camp, harbours,
flotillas, the sea; the sight of all this gives me the greatest pleasure.
Our camp, not a musket-shot from the sea, is very pretty, at a
distance it would be taken for a beautiful village. In truth, it is
not very comfortable, as we have to lie on a little straw, the bed is
by no means good, but one is not so badly off here as I expected.
Now, also, I am used to it, and it is not physical privation or fatigue
that troubles me. Three days after my arrival, a detachment was
embarked, of whom I was one. We were eleven days at sea, and
you would not suspect that in this time I have been present at three
naval engagements, two of them sharp enough. You should see the

account in the papers, but I think that some particulars will be of interest to you, when you know I was there.

As we went out, the English came to attack us with several frigates, brigs, and corvettes; we were rather surprised, for we did not expect to fight, and hardly any of the crew had ever seen the sea. We knew no sea terms for the management of the sails, or gun drill for firing the cannon: but we had to perform both duties, both quite strange to us. When we were told to let go a rope, we hauled upon it as hard as we could, and this at first caused some confusion, and took us nearer to the enemy than we wished. However, in a short time, we got used to our work, and we kept up a smart fire with the help of the forts and coast batteries; the enemy were compelled to haul off, and we got quit of them for some slight damage.

Two shots came on board the gunboat where I was without doing much harm. After this skirmish we anchored in the roads, and stayed there pretty quietly for some days; I was only sea-sick for a quarter of an hour.

In the quiet days we were practised in manœuvring, and lost no time in putting our theory into practice, for there was a signal that a flotilla was coming from Calais; and either to make a diversion, or to protect it, we made ready at daybreak. The English soon perceived that we were in motion, and attacked us furiously: we received them just the same way, and the combat was sharp enough for an hour and a half; the enemy were again obliged to haul off, and it is said were considerably damaged. On our side we were very fortunate, for there were only three or four men wounded, some masts cut, and other injuries, slight enough. In our gunboat there was only one shot that went through from starboard to port, and killed no one. The Dutch fleet was not as fortunate: all the way from Dunkirk here it had to keep up a fight with forty-seven sails, three or four of them being line-of-battle ships; in the evening it came in sight, continually harassed by the English, and keeping up a vigorous defence.* Some of our line were engaged, but it did not last long, as the enemy suffered severely from the batteries and forts on the coast. The Dutch had eighty men killed or wounded. It is time, my dear, to finish this gazette, which may weary you, but it amuses me to write it.

Your loving brother,
THOMAS BUGEAUD.

---

* English vessels at Wimereux, 'Immortalité, frigate; Hebe, 32 guns; Arab, 20 guns; and the remainder of the detached squadron. Only damage, a nine-pounder gun disabled.' *James' Naval History*, vol. iii. p. 311. See also pp. 312 and 313 for Action with Dunkirk Flotilla. Only small vessels were suitable for the service, on account of shoal-water.—ED.

Napoleon had invented several methods for keeping the enemy at a distance. He established several lines of submarine batteries, armed with heavy guns, covered by high tide, and uncovered at low water, so that the fire seemed to advance and retire with the tide itself. Five hundred pieces of the largest calibre were placed in battery upon the reefs the English call 'the iron coast,' and forts built out at sea prevented the enemy's approach to the harbour. Several of these batteries fired hollow projectiles.

Everything was ready, only waiting for a fair wind and favourable weather. The English had recourse to their usual plan of organizing a confederation. Admiral La Touche Tréville died; Villeneuve, who succeeded him, did not carry out the plans with sufficient dash. The Emperor began by abusing Austria and Villeneuve.

The violence and injustice of the Emperor's expressions vexed Admiral Decrès. 'Villeneuve is a wretch, who must be dismissed with ignominy,' cried he; 'he has no power of combination, no courage, nor general energy, he would lose everything to save his skin.' He was raging thus in the presence of Monge, for whom he had a real friendship, notwithstanding the known opinions of the savant, who had remained a republican. Annoyed at Napoleon's rage, Monge went and told M. Daru, first secretary for war. Daru went to the Emperor. Misinformed as to his master's intentions, and the cause of his displeasure, he waited in silence; the Emperor came to him, and cried, 'Do you know where Villeneuve is? At Cadiz!' And detailing to M. Daru all the plans he had been hatching for six months, attributing their failure to the cowardice and incapacity of the men he had employed, he broke out into invectives and abuse. All at once, as if he had eased his soul by this outburst of passion, he said to M. Daru, ' Sit down and write.'

A powerful effort, and the natural play of a fertile imagination, says M. Guizot, had caused him to revert to the combinations that were to make his enemies tremble, and ensure him over Austria the triumph which he had missed over England. The plan of his campaign was arranged; all his thoughts turned to execute his will like lightning.

CHAPTER V.

AUSTERLITZ (1805).

OUR land forces were now to find themselves in their real
element; and very soon great excitement was to ensue
after the abortive enterprise of the camp at Boulogne.
The capitulation of Ulm, the battle of Austerlitz, the
reconstruction of Austria, were destined in this same
year (1805) to announce to Europe the accession of a
new Emperor. By some of the continual chances of
war our young soldier was only a spectator of this
grand drama until the day of Austerlitz. He writes
to his sister from Saint Quentin that after the daily
alarms, embarkation and disembarkation at Boulogne,
the march was as pleasant as travelling; after an
hour's rest he used to go and see anything curious
in the town where they halted. Another letter :

To MDLLE. PHILLIS DE LA PICONNERIE.

Augsburg, 18 *Vendémiaire*, 1805.

MY DEAR LOVE,—I only rested one day at Strasburg ; we
crossed the Rhine, and made forced marches that have wearied us
very much. We move off very early every day, and do not stop till
night. All the army marches as sharply, and our *little man* drives
the ship with astonishing speed. Good feet are wanted to second
the activity of his mind. You can judge of the speed of our march
when you know that we have gone eighty leagues in a week, a great

VOL. I.   D

deal for loaded troops; for besides our packs we carry on our backs all our campaigning kit—kettles, canteens, picks, spades, &c.

I am absolutely tired out, and cannot imagine how the body can support such constant fatigue. Again, if we had but a good bed when we get to our quarters: but not a bit of it, we only have a little straw, and even that after three or four hours' delay, and often we can only lie in the open round a fire. Hunger is another tyrant. You can imagine whether ten thousand men coming into a village can easily find anything to eat. What distresses me more is the annoyance of stealing from the peasantry; their poultry, their bacon, their firewood, taken from them by grace or force. I do not do these things, but when I am very hungry I secretly tolerate them, and eat my share of the stolen goods. All this plainly shows that hitherto I have only seen the rosy side.

But do not suppose that I am wanting in strength and courage to bear these evils, though I do seem to express disgust. On the contrary, I endure them with patience, and try to fill my place honourably. I assure you I will die or distinguish myself. I am most anxious to win the cross of merit; and only want an opportunity.

There has been fighting already, and we had the best of it. On the 16th four thousand prisoners were taken, whom I have seen march by: there were several officers of good appearance, many of them covered with blood. It is stated that General Murat has blocked eleven thousand more men three leagues off, and that we shall march to-morrow to compel them to surrender more speedily.

Do not be surprised if I am a long time without writing to you, perhaps two months.

Adieu, my dear Sister,

Your brother Thomas,

3rd Company, 4th Battalion, Imperial Guard, Grand Army.

Linz, in Austria, 16 *Brumaire,* 1805.

Till now, my dear, I have had no time to tell you anything about the campaign we are making, or rather have already made, for the Emperor allows us to count it as a campaign already on account of our brilliant success. I have hardly had breathing time; we have been always on the run, either to cut off the enemy, or to pursue him; I take advantage of a little rest to entertain myself with you, and to describe at large the various actions and operations that have taken place.

After Strasburg we made long marches, crossing the principality of Baden, and the electorate of Wurtemburg, then entered into Swabia. The enemy fled before us; the first affairs took place near Augsburg, where we made five or six thousand prisoners. Several small affairs, that took place before the capture of Ulm, were always to our advantage, but it was at Ulm that we secured a complete success by the quick and skilful manœuvres of the French army. The enemy found themselves divided and were obliged to surrender; I have had the pleasure of seeing twenty-eight thousand men march past, who had laid down their arms. It was a fine sight. The army was arranged semicircularly in échelon on a low hill that surrounds Ulm; the Emperor was on a rock, near which we were formed up, he was surrounded by the principal generals of the army, and watched the enemy's army pass, as it were at his feet, coming out of one of the gates of the city, and going in at another after laying down their arms. He watched it all with a quiet and modest glance, warming himself by a fire we had lighted for him, where by the way he burnt the grey riding-coat that he seems to regard rather superstitiously. After seeing the enemy parade in this beautiful way, we reversed and turned back to Augsburg, where we made but a short stay, for the Emperor will take no rest until he has entirely conquered his enemy.

We crossed Bavaria, entirely cleared of Austrians by our advanced guard, and rested two days at Munich, the capital. It is a fair city, but offers none of the conveniences or pleasures that are to be found in our French towns. The enemy were entrenched on the banks of the Inn, the river that divides Austria and Bavaria. They were driven off without difficulty, and we have marched here as easy as travelling, except for some little skirmishes. On the route we saw occasionally places where there had been a little fighting. Only some five or six Russians were to be seen on the field of battle: no French at all, no doubt they had been buried. Just as I am writing to you, two thousand prisoners have reached this town, Austrians and Russians in equal numbers, taken yesterday and the day before. The fighting was sharp, and the advantage all on our side. Report says that our camp is twenty-five leagues from here, and that we are only forty-eight post leagues from Vienna. I fully believe that, if they do not come to terms, we shall soon see that famous capital, for the enemy seem in no condition to resist us; they defend themselves so badly that we are nearly sure to beat them. No doubt you suppose that, with such a quantity of success, I have been often in action, and my life twenty times in danger. Well! not in the least, my dear; I have hardly run any risk, our corps has not been engaged yet, and this is unfortunate. There is nothing to hope for, as perhaps we shall not be in action at all this whole campaign; and then no promotion! In war it is not the fighting that is to be feared; on the contrary, it is often wished for as a deliverance from the suffer-

ings, weariness, and privations that are more cruel than death. I
can assure you that one day, when we were in front of the enemy,
that is to say, in the second line, but very near, it rained, snowed,
and hailed by turns, and I twenty times wished they would let us
charge. We were obliged to remain in the ranks, carrying our
packs, unable to light a fire, with nothing to eat, having had no
bread for four or five days, wet to the bones ; and that went on all
day and part of the night, till we took possession of a very strong
village that the enemy had held. I was weak enough that day to
wish for death, and longed for one of the shot that I saw rush through
our ranks. If we had received the order to charge at such a time,
we should certainly have put everything to death. I do not tell you
of the horrors of war, the villages sacked, the wrongs and barbarities
that it brings in its train. I keep such tales for the happy time
when we shall meet again. Now I will only tell you that the profession of a hero is so much like that of a brigand that I hate it
with my whole soul. A man must have a heart of stone, destitute
of all humanity, to love war.

Your loving brother,

Thomas Bugeaud.

Brunnen, 4 Frimaire, 1805.

You did not expect, my love, that my first letter would be written
from forty leagues beyond Vienna, that is to say, from the capital of
Moravia. I wanted to write to you from the proud capital that we
have just humbled, but we only passed through it. I hardly saw
enough to tell you anything about it, but I must say something, or
you will tell me I do not know how to notice anything.

Vienna is situated in a very small plain ; the neighbourhood is
very populous, and the villages so many and so beautiful that the
whole plain might be taken for one immense city. But the pleasure
houses that these villages are composed of are not adorned with the
beauties of nature, as is the case at Paris. There are no charming
English gardens to be seen, no groves, no hedge-row elms, and
labyrinths such as form the charm of these sort of dwellings. The
houses are quite bare, with only some trees giving a little shade.
Approaching the city on the side towards France, there is a great
suburb, handsomer than any at Paris. At the end of this suburb
is an open space, at the end of which stands the Emperor's palace,
close to the gate of the city. The inside is very mean, there is no
ornament about it, and I venture to say that the court is not twice
as large as that at La Durantie. On the other hand, it is said that
the apartments are of unrivalled magnificence. As for me, the only

fine thing I saw was a pair of colossal statues at one of the gates. The rest of the city presented nothing of interest; but the houses are almost all well built. What surprised me was the confidence prevailing everywhere in the city; the shops were open, ladies, even the most elegant, passed among the French soldiers in the streets, and the faces were as calm as if we had been in the depths of peace.

Oh! my dear Phillis, how my heart bled when I saw that we passed this city by, when the capture of it seemed as if it ought to be the limit of our labours and miseries. I conjured up a very lamentable picture of my future lot; I already attributed Alexander's ambition to our Emperor, and imagined myself one of the old Macedonians, whom he dragged about the world, and who sighed unceasingly for their families and country. By way of consolation, we marched the whole night, and in three days have made forty and some odd leagues. On the march we saw a place where there had been a fight. Joseph Debetz was in action there; and I was in fear for his life when I saw a number of dead, both French and Russians I looked at the buttons, and saw several of the 75th, his regiment, among the killed. I passed on thinking our friend dead, for I had been told that a great many officers were killed; but in a village near I found a soldier of his corps, who told me he was well, and he afterwards sent me his compliments.

At last the Emperor has restrained his thunders, to our great astonishment; for we are halted in this town, without much idea of the reason, for, though we are in the middle of everything that goes on, our ignorance is complete, and we are real machines. The inaction of the troops makes me hope that perhaps a treaty is just being made. It is even stated that we shall soon go back to Vienna.

The day when I turn my steps backwards towards my beloved France will be a joyful one for me. No longer will the days' marches seem long to me when every step is bringing me nearer to my family, and especially to my dear sisters. I have always been very well, but a heavy cold has caught hold of me here. This is a fine way to cure it; we are always under arms, being reviewed, or inspected; indeed, we have a little too much tyranny; after a march of five hundred leagues, we are obliged to be as well turned out as at Paris, and if we fall short on the smallest point we are punished or reprimanded as if for a capital crime.

Brunnen, the Capital of Moravia, 19 *Frimaire,* 1805.

Do not be surprised at my silence, my dear, the speed of our march, and the little rest we have had, have given me no chance of writing to you lately; but to-day I shall make myself a little compensation. An illness of the Emperor delays us in this village for two or three days, and this gives me a moment to communicate with you. As I know you are curious to hear all particulars, I will resume my account of the campaign from Augsburg. After my return from Ulm, we left that city, and made our way straight to Munich, the capital of Bavaria, and rested there three days. We then crossed the rest of Bavaria to march against the Russians, who were upon the banks of the Inn. The enemy kept on retreating, and as far as Vienna there were only some slight affairs with their rear-guard. So we crossed Austria like travellers, and after a halt of three days at Lentz, we reached that proud capital, and its capture seemed to be the limit of our labours and miseries; but, alas! my dear, what was my surprise and grief when I saw that we were crossing the city without a halt!

At a short distance from Vienna a large number of prisoners were taken, and a large park of artillery captured. Next day we reached the scene of a very sharp conflict with the Russians which had just taken place; the dead covered the plain on both sides of the road. I looked at some of them to see the different regiments that had been engaged; and saw several of the 75th. I inquire and am told that this regiment had suffered considerably and lost a number of officers; but learnt, at last, that Joseph is well, and got off with a few knocks on the head. We entered Moravia and have stayed some days in the capital, where I still am. There is talk of peace; ambassadors have come, but no doubt the conditions have seemed tco harsh to them. The enemy preferred to try the hazard of a battle, they concentrated their forces at a distance of four leagues from here; their army was formidable, and the two Emperors commanded in person.

Three days before the battle we had orders to leave the town, and encamped a league from the enemy. The Emperor came there himself and slept in his carriage in the middle of our camp. For the three days that passed before the battle he was always walking through all the camps, and talking to the soldiers or their leaders.

We gathered round him. I heard much of his talk; it was very simple and always turned upon military duty. At last, on the eve of the battle, the anniversary of his coronation, he issued a proclamation exhorting us to behave with our usual intrepidity, and promised to keep his distance as long as victory followed us. 'But,' said he, 'if by mischance you hesitate a moment, you will see me fly into your ranks to restore order.' Then he promised to give us peace after this battle, assuring us that we should go into cantonments.

We replied by shouts of joy, the harbingers of glad success. Torches were lighted and the bands played while the whole army sang songs with eagerness. It seemed that every man was celebrating his return home, and felt the joy one experiences at seeing father, mother, and brother. Yet how many of these happy men were not to see their country again!

At daybreak the drums and trumpets announced the fight; a start was made with shouts of ' Vive l'Empereur.' The charge is sounding. These words are repeated again louder, and carry terror into the enemy's ranks. We charged like lightning, and the carnage was horrible. The balls whistled. The air groaned with the noise of cannon and our threatening voices, closely followed by death. Very soon the enemy's phalanx was shaken and thrown into disorder, at last we overthrew them entirely. One point withstands us, the batteries in a moment are taken, the gunners cut to pieces at their guns, and any that escape our steel either seek safety in flight, or a slower death in the lakes. Nothing has ever been seen, my love, like this memorable battle. In the opinion of the oldest soldiers it is the most bloody that has ever taken place. I will not describe to you the horrors of the field of battle; the wounded and dying imploring their comrades' pity. I prefer to spare your feelings, and confine myself to telling you that I was very much affected, and wished that emperors and kings who make war without reasonable grounds could be condemned for their whole lives to listen to the cries of the unfortunate wounded, who remained three days upon the field of battle without having any relief or assistance. The Russian loss is innumerable; what is certain is that there are to be seen at least sixty Russian corpses on the field of battle for one French; and it is only in one spot that I have seen nearly as many French as Russians.

Since that day there has been no more fighting. The two Emperors met in our presence; it is stated that the German promised whatever the French one chose to demand. The troops are retiring; we return to Vienna to-morrow, and I hope we shall not be long before we take the road to Paris. When we get there I ask for leave, and fly home. It is by your side, close to all of you. that I hope to get a recompense for all my fatigues, and to forget my troubles. One moment will blot everything out, as I embrace you with a full heart.

The Emperor has made a little harangue in a proclamation that has been read throughout the army. It expresses his approbation of our bravery, and commences with these words—' Soldiers, I am satisfied with you.' Then he promises us a peace worthy of us, and announces our speedy return to our own country, and the joy of our countrymen at seeing us. The speech winds up—' It will be enough for you to say, "I was at the battle of Austerlitz," for men to exclaim—" Here is a brave man!" '

In reading these letters of an obscure vélite, do we not seem to hear the whole Grand Army revealing its inmost thoughts to the world, imbued by turns with a sadness verging on despair, or an enthusiasm reaching to superstition ? We have only to observe in what cities these fraternal outpourings are written. At this simple enumeration of capitals do we not see the great shadow of the modern Cæsar depriving the ancient House of Hapsburg of its German electorates and Slav kingdoms, tearing the imperial crown of the West from the only heir of Rudolph, refashioning the world with blows of an axe, to borrow a celebrated expression? What an almost supernatural effect must this man have produced upon the generations born to contemplate him, or to feed his glory! And yet how many obscure heroes dragged in his train begged for mercy from the future prisoner of Saint Helena, seeing, like Alexander's Macedonians, in every river the extreme boundary of their conquests, every important city the aim of their labours!

Having achieved his two corporal's stripes upon the field of Austerlitz, the future Marshal of France, who carried the golden baton—dotted with bees—in his pack, was sent back to France. It was from Courbevoie, the dépôt of the Imperial Guard, that he sends this good news to his sister, the 26th of February, 1806. The date of his letters is no longer in Republican terms. His glorious master had abolished the traces of the Revolution.

To Mdlle. Phillis de la Piconnerie, at Bordeaux.

Courbevoie, 26 February, 1806.

At last, my dear, here I am back in Paris. On arriving I found, as expected, my promotion as corporal in the guard. My captain informed me, and the proofs of his good opinion that he gave me are the first pleasures I have had in my new profession. He told me that he was very sorry that he could not get me made quartermaster-sergeant, that he did all he could, but that, unfortunately, other young men had better interest than his could be, and that was the only thing that stood in my way. 'Besides,' he said, ' you ought to be satisfied with the rank of corporal; it is more important than you suppose, and may carry you a long way, especially as you gained it in a campaign. A man must go through it to go further; one step more, and you are a sub-lieutenant in the line.'

I await this step, my love, with much impatience, because it will give me the means to recover my liberty if I choose, and by that means draw near to you. At this moment I am compelled by prudence to abstain from such a pleasant meeting. You know, and you have often told me, that it is necessary to consider the future, 'that a man must not sacrifice the interests of his forty years to the wishes of the moment, and that it is wise to draw back for a better leap.'

Well, my dear, that is what I wish to do. It is to our friend-ship, which will, I hope, last more than forty years, that I sacrifice the pleasure of meeting you; but if I can gain the epaulette, no further ambition will be able to stop me. I shall fly to you, to you all, and doubly rejoice, for I shall have in some measure gained the liberty of resting at home, if my taste does not incline to soldiering. It would be impossible to get leave at this moment. I am attached to the new corps of vélites, and their instruction absolutely requires the presence of all the non-commissioned officers.

Adieu, dear Phillis.

Your brother,   Thomas.

On the 6th of April, 1806, two months afterwards, Thomas announced to Phillis, from Paris, his appoint-ment as sub-lieutenant in the 64th Regiment of the Line. Corporal of the Guard then was an equivalent rank to sergeant-major in the Line. He now has his epaulette, and says, 'When I think that I have at

last escaped from the miseries, it seems to me that it
is a dream, and a very agreeable dream.'

To MDLLE. PHILLIS DE LA PICONNERIE.

Paris, 6 April, 1806.

You had, my dear, a great idea of my deserts when I told you
that I was corporal. What would you think now if you knew that
I am a sub-lieutenant? When I come to think that I am at last
escaped from the unpleasantnesses of the military profession, it
seems to me that it is a dream, and a very agreeable dream. When
I was positively told of my new appointment, I wanted to tell you
all about my new regiment, and that has delayed me; for I do not
know yet what I shall be appointed to, and have a great notion I
shall not receive my commission till the *fête*. I suppose I am not
on the active list, for it is said that most of those who, like me, have
been made sub-lieutenants will be at the heels of the regiments. So
I have taken steps to avoid being one of them, and have obtained a
formal promise to be placed upon the active list. I have had the
good fortune in all this to be in the company of a captain, with
whom I was in two or three engagements at Boulogne, and who
thought he saw some courage in me. Added to this regular conduct
I have a little dexterity in making myself useful in moments of
difficulty, and these are the causes of my promotion.

I count with great impatience the moments that divide me from
a leave that must be granted. Adieu, my good sister.

Your brother,   THOMAS.

But there soon came disenchantments to cool this
charming delight. After a stay at Besançon, he was
again sent into Germany. It is true the Emperor
had no railways; but his valiant troops skipped from
north to south, without a thought of danger or fatigue.
A letter dated from Waldhausen, in Franconia, August
6, 1866, shows us the lieutenant face to face with a
surly colonel. From that time he becomes melancholy. ' Yes, my dear, I shall leave off soldiering
as soon as we have a Continental peace. Every day I
confirm myself in this resolution. The future has to

be considered, for I see plainly that this is not a profession for life.'

To Mdlle. de la Piconnerie.

Besançon, July 9, 1806.

No doubt, my dear, you believe that I am far away in Germany. Well! I am still in France, and this is the way. The dépôt of my regiment is at Besançon; and as that town was on my road, I went to pay my respects to the major commanding it. He has kept me here as he wants officers, and the battalions at the front have their full number.

The town is charming, but I have little time to enjoy it. I work hard at all that an officer cannot get on without knowing. First at drill, then again at the financial administration of corps, and military law. All this will not allow me a moment, because I do not choose to be ignorant of anything that makes a well-informed soldier, and can only be learnt by study or long practice.

The fat major is very good to me. He is lively, speaks kindly, and is really the most amiable of superior officers. He has confidence enough in me to give me the command of a company, which has no other officers.

My journey here has been very pleasant; I always travelled with pretty women, or sensible men, across beautiful country. Moulins and Lyons are the finest towns I have seen, but Lyons is especially magnificent, not so much by buildings as by the peculiarity of its position. On one side, the town lies against some very fertile hills, on the other side is a vast and fruitful plain. The Rhone traverses it, and surrounds it on the eastern side, then joins the Saône, a little below, so that a portion of the city is on an island. Though this city is very populous, it is dull at this moment, for trade is annihilated.

I hope you have been told the reasons that prevented my going to Bordeaux; in truth, the expense of my outfit had put me much in arrear. When leaving Paris, I examined my purse to see if it would take me to Bordeaux; but I found with pain that it would only just take me to La Durantie. When I got there, I found a very hearty welcome, but very little money. So on my departure, I only asked for ten louis; but Patrice made me a present of a mare which I sold on the way, and that was a great help to me.

Write to me, my good sister,

Thomas Bugeaud,
Officer, 64th Regiment, Besançon.

To Mdlle. Phillis de la Piconnerie, at Bordeaux.

Besançon, July 19, 1806.

My dear Phillis,—How confused I am! Perhaps you may not believe it, but I thought I had answered you. My affection suggested some doubts, and thinking carefully, I found that I was in arrear. This forgetfulness may surprise you, but your astonishment will cease, when you think that, as my thoughts always run upon you, I fancy I have written what I only thought. I have to make a calculation in order to remember, because I have several ways of communicating with you: that by letter is too dry; my ideas are shut-in by certain rules, that deprive them of expression. But when I walk alone it is very different. Then I give free course to my feelings. They jostle, overturn, and mount upon each other: then, without consulting me, fly like an arrow off to Bordeaux. Your brother is a little mad with his castles in the air, but at those times he deserves your friendship, for he always put you in the best place.

Since I have joined, I have spent a very active life of it. I have no time for mischief; I am doing the duty of adjutant-major, and this puts on me the drill as well as the police of the whole battalion. Perhaps you will not be sorry to know how my time is employed. This is it: drill from five in the morning till seven; from seven to nine study in my room; at nine I parade the sergeant-majors, and take them to the major in command, to receive his orders for duty; at ten I have all the non-commissioned officers, and instruct them in the theory and practice of soldiering; at half-past eleven I inspect the men for guard; from noon till three I am tolerably free, but I have the interior administration of a company, and that takes up some of this time. At three I go to dinner; then to the café, to read the papers. This brings me to five o'clock, when drill begins again and lasts till seven. After that I go for a stroll or pay some visits, and come back to my room to work till eleven. Add to all this bustle four or five changes of clothes in the day, and you can fancy if I have any time to rest. The post of adjutant-major is hard, but I would be glad to take it, because I should have the rank of captain, and that gives some prominence where the work is well done.

Adieu, my dear Phillis,

Your brother Thomas.

To Mdlle. Phillis de la Piconnerie.

Waldhausen, in Franconia, August 6, 1806.

I only received your letter after my return to the Grand Army. It arrived in the nick of time, for I was tired to death. Two days before I had been sent to a lonely village to command a detachment ; I had not become used to my rude habitation, and wanted something pleasant to restore me to my usual happy state. For I am quite in hopes that you will now change your opinion, and that you will have made out an explanation of the causes that prevented my journey to Bordeaux.

Duty laid a strict injunction on me to join at once, and political news also hastened my departure. A war with the North was reported ; my regiment lay in that direction, and I had every reason to expect that it would be on the march before I could reach it. It would have cost me a great deal of money to follow it alone, and I might have had the pain of hearing that it had come in contact with the enemy before my arrival. These I think are valid reasons enough, but they are not all ; when I got to La Durantie, I found I had not a penny, and the little money I could get to meet the cost of a long journey would not allow me to visit you. I thought it was wiser to go at once to the regiment, and ask for leave when my savings will allow of my making this much-desired journey.

I think I told you of the kindness of the major (the second personage of the regiment), and the good reception he gave me. Well, my dear ! the colonel's was as bad as his was good. He has a very harsh manner, and always seems as if he had a spite against one. He hardly said four words to me, and his first were, ' You have been expected a long time, sir.'

I made haste to ask his commands, so as to quit him the more quickly, determining not to go and see him very often. If I intended to continue my military career, I would manage to find a way to get into his good graces; but as I reckon upon abandoning the profession altogether, I will not take any trouble about it.

Yes, my dear, I shall leave off soldiering as soon as we have a Continental peace. Every day do I fortify myself more and more in this intention. The future has to be considered, and I see plainly that this is not a profession for life. I allow that an officer finds a good many pleasant things in it ; but it is only good during youth, and men often find themselves in very unpleasant positions. The devil must be taken by the tail, to provide the turn-out that is required, and a man often runs the risk of spending all his fortune ; and I should do this certainly if I remained, as the way to attract notice is to make a display. Then, if one has the misfortune to displease the chief of the corps, he compels one by main force to send in one's papers, and in a moment you lose ten years' service. Every day do I see officers in this case. That alone would be enough to make me retire, and I do not wish to expose myself to loss of years which I might employ to greater advantage. Just now I have gained more than lost, having travelled much, seen the world, and have not devoured my little portion.

My travel into Germany was most easy. I always had a carriage-and-four which cost me nothing, and I was glad to offer a place to ladies going the same way. At this moment I only need pride and fierceness to be like the seigneurs of old times; for I really have a barony under my orders. I have five villages under my command, occupied by my detachment. I have only to speak, and I am instantly obeyed. Yet, with all these advantages, I find it very dull; I have no society but that of the peasants, and no books.

You will oblige me, my dear, by giving me your advice as to my desire to leave the service. When you give it me, observe that in the present state of things there cannot be any more speedy promotion, as there was in the time of the Revolution. Four years must be spent as sub-lieutenant to qualify for lieutenant, as many for the rank of captain, and so on. I tell you plainly, the miseries of war, the pillage, the vexations, the cruelties, the ruin of the inhabitants, often make me detest my profession. It only pleases me when I think of glory, and the great men who have made themselves famous. But that is a gust of wind that is soon passed.

The poor inhabitants must be entirely ruined. All devour them, from the private to the General in command. There are Generals who give entertainments and banquets which cost as much as 600 florins (1350 francs), and all at the cost of the people. Keep this to yourself. I assure you that I spend nothing but what I am obliged, and that the innkeeper benefits by me.

Adieu, my love.

Your brother,   THOMAS.

CHAPTER VI.

POLAND (1806).

THE Treaty of Presburg was signed. and Napoleon
organized the Confederation of the Rhine on the ruins
of the German Empire. Europe might expect a
peace. But the interlude had hardly begun when
it was almost over. There was to be no rest at
this period.

Less than a year after the battle of the three
Emperors Prussia attempted to eclipse Austria on
pretence of revenging her. A rash idea, destined to
be dissipated by more disgraceful and more really
decisive reverses than had befallen her rival. The
battles of Jena and Auerstadt, the capitulation of
Erfurth, and some actions now forgotten, delivered
the kingdom of the Hohenzollerns to Bonaparte.

Like the descendants of Maria Theresa, the heirs
of the great Frederick begged for Russian support,
and Napoleon found his old Moravian opponents in
the steppes of Poland. Sub-lieutenant Bugeaud performed this new triumphal march in the French army,
and gained a bitter remembrance of it to carry with
him all the days of his life, for the day of Pultusk
brought him his first wound. as that of Austerlitz
had beheld the winning of his first stripes.

Warsaw, 29 December, 1806.

I have been wishing to write to you, my dear, for the last four or five days, but I had hardly begun when a sudden order came to go in pursuit of the Russians. The drum beat, we made a start, and having left Warsaw, we passed in succession the Vistula and the Bug, at a distance of about seven leagues. During the night we had carried the enemy's entrenchments at the point of the bayonet, and driven him towards the Neva. It was on the 24th that this took place: on the 25th there was only a small cavalry skirmish: but on the 26th an army corps found itself placed before the enemy in a little plain near the Neva.* We were very inferior in numbers, for our forces had not all come up, among them the artillery, as the roads were so bad. However, there was no hesitation to attack, for we are always used to conquer. The chief part of our force was posted on the left, for the enemy threatened to outflank us on that side, thanks to a wood that covered them. On our right we had only three battalions of our brigade, unsupported by any cavalry. With this handful of men we attacked a great line of infantry, protected by several batteries, and supported by a large force of cavalry. Our impetuosity threw them into disorder; they fled on all sides, and the guns would have been in our possession if the deep mud had not prevented our moving speedily. A man could hardly drag his legs out of it. At this moment the cavalry charged our left, which had no time to form, because all the men were stuck in the mud, and could only move very slowly. Notwithstanding their terrible fire, the two battalions on the left were overthrown and driven upon the first, where I was. Happily we had time to form square, but we were afraid we should be thrown into disorder by our own comrades in their attempt to escape from death, and we were compelled to kill a good many of them to save the rest, because they were between us and the cavalry. We waited till the mass was within twenty paces of us. Suddenly a fearful discharge confounded and stopped the horsemen—they fell like hail; the rest were seized with a panic, and a shameful flight deprived them of the small share of glory they owed only to the dreadful state of the ground. During our short reverse the enemy's gunners had bravely returned to their pieces, and their infantry had rallied. So we had to encounter a much superior fire. We bore it well, and when we had fired all our cartridges, the officers collected any they could from the killed, and gave them to the men. Hitherto I had been lucky, but a ball came, and struck me just above the left knee. A soldier came and took me by the arm to lead me to the ambulance;

---

* Narew.—*Alison.*

but when he had gone a few paces my conductor was killed by a bullet. So I was left alone in the mud, and, to add to my misfortunes, some fresh squadrons of cavalry came by the rear of our square, and passed just where I was. I had no resource but to feign death; and they were no more successful in this charge than the first. A man picked me up, and led me to a village, where my wound was dressed.*

To make the scene more tragic, the house where I was caught fire. I dragged myself as best I could to another quarter, and from there was carried to Warsaw, where I now am pretty comfortable. My only fear is that I shall never be able to march comfortably, for the tendon is touched. I never rightly knew how the action ended, but think it was to the advantage of the French.*

I have told you my misfortunes—now to cheer you up I will tell you my good luck. I was made a lieutenant a week ago by the Emperor at a review he held here. This is consolation!

Your brother, who loves you,

Thomas Bugeaud.

The following letter, also from Warsaw, mentions the wound; it led to no bad consequences. A certain difficulty in some movements was the only thing that in future reminded the Marshal of this almost inevitable consequence of the profession of arms. As for his horror at the ruined villages, the plains strewed with corpses, the wounded left without help, the fruitless appeals addressed by the living to their friends of the day before, whom they were never to see again, the wars in Spain, France, and Africa, will show how far the new-made officer was cured. Again, how many mighty men of war have been affected like the heroine of Domremy by the first action, who were destined afterwards to sacrifice whole generations with the carelessness of Catherine the Great!

In this letter the young officer's tone is curiously

---

* *See Alison's Hist.*, vol. vi. p. 35. Battle of Pultusk.

changed. We find him a very civilised man of the world, and we would wager that his enforced detention at Warsaw—that Capua of the North—went a long way in the change effected. Certainly the society of the Polish ladies, those enchantresses, very much aroused the animation and wit of the young Frenchman, who sometimes seems to us somewhat worldly-wise and experienced for a young officer of twenty-two.

To Mdlle. Phillis de la Piconnerie.

Warsaw, 21 *February*, 1807.

Be comforted, my dear, I am not crippled! I shall be able to march easily, but perhaps shall never be quite so strong for forced marches; for this, added to a sprain I have had, gives me but a poor leg. I was almost entirely cured by the time of the Carnival, but having chosen to go out too soon, and even having spent the night at a masked ball, my wound broke out bleeding again, and I was as bad as before for a few days. Now it is getting much better, and I hope that in a few days I shall be in condition to rejoin my corps.

I fancy I hear you saying, ‘He is always the same giddy fellow; he will never change!’ Perhaps you are right. However, if I went out too soon, it was because I was very anxious to join my regiment, and had to walk about to get used to severe marches. . . . . .

I am quartered upon a miniature-painter, who is much thought of; and it makes his house very agreeable that he and his children are very good 'musicians. Though still very young, they speak six or seven languages, among them French, with considerable purity.

I am absolutely in the midst of the arts and sciences. I never felt before what it is to have no talents; I think of it every moment. Why was I born in a cursed country where the arts and sciences are almost ignored? . . . . .

In this country they are very much tainted with nobility. The gentlemen are unbearably proud, especially towards their own peasants, who never approach them without kissing their feet, or making a show of doing it. They were very much surprised that the French took no more account of a palatine, or gentleman, than of any other burgess. As we do not know how to bow our heads to the ground, we have been considered unmannerly.

Lately, two ladies were rather stupidly telling stories of French incivility before me. One said, 'To-day an officer very rudely asked me to show him where his quarters were.' The other said, 'Madam, this is much worse. Two officers all over mud were quartered upon me the other day. They were shown into my apartments; I went out to give some orders, and these gentlemen, thinking themselves at home, changed their boots and shirts—in a word, made their whole toilette.' I instantly thought of revenge, as this feeling is natural to us; and fancied that the best way was to vindicate the French women. 'Ladies,' said I, 'we are trained in camps, and it is not surprising that our manners sometimes partake of the roughness of our employment. But if you knew the ladies of France, you would judge much better of the nation. They are polite and modest, they have the tone of good society, and especially much fairness and kindness; never do they utter in conversation the smallest word that could annoy anyone. They are dainty, and display a multitude of little attentions that charm every-one, even the persons who at first thought themselves neglected. They are virtuous, but no prudes; on the contrary, gaiety and enjoyment are their most graceful attributes. In a word, ladies, they have in general all the amiable and solid qualities that a reasonable man, a fool, a giddy-pate, or a philosopher could desire. Oh! my dear country, when shall I revisit you?'

I saw my two Poles blush and bite their lips, but neither said a word. I was silent, and saw that the portrait of my country-women I had drawn had gained me a little consideration.

They no doubt thought that a man who was able to see so many qualities in their sex, could not fail to perceive those that were wanting in them.

I think, my love, I have chattered enough for to-day; yet I do not choose to go to bed before assuring you that I am the most tender of brothers,

THOMAS.

When cured of his wound, Lieutenant Bugeaud had to return to France, to the dépôt of his regiment at Besançon. He passed through Berlin, and stayed there some time. His observations are short, but effective. He writes: 'We are really esteemed in this country, as much on account of our success as for our freedom from pride. They compare us with their own officers, who were vain and insolent; they got no advantage from it.   Alas! their pride is much abased.'

When Lieutenant Bugeaud wrote these words, three-quarters of a century ago, he was far from prophesying that the Prussians, then so humiliated, would one day enter Paris, seventy-four years afterwards, as victors, and encamp on the Champs Elysées before the triumphal monument erected to the Grand Army.

To MDLLE. PHILLIS DE LA PICONNERIE.

Besançon, May 28, 1807.

MY DEAR PHILLIS,—After a journey divided between storms and pleasures, I happily reached Besançon, where one of your good long letters was already awaiting me. Thank you for your advice, always good and prudent, though it is only founded upon your simple judgment. It will please you much that I have quite determined to remain in the service. False hopes had long made me form other plans; but when I saw that I was mistaken, I altered my views, and fully determined not to be so weak again.

I am forgetting to tell you of the miseries of the journey. I was travelling with two captains near Frankfort-on-the-Oder, when we were stopped by some partisans, who were nothing but Prussian prisoners escaped into the woods. They robbed us of everything that we had : I could only save six louis and a ducat that I had sewn into my waistcoat. At Berlin I got an attack in the throat that nearly killed me. A kind doctor attended me for twelve days, and would not take any money, saying that he was too glad to have made the acquaintance of a French officer. We are really much considered in this country, both on account of our exploits and our want of pride. They compare us to their officers, who were empty and insolent. They do not gain by the comparison—their pride is greatly abased. Berlin is quieter than in the time of the king, according to the statement of the inhabitants ; provisions much cheaper, though there is less trade.

I do not in the least expect to join the legions that are in process of formation. Except the Imperial Guard, or the Royal Guard of Holland, which I do not like at all, there is not a corps for which I would exchange my own. According to appearances, I shall be captain in three years.

Adieu, a thousand regards.

Your brother,   THOMAS.

To MDLLE. DE LA PICONNERIE.

Besançon, 1807.

Though I have become somewhat of a philosopher, I have at this time some vexations that I endeavour in vain to stifle. The Government has just appointed a stranger to the regiment to the post of adjutant-major, to which I aspired. The Major is vexed at not having an officer of his own selection. This is a chance that will not occur again for a long time. The adjutant-major has not come yet; I am performing the duties, and showing a brave face to fortune.

I should be very glad to get on General Souhans' staff—it is very pleasant with a kind General. The place of captain attached that I might get is very nearly the same as that of aide-de-camp. He transacts all the business relating to the duties of the division, and a large portion of the General's correspondence. He is obliged to have two horses in war time; the pay is 180 francs a month, and forage, which is very nice.

Adieu, my dear Phillis.

Your brother,   THOMAS BUGEAUD.

Thus, wounded at Pultusk, and unable to follow his comrades in arms, he did not see the battle of Eylau, a contestable victory, the achievement of Murat's horsemen more than of Bonaparte's combinations, and a premonitory sign in the eyes of Benningsen, the Russian Commander-in-chief, of a startling retaliation ; nor that of Friedland, ' the daughter of Marengo,' as said the Corsican hero in the imaginative language affected by the people of the South ; nor the other various military events that led to the peace of Tilsit.

What an error of the conquering autocrat was the

imperial Utopia destined to increase the Empire of the Czars with Bessarabia and Finland, to alienate Turkey and Sweden from France, and, lastly, to prepare in the regions of the North a centre of resistance to the desires of its author !   The vanquished of Austerlitz and Friedland became, thanks to combinations, less worthy of Cæsar than of Charles XII. ; the heir-presumptive of Constantine was to bring about the fall of the 'great man,' whose friend he proclaimed himself before a gallery of kings.   Anyway, the Treaty of Presburg was going to secure a moment's repose to Europe, exhausted and out of breath ; while no one could then prophesy all its results.

CHAPTER VII.

IN SPAIN (1808–9).

THOMAS BUGEAUD had been for two years a lieutenant of Infantry of the Line (June 30, 1808) when he obtained leave for six months. This was the first time since his enlistment that he made so long a stay in Périgord. Home-life, the affection he so much needed, his native air, inspired him afresh with disgust at military life,—a disgust that he had so often displayed in his letters to his sister Phillis. So he decided, one fine day, to break with the past, and it was without hesitation or regret that he wrote to the Minister and sent in his resignation. His sister, Antoinette, offered to carry his letter herself to the post in the town. But, on consultation with her other sisters, she carefully locked up the important missive enclosed in a sheet of paper. The young man, delighted at having made up his mind, and proud of having regained his liberty for ever, set himself seriously to the study of agriculture with the help of his sister Phillis. Nevertheless, he was beginning to be surprised at the Minister's delay in acknowledging the receipt of his resignation, when, instead of the final release that he expected, it was an order to join his regiment that he received.

All was explained; his sisters' plot was discovered and forgiven; and the poor officer, who had so gladly renounced the glorious profession of arms, went to join his regiment, the 116th of the Line, which had just been sent to Spain.

The peace of Tilsit might have made Sub-lieutenant Bugeaud believe for a moment that his desires would be fulfilled. Isolated from all Europe by the checks to her allies, and especially by the bad faith with which she had repaid their assistance, England would be forced, in the opinion of the politicians of the time, to behold, as an envious but impotent observer, the elevation of the Empires of the East and West, the two divisions of the civilised world.

But the new pacificator of Europe had not despoiled the conqueror of Italy and Austria in order to spend the latter part of a career already so eventful in the administrative organization of his dominions. One day this indefatigable winner of crowns noticed Spain, and having at a single glance comprehended its resources, and its strange government, he determined to conquer it.

Soon afterwards Charles IV., the possible heir of the crown of France, placed the States of the Emperor Charles V. and Philip V. in the hands of Monsieur Bonaparte, Lieutenant-General of the armies of Louis XVIII., who interfered in the internal discords of the Peninsula in the name of outraged morality.

The people displayed a less accommodating humour than their King. Everything on which Bonaparte had reckoned seemed to turn against him. The young Spaniards learnt in a new kind of catechism that Satan was in three persons, Napoleon, Murat, and Godoy.*

---

* Manuel Godoy, Principe de la Paz, Minister to the King of Spain.

With the feverish activity peculiar to the people of the South, who are condemned by the consequences of efforts as excessive as they are momentary to ages of stagnation, the Spaniards organized, in a few months, an insurrectionary government and a regular defence. The Juntas, equal in number to the provinces, who at first had dearly paid the penalty of local ideas, formed the central Cortes of Cadiz. From this provisional capital, continually exposed to the fire of the French batteries, were soon to issue the civil and military liberators of Spain.

Upon this rock, surmounted with a fortress backed by the ocean, which constituted the whole European empire of the prisoner of Valençay, the sword of Napoleon was to be broken. At the moment of this explosion, Madrid was not forgetful that she was the head of Spain. The War of Independence commenced on the threshold of the royal palace. The second of May saw Castillian valour, forgotten the day before, blaze forth into light, and was the commencement of an era of glory.

For the first time did Lieutenant Bugeaud fight against a popular rising. What impression was produced on the future sword of the monarchy of July, by this war, without rule or law, but undertaken, it is true, in the name of the national religion, invaded country and dethroned king? The following letter, which does not appear to reflect the ferocity so long attributed by fable to 'the general of Transnonain,' will answer that question:

To MDLLE. ANTOINETTE DE LA PICONNERIE.

Madrid, 10*th May,* 1808.

Your conscience is very tranquil, very approving, my dear Toiny; because I have not written to you ten times, you think you have nothing to blame yourself for. Well, you are wrong, you are very much to blame, not only for the harm you have done, but for the good you have neglected to do. Do you think that a poor soldier, away from any kind of pleasure, is not worth consideration, and ought you not to have relieved his weariness with several long letters? Remember that I read them at least six times the first day every two hours, and think of them meanwhile. I spend a happy day. Thus you are to blame. This is demonstrated, and so for the future be more wise.

You do not expect to hear the sound of guns and musketry; well! put cotton-wool in your ears, for you will be cannonaded. The populace of Madrid took a fancy to revolt on the second of May. They seized upon straggling Frenchmen and cut their throats, then ran to the arsenal, took possession of it, dragged out guns, seized upon firelocks, and began a little war in the streets with some French pickets. On our side we were not inactive. The assembly was beaten, we hurried to the city, and their success was but brief. We attacked them vigorously upon all points. They were overthrown, their guns taken, and in one hour this confused mass existed no longer. The same day a good many of the guilty were shot. We lost some men in this action. I got out of it for a bruise and a slight scratch. The insurgents wished to murder our sick in the general hospital, but the strongest of these broke open the stores of arms and exterminated their assailants. Peace appears to be restored; but there is no depending on it, though the Prince is doing his utmost to quiet minds by his proclamations and his generosity to many of the guilty. He behaved with humanity, stopping our vengeance at several points at the moment when the carnage was most dreadful.

I assure you I am not much at ease when walking through the streets; I always have my hand on my sword, for there were daily assassinations before the revolt, and these gentlemen took our moderation for weakness. Now they are more gentle. Do you think that this little life is better than the gun and game-bag that you tell me of?

I assure you it is not a good time for playing the flute at night under a beauty's windows, and besides we have no leisure. So the article of love goes but badly in general. Every one complains of a dearth of intrigues, and perhaps I am one of the most lucky, though that is not much. A pretty little French milliner promised to love me for three days, and to go on after that if I am alive. She says, by way of reason, that our loves being birds of passage one cannot promise for long. My answer was that the proofs must not be migratory, and begged for some on the spot that they might be permanent. The answer was that if I got them, perhaps in three

days I should not ask for a continuance, and must wait. I yielded
to these grand reasons, but asked for pledges; and was given a
ring and lent the *Lettres à Émilie*. I begged her to read them
with me in order to furnish me with applications. You have the
whole account of my Spanish loves, for you know that we have
them in every country. You do not tell me about the truffles, nor
'Polisson' [Bugeaud's dog]. My love to all relations and friends. As
for you, you shall have nothing till an answer comes.   BUGEAUD.

This explosion of patriotism, extraordinarily exaggerated in importance by the fertile imagination of
the Spaniards, was in reality the commencement of the
war, most sacred, most embittered, and most glorious
to the people who maintained it, mentioned in con-
temporary European history.

Less than a year after the revolt of Madrid, Lieutenant Bugeaud was engaged in the capture of Saragossa. What man awake to the name of patriotism
knows not the legend, if not the history, of this epic
defence? In every age a town of Iberia has been a
self-devoted holocaust for the national glory. Saragossa was a match for Saguntum and Numantia. And
so the French were imbued with admiration for this
improvised army, these public or private edifices
transformed into fortresses, these heroic leaders torn
from the charms of indolence, like Palafox,* or the
peace of a monastery, like Merino.† The young
officer's letter bears the impress of sadness; and
shows the reader all the admiration he felt for this
people with whom he was compelled to fight.

To MDLLE. PHILLIS DE LA PICONNERIE.

Bivouac before Saragossa, Feb. 12, 1809.

I have received, my dear Phillis, your little letter full of great reproaches, and, as I do not deserve them, I will not make excuses. I

---

* Defender of Saragossa.
† The Cura Merino, a guerilla leader who did much harm to the French.—ED.

wish to direct your anger and mine against the Spanish assassins, who murder a great many couriers, though all precautions are taken. So complaints about correspondence are universal. The colonel of the regiment has received your letter of inquiry about me; he tells me he will answer it, but, for fear he should forget to reassure you, I do not miss the chance of an officer who is going to France as escort to a wounded general. I can write freely to you, for he will post the letter after passing Bayonne, and so there will be no fear of its being opened.

We are still before this cursed, this infernal, Saragossa. Although we took their ramparts by storm more than a fortnight ago, and are masters of part of the town, the inhabitants, stirred up by the hatred they bear us, by the priests and fanaticism, seem to wish to bury themselves under the ruins of their city, after the pattern of old Numantia. They defend themselves with incredible determination, and make us buy the smallest victory very dear.

Every convent, every house, holds out like a citadel, and every one has to be besieged by itself. The whole is disputed foot by foot, from the cellar to the loft, and it is not until everyone is killed with bayonet thrusts or thrown out of window that we call ourselves masters of a house. As soon as we have conquered one, there come upon us from the next house, through holes made for the purpose, grenades, shells, and a rain of musketry. It is necessary to raise barricades and cover ourselves very speedily, till measures are taken for attacking this fresh fort, and that can only be done by piercing the walls, for traversing the streets is impossible; the whole army would perish in them in a couple of hours. It was not enough to make war in the houses, it is carried on beneath the earth. An art no doubt invented by devils leads the miners beneath the building held by the enemy. A large quantity of powder is laid there, fired at a given signal, and the wretches fly into the air or are buried beneath the ruins. The explosion makes the enemy evacuate the neighbouring houses in fear of the same fate. We are posted very near, and rush into them as quick as we can. This is how we make our way in this wretched city. You may imagine how many men such a war must cost. How many young fellows, the hope of their families, have already perished among this rubbish! Our brigade has already lost two generals. General Lacoste, of the Engineers, a young man of the greatest promise who was not long from school, but already made one of the Emperor's aides-de-camp, has fallen a victim to his devotion, as well as so many others. There is not a day when there are not some officers among the dead—many more than in proportion to the soldiers, because the enemy, firing with certain aim when we make the attack, select their victims.

Oh! my dear, what a life, what an existence! It is now two months that we have been between life and death, corpses and ruins. If we get all the advantage from this war that is expected, it will be bought very dear. But the most fearful thing is to think that our labours and our blood may not be of use to our country. I always remember these lines of Voltaire.—

> Encore si pour votre patrie
> Vous saviez vous sacrifier ;
> Mais non, vous vendez votre vie
> A ceux qui veulent la payer.*

Who can foresee the end of so many ills? Happy they who may catch a glimpse of it.

I write very sadly to you, my dear; but what would you have? One's mind is affected. No doubt if I had hopes of seeing you again soon I should be more cheerful; but alas! that moment is far removed. While waiting its coming, may God preserve your health and happiness, and He will grant my most cherished desires.

A thousand loves to Toiny and all your family.

THOMAS BUGEAUD,
Captain in the 116th.

Saragossa was at last conquered, and Palafox went to swell the number of his countrymen detained in France until the terrible reckoning of 1814. This siege, almost as much renowned to the north as to the south of the Pyrenees, was worth captain's rank to Lieutenant Bugeaud. And yet at this time the future Duke d'Isly seemed less concerned about his promotion than about that Périgord which he so ardently desired to revisit in order to resume his former habits there.

To MDLLE. PHILLIS DE LA PICONNERIE.

Pampeluna, 20 March, 1809.

How can I contrive, my dear Phillis, to express to you my joy and my sorrow? These two feelings present such a contrast, that it

---

* If only you knew how to sacrifice self for your country : but no, you sell your life to any that will buy it.

is hard to believe they can exist in one head at the same moment. However, that is what has happened to me to-day, but it is true that my sorrow is greater than my joy. To talk of the bad first.

You know I was in hopes that my return to France, or a journey into Germany, would procure me the great pleasure of being a witness of the first day of your happiness. In addition to this pleasant anticipation, there was the expectation of a journey to Bordeaux, by the colonel's orders, to buy musical instruments for our regimental band. I had the order in my pocket, and was ready to go, when the order to turn back into Spain arrived; my captain was ill, and no officer with the company but one only eighteen years old. The colonel told me he could not send me away, for a grenadier company could not go on a campaign without an officer to command it. Imagine my annoyance at the information, but I could not say a word. There was talk of another siege, it would have risked the loss of all I had won at the siege of Saragossa. So off I went, and here I am at Pampeluna, where we have this morning been reviewed by the governor. While we were under arms, the colonel also was preparing a surprise for me as I am doing for you now, called me, addressed me as captain and handed me my commission! This is the cause of my rejoicing.

Adieu, &c.,

BUGEAUD,
Captain, 2nd March.

P.S.—Our general of division is dead: that is the fifth since our entrance into Spain, four by the enemy's fire, and one by the prevailing sickness.

TO MDLLE. HÉLÈNE DE LA PICONNERIE.

Saragossa, 30 April, 1809.

MY DEAR HÉLÈNE:—Your kind letter found me at Saragossa, where I have been for several days. A false alarm made us leave our cantonments to concentrate near the capital. Now it seems that the enemy have not made offensive movements. We have lost a good deal by these changes: the soldiers do not get such good food, we have to take up new ways, and change our mode of life according to the places we are sent to. Certainly I do not think that it would be advantageous to get into the guard with my rank, and those who say so are much mistaken. A captain in the guard ranks with a chef-de-bataillon in the line, and he can only exchange as such, indeed there are several who have gone out as majors.

This is a very evident advantage. Now to consider the difficulty that there is to get the rank of chef-de-bataillon in the line. There are eight captains for each chef-de-bataillon, and so there are eight candidates. Now I am the youngest captain of my regiment, and so have no ground to hope to be chosen in preference to my comrades. Let us then try to gain at once a rank that I cannot win here for a long time.

I am very thankful for the remembrances of the C——. Please inform them of my thanks for their kind wish to be useful to me, and my great desire to be in a position to know them better. I embrace you with my whole heart.

BUGEAUD,
Captain Light Company of the 116th.

Fortune was already turning against the man she had loaded with favours. The resistance of Spain was preparing the public mind for the fatal campaigns of Russia and Saxony.

After a short stay at Saragossa, the new-made captain twice crossed the north-west of Spain in search of the unapproachable enemy whom the Grand Army was never to bring to submission. These marches and counter-marches, that go to make up almost all wars of this kind, caused him to be present at the combats of Moria and Balahite,* and gained him the epaulette of superior officer.

---

* Mgr. the Duke d'Aumale has told us a good deal that is interesting as to the importance Marshal Bugeaud throughout his life attached to his campaign in Spain. ' It was the subject he opened most willingly and most frequently,' said the Prince. ' The sieges of Saragossa and Lerida, his campaigns in Aragon, came over and over again in his talk. He told of the battles with fire and animation, and loved to remember that time. His accounts were also full of points. How many times in Africa, at the bivouac fire, have we spent the whole night, not quite to our satisfaction, listening to the Marshal. He slept but little and when he pleased ; this was not the case with his aides-de-camp and me, who were often falling asleep, but kept nearly awake by our respect. How often, when an officer complained of being forgotten or sacrificed, have I heard the Marshal say to him, " If you had only lived in the time of the Empire it would have been quite another thing ! After the campaigns in Germany, after Austerlitz, Pultusk, the wars in Spain, the sieges of Saragossa, Lerida, and the rest, I was a captain,—an old captain, do you understand ! and not decorated. We did not think of complaining then." '

To Mdlle. Phillis de la Piconnerie.

Saragossa, 29 September, 1809.

I did not choose to answer your last letter immediately, my dear Phillis, because I waited to be able to tell you something positive as to the commission you gave me about the Spaniard. At last I determined to mention it to Combemoreau himself. I discharged it with exactitude to please you as well as our relation: but I did nothing for the Aragonese peasant. I detest that class of assassins and fanatics too much. However, the brother of Gregorio has showed me much gratitude for the information I gave him.

We remain at Saragossa, to our weariness and the draining of our purses. Everything is so dear, that the pay of lieutenants and sub-lieutenants is not enough for them to live upon. This wretched city still feels the disastrous effects of the siege. It is depopulated, and the inhabitants that are left are so mournful that they freeze everything around them. No amusing society, no *tertullias* (evening parties). All remain shut up in their houses.

I cannot tell you how weary I am of this town: I go so far as to wish to be campaigning to get away from this cursed place. The only resource we have against this weary time is to eat, drink, and sleep; and the only eatables here are brought us by Frenchmen, who, attracted to the army by interest alone, take advantage of the circumstances to devour our substance. Our future does not appear likely to be brighter. If peace is not made in Austria, affairs here will go dragging. We are strong enough to beat the enemy, but not to pursue him after the victory. This cursed Peninsula is so large and so mountainous, that it would take three hundred thousand men to hold it in such a way as to ensure its speedy subjection. What we have done till now is of hardly any use. We have occupied several provinces which have risen again as soon as we left them; and even those we hold to-day are filled with little parties who, too weak to attack the army, fall upon small detachments, badly escorted convoys, couriers, orderlies, &c. But this is melancholy talk enough; I must repair the effect it has had by telling you that nothing is wanting to my satisfaction but a better political condition. I am in a regiment that I look upon as a second home; my comrades like me; I think my chiefs value me, for they give me daily proofs of it; I command a fine company, well clothed, well disciplined, that cannot fail to get me credit when there is an action. What is wanting to my happiness? Could I reasonably hope for such a good result when I entered the service without interest, without those brilliant talents that enable a young man always to make his way if he knows how to use them? By the way, it is as well to let you know that I expect to remain a long time in the new rank I have just gained. It is not uncommon to see captains who have been so for fifteen years. There are in a regiment twenty-eight captains; there are so many competitors for one place of chef-de-bataillon that may chance to be vacant; I tell you all this that you may not be impatient in a few years' time. If I am a superior officer by the time I am thirty-two, I shall be well pleased.

I am very anxious to know if my business with Patrice is settled. Do you know I have written to him twice, now several months ago, and he has not answered?

Tell me what has become of Dubois in the turmoil. If you could give him a useful present, you would do me a favour.

If you know any young men who wish, or who ought, to enter the service, well brought up, and able to write a good hand, you may, in my name, boldly advise them to go before the Prefect and engage for the 116th regiment: the depôt is at Aire, in Gascony. I promise them that, if they have the qualifications named above, they will be sergeants within six months. If you are interested in some of those who embrace this career you must inform me of their arrival at the dépôt. I will ask to have them sent to the battalions in the front, and then I will give them a good pat on the shoulder till they get the rank of sub-officer, and then it only depends on themselves to get made officers. . . . . . .

I go after game here whenever I have time. I kill a great many fat quails, very often I have wished you could have a dozen of them.

Just as I am writing come two bits of news : one—neither good nor bad—is our departure from Saragossa on an expedition: the second is this, very bad for the regiment. There were coming to us from the dépôt two hundred pairs of shoes, four hundred sets of clothing, cloth for all the officers, epaulettes, thirty soldiers and twenty-nine musicians with their instruments. The insurgents in the mountains have attacked and taken this convoy, and that is a loss to us of 40,000 francs. That of our band, especially, will not be made good for a long time. Adieu, dear sister.

Thomas Bugeaud.

To Mdlle. Antoinette de la Piconnerie.

Barbastro, a town of the north of Aragon,
not far from the Pyrenees, 1809.

I received your kind letter. my dear Toiny, just at the moment when I had reached Saragossa, and found myself in front of the enemy; it made me for a moment forget that the cannon roared; and when we got the order to attack, the only painful feeling I experienced was that I could not read it a second time. So after the affair I fully recompensed myself. I read all you told me quite quietly; how delightful to hear what goes on in the country! But, here I have written a page, and told you nothing yet.

To begin, you know, perhaps, that after our return to Bayonne, in Spain, we were sent to Burgos, in the kingdom of Leon; that afterwards we made our expedition into Galicia, and went nearly to Corunna. Now take the map and follow me.

Here I am on the march to return to Leon, crossing the mountains and country of Vierys. Reaching the capital of the kingdom of Leon we find a gathering of troops, who are going on an expedition into the Asturias, and informed that we are to join them. We start by the steep cut road that leads to Oviedo, and the day before we ought to arrive at that capital, our brigade receives an order to turn back and go into Aragon, where the horizon was beginning to darken. We set off by long marches to return to the scene of our former glory. We rapidly cross Leon, Old Castille, the south of Navarre, and at last reach the plain of Saragossa. What was our surprise to see all the baggage of the army in retreat, and all arrangements made to abandon a town that a few months before had cost so much trouble! We learnt that General Blake, having heard that the 5th corps had quitted Aragon, and that there were not more than 10,000 of the 3rd, had united 30,000 men of the armies of Valencia and Catalonia to seize upon our conquests, and was not more than two leagues from the capital.

The little French army was making a good show in presence of the enemy who were posted in the village of Maria, which is in a valley fringed by rather high mountains, and this favoured our small force. However, General Suchet had every reason to fear that he would be crushed by numbers, and for two days had been avoiding a general engagement in order to await our arrival. It was the 17th of June, at noon, that we effected our junction. It was announced to the army in order to give them confidence, and we immediately took our places in the line after having marched seven leagues; it was then I received your letter. The enemy, impatient to reach Saragossa, attacked us; as soon as he moved we went at him and in a moment the whole line was engaged. General Suchet made several very able manœuvres, and the last decided the contest. While all the cavalry having gained the left flank of the enemy charged between his two lines, the whole of the infantry attacked in front with the bayonet. The boastful bands could not resist our impetuosity. They broke on all sides, and in less than half-an-hour we had gained a complete victory. The enemy left in our hands twenty-seven guns, three colours, a quantity of baggage, ammunition, a great number of killed, wounded, and prisoners. Among the last were two generals and several superior officers.

In this battle I became by chance captain of a light company. I had been sent with my company of the centre, under the orders of a captain of the light company of the same regiment who was senior to me; we were skirmishing in the olive-groves and in a village on the bank of a little stream called the Warba; a post of consequence to keep. The poor captain of the light company was killed by a discharge of grape, and so I found myself commanding. The enemy tried several times to carry the post, but we always received them with such a sharp fire that they were obliged to drop their intention after leaving a number of dead before our shelters, from which we fired point-blank. By this means we prevented the enemy from passing by the only practicable road to turn the left of our army. It is true we were supported by a squadron, but they had no occasion to charge.

After the battle General Suchet came to the regiment, and asked who were the captains commanding the skirmishers in the village. I was put forward. He said, ' He must be saluted as captain of the Voltigeurs, for he looks to me like a skirmisher.' It is right to tell you that I had a double-barrelled gun in a sling at my back, and this, added to the rest of my equipment, gave me a very swaggering look. I gave my thanks, and here I am commanding the green epaulettes and bugles. This does not suit my stature very well; but it is true that I am not cut off from the Grenadier company, and that is worth more, at least in respect of promotion.

After Moria came the combat of Balahite, where we took from the enemy all the guns he had left, and a number of prisoners. After this we crossed Aragon by forced marches, and here we are at Barbastro resting a little.

I cannot write any more to you as I have to take advantage of an opportunity of sending to Saragossa, and that does not happen every day. I beg you will tell Phillis about me, and Patrice and all the family, and you may, if desired, send my letter round.

Thomas Bugeaud.

To Mdlle. Phillis de la Piconnerie.

Saragossa, September 2, 1809.

My dear Phillis,—I do not like to lose a moment in telling you anything that happens to me, good or bad, because you take the same interest in it as I do: it would, indeed, be treason against friendship not to tell you everything. Well, you must know that I have been made captain of Grenadiers, that I command the first company, composed of a hundred and twenty of the finest men in the regiment and best behaved. Thus I hold an honourable position that I had no right to expect with my short amount of service. Another thing that should also go into the account is, that it is worth 600 francs more a-year. So here I am, a little lord with an income of 2400 francs. You can well understand that with this I am no longer obliged to live upon my little fortune, so you must be less careful in dealing with it.

I have nothing now to tell you; we are inactive, though surrounded with enemies, timid ones it is true, on account of their numerous defeats. It may be supposed that we shall make some attempt towards the end of this month, when the heat will be less.

I have mentioned Barbastro to you in another letter, we left it in the following way; a chef-de-bataillon, posted fourteen leagues from Saragossa, was attacked before day by a handful of insurgents; terror got the better of him, and he fled with all of his battalion he could collect, leaving two or three companies at the mercy of the supposed enemy. Not content with this cowardice, he immediately wrote a report to the General-in-chief that he had been pursued by a considerable force, had lost a part of his battalion, and only got in after a terrible contest. What happened? Why, the said companies, braver than their chief, chose to await a serious attack before retiring; day came, they saw the weakness of the assailants, issued from the village, and saved the position. But the General, before he knew this, sent out his orders to all the troops to concentrate with all speed upon the capital. This is why I have left the agreeable Barbastro.

It is supposed that the chef-de-bataillon will be cashiered. Adieu, your devoted brother,

THOMAS BUGEAUD,
Captain of Grenadiers in the 116th.

After the combat of Balahite Commandant Bugeaud constantly followed the fortunes of Marshal Suchet. And so a few months after these engagements we find him in Catalonia engaged in the war of sieges that took place in that province.

CHAPTER VIII.

LERIDA (1810–14).

AGAIN we will leave the actor in the siege of Lerida
himself to relate how this strong fortress lost its old
reputation of impregnability.

To MDLLE. ANTOINETTE DE LA PICONNERIE.

Lerida, 4 June, 1810.

I have written to you, my dear Toiny, by my Colonel, who is
gone to France, but as that letter may be delayed a long time before
it reaches you, and I do not like you to feel as if you mig'.t complain of me, I am going to address another to you. I hope you
will cease to think that I make a favourite of Phillis, especially
when you recollect she wrote oftener to me than you did, and it
was but fair that I should answer her. Difference in affection has
nothing to do with it, and I think I love you all equally—that is,
all very much.

You leave politics and war to Phillis: you only want historical
descriptions. Nevertheless, should not you be very glad to have an
account of the siege and assault of Lerida? And after that I will
tell you of the effect that our vigorous attack has produced upon the
beauties as well as the plain ones.

The trenches were opened very near the works, with the audacity
that is characteristic of the French Army.* The works were con-

---

* At only 300 yards from the bastions.—*Napier's Peninsular War*, vol. iii. p.
152. Ground was broken April 28, the citadel surrendered May 12. Suchet
assaulted with converging columns, that, when the ramparts were carried, drove
all the inhabitants, women and children, into the citadel. He then commenced

tinued with ardour when it was known that an army was coming to relieve the enemy. Nothing was suspended on that account; only the cavalry and some few battalions were detached to meet 12,000 of the best Spanish troops. The combat took place within sight of the city, and a diversion was attempted by a sortie of 2000 men. Victory speedily declared itself in our favour. It was a brilliant charge of the 13th Cuirassiers and 4th Hussars that decided this affair, an everlasting triumph for our cavalry. The enemy's ranks were fearfully crushed, his infantry, put to the sword and broken, were obliged to lay down their arms, and not one man of the first division—7000 combatants—managed to escape. The cavalry only owed their safety to a speedy retreat. The garrison was not much more fortunate; they were driven back to the gates with the bayonet behind them.

In a few days batteries were established, and fired on the works, without much luck. The fire of the Castle crushed them, and in three hours they were silenced, and others had to be constructed. The bad weather was against us. However, five days afterwards forty guns were in position, and opened two large breaches.

The enemy must have expected the assault on that day; they were deceived by attacks made upon some formidable redoubts they held on another side, that were very bravely taken. Next day the assault of the place was ordered, ten picked companies, mine being one of them, were in orders, and assembled in the trenches nearest to the breaches.

About six in the evening, at the signal of four cannon-shots, we dashed on like lightning. The walls were escaladed, the works were entered, several barricades were broken, and our enemies perished in crowds under our blows. A gate leading to the quays delayed us a moment: then several of our brave men were killed by a point-blank discharge. At last the gate was broken; we entered in a mass, racing with one another. Every man wanted to be first to strike, nothing could stop us—bayonets, shot, and pikes could not daunt our ardour. I have the luck of penetrating the mass with my company; I am the first to reach a fortified post, and I cut off a lot of the enemy whom we treated to the edge of the sword and the bayonet. The redoubts, the guns, the city, all fell into our hands. The terrified Spaniards took refuge in the citadel and carried alarm with them. A number of the inhabitants also took

---

such a furious bombardment that the governor felt constrained to surrender to spare the misery of so many helpless persons. The Spaniards were considered to have been badly handled, as the attacking army was not more numerous than the defending, instead of four times as large according to the rules of siege operations. Napier —ED.

refuge there. The soldiers, greedy for pillage, scatter themselves about among the houses; carnage ceases, and gives place to scenes of quite another kind; the conquerors are everywhere seen in the arms of the vanquished—Carmelites, grey sisters, old women, young nuns, all experienced the transports of our Grenadiers, and several of them are said to have cried out, ' Oh, if we had known that this would be all we should not have been so much afraid.'

The day after this terrible one, the forts were terrified into offering to capitulate, and so in a short time we made ourselves masters of a formidable city that had seen the great Condé fail at the foot of its walls, and that the Duke of Orleans only took in 1707 after thirty-three days of open trenches. But the greatest advantage of our victory is that it has turned the minds of all the women in our favour. They were breathing nothing but revenge and detestation; to-day they have become so kind and gentle that there is no more need for an assault. By way of formality they exact the honours of war, and these are always granted them. We stay some days at Lerida ; and already there is a talk of sieges of Valencia and Tortosa. Always beginning again!

Your brother,

Thomas Bugeaud.

Time passes, King Joseph has already lost and then regained his capital, where he only displays his power by acts of clemency, using in vain the most noble attribute which the constitutions of the age leave in possession of the rulers of the State. In the various provinces of the Peninsula the work of conquest only eventuated in barren victories. Catalonia is divided into departments, organized upon the model of those of France; but the strong towns, the mountains, the isolated villages, everything that is guarded from our arms by art, nature, or solitude, still resist the invaders, and shelter the soldiers of independence. The heroic and patient adversaries of the Moors, waked up by the sound of the guns of Saragossa, and encouraged by daily partial successes, sustain the military ardour that enables them to hope for a final victory.

To Mdlle. Phillis de la Piconnerie.

At the bivouac of Tivisa (Catalonia), eight leagues from Tortosa, on the left bank of the Ebro, July, 1810.

I am sorry to hear nothing of you, my dear Phillis, but I do not blame you. There are so many couriers intercepted I am very much afraid that either my letters have not reached you, or that your replies have fallen into the hands of some Spanish partisan, who probably has made very little account of what is so very dear to me. If these gentlemen would wish to be reconciled to me, let them send me your correspondence. I would content myself with making them prisoners : but, as they have not been gallant enough to do it, I declare war to the death against them, and, as often as any of them fall into my hands, I will send them to Pluto to teach them how to live.

I told you in my former letters that you might dispose of my little revenue as you pleased without being obliged to consult me.

I have given you an account of the siege of Lerida, and that I had gained some credit there. If I had possessed the least interest I should have been made a lieutenant-colonel. My colonel asked for this promotion for me, and Pascal told me he saw the application in the report that the general of division sent to Count Suchet. I do not know if it reached the Government. But I am not without some hopes, and two consecutive fights we have just had at Tivisa have refreshed them. The 116th Regiment has gained much credit. I will tell you this in place. I am going to begin by making you perfect in our earliest operations.

The Third Corps marched on the two sides of the Ebro towards Tortosa, to besiege it. This movement seemed to be in combination with Marshal MacDonald, who commands in Catalonia ; but it seems that the shattered condition of his army, and the deficiency of magazines in this wasted country, prevented him from starting as soon as we did. Notwithstanding this difficulty, General Suchet established his head-quarters at Xora, formed the blockade of the bridge-head of Tortosa, which is upon the right bank, and pushed up our division on the left bank to within two leagues of the place. He established two flying bridges for communication, the one at Tibinys, the other before Mora. Care was taken to protect them by field-works. However, the Spanish army, not being attacked on the side of Taragona, turned all its attention to us. General Odonilla issued a proclamation, in which he exhorted all the inhabitants to join the army in order to throw us into the Ebro. He named for points of concentration Falcet and Tivisa, from which it was easy for him to hinder our communications, as well as the navigation of the Ebro. In fact, three thousand Spaniards and some hundreds of peasants came to occupy Tivisa. A similar number proceeded to the other point, at only four leagues distance.

General Suchet, informed of this, ordered the 115th and 116th on detachment to attack the men at Tivisa. The combat was not bloody; the enemy gave ground as soon as we met, leaving in our power a very few prisoners and some stores.

We remained holding this place to the number of seven hundred; the 115th returned to Mora.

On the sixteenth of July we were attacked by six thousand men, commanded by three generals. Our forces being dispersed over various hillocks that it was important to guard, it was not difficult to drive us from them. However, we only yielded foot by foot, and when being attacked by very superior forces we had reason to fear that we should be surrounded. We made several brilliant charges, but at last were obliged to yield to numbers. We were successively deprived of all our positions, and found ourselves forced to retire by the road to Mora. I was entrusted with the duty of covering the retreat, during which I lost nineteen men; but having stopped the enemy in several places, I prevented them from taking advantage of the disorder that reigned in the column, as they could not have failed to make a great many prisoners.

General Abbé re-formed the column on a plateau covered with vines, and bounded by rather difficult ravines. The enemy manœuvred in three columns; two tried to turn our flanks, and the third attacked us in front. A little audacity, with the help of a simple trick of war enough, got us out of the scrape. We had just received three fresh companies: two were placed at the head with mine, the third extended on the flanks to drive off the skirmishers. In this order we resolved to charge the centre column with the bayonet, judging, with reason, that the ravines would prevent the others from taking part in the action for some time. We had been fighting all day in white linen chakos;* we took them off and having done this rushed upon the column with the greatest vivacity. Astonished at our audacity, and supposing by the change of ornament that we had received a considerable reinforcement, they only fired once, and were thrown into horrible disorder. Without giving them time to rally, we pursued them with the bayonet at their flanks to the foot of a high hill, where they broke, leaving in our power their wounded and a great many prisoners. The rest, terrified at the defeat of the centre, escaped

---

* Probably cap *covers* that they took off. —ED.

into the mountains. We pursued them till night, killing and wounding a large number of them.

This combat is a very evident proof that it is not numbers that decide the victory. A body inferior in number to its enemy, but composed of brave men, and directed by a man of skill, should fear nothing. It may encounter a momentary check, but its constancy and determination will furnish its chief with the means of seizing a fortunate opportunity, and repairing everything in a moment.

This little victory only served to prove our superiority; for, with a thousand men, we beat six thousand ; but the results were not considerable enough to make the enemy abandon their projects. They were reinforced at Falcet ; we at Tivisa. In a few days there will be a battle. The victory is not doubtful, they will be beaten ; but I do not expect the action will be decisive, because the difficulties of the ground do not permit the action of our cavalry, and present a thousand ways of escape to a beaten army.

We lost in the affair of the 16th a chef-de-bataillon (we had one in succession who replaced him), three lieutenants and sub-lieutenants, twenty-two soldiers and sergeants, and forty-eight wounded. A very slight loss for so serious a conflict, with several bayonet encounters.

I think I shall be able to tell you that I am a member of the Legion of Honour. There are fourteen crosses for my regiment. The list is made, and I am at the top. It has been forwarded to the Chancellerie, and we expect our patents every day. As to the lieutenant-coloneley, that is not so certain. However, as I have already told you, there is still hope. After the affair of the 16th, General Abbé said to me, 'Young man, I think I may promise you that you will be chef-de-bataillon before the end of the year.'

I tell you rather shamelessly of these flattering words addressed to a young man who follows the profession of arms, but I hope it will not go beyond the family, and that you will judge me well enough to think that it is my great confidence in you that makes me thus communicative.

Write to me twice for once, and tell me the same things over again, for the roads have never been less secure. As we advance in our conquests, the brigands multiply in our rear. There must be no army for us to go to work with them.

BUGEAUD.

Who could then foresee that the year 1812 which had just commenced, would see the Grand Army disappear among the snows of Russia, while in Spain every day brought on the capture of a fortress or the destruction of a guerilla? However, this desperate warfare was not nearly concluded.

Marshal Suchet, the most notable organizer of the conquest of the Peninsula, made himself master of the city of Valencia and received the title of Duke.

To Mdlle. Toiny de la Piconnerie.

Camp before Valentia, 1 January, 1812.

We crossed the Guadalaviar on the 26th, and after a rather sharp encounter the city was very closely invested. General Blake, president of the insurrectionary Junta, is inside with 15,000 men. The rest of his troops have escaped to Alicante. Our army is superb, full of confidence, and rejoicing in an excellent spirit; that of the Spaniards, on the contrary, is entirely discouraged by its numerous defeats, and will soon be in want of everything. This difference of situation must very soon cause the fall of Valencia, and the conquest of the kingdom of that name.

We opened the trenches last night, all is going on most excellently.

Adieu, &c.,

Bugeaud.

Among the letters of Thomas Bugeaud to his family—precious letters, for which we are indebted to M. Robert Gasson-Bugeaud d'Isly, owner of all his grandfather's papers—we have found one dated from Barcelona, and addressed to an old servant of the family of La Piconnerie. We publish it, and think there is no need to call attention to its affecting simplicity and the exquisite sentiments it contains.

To M. Pierre Lionnet, at Bordeaux.

Barcelona, 3 September, 1812.

I was glad to receive your letter of congratulation; I even ought to say I was flattered by a good and old servant like you having preserved the remembrance of a man whom he only knew as a little child: it is more than a remembrance, it is interest and affection. I assure you I am very sensible of it. I have often thought of our estimable Lionnet, and always considered that he must be happy, for I knew that he possessed the qualities that must attract the friendship of the masters whom he served. I do not know why he left the family of Lajudie, but I presume that it was not his fault, and that another situation must have made up for the loss. If I was mistaken, my dear Lionnet, address yourself to Mdlle. Phillis, she has some funds of mine, and will send you some help. You need only present my letter to her, use it without formality or scruple.

It is true, my dear Lionnet, that I have prospered in the profession of arms; it has cost me more pain and self-devotion than it does others. I was without interest and without the brilliant education that promises great success; I have gained my rank by much toil, danger, and privation. I am well in health, and feel myself strong enough to make fifteen campaigns if they were wanted for the safety of our country, which cannot be.

Our affairs in Spain have been rather a failure, but I hope that we shall restore them in the coming campaign.

Adieu, my dear Lionnet, keep well, and believe in my attachment to you.

Thomas Bugeaud.

To Madame Puyssegenez (Phillis de la Piconnerie).

Granollers, 1813.

My dear Phillis,—I have delayed writing because I wished to tell you something definite as to my position. Fortune is very capricious towards me, she serves me in action, everywhere else she deserts me. You know I had a well-founded expectation of being appointed colonel. Well, the minister sent me a major's commission for the army of reserve at Montpellier. Marshal Suchet was very much annoyed at it. He spoke to me with the greatest kindness, and changed my destination, giving me the command of the 14th of the line, and wrote again to the minister to press for my appointment as colonel to this regiment or to some other. This is my position. Henceforth please address me Major commanding the 14th of the line, 1st division of the army of Aragon and Catalonia.

I am going to join my regiment which is at Girona.

On the 16th I was attacked at Saint Vincent by nine battalions eighteen hundred horses, and four guns. It was not a fair match we had to halt, after delaying the enemy long enough to allow the troops from Barcelona to reach the fortified position of Esplugas. By the help of some small entrenchments, I maintained myself two hours upon the right bank, and killed and wounded three hundred men of the enemy. My loss was seventy wounded and seven killed. A horse which my servant was bringing me was killed. I cared for him very much. It was an Andalusian that I had owned for three years.

The Marshal gave me a lot of praise for my defence of Bobregal. That is worth more than nothing. The enemy's project was to capture the garrisons of Saint Vincent and Molinos del Rey. Having missed their point they retired, and we resumed our positions, and kept them till the 19th. I learn that the advanced posts are pushed near Barcelona.

I think I told you that the convoy of money, that had my 7000 francs, was robbed near Toulouse of a box with 10,000 francs. We are bringing an action against the carriers, but am afraid we shall lose, my loss will be 1800 francs. Our pay is five months in arrear. I begin to be short of money. I think Marshal Soult's army is doing well, and there is no fear that the English will penetrate further.

Love to all,

Your devoted brother,

Thomas Bugeaud.

P. S.—An important personage has crossed Catalonia, who, they say, goes to propose peace to the Cortes. I look upon this negotiation as very difficult. Send my letter to Toiny and Hélène.

To Madame Puyssegenez.

Saint Vincent, near Barcelona, 22 December, 1813.

My dear Phillis,—Perhaps you will see in the Gazette that on the 10th of this month I captured a picket of thirty-five horse and an officer. I received flattering compliments from the Marshal. That is all I have got for three years. His desire to keep me in his corps d'armée has done me much injury. I should be colonel to-day if I had been major a year, and as I might have been, and his Excellency did not choose, under the excuse that he kept a regiment of his army for me.

A little Spanish servant has robbed me of nearly 800 pieces of Spanish gold; in return I have made booty of two fine horses worth 80 louis, that only cost me a little money, that I have made into a fund for the soldiers who were on the expedition. Each of them had 66 francs. Their cavalry is very well mounted

A letter from Mont Marsan tells me of a victory gained over the Anglo-Spaniards before Bayonne. Marshal Soult's manœuvres, if they are as said, were fine, wise, and bold.

Ah, my dear Phillis, when shall we meet? When shall we cease to disturb the world? Ah, without patriotism, how weary I should be of the first of all professions! You will find me aged, I am beginning to turn grey; do not tell that to the fair ones of the country, they would take advantage of it, and I hope with a little attention to my toilette I may partly conceal the ravages of time.

Your devoted brother,

BUGEAUD.

Although the Duke of Albufera had managed to establish an appearance of organization in the kingdom of Valencia, whence King Joseph sometimes received assistance, none the less was it necessary daily to fight the little armed bands that intercepted all our communications and were supported by the English. The Spanish insurrection was at last to gain its point. But before leaving this country, to which he was attached by five years of struggle and fatigue, the late vélite of Austerlitz reproduces his first victories and gains the epaulette of Major (lieutenant-colonel).*

---

* In the *Memoirs of Marshal Suchet*, that excellent book written in 1826 by the soldier himself, there is often mention of Chef-de-bataillon Bugeaud, who gave proof on several occasions ' of capacity and intrepidity ;' notably at the combat of Ordal. It is interesting to give an extract : 'A section of Sappers marching with an advanced guard were among the first to reach the redoubt with the Voltigeurs. The enemy made an obstinate resistance, and twice drove us off. A second redoubt, placed very high and very near, crushed the assailants with its fire when they had made their way in. General Mesclop with his sword drawn brought them back with beat of drum; Chef-de-bataillon Fenchères was wounded, and several brave men perished in the shock. At last the redoubt remained in our possession ; almost all its defenders were killed. Immediately, Marshal Suchet advanced Habert's division to the left upon the road, and General Harispe's reserve followed Mesclop's brigade. The battalion of the 116th, led by Commandant Bugeaud, made a movement to turn the second redoubts by the left ; they were at the same time attacked in front, as well as the retrenchments that supported their flanks on the crest of the hill. All were carried with a rush, and the enemy retreated, leaving many dead and wounded, covered by his cavalry.' Also vol. ii. p. 315. ' Bugeaud's battalion leading, ran up and restored order.'—*Mémoires du Maréchal Suchet.* (See *Napier's Peninsular War*, vol. vi., book xxi., ch. ii. p. 56. Combat of Ordal, Sept. 13, 1813. There were 1200 men under Col. Adam.—ED.)

To Madame de Saint Germain (Antoinette de la Piconnerie).

Saint Vincent, near Barcelona, 22 December, 1813.

My dear Toiny,—You do not write to me any more. Do you think that I do not care to get letters from you? You are quite mistaken. I love you, and consequently love to hear from you. I allow I write little ; but you write still less, though you could do so more easily than I can. Every day I have five or six letters to write, without counting a good deal of other pen work. I have besides, important business, and it will be much worse when I am colonel. Then you will owe me three letters for one. Do you quite understand?

Some time ago there was some news of me in the Gazette. It is possible that you may again see in it that I captured an English picket of thirty-five horse and an officer. They might say God-dam ! as much as they liked, but they had to capitulate.*

I am well in health, but a little sick at heart, yet I am not in love.

There is a singular fate against my promotion. I often have a chance of attracting observation ; my chiefs all say that they wish me success, and I get nothing ! Patience and the armour of patriotism.

Adieu, dear sister : best regards to your husband.

Bugeaud,
Chef-de-Bataillon.

To Madame de Puyssegenez (Phillis).

Girone, 13 February, 1814.

I wrote to tell you I was made major, and that his Excellency had given me the command of the Fourteenth to recompense me, if possible, for the minister's harshness. I have the certainty that his Excellency the Marshal has done all he could for me. A letter from the War-Minister proves it. He tells me he is desired to express

---

* *Napier, Pen. War,* vol. vi., book xxiii., cap. vi., p. 481. On the 9th, Suchet pushed a small corps by Bejer, between the Ordal and Sitjes, and on the 10th surprised, at the Ostel of Ordal, an officer and thirty men of the *Anglo-Sicilian* cavalry. This disaster was the result of negligence. The detachment after patrolling to the fron thad dismounted without examining the buildings of the inn, and some French troopers who were concealed within immediately seized the horses and captured the whole party.—Ed.

to me the Emperor's satisfaction at my good conduct at Ordal and on every occasion. I preserve this letter among my archives.

I send you a letter of good General Harispe, though my doing so shows some vanity. It is indeed extremely flattering, but from a sister I fear no criticism. You will see that I must be very unfortunate if I am not a colonel very soon.

I have a very fine regiment which I much wish to keep. I do not know the 9th Light. I am aware that it has a brilliant reputation, but it must have lost most of its old soldiers.

The third part of our army, half the cavalry and all the light artillery, have marched for Lyons. We are on *Ter*, and I think we shall soon be on the *Fluria*. There has been no fighting since that on the 16th. The general orders relating to that affair mention me in a very flattering way. I will compel the minister to give me promotion.

Our pay is reduced by a fifth as long as there is an enemy upon the soil of France. We get no pay; I shall soon be obliged to ask for money. I am, and long shall be, a poor devil. There are no riches to be gained in the profession of arms when it is honestly and nobly practised. But for the high pay of the kingdom of Valencia, I should be without a sou. There must be love of glory, for we get nothing else and buy it very dear. Our condition is most deceptive, and yet one becomes most incredibly attached to it; so much so, that it is very painful to become a civilian again; even when our physical powers no longer allow us to serve, we always want to run after this phantom of honour and glory. It was thus that Gil Blas left his pretty country at Livia to return to the court where he had experienced all the tricks of fortune.

A thousand loves.

THOMAS BUGEAUD,
Major.

To MADAME DE PUYSSEGENEZ (PHILLIS).

Moxente, 29th April, 1814.

MY GOOD PHILLIS,—I received your letter of the 1st of April yesterday. It is very good, for it is very long, and I bargain with you to continue in the same style. The couriers come in regularly every ten days.

It is true that Colonel Rouelle has been made a general, and it is also very true that I had the greatest hopes of succeeding him in the 116th regiment. They were based upon the positive promises of the Marshal Duke of Albufera, and the wish of all my chiefs and comrades that it should be so. Everyone looked upon me as a colonel, and the officers congratulated me on it ; but often the things that seem most certain escape us at the moment we think we hold them. Success in the profession of a soldier depends much on chance and luck. It is not enough to be a good player, a man must be likewise lucky. Until now I have had the happiness of finding several opportunities of bringing myself into notice. Just lately again, at the combat of Yecla, the Marshal Duke of Albufera told me, ' Monsieur Bugeaud, a month ago I asked for a regiment for you, and you have just established a fresh claim. I greatly hope that you will have the 116th, at least I will ask for it till I have got it.' After that you see that I might hope. Well, my dear, yesterday we received a letter addressed to the administration of the 116th from M. Chevalier, major of the 11th, to inform us that he is appointed colonel of the 116th. General Rouelle is quite distressed at it.

So my promotion is stopped till there is another bit of luck. I have desired Hélène to give you a long letter in which I tell her all about our combats of the 10th, 11th, 12th, and 13th of April.

One of our countrymen, M. Meselop de Bergerac, has just been made General, he is a great friend of mine : I enclose two of his letters written to me after some small expeditions in which I was fortunate.

It was unlucky for me that they wanted to do too much for me. If an officer's cross had been asked for, it would have been got. A colonelcy was asked for—a much better thing, for it is the road to everything, and therefore I shall have nothing.

I think the Marshal is not on good terms with the War Minister, because at first he only addressed himself to the Major-general (Berthier). Now that the latter is ill, the Duke de Feltre* does not care to be of service to the Marshal. Alas! it is on all these petty feelings that our promotion is dependent, when His Majesty is not with the army.

Love to Patrice and all.

THOMAS BUGEAUD.

To MADAME DE PUYSSEGENEZ (PHILLIS).

Barcelona, 29th August, 1813.

I am at Barcelona, my dear Phillis, as a bit of a change from the life in camps and mountains. This city is beautiful, and well worth a journey of several miles to see.

---

* Clarke.

I hear that a courier is to start for France to-morrow, and will not lose this chance of telling you that I am well and always love you.

It is probable that we shall not be long before we come near to France. The force of circumstances draws us that way, but our immediate enemy does not drive us. The army of Aragon is still respected. Since we retreated we have not fired a shot.

My heart is torn with all that I hear of the army in the north of Spain. It is very sad for us thus to lose the fruits of our splendid labours, &c., &c., &c. I say no more. I suffer too much.

Adieu.

I embrace you most heartily.

BUGEAUD.

The Emperor had an especial esteem for Marshal Suchet, and he considered him 'one of the best French generals.' 'What he writes,' said Napoleon, 'is worth even more than what he says, and what he does is worth more than what he writes—just the contrary to many others.' The commandant of the two armies of Aragon and Catalonia had noticed his officer Bugeaud. Between the young corporal of Austerlitz, the future Duke d'Isly, and the Marshal Duke of Albufera, there was thenceforward a kind of mysterious relationship of honour, kindliness, and glory. Napoleon said that if he had possessed two marshals like Suchet in Spain, not only should he have conquered the Peninsula, but he should have kept it. That just, conciliatory, administrative mind, that soldierly tact and courage, had gained for him incredible success. Napoleon added, 'It is vexatious that sovereigns cannot create men like that.'

The five campaigns made by Marshal Suchet in Spain as General-in-chief will remain as an imperishable example of everything requisite in wise combinations, audacity, and dexterity for establishing the domination of a foreign army in the midst of a great people rising against them.

It was on the 1st of January, 1814, that the invasion of the allied armies commenced on all the boundaries of the empire, except on the side of the Alps, still covered by the Viceroy Prince Eugene Beauharnais at the head of the army of Italy. As soon as war was kindled in the heart of France, it was necessary to take into consideration the relinquishment of the occupation of Spain, and to evacuate the kingdom that the Treaty of Valençay restored to King Ferdinand.

On the 14th of January, by orders from the War Minister, the Duke de Feltre, ten thousand foot-soldiers, and two-thirds of the cavalry, quitted Barcelona. This first column was directed upon Lyons, to be followed speedily by the last remains of our army of occupation.

Commandant Bugeaud went with the last portions, and left Spain at the same time as the General-in-chief. The instructions were to hold back the enemy before him, either to secure the safety of the garrisons or to protect the territory of France, and make his arrangements to do his part in covering the heart of the threatened empire.*

---

* In the certificates of service given to Colonel Bugeaud I find, under the heading, 'Distinguished behaviour, wounds,' the following entries given complete:—

CAMPAIGNS IN SPAIN.

At the storm of Lerida, 13th May, 1810, the breach was scaled with courage, but the assailants on reaching the quay were stopped by the active fire of six light guns and a number of muskets. Captain of Grenadiers Bugeaud, at the head of his company, rushed upon the guns and spiked them. On this occasion he himself killed several soldiers and gunners.

On the 15th of July, 1810, at the combat of Tivisa, Captain of Grenadiers Bugeaud was ordered to protect the retreat. He did so with the greatest coolness and courage, and was the first to resume the offensive, which decided the result of the combat.

At the siege of Tortosa the enemy made a general sortie on the 28th of December, 1810, Captain Bugeaud with his company cut off four to five hundred men, bayonetted a large number, took some, and chased the rest as far as the glacis. This action gained him honourable mention in general orders.

During the siege of Tarragona, May 11, 1811, Chef-de-bataillon Bugeaud was sent with seven companies to relieve the garrisons of Amposta and La Rapita. Attacked by four battalions and three hundred horse at daybreak, he fell on the enemy's flank, beat them completely, rescued the two garrisons, took five guns served by English gunners, a hundred and fifty men, and a colonel.

On the 1st November, arriving at Barrocca to reinforce General Mazzuchelli with six companies of the Fourth Italians, he caught sight of the band of Duran, composed of two thousand five hundred foot-soldiers, and three hundred horse, in pursuit of some companies of the First Italian Regiment. He attacked this enemy in flank, made them lose hold, drove them from several strong positions, and compelled them to retreat, leaving a large number of killed and wounded. On the 3d he was detached to go to the relief of Alumnia, and on the 4th he was attacked by all the bands united, to the number of six thousand foot-soldiers and eight hundred horse. He was frequently surrounded during the retreat he made from Alumnia to Muela ; but he always broke the enemy who attacked his line, repulsed several charges of cavalry, and reached Saragossa with two-thirds of his men, including his wounded, nearly all of whom he brought off.

On the 20th of November he was detached by General Musnier against the band of Campillo. On the 23d, at midnight, he surprised the cavalry of that chief, killed twenty men, took thirty-two horses, twelve soldiers, and the commanding officer. He immediately marched against the infantry, hoping to surprise them, but could only reach them at daybreak ; he fell upon them very speedily, killed several officers, about a hundred men, and dispersed the rest.

The 1st of September, 1812, he was detached with four companies and twenty-four horse to destroy a collection of guerillas in the valley of Concenteyna. He attacked them at daybreak and dispersed them. As he returned, these brigands joined by a large number of peasants attacked his flanks. By a pretended flight he drew them into an open space, where he killed three hundred.

The 26th of December, 1812, he was ordered to surprise the garrison of Ibi, three companies and forty horse. One of his detachments alarmed the enemy too soon, nevertheless he took two hundred and sixteen men and fourteen horses, a captain and a lieutenant of the dragoons of Almanza.

At the combat of Ordal, Sept. 13, 1813, he determined the capture of the redoubts and the position by a vigorous attack on the right flank of the enemy, carried out with four companies of his battalion.

On the 13th December, 1813, an ambush that he placed near the pass of Ordal captured thirty-five English horse and an officer.

CAMPAIGN IN FRANCE.

The 14th of June, 1815, he was in charge of the left attack upon the Piedmontese line. He seized upon Conflans (Savoy), beat the Chasseurs Robert and the Regiment of Piedmont : he made two hundred prisoners, and killed or wounded five or six hundred men. On the 23rd he captured a company at Moutiers. On the 28th he was attacked by seven thousand Piedmontese and Austrians under the orders of Marshal Trenck. He retook the town of l'Hôpital three times at the head of his Grenadiers, and threw a column of two thousand men who tried to turn his flank into the river. After seven hours' fighting he held possession of the place. In this affair he killed and wounded twelve hundred men, and made five hundred prisoners. His force was fifteen hundred men and forty horse.

CHAPTER IX.

1814 AND 1815.

THE first of January, in the year 1814, was a sad day
for France. The armies of the coalition hedged
our frontiers ; on all sides the cities and territories
were overrun ; lastly, a bloody and obstinate strife
was waged around the capital. During the short
campaign in France, when all the resources of a
wonderful mind were developed, hope did not abandon
Napoleon I., until the last moment, when he saw that
everything was slipping from him. Victory at last
was weary of following him ; the army was worn out
and its strength exhausted; the marshals were glutted
with plunder, their devotion exhausted.

On the evening of December 3, the Emperor
left head-quarters, and went to Paris to receive as
formerly, in prosperous times, the great bodies of the
State assembled at the Tuileries. A piteous and
heart-rending comedy !

The sovereign's reply to the embarrassed compliments of the Senate was short and significant.
' Bearn, Alsace, Franche-Comté, and Brabant are
invaded,' said he. ' The cries of these members of
my family distract my soul. I summon the French
to the assistance of the French ; I call the French, of
Paris, Brittany, Normandy, Champagne, Burgundy,

and the other departments, to the aid of their brethren. Will they leave us to misfortune? Peace and the deliverance of our territory should be our rallying word. The stranger will flee or sign peace on terms of his own proposing, at sight of all this people in arms. This is no time to speak of recovery of the conquests we have made.'

France made no response.

Two months later, the Senate, in obedience to circumstances, and following the will of the nation, as well as their own instinct, put the climax to the defection and registered it. On the 3rd of April, 1814, a proclamation from the Senate announced that ' Napoleon having forfeited the throne, hereditary right is abolished in his family, and the people and the army are released from the oath of fidelity.' Two days afterwards the house of Bourbon was restored in France.

To resist the decrees of fate would have been madness. The people also, wearied and ruined, impatiently clamoured for peace. As for the army, it must be avowed that it gave the new government a cordial reception. Excepting a few generals and soldiers, who remained faithful, and who were attached to the Emperor by some special favour or personal bond, all received the accession of King Louis XVIII. with acclamations and enthusiasm.

The army of Spain, with which was Major Thomas Bugeaud, had been neglected and sacrificed by their master more than any other corps. The letters written by the young officer during the six years he passed in Spain often express great discouragement, and very pardonable disgust. In spite of most brilliant deeds of arms, the reiterated recommendations of his immediate superiors, even those of the commander-in-chief of the army of Catalonia, Marshal Suchet, remained without result and unanswered.

It seems that this neglect arose from carelessness in the offices, and the ill-feeling of the War Minister, the Duke de Feltre, against Marshal Suchet, the Duke of Albufera.

Although Thomas Bugeaud had won his corporal's stripes on the field of Austerlitz, the son of the Marquis de la Piconnerie, enlisted at twenty years of age among the vélites of the guard, did not long remain subject to the spell of the great conquering Cæsar. We have seen him several times during the campaign in Germany ardently longing with sighs to return to his country, and the long and curious correspondence he kept up with his sisters at this time frequently contains bitter criticisms on the profession of arms, which he had entered against his inclination.

When the royal family returned to France, the 14th regiment of the line, in which Thomas Bugeaud held the rank of Major, was ordered to garrison Orleans. In a short time came his appointment as Colonel. We give his letter informing his sister of this happy event. It is almost always to his elder sister Phillis, his faithful and devoted confidante, that the Marshal's long correspondence is addressed, beginning in 1804, on his enlistment in the vélites of the guard, and affectionately preserved in the family.*

---

* Statement of service of Marshal Bugeaud de la Piconnerie, Duke d'Isly (Thomas-Robert), son of Jean-Ambroise and of Françoise de Sutton de Clonard, born 15 October, 1784, at Limoges (Haute Vienne), married 30 March, 1818, to Demoiselle Elisabeth Jouffre de Lafaye (Official permission, 27 December, 1817), died at Paris, 6 June, 1849 :—

Vélite in the Grenadiers of the Imperial Guard . . .	29 June, 1804.
Corporal	22 December, 1805.
Sub-Lieutenant in the 64th Regiment of the Line . .	19 April, 1806.

Nothing was concealed from his sister. He communicated to her his impressions, his secret thoughts, all the actions of his life. We know of nothing more touching than this tender and filial affection of the

Lieutenant	21 December, 1806.
Transferred to the 116th Regiment of the Line	1 July, 1808.
Captain	2 March, 1809.
Chef-de-Bataillon	2 March, 1811.
Major in the 14th Regiment of the Line	10 January, 1814.
Colonel	11 June, 1814.
Reduced, and placed on half-pay	11 November, 1815.
Received upon the Reduced Pay List, in accordance with the Order of 5 May, 1824, to date from	1 July, 1828.
Colonel of the 56th Regiment of the Line	8 September, 1830.
Maréchal-de-Camp (Major-General)	2 April, 1831.
Commanding a Brigade of Infantry at Paris	30 November, 1832.
Commander-in-Chief of the Town and Castle of Blaye	31 January, 1833.
Unattached	22 July, 1833.
Commanding a Brigade of Infantry at Paris	8 October, 1833.
Commander of the Forces, Province of Oran	23 May, 1836.
Lieutenant-General	2 August, 1836.
Unattached	1 October, 1836.
Commanding the Active Division of Oran	1 March, 1837.
Inspector for 1837 of the Infantry Forces under his command	22 July, 1837.
Returned to France	12 December, 1837.
Unattached	1 January, 1838.
Commanding the Fourth Infantry Division of the Corps to assemble on the Northern Frontier	22 January, 1839.
Unattached in consequence of the breaking up of that corps	25 May, 1839.
Member of the Cavalry and Infantry Committee	31 January, 1840.
Governor-General of Algeria	29 December, 1840.
Marshal of France	31 July, 1843.
Relieved of the Government of Algeria	29 June, 1847.
Commander-in-Chief of the Army of the Alps	29 December, 1848.
Died at Paris	6 June, 1849.

CAMPAIGNS.

1804, on Coast; Vendémiaire, year xiv, 1805, 1806, 1807, with Grand Army; 1808, 1809, 1810, 1811, 1812, 1813, and 1814, in Spain ; 1815, Army of the Alps ; 1836, 1837, 1840, 1842, 1843, 1844, 1845, 1846, and 1847, in Algeria.

WOUNDS.

Gunshot wound of the left thigh at the Battle of Pultusk, 26 December, 1806.

DECORATIONS.

Member of the Legion of Honour	6 June, 1811.
Officer	17 March, 1815.
Commander	8 May, 1815.
Grand Officer	24 December, 1837.
Grand Cross	9 April, 1843.
Knight of Saint Louis	20 August, 1814.
Created Duke d'Isly by Royal Ordinance	18 September, 1844.

soldier towards her who stood in the place of mother to him, and by whose side were passed his earlier years in the old home of La Durantie. This deep feeling never failed. Madame de Puyssegenez throughout her life retained the ascendancy she had possessed over her brother during his infancy and youth.

To Madame de Puyssegenez (Phillis).

La Ferté-Saint-Aubin, near Orleans, 12 July, 1814.

Dear Sister,—This very moment I am informed that the King has made me a colonel by a decree of June 11. So I was a colonel when I was at Puyssegenez. Fortune is wonderfully kind to me, and seems to reserve my pleasures so that I may be continually receiving one. So she did not choose me to know of my promotion while I was with you ; it would have been too much good at once.

The favour I have just received is very great, considering the actual circumstances. Several old colonels were asking for the 14th. If I had not been appointed, I should have had to compete with fifty-seven majors my seniors. And most likely I should have been sent about my business with half-pay.

I request you to inform the whole family in Périgord of my appointment, and ask you afterwards to send my letter to Hélène, who will tell Toiny; but no, I think, though very busy, I will write to Hélène, and you need only undertake Périgord.

I shall reach Orleans to-morrow, and shall enter it at the head of 1100 men in fine order. Marshal Suchet, who saw us when he came to Vierzon, told me it was the finest and largest regiment in the whole army. Everything is going on as well as I could possibly desire. The only thing wanting to my complete satisfaction would be to keep the brave officers, who have contributed so much to my being appointed their colonel. I fear a good many of them will be lost.

I shall be able to write little for a fortnight. I shall have much to do for the new organization of my regiment. My most hearty love to every one.

Bugeaud,
Colonel of the 14th.

The city of Orleans, ardently Royalist, was very eager to celebrate the return of the princes after their long exile. The newly promoted colonel enthusiastically joined in all these manifestations, and especially in the fêtes given by the city on the occasion of a visit of the Duchesse d'Angoulême.*

Thus passed at Orleans the first period of the Restoration, without incident, until the return from the island of Elba. It has been stated that in March, 1815, at the time of the Emperor Napoleon's landing at Cannes. Colonel Bugeaud, having proclaimed that he was going to fight the usurper, himself gave his soldiers the signal to desert the royal cause. According to an account then current, Colonel Bugeaud did not even wait to leave Orleans before declaring himself, but made his soldiers mount the tricoloured cockade in the suburb Bourgogne.

'We believe these statements are unfounded,' says

---

* It is to M. H. de Lacombe that we are indebted for all the information relating to Colonel Bugeaud's stay in Orleans, and the communication of a very curious document that bears strongly the impress of the time. It is a little printed sheet, surmounted by a shield with fleur-de-lis, with this heading. 'Verses made on the occasion of the Fête, given by the city of Orleans to the officers of the garrison.'

AIR—*J'ai quelque foies chanté la gloire.*

Loin de notre bonne patrie
Naguère nous portions nos pas,
Et le printemps de notre vie
N'était semé que de combats ;
Aujourd'hui le sort, moins sévère,
Nous a fait un double présent :
En *Louis* il nous donne un père, } *Bis.*
Et nous fixe dans Orléans.

Allez, nous dit ce bon Monarque,
Vivez heureux, il en est temps ;
Je veux qu'une joyeuse Parque
File les jours de mes enfants,
Les plaisirs, les jeux, la tendresse,
Ici rempliront vos loisirs ;
Mais au milieu de votre ivresse } *Bis.*
Donnez à Mars des souvenirs.

And there are two other couplets of the same style. The whole is signed. Colonel Bugeaud, Colonel of the 14th Regiment of the Line.

At the bottom of the sheet, 'At Orleans, from the Press of Rouzeau-Montaut, Printer to the King, the Mayor, &c., Rue Royale, No. 11.'

M. H. de Lacombe. 'First, it is established by official documents that the scene supposed to have taken place in the Faubourg Bourgogne is imaginary. Some mischievous speeches having passed among the soldiers of his regiment, Colonel Bugeaud immediately checked them. Marshal Moncey, first inspector-general of gendarmerie, had informed the Minister-at-War of the reports current on this matter.' There was no imputation then cast upon the conduct of Colonel Bugeaud, and yet he had left Orleans several days before. He had already reached Montargis, where he was to operate with the army corps intended to oppose Napoleon if he should advance from Burgundy. The Minister-at-War, the Duke de Feltre, wrote on the 16th of March, 1815, to Colonel Bugeaud, concerning the bad spirit some of his soldiers had exhibited at Montargis. ' I know, it is true, that, full of zeal, and a sense of your obligations, you, as well as the officers, have done all you could to restrain the men, and keep them to their duty. But these measures are not sufficient.'

Now, these very acts of factious insubordination that took place in the 14th of the line had been very much exaggerated. Even before he received the War Minister's letter Colonel Bugeaud had written to the prefect of the Loire to deny them. The prefect had immediately forwarded Colonel Bugeaud's protest to the minister's office. The Minister-at-War received the document from the prefect on the same day that he had addressed to Colonel Bugeaud the missive given above. He immediately wrote a second letter to the Colonel, thus expressed, to be found, like the former, among the archives of the office of the Minister-at-War :—

Paris, 17 March, 1815.

Monsieur le Colonel.—I have this moment received, with a letter from the prefect of the Loire, a copy of that in which you complain of the disadvantageous reports current as to the bad spirit of some soldiers of your regiment. A report has indeed reached me on this matter, that led me to write directly to you on this very day. I am glad to learn that this report has no sort of foundation, and that you, your body of officers, and all the soldiers under your orders, are animated by feelings that give the greatest assurance of their fidelity to his Majesty. I will cause inquiry to be made for the authors of these false reports.

From these documents it clearly appears, therefore, that if Colonel Bugeaud joined in the rising of the Hundred Days, he did not in the least take the initiative. He gave his adhesion when the event had taken place ; and setting aside the question of dynasty, there only remained the military and national question against the reconstituted coalition.

But, though quite false, these reports had the fatal effect of causing Colonel Bugeaud to be treated as an enemy and object of suspicion under the Restoration. Thus it was that the government of Louis XVIII. and the country were deprived of an able servant.

M. de Lacombe adds, ' I learn from a very trustworthy source that a very royalist officer, Commandant Count l'Esclaibes, who was a friend of Colonel Bugeaud, and knew his bravery and his sentiments, wished to put an end to this unjust disgrace, and give this valuable support to the monarchy. After the Hundred Days at the Tuileries he presented Colonel Bugeaud to the Duke d'Angoulême, president of the high commission on the army. The conversation was excellent and left a good impression, but unfortunately had no practical result.'

In the correspondence of the Count de Chambord there is a letter dated October, 1848, in which that prince expresses his rejoicing at the patriotic inclinations of Marshal Bugeaud; and adds that Colonel d'Esclaibes had long ago informed him of them.*

---

*   *Venice, 13 October, 1848.*

To Monsieur X.

. . . . . I take advantage, my dear friend, of a safe opportunity to thank you for the various letters you have sent me for some time. I have read with much interest the accounts you give me of the condition of things and minds; but what has struck me most is to see men of courage and ability of different parties forgetting their old divisions, and uniting in their efforts to save society from approaching destruction. This is a happy symptom that should confirm our hopes for the future. I am especially rejoiced at what you tell me of the good disposition of Marshal Bugeaud. I am not surprised at it, for the excellent Colonel d'Esclaibes, whom we have had the misfortune to lose and who was his friend, had taught me to know him long ago. By his military talents, his great ability, his firm and energetic character, and the influence he exercises over the army, the Marshal may be called to render the most signal services to our country, under existing circumstances. As for me, whose motto has always been "Everything for France," my wish, my sole ambition, you know, is to serve my country, to devote myself to her and those who will assist me to save her, and give her rest, freedom, prosperity, and greatness. Such men may always count upon my entire recognition. They will always find me ready to hold out a hand to them, wherever they may come from.

(Signed)   HENRY.

CHAPTER X.

THE HUNDRED DAYS (1815).

THE return of the Emperor from the Island of Elba had again kindled the war in Europe, and the frontiers of France were bristling afresh with a hedge of bayonets. The 14th of the line, which was intended to form the advanced guard of the army of the Alps, was still under the orders of Marshal Suchet, and had, this time, to contend with the Austro-Sardinian army holding the valleys and defiles of Savoy. Our military glory, so soon destined to be obscured upon the field of Waterloo, darted forth a last flash upon the frontiers of Italy, and it was to the brave colonel of the 14th of the line that we owe this heroic feat of arms.

This glorious incident of war, remaining almost unknown amid the frightful crash of the colossus of empire falling into ruins, seems to us like one of those final radiances that sometimes illumine the sky as the orb of day is vanishing. Might not there be a curious similitude in the idea that the young colonel who, in an obscure corner of Savoy, just before the disaster of Waterloo, accomplished the last gallant action that adorned the imperial era, should, after a long enforced sleep of fifteen years, awake as the most accomplished soldier of his time, the only great warrior of the monarchy of 1830 ?

The commencement of hostilities had been fixed for the 15th of June. The 14th, which was stationed at Chatelard, among the mountains of Banges, in Savoy, had received orders to descend into the valley of Tarentaise, guarded by a Piedmontese corps, and to take possession of the small towns of Conflans and l'Hôpital.

It was then that Colonel Bugeaud, in conformity with orders received, attempted one of those bold strokes in which he had so often succeeded in Spain. A battalion of the enemy (*batallion* Comte Robert), was established as advanced picket at Saint Pierre d'Albigny. Colonel Bugeaud resolved to surround it. and make it prisoner with hardly a blow. With this object he despatched three companies by a mountain-path that came out about half a league in rear of the village, and ordered them to lay in wait. Then he attacked in front with the rest of his force. One part of the enemy's detachment was captured or killed, the rest ran away and fell into the ambuscade prepared ; not a man escaped, and by four in the morning the whole Piedmontese battalion was captured.

In this combat Colonel Bugeaud himself made two prisoners, who turned out to be two Frenchmen, MM. de Polignac and de Macarthy, commissioners of Louis XVIII., with the Austro-Sardinian army.

We will leave the account of it to Colonel Bugeaud, who relates this episode in a letter addressed to one of his sisters, dated August 3, which we shall find below. A Piedmontese brigade, 3000 men strong, had come in haste to support its advanced picket, getting no communication from it. It came in contact with the victorious 14th, was routed after a pretty sharp conflict, and retired, leaving with its opponent, 200 prisoners, its wounded, its dead, and the possession of the towns of Conflans and l'Hôpital, not even attempting to defend the approaches, which the 14th occupied conformably to orders received.

Some days later Colonel Bugeaud, seeing that the enemy continued to commit the same blunder, and that their advanced posts did not sufficiently guard their lines of communication with the main body of their troops, again gave himself the pleasure of capturing a battalion posted at Moutiers as an outlying picket. He employed the same method that had previously been successful, brought upon the enemy's line of retreat a detachment which had to march for eleven hours by horrible roads, then attacking the picket in front, took it between two fires, and forced it to surrender.

It would seem that Marshal Bugeaud must afterwards have especially had the remembrance of these two exploits in his mind, when he wrote in his ' Maxims of the Art of War:' ' Efficient guards must always be distant, and equally must it be impossible for the enemy to penetrate through the chain of the advanced posts unobserved. A fault often committed by the chief of a detachment posted on outlying picket, at a great distance from a numerous force, is to surround himself with precautions calculated to prevent himself from being surprised, but to leave behind him a considerable space in which a party of the enemy may lie in wait, and fall upon the detachment when it, attacked by superior force from another side, thinks it can easily retire to its own forces, then it is captured, and uncovers the space it was ordered to occupy.'

This was a happy commencement for the army of the Alps ; to be followed by a combat still more glorious, that might have gained a great reputation, had not at the very moment the bloody day of Waterloo absorbed the attention of France and the whole of Europe by the vastness of the strife of which it was the turning-point, and the incalculable consequences that followed it. But it does not displease us, while turning over this grand page of history, to tarry, in company with the valiant man of war whose life we are endeavouring to describe, among these combats obscure, but deserving illustration, that so honourably terminated the war upon our Alpine frontiers. Besides, there can be no doubt that the remembrance of this success was especially valued by the Marshal when he reached an advanced age, full of honours, for he gave a very full account of it in an anonymous pamphlet printed, in 1845, at the Government press at Algiers, from which we take some of the details that follow.

In the last days of the month of June, 1815, the 14th of the line, reinforced by a battalion of the 20th of the line, still held the two towns of Conflans and l'Hôpital, washed by the stream of the Arly, a small tributary of the Isere. Some prisoners, made on the 26th, informed Colonel Bugeaud that he was to be attacked two days afterwards by 10,000 Austrians under the orders of General Trenck, coming down the Little Saint Bernard, while General Bubna. coming from Mont Cenis with 20,000 men, was to advance by the valley of Maurienne, held on one side by the brigade of General Meselop. Colonel Bugeaud lost

no time in forwarding this information to the General-
in-chief, and judiciously requested that Mesclop's
brigade might come and join him without delay in
the valley of the Tarentaise, so as to combine their
efforts to crush General Trenck, while Bubna's
column 'should strike at nothing, and run its head
against the tête-de-pont of Montmeillan.' But Marshal Suchet had already received intelligence of the
disaster at Waterloo, and, considering it useless to
prolong hostilities, had sent a proposal for an armistice
to General Bubna. Being convinced that this proposal
would be accepted, and the forward march of the
Austrian corps stopped, he gave no orders to the 14th
of the line or to Mesclop's brigade. On the morning
of the 28th, instead of the reinforcement so ardently
desired, Colonel Bugeaud received the official bulletin
of the battle of Waterloo, and, by a singular coincidence,
the deputation of the regiment which had been sent to
the Champ de Mai for the distribution of the eagles,
joined at the same moment, bringing the eagle for
the regiment, together with the account of the Emperor's abdication.

While these unfavourable reports were spreading
through the ranks, and causing great excitement, a
sub-officer of cavalry arrived at full speed and brought
information of the approach of the Austrians. Matters
looked grave ; resistance to an enemy of considerable
numerical superiority, with soldiers disconcerted and
troubled by the cruel intelligence just received, might
have seemed a hazardous enterprise ; but Colonel
Bugeaud, inspired by ardent patriotism alone, found
some noble words that went to the soldiers' hearts,
and restored their *morale*. Forming up his regiment
in close column, he himself read the bulletin of

Waterloo, and received the eagle in the name of the country, speaking these words in a loud voice, ' Soldiers of the 14th line, here is your eagle. It is in the name of the country that I present it to you, for if the Emperor, as here stated, is no longer our sovereign, France remains. She it is who confides this standard to you; it will always be your talisman of victory. Swear that as long as a soldier of the 14th exists no enemy's hand shall touch it !' ' We swear it,' cried all the soldiers, and the officers stepped from the ranks, waving their swords and shouting again, ' We swear it !'

Happy are the soldiers led by such a chief ! What melancholy thoughts assail the mind at the idea of the grand results that our brave army of Metz might have produced in the fatal war of 1870 if at its head there had been a man of such energetic mould, who would have been able to make the grand idea of patriotism overpower the ruins of a crumbling government.

It was in this mood that the 14th was going to meet the enemy.

In order the better to resist such superior forces, Colonel Bugeaud proposed only to defend the right bank of the Arly, and to allow the enemy to pass the stream in small bodies, so as to have them on easier terms, and crush them in detail. He began by a slack defence of the positions on the left bank, so as to prevent the enemy from adopting a plan that they might have conceived if they had met with an energetic resistance, that of crossing the Arly at some distance and turning the position. With the same view he prevented the destruction of the bridge that unites Conflans and l'Hôpital. The event was as he had foreseen. When the Austrians had made themselves masters of the left bank, which had been so easily abandoned to them, they several times endeavoured to debouch from the bridge.

Every time they were received by a sharp fire from a short distance; then our troops quitting their shelter advanced upon the enemy with the bayonet, and thrust them back to the other side of the stream with considerable loss.

Despairing of forcing the passage in this manner, the Austrians passed a column of two thousand men over a ford below the town, intending to cut the line of retreat of the defenders of l'Hôpital. Colonel Bugeaud, not choosing to empty the little town, only made use of six companies of the centre to meet this movement. Though numerically inferior, the want of numbers was compensated for by an excess of audacity, and he flung these few men, with himself, upon the rear of the enemy's column, so that they, thinking that they themselves were threatened with being cut off from the ford where they had crossed the river, became demoralised, gave back, and were flung in disorder into the Isere and the Arly, having sustained a considerable loss by a well-sustained and well-directed fire. A second attempt of the same kind on another point was not more successful.

However, cartridges began to fail, and the Colonel would perhaps have decided upon retiring. if he had not been reluctant to leave to the enemy's mercy a battalion of the 67th that had on the sound of the engagement made its way by the valley of Udine and had just communicated with him. Not being able to maintain himself any longer in l'Hôpital without ammunition, Colonel Bugeaud rallied his men, and made them take up positions on the hills in the rear. The Austrians entered the deserted town and pillaged it. Meanwhile a detachment of twenty mules loaded with cartridges had been brought up; the pouches were filled, and the battalion of the 67th came up with some pieces of artillery. Their arrival was a signal to take the offensive; the 14th again rushed forward, killed or captured 1500 Austrians who occupied l'Hôpital, and effected its junction with the battalion of the 67th over a heap of corpses.

At the same moment a battalion of the 20th of the line arrived by the Chambery road. Colonel Bugeaud, seeing his force augmented by two battalions, prepared to cross the Arly in his turn, and to complete the destruction of the Austrian division, when an officer from the head-quarters' staff arrived with the information that the armistice was signed, and, to his great regret, the intrepid Bugeaud had to break off the movement just begun. But he gave himself the pleasure of waiting till the enemy themselves sent him information of the armistice, and thus had the well-deserved satisfaction of not leaving the field of battle till the next day.

So terminated this combat in which 1750 French fought for ten hours against nearly 10,000 Austrians, killed 2000 men of them, and made 960 prisoners.

After the disaster of Waterloo, 18th June, 1815, and the second abdication of the Emperor Napoleon I., 23rd June, 1815, according to the conventions with the allied armies, the French forces were to retire behind the Loire, and Marshal Suchet's corps to quit Savoy.

A letter from Colonel Bugeaud, written to his sister,

on 3rd August, 1815, is already a foreboding of the adverse decision about to be made with regard to him.

TO MADAME DE PUISSEGENEZ.

Saint-Symphorien, 3rd August, 1815.

MY DEAR SISTER,—I received your letter of 20th July at Saint-Symphorien. The one you addressed to me at the army of the Loire has not reached me yet. Your opinion agrees with mine. When I recovered from the first moment of disgust, I considered that it was right to wait at my post till I am told, ' Be off with you!' and that then I should have a right to say, ' I served my country as long as I could, and it is not my fault that I am not serving it still.' I fully expect that we shall be discharged, the proscriptions do not promise anything good.

I should not be sorry to remain upon half-pay for a year or two while things settle themselves.

Our army is obedient indeed ; very obedient. Some days since we received the white cockade. I have resumed this badge in the regiment without encountering fresh desertions.

You may feel sure I never will join in a civil war unless compelled by persecution. I am too much of a Frenchman ever to shed the blood of my fellow-citizens as long as they do not threaten my life.

I am in daily expectation of leaving this country and going to Clermont. You can write to me at Roanne till further directions ; your letter will follow me.

You will no doubt like to see our deed of submission ; I send you an exact copy of it :—

' SIRE,—The officers, sub-officers, and private soldiers of the 14th Regiment of the line, present to Your Majesty the homage of their complete submission. We unreservedly range ourselves under the banner of the lilies. The fate of the country is henceforth combined with that of your sacred person. This fact will be the warranty of our fidelity and love.

' May all Frenchmen, forgetting their divisions, only make one great family, and have like us but one cry, " Long live the King, and France in all its integrity !"

' You will experience our devotion, Sire, if ever this integrity should be threatened.'

(The signatures follow.)

I have received a long and kind letter from Hélène, and answered it. Ask her for my letter of the end of July, it will interest you. I give her accounts that I have not sent you; in your turn I am going to give you some that she has not received, and you may send her in exchange.

On the 15th of June, at two in the morning, I surprised the Piedmontese advanced posts at Saint-Pierre d'Albigny. I entered the town with the first of the Voltigeurs. I heard two men galloping away down the street. Having no mounted men I pursued them myself, and cutting them off at the turn of the road, I made them prisoners.

' Who are you ? '

' French travellers.'

' French travellers at such an hour, armed and in the enemy's lines. I cannot recognise you as such. No, gentlemen, you are not Frenchmen.'

' Yes, sir, we are ; and as we must tell you, we are French émigrés. We left our country to escape from Bonaparte and serve the King.'

' Ah, I understand, you are royalists, but foreigners and not citizens of France.'

' Sir, we are Frenchmen on honour; we are on the road to it, and it is not very clear that you are on the same course.'

' Gentlemen, do not compel me to abuse the power I have over you and say harsh things, which your own conduct may easily give occasion to. We will break this off. You will be taken to head-quarters with the other prisoners, and you will be able to explain to Marshal Suchet.'

I was in haste, and went on my way without ascertaining the names of my prisoners. In the evening I heard that one of them was M. Jules de Polignac, and the other M. de Macarthy of Toulouse ; that they had been several days upon the frontier establishing communications with France, and giving information to the Piedmontese of all the movements of the French army.

The Marshal had them taken to Fort Bareau ; but I soon learnt that they had quietly been set at liberty.

Three or four days ago I received a letter from M. Macarthy asking me to let him have for 1000 francs a couple of carriage-horses belonging to him, which I had taken in the affair of Saint-Pierre.

I answered him, that considering the Macarthys of Toulouse are relations to those of Bordeaux, who are my cousins, I could not consider these horses as fair booty, and that he might send for them, not for the 1000 francs, but for nothing.

I added something, to say that this was not the least in consequence of circumstances, but owing to the name of Macarthy.

I love you all, and embrace you a hundred times.   Adieu.

BUGEAUD.

To MADAME DE PUISSEGENEZ.

Clermont, 27th August, 1815.

Progress is being made with our disbandment. This will take up at least a month, and will delay by so long the pleasure I shall have in pressing you in my arms.

The councils of administration will be provisionally kept up, to give-in their accounts with the records and stores. That of the 14th is to be merged in the legion of the department of Côte-d'Or, and said to be intended for the nucleus. If any colonels receive employment in each legion, I am almost assured I shall be among those chosen. The Marshal has told me several times, ' If any one in the army ought to be employed, it is you.'

As soon as we are disbanded, if circumstances permit, I will go and see you. I shall travel on horseback by cross-roads.

You will be glad to hear that several persons of distinction of the department of the Loire have joined in requesting their deputies to ask the King to give me the legion of the Loire. I have letters to this effect from M. de Montenac, and the Marquis de Talame, peer of France. I do not reckon much on its success, but am flattered at this proof of goodwill which I owe to the good conduct of my regiment, and to a slight service that I did to the people of the country. This is it. A band of Austrian hussars were wasting the country. pillaging. robbing. violating, &c. I went after them with eight mounted officers. We caught them at the village of Regny, and took them all.

I have received a long and kind letter from Hélène. She thinks a great deal about me. The people of the South, or at least the royalists, are covering themselves with shame by a quantity of murders. They seem to wish to defy the Duke d'Angoulême rather than the King. They are in a complete state of anarchy.

The illegitimate sovereign's party did not commit such crimes. I hope that as soon as His Majesty can he will chastise these brigands with white and green cockades. Doubtless you know all that goes on in these countries. At Toulouse they murdered the General the King had sent.

In several other places the authorities appointed by the King have been unable to enter upon their duties.

Love to your husband, to Julien, to all the family, and to all the friends.

You do not tell me about my money. Will Granger pay me?

Your devoted brother,
BUGEAUD.

On the 16th of September, 1815, as he had foreseen, Colonel Bugeaud was disbanded, as a brigand of the Loire, and ceased to belong to the army. Perhaps we may find an explanation of this proceeding on comparing it with an incident that is rather obscure, for unfortunately no letter of the Marshal's nor any formal document gives information about it.

We have seen that the former major of the Spanish wars had received his colonel's rank from Louis XVIII., 11th of June, 1814. There is no reason to doubt the sincerity of the Royalist feelings displayed by him at Orleans. The son of the Marquis de la Piconnerie had, besides, no strong bonds of gratitude to attach him to the Emperor. Then came the Hundred Days. Together with the whole army the Colonel took his place beneath the standards of the usurper, and, under the orders of his commanding officer, proceeded to join him with his regiment at Auxerre. What took place afterwards? The Colonel of the 14th of the line must have had some powerful enemies in the office of the Minister-at-War, for they managed to deprive him of his regiment. The order was given by the minister, but not carried into effect. Why?* The curious autograph letter of the Emperor now in our hands will tell us.

Monsieur le Colonel Bugeaud, I am satisfied with your conduct. The command of the 14th Regiment of the line, with which you

---

* In the statements of the Marshal's service obtained from the War Minister's office, there is no trace to be found of this strange proceeding. The autograph letter of the Emperor is the only document alluding to it.

joined me at Auxerre has wrongfully been taken from you. I have given orders for it to be restored to you, and in proof of my satisfaction have appointed you commander of the Legion of Honour.

Signed, NAPOLEON.

Paris, 8th May, 1815.

Let us endeavour to establish the facts. No doubt this must have passed, perhaps even without the knowledge of Colonel Bugeaud. His protector, Marshal Suchet, who showed an especial appreciation of the brilliant soldier of the Catalonian army, had been informed of the injustice about to be inflicted upon his comrade in arms, and managed to obviate it. He was easily able to persuade the Emperor to revoke his minister's decision, by showing him how important it was at that critical moment to favour and secure to his side such a valiant soldier as Colonel Bugeaud. Thence arose the imperial letter and the quite unexpected nomination as commander of the Legion of Honour.

Indeed, Thomas Bugeaud, chevalier of the Legion of Honour in 1811, had been made an officer of the order on March 17, 1815. Two months afterwards he was commander ! This politic nomination was a dexterous action of Napoleon I., who evidently wished by an especial favour to attach to himself one of the youngest, cleverest, and most steady colonels in the army. We have seen at Conflans and l'Hôpital in what brilliant fashion Bugeaud showed that he deserved the high distinction which imperial favour, by a kind of divination and prescience, had granted him beforehand. Notwithstanding the Colonel's fine feat of arms. notwithstanding his services, his name and his friends, it is certain that after Waterloo and Napoleon I.'s abdication, his determined enemies at the War-Office produced, at the right moment, this unexceptionable proof of the good-will of the usurper, and took advantage of it to procure the insertion of Colonel Bugeaud's name among those who were discharged.

CHAPTER XI.

COUNTRY LIFE (1815–30).

Colonel Bugeaud in Périgord, 1815-1830—His Attempts at Agriculture—His Activity and Taste for Field-work — He founds an Agricultural Meeting—His Marriage with Mademoiselle de Lafaye—Transformation of the Country in an Agricultural point of view—The Soldier Labourer—Colonel Bugeaud and the Peasants.

This period of fifteen years, 1815 to 1830, during which the brilliant soldier found himself compelled, by events, to abandon military life, was far from being idle. The brave, indefatigable officer carried with him into his retirement the same ardour, devotion, and activity, that had already filled the first part of his life. Besides, this was not the first time he had engaged in agriculture, and farming had long ago attracted him. We have told how it was that several years before he had missed breaking off his career, and devoting himself entirely to the management of his little domain.

In 1815, the object of his life was to be completely changed. We find in his manuscript notes, a sort of biography dictated by himself to one of his daughters, the account of his first attempts, and the inauguration of the first agricultural society established in France.

'Struck with the wretchedness of the people of his country, he found the cause in the system of agriculture, namely, fallowing in its most primitive state. He saw that if he could not serve the State with his sword, he might still be useful to the country-people by teaching them how to improve their condition by a more intelligent system of labour. He undertook this mission with infinite eagerness, and it had a great effect in consoling him for the loss of a career that offered him the most brilliant prospects.

'A lady, as good as she was beautiful, soon united her lot to his, and the soldier was nothing more than a most active and zealous agriculturist. By daybreak he was in the fields leading his labourers, and himself showing them how the work ought to be done.

'In order to speak with more authority, he had very speedily learnt how to hold the plough, use the scythe, and all the agricultural implements as dexterously as the most practised workman. And he especially opened the minds of the tillers of the soil by his teaching, and stirred up the neighbouring townsfolk to a taste for agriculture.

'However, he soon perceived that if his efforts stood alone, they would not be able to conquer the bad habits that had been the rule for centuries. His idea, therefore, was to unite all the landowners of the canton into a society. As soon as he could show a favourable specimen of the effects of the course of cropping that he had selected with reference to the nature of the soil and climate, he assembled all his neighbours. After a breakfast, there was an inspection of the fields; they were delighted with the excellence of his artificial grasses, roots, and all his cultivation of a kind quite new to the country. Actually, enthusiasm was displayed, for no one believed that these lands were capable of producing such things.

'Colonel Bugeaud had previously prepared papers for the formation of a company, and a programme of

the encouragement to be given to agriculture in the
canton. He took advantage of the general feeling
to lay it before the party, and all present signed.
Thus was organized the first agricultural society*
of La Dordogne, and we believe in France : this took
place in 1819.

'The society prospered, and caused such progress
to be made in the canton as astonished the neighbouring cantons. Colonel Bugeaud stirred them up
to imitation, and had the happiness of becoming the
promoter and organizer of several other societies.'

At the beginning of the year 1818, Colonel
Bugeaud married Mdlle. de Lafaye, of one of the most
respected families in the country. Here is a very
interesting letter addressed by the impatient betrothed
to his future father-in-law, in which the Colonel
describes his whole self with original and delightful
frankness.

Excideuil, 27 *October*, 1817.

Sir,—I trust you will excuse a very natural impatience in one
who aspires to the happiness of becoming a member of your family.
It is impossible for me to wait till St. Martin's day to ask from you
an answer upon which my happiness depends. You had the
kindness to promise it to me in a few days. It is only indirectly
that I have learnt that you have fixed a more distant period. You
had not told me; I may then surely beg you to fulfil your first
promise, without your being able to impute indiscretion to me.
And why should you defer a moment so much desired by me?

Shall you know me better in a fortnight? Have you not had
time enough for consideration? Have you not been able to get all
possible information? In mercy, sir, do not defer giving me a
certainty. Consult your own heart; it will tell you, for it is kind,
that you cannot leave me longer in this cruel expectation.

But it is especially your daughter whom you must consult, if you
have not already done so. I hold above everything to her own well-

---

* Comice Agricole. Comitia, public assemblies of the Roman people. — *Smith's
Dict., Greek and Roman Antiquities.*

considered choice; otherwise there will be no happiness. I am
also sure that you will do nothing distasteful to her; your intentions
on this matter are well enough known, and your character would
point them out.

I know that some persons have cast doubts upon my temper.
Soldiers are said to be generally despots, being used to command; I
can only refute this idea by defending myself and my comrades.
I will therefore confine myself to observing that there is no
military man who is not under command more, perhaps, than
he is in command, and that this graduated subordination beginning with the private and only terminating with the chief of the
state, teaches all to obey as well as to command. Assuredly a rich
only son, who has never left home, has much more the habit of
absolute command than a marshal of France, and it would be a
good thing for spoilt children to be in the service for four or five
years. I fancy their tempers would be improved by it.

My fortune is not what M. Festugières thought, upon what
grounds I know not, for I have never exaggerated it beyond the
reality. I have 78,000 francs either in my pocket-book or well
invested. I will immediately make a purchase to that amount, if
you require it. I have, besides, my pay, worth about 3000 francs.
I allow that this is little in the general way of considering these
things. Your daughter is more wealthy: I wish she were not so
well off, or that I were more so, and that would be better. However, my means are sufficient according to all my wants; and I
should not desire any more unless it might be as a means of level-
ling the difficulties that stand in the way of a union, that I desire
more than I have ever wished for anything in the world.

My messenger has orders to wait for your answer till to-morrow;
I reckon upon your kindness not to keep me in suspense any longer.

Accept, sir, the assurance of my feelings of respect and my complete consideration.

BUGEAUD,
Infantry Colonel.

Colonel Bugeaud having returned home, where
he soon became head of his family, could not
remain inactive. His vivid imagination, elevated
mind, and heart always full of a wish to do
good, required occupation to make him forget the
field of battle. He soon found it. An immense
sphere was opening before him. Limousin where he

was born, Périgord the land of his adoption, were then
far from being reckoned among our most fertile provinces. There was wide-spread misery. 'The colonel
looked around,' as we are told by M. de Bezancenetz,
an Algerian, an actual worshipper of Marshal Bugeaud.
'He saw a land sparsely covered with heather, further
off vast lands without vegetation, scorched up as if
wasted by fire, with only a crop of grey rocks like the
bones of an abandoned cemetery. He looked another
way; on the hill, meagre vine-stocks only just pushed
forth their stunted branches ; in the valley, marshy
meadows scarcely produced sedges enough to feed the
few lean cows dolefully browsing there. Here a
scanty chestnut-grove with mutilated trees ; there a
copse-wood with foliage turning yellow before its
time. The veteran of thirty was greatly excited.
He went to see if the arable land was in better condition : alas! half of it was fallow, and what had been
turned by the plough seemed only to promise half
profits to the cultivators.

'The Colonel reached a farm-house by a broken-
up road, choked with rolling stones, furrowed with
ruts. Children in rags, half naked, played upon the
manure-heap where the fowls scratched and the pigs
routed. He entered the house by a broken door.
The only openings of the one habitable room were
two small windows, without casements, and only
provided with an inside shutter closed at night when
there was no need for light. Thick planks put
together into the shape of chests, covered with straw
and a few rags over them, were made to serve as
two beds for the use of the whole family ; an old
worm-eaten chest. a bread-board, two benches and
two stools, completed the farmer's furniture. The

floor was of uneven, trodden earth, the stairs were a step-ladder leading to an almost empty loft. Such was the appearance of the farm-houses of Périgord in 1815, when the disbanded colonel came to take up his residence in the country.

' He who now travels in the country colonised by M. Bugeaud,' adds M. de Bezancenetz, in 1852, 'cannot imagine that in so short a space of time as fifteen years the aspect of the country could have been so changed by the influence of one single man. When he admires the fields with such even furrows, and covered with flourishing crops of corn, the artificial meadows with such rich, thick sward, the main roads thickly metalled, the smiling and comfortable farms, the healthy and well-clothed villagers, he cannot believe that this plenty and prosperity only date from some twenty years back. Why should it not be so? The very inhabitants of the country being used to the miracle, only have a confused remembrance of the past.

'Colonel Bugeaud's attempts had at first been viewed with mistrust. When the peasants saw him undoing and destroying everything in his domains, they shook their heads, and the owners of property boldly declared that the innovator would ruin himself. Each new trial, every implement unknown in the country, were the objects of malignant curiosity and criticism from all. What was the use of those harrows? Their teeth would never break the clods as well as the old peasant's mattock. What was the use of these stone-rollers, to part the grain from the straw? The flail known from all ages did its work much better. Did not the Colonel also entertain the crazy notion of having the harvested corn trodden under the feet of horses on the threshing-floor. Clearly the Colonel was possessed with a mania for novelties that would bring him to ruin and the most melancholy results.

'But when, after a few years, the most obstinate could no longer keep out the light, when they saw that instead of being ruined, the innovator had considerably increased his income, there was a truce to disparagement. People even began to allow that M. Bugeaud sometimes had good notions, and at last came imitation. This was what the Colonel waited for. The improvement of his own property was only half his projected work; his wish was to regenerate the canton, the arrondissement, the whole department.'

He had rebuilt his houses; the men who worked for him were better clothed, better fed, more intelligent than their like. Again, by his care a school for the children of his commune had been established in a house of his own. But that was not enough; the good must be propagated from neighbour to neighbour, like contagious diseases of other days. So the Colonel, far from repulsing those who seemed inclined to proceed with him on the course he was pursuing with so much success, placed himself entirely at their disposal. He helped them with his advice, gradually brought them to his views, and one morning, as he has told us himself, the agricultural society was founded.

It was a great day for Colonel Bugeaud. In his ideas the existence of an agricultural society was a fountain of prosperity to the country to whose progress and welfare it was devoted. He said, 'Agriculture being a science of local practice, the clever men of the locality must select the processes most suitable to the different localities. This is the original idea of agricultural societies.'

It was not in his own department alone that he desired to establish these gatherings of practical agriculturists, but all over France ; later, he moved in the Chamber that a sum of two million francs should be allotted for promoting the establishment of similar institutions in all the cantons of France, so that two hundred thousand persons might be morally associated in the same work of regeneration . . . . . His dream was realised ; and under the Second Empire annual district agricultural society meetings were established throughout our territory. Never should it be forgotten that this idea, so simple and so fruitful in results, is due to the initiative of Colonel Bugeaud.

He said on one occasion in the Chamber, ' It is all very well to colonise Algeria, but it would be still more interesting to colonise the great plains of Brittany and Bordeaux. A portion of the army might be thus employed, and villages built there, on the camp principle, but on a convenient plan for agricultural work ; the troops might occupy them with the double object of being taught the art of war, and of cultivating the adjacent land. When the ground had been brought into such a state that families could live upon it, these villages and their dependencies might be sold or leased out.

' Some persons who have not observed the vast resources of agriculture are uneasy at the increase of population. It is said there are too many people ; I will undertake to prove there are not enough. We could feed, and feed better, more than twice as many. Certainly the population is at this moment ill arranged. There are too many in the towns, but I would undertake to employ all the excess of Lyons, Bordeaux, Rouen, Marseilles, and Paris, in the country of Limoges.'

These notions of the 'soldier labourer' spread in the neighbourhood. The seed bore fruit, and his example and advice were so well followed, that the canton of Lanouaille soon became, from an agricultural point of view, one of the most advanced parts of half the central provinces, and of the entire south. The movement did not stop there, and the mode of cultivation that he advocated spread over Périgord and some of the Limousin; agricultural societies were established in several cantons, and the whole country presented a new aspect.

Colonel Bugeaud was adored by the peasants. His address being affable, encouraging, and grave, and his fatherly solicitude had a great share in the success of his enterprise for agricultural and moral regeneration. He succeeded in improving their generous but rather hasty natures. So the peasant of Périgord still carefully retains in his memory the recollection of the master of La Durantie. In his familiar talk by the farm fireside, on a bundle of straw in the barn, before the church, as on the occasion of the rural solemnities at the distribution of premiums, his language was simple, energetic, and plain. He always contrived to teach the labourers a great deal they did not know, and to correct their ideas about what they knew imperfectly. He talked familiarly with them, politics, work, agriculture, even social economy, so as to make them understand the hardest questions.*

Amid these absorbing occupations and pure enjoyments did the years of the Restoration pass with Colonel Bugeaud. He took but little part in politics, refusing to be present at such republican and Bonapartist meetings as kept alight the holy fire of the revolution at Perigeux and Limoges.

The young Colonel, though he had been so stupidly set aside by the Government of the Restoration, did not feel any aversion to it. In fact, he could reckon among the influential men of the day some intimate and devoted friends, who bitterly deplored that so many brilliant and solid qualities should be buried deep in Périgord, and never guessed the wonders and transformations accomplished in his province by this able man, with his energy and perseverance.

---

* We give a sentence from one of his speeches in patois with the French :

'Ni la liberté, ni l'art d'écrire et de lire, ne vous donneront du pain, des habits, des souliers, une bonne maison, des meubles et le reste. C'est peu de chose que la liberté, quand elle n'est pas accompagnée d'aisance. La misère, mes amis, est la cause de votre ignorance; c'est aussi la seule oppression qui pèse sur vous, et c'est le plus dur de tous les esclavages.'

' Si èrâ librei, si sabia letzi, voû dounŏriŏ co dô pŏ, de' lâ vestâ, dô sutzou, 'no meïtzou, dô meubei. . . . E sabi io qué ! . . . . Sei paobrei, qué volei sobei? E à cŏ qué voû abrâco, lo misèrio ! . . . . qu'è loû pû terriblé de toû loû esclavatzei !'

CHAPTER XII.

REVOLUTION OF JULY (1830).

THE day after the revolution of July, Colonel Bugeaud made an offer of his services, believing war to be imminent. In the month of September he was appointed to command the 56th regiment of the line, in garrison at Grenoble. Though very much engaged in the instruction of his regiment, he followed the course of politics at Paris with great interest, showing equal aversion for the manifestoes of demagogues, and the warlike declarations that were published, on the tribune, by the press, and in the street.

We have read several letters expressing this feeling in sharp, eloquent, and practical language, where it is easy to recognise not only the good citizen, but the soldier, and the statesman called to the highest destinies.

These letters were written from Grenoble by the Colonel of the 56th to one of his best friends, M. de Lacombe, a royalist, who had very much regretted that the brave officer was unemployed by the Restoration. We give one of these letters, written ten days after the appointment of the minister who repaired the omission, M. Casimir Périer, 13 March, 1831.

Grenoble, 23 *March*, 1831.

MY DEAR FRIEND,* —This minister offers us some security, and I hope he will be supported, even though there may be a limit to his kindness, for we require a little stability to re-establish order and confidence, without which we should be weak at the moment of danger.

Unhappily the tendency of the press does not leave much hope that the new ministry will be successful; the press, that indispensable auxiliary to a representative government, seems only to be able to live upon troubles and fights. If it carried on the war disinterestedly, unconcerned with defeated or dissatisfied ambitions, it would do well; but it is only too clear that, since the days of July, it is in great measure the organ of those who could find no place at the feast. This is the root of the injustice and bad faith of accusations that render it almost impossible for ministers to fulfil their office. It is very lamentable that a handful of private persons thus disturb the industry, the peace, and the future of the whole of France.

Do you really think that the majority in towns (I do not say of the nation, for there would be no doubt of a negative) is desirous of war, as is stated in the *Tribune*, the *National*, and the *Revolution?* Even if such were the case, that should not determine the course of the government, for the opinion of the multitude on war is like a blind man's on colours. There is no matter less understood even by those who are actually engaged. It is evident that, on the faith of these journals who have talked nonsense by the fathom on this point, a certain public, especially the commercial men, desire it unblushingly, because they expect that a better future will arise from it. About the means of carrying it on, the number of enemies we shall have to meet, the disorders at home that would arise in consequence of possible defeats, they have never thought at all. A better proof of this than all sorts of arguments, is that they wished to make us declare war six months ago, when we could not put 40,000 men in line. Even to-day is our army really ready to strive against Europe? The infantry could not put 200,000 men in line. We really have no more than 75 regiments in France. I allow them an effective of 2500 men, which would make 2100 fighting men,

---

* We are indebted for this letter to MM. Hilaire and Charles de Lacombe, of Orleans, sons of the friend to whom Marshal Bugeaud addressed it.

to judge by my own regiment, or 157,500 for the army. The cavalry cannot have 30,000 mounted men, the artillery and engineers 20,000. This makes 207,000; few to make head against Europe.

If war is absolutely determined on, the first thing to be done would be to organize 400 or 500 battalions of National Guards or volunteers, and equip and drill them very quickly. This is no small business, but all these superficial writers think it can be done with a turn of the wrist. Add to this, that the army wants teaching, and that the cavalry and artillery are not ready. And yet these impudent praters* do all they can to embroil us with all the world.

They ought to be thankful to the Government for not listening to them; at the present time they should chatter no more. The armies of Germany would be at Paris; 400,000 or 500,000 good troops are not to be stopped by tumultuous gatherings. The more numerous such are the better they are beaten.

At the present moment we should have ten times more chance of success: our army would make a good advanced guard for the nation, some peoples would assist us, and by the end of the year we should have a formidable army. But what expense, what losses, what misery! It makes one shudder. The advantages would be very dearly purchased. Certainly I should only gain by war: I should be killed or get promotion. And yet I do not desire it, for, above all things, I fear civil war and republican anarchy.

My regiment goes on improving, we are fairly good in drill, and

---

* This letter shows that the notorious hatred of the brave Marshal Bugeaud for the members of the press was of ancient date. Though he had so much force of character, such a strong contempt for fools and danger, he could not read a calumny against himself in a newspaper without a shudder of indignation. The journalists and members of the opposition, knowing this unfortunate peculiarity and weakness of the Marshal's, abused it strangely. The more they knew that he was sensitive, and took all the infamies laid to his credit seriously, the less they spared him their attacks and diatribes. His exasperation was unbounded when he saw in some papers his intentions unrecognised, his actions falsely interpreted, his words travestied. He immediately wanted to reply to the article, refute it, and confound the malicious calumniator. It was in vain his friends endeavoured to convince him of the inutility of defence, and make him understand that silence and contempt were the only arms to use against these wretches. The Duke d'Aumale told us, ' It was not always easy to hold him back. How often the ministers were embarassed! Although the Minister-at-War had the Marshal under his orders, he did not much care to venture on a prohibition. In reality it could not be forgotten that the Marshal was the chief personage in the kingdom. My father would send him one of his aides-de-camps as an ambassador. I was myself sometimes desired to advise him to desist.' Even to the end of his life did the Marshal maintain the violent hatred he expressed as Colonel for the journalists and tribe of pamphleteers

we are even giving a certain amount of instruction for war. I am now taking pains to form their ' moral,' without which there is no army.

BUGEAUD.

Marshal Bugeaud's younger daughter, the Comtesse Feray, who has been kind enough to assist in our work, has taken the trouble to arrange some valuable notes upon the domestic life of her illustrious father. It is thanks to her and her affectionate remembrances, that we have already been able to give our readers those charming pages that portray the childhood and youth of the great soldier down to the smallest details. This has reference to the year 1830 :

The start for Grenoble was very painful. How many tears were shed. My mother was sorry to see my father re-enter public life. We had been so happy! The apartments awaiting us were gloomy, in a narrow street. The new Colonel soon became idolised in his regiment, and was the object of touching attention during the severe illness that kept him a long time in weak health. A few months after our coming, the youngest of my two brothers was carried off by brain-fever. Leo was three years old. Like my elder brother he was singularly beautiful, and his over-developed intelligence had always made us anxious. There are griefs that cannot be described. I shall never forget that of my parents. Kneeling in a corner of the room, I prayed to God to take me and restore my brother. No more fervent prayer has ever been sent up to heaven. My sister was beginning to understand resignation, and wept beside my mother.

My father was not made a general as had been promised. His injured health did not improve. He asked for leave, and the whole family was delighted to return to the modest rural life of La Durantie.

How delighted were the friends and peasants to come and meet their master, when he resumed his agricultural occupations. My father was very uneasy about my mother's health ; he bought a house at Excideuil, where we were to settle ourselves. It was a very plain residence, but we were so happy there. Fruit and flowers in the garden, and sun everywhere. My father was always trying to make it pleasanter, and we all loved the bright house. How much might be said of the influence that a habitation may have over the life.

This new dwelling soon became the rallying place of all the society of the town and neighbourhood.

My father had been elected Deputy, and made General on the 2nd of April, 1831. He was in command at Paris, and we were expecting him in the country, when, in the month of January, 1833, my mother received a letter from him, and burst into tears. My father informed her of his departure for Blaye; the King had not allowed him time to refuse when he gave him the order, still less time to consult his wife, adding that the commission was a difficult one, that he would perform it as he had done everything entrusted to him, like a man of heart and honour. 'Poor Tom!' said my mother, 'he thinks other men are as good as he is, through everything he always believes in their justice. It does not matter, in spite of his disinterested devotion, he will be abused by excited factions. The King sacrifices him without recollecting that he has a family, and in the confusion of parties the Government will not support him.' My mother was not entirely wrong.

Before entering upon the details of the episode of Blaye, it is interesting exactly to establish the bent of General Bugeaud's mind, as Deputy for Excideuil, and his connexion with the politicians of the time, by his correspondence now in our hands.

We give a letter, dated 7th July, 1832, written by him to one of his best friends, M. Gardère, a rich merchant at Paris, who was always the confidant of his most secret thoughts. Detained at La Durantie by business and farming, General-deputy Bugeaud, not having any command, was not at Paris when the troubles broke out in June, 1832.

La Durantie, 7 July, 1832.

I am really ashamed, my dear Gardère, of having been so long in answering your original and kind letter. Believe that the cause is not indifference, and that I love you as much as any one after my own family, for you deserve it.

Yes, you may well tell me, 'Hang yourself, good Crillon.'*

---

* 'Pends-toi, brave Crillon, on a vaincu sans toi.' Message of Henri IV. to Crillon, after the victory of Arques, from which Crillon had been absent.—ED.

Perhaps I should have hung myself if the *bousingots* had won. You may imagine how I regretted that I had not had my share of the blows given to these implacable enemies of the tranquility of France, and that I shall make sure of being present in future. I think they were not struck hard enough. And what do you think of the crotchets about the state of siege raised by the very men who had demanded the same measures against La Vendée with such pertinacity. They say the war is finished at Paris. What! are not the secret societies always at war?

Are they to be always allowed to make their attacks, and when defeated to entrench themselves behind absurd forms of law? If it were so, it would be necessary to make no prisoners, the laws being impotent to punish these great criminals.

What do you think of these fine fellows who wish to carry the war into Poland and Italy, who expect with their civilian pouch-belts and their enthusiasm that they can overturn all the armies of Europe, who, on the first gun-shots, hide behind barricades that they do not know how to defend, and fire through cracks and holes. What! You want to overthrow a million of Germans and Russians, and you do not know how to defend the traverses of a fortress?

How would you meet the fire of a thousand guns, and the charge of 20,000 horse in the open country? You fancied, no doubt, that a quarter of Paris would be sent after you, mounted upon trucks? But the combats of the 5th and 6th of June have proved that would not be enough for the *exubérants*.

Is it true, as stated in the papers, that there is a general complaint at Paris of the state of siege? I did not believe it.

What will be done with those scoundrels Garnier-Pagès, Cabet, and Laboissière? Certainly they are guilty. They have shown us their plans so plain that there is no room to doubt!

Garnier is the most dangerous of all, and the most perverse. God grant that the jury may do their duty by them.

I thought of resting in Périgord. Vain hope. I am overwhelmed with visits; the interests of many are at stake: there is no end to it. Lately a young man came from the further end of the department, and stayed with me a day, without telling me what he came for, it being his first visit. Next morning I said to him, 'Sir, no doubt your visit has an object; what is it?' 'General, I have come to ask you to get me a place.' 'What place?' 'I do not know: whatever you think I could hold.' 'But, sir, I do not know you; and if I knew you I have no places at my disposal to give you, or means of applying for vacancies to be made for you to fill.' He went away after making a very good breakfast.

Though I find great eagerness for places, I find much less for the public good. I am striving hard to establish agricultural societies, and cannot succeed.

I am full of business. I am building a barrack for gendarmerie at Lanouaille: I am building at Excideuil, where I have my hay and my harvest. So you must excuse my delay. I have fifty people to answer.

Adieu, my dear friend; I think it will not be long before we meet; and yet I should be glad if it was not till October.

Love to Pascal.

B.

We find about the same time a letter from Madame Sermensan (Hélène de la Piconnerie), the Marshal's sister, which deserves to be quoted.

MADAME SERMENSAN TO GENERAL BUGEAUD.

Hanguiran, 22 April, 1832.

MY DEAR BROTHER,—I have just received a letter from M. Reculet, and one from Chéry-Colomb, expressly to tell me of their pleasure and admiration at your letter to the Minister-at-War, refusing a command at Paris, that they read in the *Memorial* of Bordeaux. It certainly gave me great delight; and once more did I feel proud that the same blood flows in our veins.

I went back to the year 1816, when M. de Montureux wrote, 'He is a dangerous man, who must be watched, for he is the rallying point of all the half-pay officers.' At the same time M. Lainé wrote to the Duke de Feltre to know in what class you were placed in the famous categories; the office reply came, 'He is in the 14th class;' and the minister added below with his own hand, 'That is to say the worst.'

How grieved I was at that letter; how it told me in large print, Do not deceive yourself any more: your brother will never get employment under such a government.

And this very dangerous man only wished, as he does now, to encourage every one: for instance, he preached obedience to the law; he occupied himself with agriculture, main roads, and anything to the public advantage. He was a zealous maire, respected by every one, &c., &c.; and yet the Government thought him unworthy to resume his rank in the army. Oh, shame! but other times, other manners.

One thing alone, my dear, gives me real pain, to see that you are

undecided about returning to the Chamber next year. I understand
the dog-life that you lead, I understand all the discomforts of your
position, especially separated from those you love ; but it is worthy
of you to persevere in supporting the Government; and the ministers
are to be admired for their bravery, and bearing the attacks of all
these desperadoes with so much dignity-—Maugnin, Salverte, and
the rest. I read the papers twice as carefully since you have been
in the Chamber. There are days when I am raging at their bad
faith, others when I pity them ; the discussion is so stormy upon the
head of *subjects* that it will be difficult for them to find a suitable
substitute ; and I cannot understand how, after M. Montalivet's
explanation, they could continue to make such a disturbance. It is
evident they are choking with rage, and are in search of a subject to
vent all their bile upon.

The wretches! I despise them too much to hate them :
but I cannot believe that such an opposition is a necessity for a
representative government. By the rule of contraries, my admiration for the ministers is doubled, especially for M. Casimir Périer.

A national reward has been voted to M. de Richelieu. I do not
cast any doubts upon his deserts, but according to my notions he is
nothing to compare with the president of the ministers. His courage
and devotion are much above those of heroes who win battles.
They peril their lives, it is true ; but if they meet an honourable
death their memory will live with honour in history, while
M. Casimir Périer every day sacrifices his life, steeped in
bitterness, his rest, his reputation—indeed his happiness. And
perhaps this complete devotion, which is the saving of France,
will meet with nothing but ingratitude. Happily, men of his
temperament must find their sweetest reward in their own heart.

After all I see, my dear, I have no more ambition for you.
Thoroughly perform your work as deputy, and quietly return to hold
your plough, amid your family and all your cares ; there is no real
happiness but that and an honest competence. It was said of old
time, As happy as a king : the phrase might be inverted now.

I thank you a thousand times for all your kind speeches to me,
and generous offers. I never expect to be in want of the needful, for
my expenses are too well regulated. . . . . .

My young couple are admirable in orderliness and economy, and
their love seems stronger every day. Azia is indeed very remarkable
for her precocious judgment.

It is too charming to be successful when one arranges the
marriage of a son of twenty-three. I have good news from Excideuil
and Puissegeney. Good Eliza has sent us a capital truffled turkey,

we had a party of the neighbours to eat it ; and we drank the health of that worthy and excellent woman, and of General Bugeaud, the good and loyal deputy.

Phillis tells me that your little daughters are getting very pretty; all the better, for I am like the men, I do not care for ugly ones.

Adieu, my good brother, I love you as you deserve.

HÉLÈNE SERMENSAN.*

P.S.—I will write to Pascal immediately. Meanwhile, kind love to M. Gardère, and all the Clonards.

---

* Colonel Louis Sermensan, now commanding the 50th regiment, is grandson to two sisters of Marshal Bugeaud. Hélène de la Piconnerie married Sermensan, and Phillis de la Piconnerie married M. Lignac de Puyssegenez. Thus his father, M. Sermensan, married his cousin, Mdlle. Puyssegenez. As legatee of his maternal grandmother, Phillis, Colonel Sermensan had in his possession most of the letters and documents relating to his great uncle the Marshal. They then came into the hands of the Marshal's daughters. The name Puyssegeney, the name of a fief, is spelt in various ways. Thomas Bugeaud himself wrote just as often Puyssegenez, Puissegenez, Puyssegenetz.

CHAPTER XIII.

THE DUCHESS DE BERRY (1832).

WE have now reached one of the most important
and interesting periods in the life of Marshal Bugeaud.
It is about half-a-century since the events now to be
described took place. We think the time has come
for telling the whole truth. The passions and political
hatreds that ensued upon the revolution of 1830 are
now at rest ; and we hope we may be permitted to
touch upon the earlier years of the reign of Louis-
Philippe, without ruffling the calm course of history.
Besides, our work is not polemical, and we cannot be
accused of forming a partial opinion on the facts.
We will confine ourselves to bringing to light the
incidents that personally concerned our hero, and
properly defining the portion of responsibility that
rests upon him in an event of great political importance, which was very variously considered in the strife
of parties.

From the commencement of his reign, Louis-
Philippe found himself encountering very great difficulties. However, in these critical times, he had the
rare good fortune to meet with a great minister, a
man of both rule and liberty, whose energy, political

good sense, and patriotism, were a powerful assistance in establishing his throne upon a firm foundation. Indeed, this throne had been speedily shaken by different enemies all equally determined; on the one hand, the republicans, whose hopes of anarchy the prince had frustrated; on the other the partisans of the old *régime*, who could never forgive the nephew of King Charles X. for not having refused the crown offered by the representatives of the nation. At the very moment when Casimir Périer was dying, 16th May, 1832, having put down the rising in Paris and Lyons after a terrible struggle, the Legitimists were stirring up the western provinces, and the Duchess de Berry, landing in France, lost no time in proclaiming a capture by force of arms in La Vendée. It was then that the *Moniteur* of the 11th October, 1832, announced the Duke de Broglie Minister for Foreign Affairs, for the Home Office M. Thiers, and M. Guizot for Public Instruction. Marshal Soult kept the War Office and Presidency of the Council.

In the voluminous collection of the Marshal's official and private correspondence, most kindly placed at our disposal by one of his grandsons, M. Robert Gasson-Bugeaud d'Isly, we have found a large number of letters from M. Thiers. We give two, dated the 12th and 28th October, 1832, addressed by the new minister of the interior to his colleague, General Bugeaud, the deputy of Excideuil; they show the young deputy for Aix.—M. Thiers was then thirty-five years of age—minister for the first time, asking the General to encourage him, and to request men of spirit to support 'his calumniated youth, assailed by the blasts of envy.'

Monsieur Thiers, Minister of the Interior, to General
Bugeaud.

Paris, October 12, 1832.

My dear General,—You are the first person to whom I write after the martyrdom thrust upon me, that is made to pass for promotion. The King had thought not of me, nor of M. Guizot, but of M. Dupin alone. M. Dupin desired to be absolute chief, to make and unmake at will, and especially to make an alliance with the Left, under pretence of compounding with its most moderate leaders. At any other time such a plan might have had its advantages, but at a moment when we have need to prove to Europe that the vessel has not lost its anchors, the notion of such a proceeding was senseless. Three times was M. Dupin addressed, at my urgent desire ; three times did he obstinately refuse. Then the King applied to us. I did not ask for what are called the doctrinaires, and they, more disinterested than any others, did not ask for power. But strength was needed, and where was it to be got when Dupin refused ? We went in, despairing in our hearts, for the burden is immense. But, in all conscience, where can men be found more capable, more honourable, more worthy of freedom, than MM. De Broglie, Guizot, and Humann ? Must there not be an infamous genius of calumny to find anything to say against such men ?

Support us, I beg of you; give me courage, in my great need of brave men, to support my calumniated youth, assailed by the blasts of envy. I shall be very thankful if you will write to me. I am painfully impressed by the newspapers, and am perhaps writing to you too strongly.

Adieu, my dear General, I embrace you, and wish you better health. The Chambers are summoned to meet on the 19th.

Adieu,

(Signed)   A. Thiers.

M. Thiers, Minister of the Interior, to General Bugeaud.

Paris, 28th October, 1832.

My dear General,—A man cannot display more patriotism or judgment than you do. I think exactly as you, and consider your articles in the *Journal of the Dordogne* to be very good indeed. We have decided upon using the language that you wish, to the Powers, and we have done so. I hope that we shall have Antwerp. As for La Vendée, I should like to have hold of the Duchess; I have neither hope nor wish to destroy the bands in a month. Jacque-

minot has shown some anger, but he is quieted.   There is no question
of his resignation.   We are expecting positive answers from London
on the Belgian question.   We are determined to get in.   This is,
between ourselves, a State secret.   Adieu. my dear General.   I shall
be ready to retire when the good of the country requires it.   I hope
you will soon be well.

(Signed)   A. Thiers.

On the 7th of November, the Duchess de Berry
was taken at Nantes.   It is no business of ours to
excuse or judge the means adopted for her arrest by
the zealous and ardent Minister of the Interior.   The
following letter, written by him at the moment it took
place, fully expresses the general excitement at that
time :—

M. Thiers, Minister of the Interior, to General Bugeaud.

Paris, Tuesday, 13th November, 1832.

My dear General,— I beg your pardon for not having
answered your letter.   I am so wearied, so tormented, with cares
that I hardly have time to think of the most urgent business.   You
are indispensable to us, my dear colleague.   We cannot do without
you in any way.   I have captured the Duchess de Berry, and yet I
have encountered nothing yet but folly and abuse.   Now, people wish
that we had dragged her from one tribunal to another, and given rise
to an odious scandal ; they would like to get us into a scrape, instead
of our confining ourselves to a simple precaution for safety.   I have
never seen so much injustice and bad faith.   Our project is to propose
to the Chambers to detain her as long as is necessary to the safety of
the State.   Come, my dear General, come and help us with your
advice, and your valuable vote.   Adieu.   All our friends must be
present, or we shall be lost.   I embrace you, and pray that God may
send you better health.   Adieu.

(Signed)   A. Thiers.

We think it interesting to quote here a letter of
General Bugeaud's, addressed to M. Mourgues, Prefect
of the Department of the Dordogne.   When speaking

of the Duchess de Berry, the General was far from prophesying that a few days later he would be charged with the delicate mission of being Governor of Blaye.

GENERAL BUGEAUD TO MONSIEUR MOURGUES, PREFECT OF LA DORDOGNE.

Paris, 4th January, 1833.

We shall have quite a theatrical sitting to-morrow at the presentation of five-and-twenty or thirty petitions for the Duchess de Berry; after that we shall pass to the order of the day, and draw a terrible thorn out of the Minister's foot.

The order of the day will be very significant; it will mean that things are to remain *in statu quo*. At any rate, the way is likely to be cleared by discussion.

Thus, it appears, the Duchess de Berry will not be tried, and she will only be detained until circumstances permit of her being set at liberty, on condition that she never returns.

I am well aware that the Carlists are lifting the mask, supposing that they have had a mask, for I think they have never hidden themselves. This must be attributed, not to their bravery, but to the gentleness of the Government and the laws. They are not physically dangerous, and you may rest assured that, far from becoming worse, the situation is improving every day. There are no more risings to fear; Europe respects and fears us; trade and work are prospering; everything promises us more prosperous days; there will still be some small troubles, but we shall easily conquer them.

Though General Bugeaud's mission commenced three months after the arrest of the Duchess de Berry, as he was only appointed Governor of the town and castle of Blaye on 17th of January, 1833, it is interesting to study the first instructions of M. Thiers to Colonel Chousserie, the predecessor of General Bugeaud in the post of Commander-in-Chief of the citadel of Blaye. These documents were made over to the new Governor when he relieved Colonel Chousserie.

M. Thiers, Minister of the Interior, to Colonel Chousserie, Commander-in-Chief at Blaye, Gironde.

Paris, 18th November, 1832.

Colonel.—After a long journey you reached Blaye, where you found the notification of the high command entrusted to you, and the first instructions of the War Minister.

Before giving the final instructions in the portion that concerns me, I require to know your private observations, and therefore will confine myself to facts.

It was first necessary to provide for the most pressing needs, and that is what the Prefect of the Gironde has done according to my recommendations. He is, as you must know, furnished with a letter of credit from the Receiver-General upon the special receiver of Blaye. This letter, on his personal responsibility, has been delivered to the Sub-Prefect of the arrondissement of Blaye, who will hold the necessary funds at your disposal, in proportion to the requirements.

The great vigilance you are required to exercise and to direct is necessarily divided into three portions: the interior, the exterior of the castle, and the coast.

For the first, two civil commissioners will be appointed; a commissary of police will have charge of the second; and with regard to the third I enclose a copy of the instructions sent by the Minister of Marine.

Interior supervision of the castle.*

It appears there is no reason to expect an attempt to carry off the Duchess by force, but it is reasonable to suppose that a number of plans for escape will be made.

Two persons will be placed near her: M. de Mesnard, a devoted servant, but old, and not likely to intrigue: Mlle. de Kersabiec, not less devoted, but active, enterprising, accustomed to an adventurous life; she would necessarily be the intermediary in all undertakings.

---

* The citadel of Blaye stands on the right bank of the Gironde, and commands a town of a dull and wretched appearance. Some streets of barracks, a parade, artillery and engineer stores fill the interior of the citadel. The top is crowned by an old castle, said in popular story to have been built by Roland, and that his body was carried thither after the defeat of Roncevalles. Around it is a terrace only ten or twelve feet wide, on a level with the retaining wall. From the top of this kind of parapet, sanded for the chief part of its length, and divided at regular distances by embrasures bridged by planks, the eye commands an immense horizon. On the west the river, clothed in this place with the melancholy majesty of the sea: to the north, east, and south hills covered with vines, country-houses, mills, and factories. The citadel is a cold place to live in. The winds are dangerous there, and consumptive persons soon die.—*Louis Blanc, Histoire de Dix Ans.*

Some waiting-women will probably be claimed by the Duchess. The first selection made will not be unimportant. It will not be sufficient only to be assured of their character. Who are their friends? What family do they belong to? Whether the condition imposed upon them, of keeping up no communication with the outside, might be illusory? It will be important to ascertain all this.

Books, clothes, instruments. &c., will be procured at Bordeaux. Daily communications will be kept up with that city, where the Legitimist party have always counted numerous adherents. These books and clothes must be carefully examined; and information obtained as to the tradesmen who supply them. There must be none appointed. By procuring the goods first from one shop, then another, not letting their destination be known, attempts at communication and the establishment of a connexion with the castle will be evaded.

Letters can only be received or sent open. The wrappers of newspapers must be taken off. The commissioner of police ought to have chemical means in his possession to bring out sympathetic ink if necessary.

These precautions are to be as much as possible unseen, but they are indispensable. Watchfulness at every moment, and of everything, is quite compatible with great respect, delicacy, and complaisance. The object of this perpetual supervision is to leave the Duchess no chance of escape.

I leave to you, Colonel, the charge of preparing a special regulation, and articles relating to the proper establishment of the identity of persons, in the indispensable communications, the office of confessor, the service of health, &c., &c. All those attached to the personal service of the Duchess must be informed that, once entered, they cannot leave.

It will be through you that the Duchess will receive the newspapers, which you will yourself procure; no subscription will be taken in her name.

That which it is above all things necessary to avoid is the possibility of the establishment of any direct communication, or any method of concert. Your duties and those of the civil commissioner must in no case be illusory. It is necessary that in everything and everywhere, throughout the castle, the command of which is confided to you, your presence and your action should be manifest. It is the Duchess of Berry that is confined in the castle.

Receive, &c.,

(Signed)   A. THIERS.

M. Thiers omitted no detail or precaution in his

solicitude for the great interests placed in his charge. There is in existence a confidential letter that he wrote himself to the special police commissioner employed to guard the illustrious prisoner.

Colonel Chousserie was justly jealous of his authority, and was annoyed at M. Joly being placed by M. Thiers at Blaye as special police commissioner, with a kind of commission to supervise the guard and the actions of the Commander-in-Chief. The Government very soon afterwards put an end to these disputes by nominating to the command of the fortress a maréchal de camp, the name then used for general of brigade, instead of a colonel.

Zealous though he was, M. Thiers could not retain the Home Minister's portfolio. On the 1st of January, 1833, he was succeeded by the Count d'Argout, formerly auditor of the Council-of-State under Napoleon I., Prefect, Councillor-of-State, and peer of France, under King Louis XVIII. M. d'Argout, a diligent man, conciliatory, and rather sceptical, undertook this ticklish duty without much enthusiasm ; but his political programme being accepted, he proceeded to work without hesitation.

We find in a curious book, *Les Salons d'Autrefois*, by the Comtesse de Bassanville, the following passage:

'One of those who most often and most readily opposed Mme. de Girardin was Marshal Bugeaud, at whom the Legitimists of the Hôtel d'Osmond always cast an evil eye, as they accused him of having solicited the *infamous honour* of being the gaoler of the Duchess de Berry at Blaye.' This accusation was an infamous calumny. This is completely proved by the perfectly authentic letter that I have been allowed to copy, and the history of his character leaves no doubt upon this unfortunate affair, now long past, yet which might inflict a stain upon the memory of the honourable man who did nothing but obey, like a soldier, an order that he was sorry to receive. This is the letter :

Blaye, 13th January, 1833.

It was with great pleasure, my dear F., that I heard of your appointment. I was uncomfortable every day when I thought of you thus left out. But I thought the more highly of you for bearing this without a murmur, or attacking the Government, as do so many persons who have been unable to obtain employments to which they had no right.

Your title was patent, and you made no complaint, because you knew that governments cannot always do what is right, nor do it at once ; that in every case the King and the Government ought not to be blamed for these little denials of justice that will take place under all governments, because they are composed of men, and men are not gods.

You did not expect, any more than I did, to see me sent to Blaye. This is how it occurred.

On the 30th (Dec.) I was at a court ball. M. Argout came to me, and said, ' I have always thought, General, that you were very much devoted to the monarchy and government of July. Would you accept a mission of confidence and devotion ? ' and he looked at me in a peculiar way as he said this.

' When I devote myself to a cause it is not by halves,' answered I ; ' so I will accept it, and do anything that is not against honour : the more dangerous and difficult the task, the more I shall be flattered.'

' I expected this, and am going with your answer to the King,' said M. Argout, going away.

Thereupon my mind set to work to guess what it meant. Was it assistance to Don Pedro? or a mission to Turkey? anything but Greece. I ended by trusting to chance without further thought, and stayed at the ball till five in the morning.

On my return to my lodgings I found the order to start for Blaye. I went to MM. Argout and Soult to receive my instructions. The King sent for me, thanked me for accepting, and immediately gave me his instructions.

I assure you I should have preferred taking 6000 men to Don Pedro or the grand Turk. This gaoler's business suits my character and mind very little; but I must obey, for we soldiers must not act as suits us, but march when we get the order. Besides, is it not only by this entire devotion of men of spirit that France can be made independent of factions and the factions?

Adieu, my dear F. Amuse yourself; good luck to you, and think sometimes of the poor prisoner, your affectionate

BUGEAUD.

Madame de Bassanville adds, ' I have chosen to quote this letter entire as it belongs to history, and no pains are too great to be taken in order to wipe off the dust that might sully so fair a life as that of the Marshal, whose memory is adored by the soldier. He was at the time very much distressed by public opinion turning against him, and conceived an implacable hatred to the journalists and journals whose articles were rending him so pitilessly.'

These are the instructions addressed by M. Argout to General Bugeaud on his departure.

THE COUNT D'ARGOUT, MINISTER OF THE INTERIOR, TO GENERAL BUGEAUD.

Paris, 1st January, 1833, 3 p.m.

MY DEAR GENERAL,—These are your instructions, and letters for the prefect, sub-prefect, Colonel Chousserie, M. Dufresne, and M. Joly. I add all the copies that I could get made this morning of the instructions given by me or my predecessor to Colonel Chousserie. His duty is to leave you all those he has received; but in any case I am not sorry to give them to you myself. I add the copies of instructions sent to M. Joly, that you may know everything.

The Marshal will forward you your appointment and instructions before four o'clock. I have ordered post-horses for that time. I should not be sorry if you could start before the mail; make your carriage precede it, so as to go faster. I think you should not stop at Bordeaux, as that would make you lose time, but go direct to Blaye, and forward thence the letter intended for the councillor of the prefecture with a few lines of apology and compliment. No doubt these precautions are in excess, but it is better to sin by excess than default. In your communications with Colonel Chousserie be good enough to explain to him that this measure is not a disgrace, but a matter of convenience and the good of the service, as he perceived himself when he suggested to the Government that a command of such importance should only be entrusted to a maréchal de camp.

Adieu, my dear General, I again repeat how glad I am to see a post, in which careful watch and judgment so much affect the greatest interests of the State, entrusted to such loyal hands, so dexterous and so devoted. I beg of you to have a perfect confidence in my zeal to second you in everything, and to assist you in this difficult task. Believe also, my dear General, in the sincerity of my most cordial attachment. Write to me very often, and with the most minute particulars.

CTE. D'ARGOUT.

I have taken a note of M. Desvignes and the interest you are good enough to take in him.

We believe that of all the eye-witnesses of the captivity at Blaye two persons alone are now alive— the two daughters of General Bugeaud. One of them, the youngest, the Countess Feray d'Isly, has been good enough to forward us her recollections of this time. We take the liberty of giving these freely written private notes without alteration, full of the freshness of childhood, always redolent of simplicity and truth.

My father waited upon the Duchess de Berry the day after his arrival at Blaye, and she soon saw that her position would be improved. She was able to appreciate his open and thoroughly honest character. There was an end of the excessive watchfulness she had suffered under. She received whom she liked. The persons whom she would not receive blamed the Government! Very soon after his appointment the relations of my father with the Duchess de Berry became very cordial.

As soon as we arrived, without waiting for my mother to request the honour of being presented, the Duchess sent to ask her to come and see her, and bring her children. My sister and I were both dressed fine—frock of light green bombazine, a hat of the same light green, with a colossal rose-coloured bow. I give these particulars to show you how perfect is my recollection. All the evening before

I had been receiving sermons from my mother as to how beautifully I was to behave, and Lieutenant Saint Arnaud made me rehearse my curtseys. We started with my father at the time her Highness had appointed, and she very graciously came to meet my mother in her parlour. The Duchess had risen to salute my mother from a very large arm-chair, with great down cushions; no doubt I was fascinated with the comfortable look of this chair. I at once forgot all the sermons and the curtseys, and I jumped into the chair and disappeared in the soft down. Nothing was to be seen of me but the red bow of my hat. The Duchess burst out laughing, as much at my mother's confusion as at my uncivilised proceeding; she would not allow me to be disturbed, and took another chair. Happily my sister had behaved like a well-brought-up young lady, but when she saw me in full possession of my pleasant retreat, she took courage and came and shared it with me.

After this visit, every time that we both were in the Duchess's room she gave us the down chair, by turns. The Duchess was very pleasant with my mother: when we left her room, my father went last, and she called to him, ‘General, send me your children very often; I like your little savage, it is nature.’ My sister went every day to take lessons at a school. She only visited the Duchess on Saturday and Sunday, and always took her a nosegay. Her Highness petted us a good deal, always gave us something nice to eat, and liked to see us running about in the garden. Not so much engaged as my sister, I saw her almost every day. Sometimes she would look steadily at me, take me on her lap, and give me a kiss. ‘Nini,’ said she, ‘you remind me of my boy; he is fair like you. Lots of people ask me for some of his hair; I will send them some of yours: it is just like his.’ And the Duchess used to cut off long curls of my hair. My mother was very sparing of her visits, and the Duchess was good enough to reproach her for it.

My father often went with M. de Saint Arnaud,* and spent some hours with her Highness. The conversation was always interesting, and very often exceedingly animated and cheerful. The Duchess laughed very freely at stories the gentlemen told her. At other times my father made plans with her in the expectation that she would remain in France. He told her, ‘Your Highness has been a good general of an army, and would make a very good farmer. I will come, madam, and bring my experience to help you.’ Sometimes

---

* Marshal St. Arnaud's curious correspondence, published after his death, contains some valuable information about the captivity of the Duchess de Berry, given below.

the Duchess would tell him stories of her campaign in La Vendée. The letters, published in the work of M. Henri Lecharpentier, show that my recollections are very faithful. These conversations, though I did not attend to them, have come back to my mind since I knew how to understand them.

The rooms her Highness occupied were furnished with all the luxury she was used to. She had her household, her gentlemen of honour, and ladies of honour, and all the attendants her Highness could desire. She seldom went outside the garden, often invited my father and his staff to dinner, very seldom the persons who came from Paris or anywhere else. She did not always like to receive these visits, and was always perfectly free in that respect.

The Duchess had a dog named Bevis, and three parrots; a person was entirely occupied in taking care of these creatures. The house my father lived in was not very far from the royal habitation. Though less elegant, there was plenty of room in it; his sisters, my aunts De Puyssegenctz and Sermensan, came to us. The officers and the numerous visits of my father's friends made the private life of the family very gay. M. de Saint Arnaud was a lieutenant in an infantry regiment in garrison at Blaye. My father soon found him out to be the charming, clever, and devoted man that he was, and placed him on his staff. From that moment they never ceased to be on the most intimate terms. M. de Saint Arnaud contrived the diversions. He arranged evening parties for reading or singing, and nobody was better than he was at finding out games, tricks with cards, and amusements of every sort. On the grand days when plays were acted by the officers, an exhibition of marionnettes for the children was given. The Duchess asked for an account of the entertainment, and desired a second representation at her house. In this way M. de Saint Arnaud tried in the evening to distract the minds of my dear parents from the troubles that crowded upon them, by his cheerfulness, energy, and these amusements.

I have only spoken of the good side of the situation. How often has my mother talked of the reverse of the medal! Her sojourn at Blaye would have been the happiest time of her life but for her suffering at heart from the abominable calumnies directed against my father. Not an insult was spared him! How patiently he bore the injustice! He tried to console my mother, and restrain the anger of M. de Saint Arnaud and my aunts. 'Justice will be done me later,' said he; 'the King will defend me, and it will be known that I have done my duty like a gentleman.' Poor father! what a mistake! The ministers let the talk go on; it was more convenient than undertaking the defence of the man of duty. The calumny still goes on. Only a few months ago did I hear all these infamous tales repeated by a person who was very near the King, or at least the Government of that time.

Some even dared to attack my mother. I was not spared, though only seven years old. My sister, being studious and working successfully, was respected. I was determined not to learn to read; my mother did not know how to rouse my emulation. M. de Saint Armand wanted to give me lessons that only turned into play. One morning came a paper with more horrible calumnies than usual. The title was, 'Mlle. Nini's Reading Lesson.' In this imaginary lesson of the journalists my mother was making me spell a word, and I was answering by some coarse abuse of my father. These unconscionable men were not ashamed to put such horrors into a child's mouth: the article was long and wound up with this flattering reflection, 'The gaoler of Blaye's little daughter promises to be very clever.' All present were very indignant. My mother had an idea; she called me and read me the article; the lesson was valuable. In a few months I had learned to read.

The Duchess received some strange presents, sometimes very pretty things,—a quilt of white satin, with her arms embroidered on it, dresses, a dressing-glass; other times more serious missives—a great woollen wrapper, with a bit of paper pinned to it and written, 'To warm Madame's chilled limbs.' I once saw the arrival of a pair of shoes, real wagoner's shoes, with great nails in the sole, and marked on a paper, 'To save her Highness from the damp floor of her dungeon;' and many more attentions of the same kind.

You know the history of her Highness's marriage which was disclosed by herself; so it is needless to repeat it. I can now perfectly remember the excitement caused by the birth of the little princess, Marie Caroline, born at four in the morning! A few days after the event the Duchess sent to beg my mother to come and bring us to see the little princess.

Her Highness was lying in a mass of lace and blue satin. At the side of her bed was a cradle, also blue, in which slept the little girl, and we went to see her, timidly walking on tip-toe. Her Highness told us to kiss her; the baby was waked, no doubt, by these too eager kisses, and began to cry like an ordinary mortal. The nurse was not in the room; the lady of honour, Mme. de Hautefort, sat upright in her chair, probably restrained by court etiquette. The child kept on crying. Though my mother was so timid, she could not long resist that little voice. She rose, took the little princess in her arms, and gently soothed her. I think I can still see the Duchess de Berry's look of thanks to my mother. I very soon resumed my habits with my dear Duchess; only Bevis and the parrots got no more of my favours—all my love was for the sweet little princess. I was at the height of happiness when her Highness made me sit down in her great chair, and allowed me to hold her little girl for a few minutes, and nurse her in my arms. Poor infant! her course upon earth was very short. I was really sorry when she died.

The day before the Duchess left Blaye for Palermo she received some shrubs with the usual paper, 'To shade Madame's prison.' 'They are delightful,' cried the Duchess; 'to imagine that I should stay here till these lilacs could give me shade! Here, my children, I give them to you: plant them in your garden at Excideuil.' These lilacs. violet, of a kind then very rare. lived a very long time; they were known by the name of the Duchess's lilacs; the white ones could not bear the cold.

Next day, a very hot one. we were on the quay to see the Duchess's departure; her Highness saw my mother standing a little way off, and gave her a most affectionate farewell,* kissed us, and let us embrace the little princess.

The crowd was great; persons of all parties were mingled upon the quay, hoping for some accident that might prove to this mass of witnesses that the infant was not the princess's. and that the infamous governor had provided a supposititious child. Just as she was going down into the boat the Duchess turned, and looked anxiously for the nurse, who was separated from her by some persons. Just then a ray of the sun was shining on the child's face; the Duchess stepped forward hastily, and gave her parasol to shelter her child. There was a murmur in the crowd—no longer any room for doubt. This scene is very clear in my recollection, though I did not understand the meaning of it; M. Veuillot has described it in one of his books.

During the voyage from Blaye to Palermo her Highness. at the instigation of the captain of the vessel who chose to act the zealot, for a moment forgot that she had found a devoted and safe friend instead of a governor, and spoke very harshly to my father. I do not know the circumstances well enough to give an account of it. However, as she was very kind, she very soon resumed her former feelings. and expressed to my father her regret for this capricious freak in very warm terms.

This episode was related by the captain according to his fancy, and several journalists commented upon it most malignantly to my

---

* Reaching the Porte Dauphine, Marie-Caroline, seeing the governor's two daughters and their mother, bent to embrace them, then turning to Madame Bugeaud, whom she knew to be endowed with a fine character and a merciful soul, she said, ' I hope you will soon see your husband return quite well.'

father.   Some letters written by the Duchess to my father after his return to Excideuil prove what I have stated.   Alas! the wicked cannot be prevented from talking.   The truth is known to intelligent Legitimists.   Justice has been done to my father's character. Since I have known the history of that time I think that the real friends of her Highness the Duchess de Berry, and the king her son, might have shown their devotion to the august prisoner by more tact and silence.

CHAPTER XIV.

DUCHESS DE BERRY (1832).

AT the distance of half-a-century may not an impartial and unexcited historian go back to the past and bring to light every document emanating from the actors in a great political drama? Among the documents laid before us, we know none more interesting than the *Journal of the Citadel of Blaye*. This precious manuscript is written by the very hand of General Bugeaud, of Madame Bugeaud, and the General's aide-de-camp, Captain de Saint Arnaud. It is a simple paper book, decorated with the stamp of the citadel of Blaye. The Governor, a man of method, committed to it the chief events of the day, copied the despatches he received and those he sent to Paris, both to Count d'Argout, the Minister of the Interior; and to Marshal Soult, President of the Council, War-Minister. There are also notes written by the ministers, generally by their own hand.

To understand what was going on we must transport ourselves in the first place to the year 1832. Louis - Philippe, sovereign in fact and by national right—this is indisputable,—found himself placed in a most critical and most perplexing situation imme-

diately after the arrest of his niece, the Duchess de
Berry.

Without wishing to detract in any way from
the high qualities of heart and mind, the nobility and
energy, of the heroic princess, it is impossible to deny
that at this moment her Royal Highness had raised
the standard of Civil War in France. As a State
prisoner she would certainly have been immediately
set at liberty, if the opposition press—the Republican
papers——had not as soon as she was captured published that the young princess was in a condition that
her widowhood rendered disgraceful, as there was no
knowledge of a previous secret marriage.

The Carlist party, as were called the partisans of
the elder branch, did not hesitate a moment to give a
denial to the alleged condition of the princess. Thus
King Louis-Philippe's Government found themselves
driven to a painful and terrible alternative. To get
out of the difficulty and rebut the calumny, they
must choose between two alternatives. To set the
Duchess at liberty immediately was to declare themselves guilty in the eyes of the Legitimists of an
infamous lie; and to assume the odious responsibility
of having been desirous of dishonouring a noble princess of royal blood, the King's own niece, in order to
overcome a dynastic opposition. To keep the Duchess
in captivity, so as to establish the fact of her condition, the secret marriage, and the birth of the
royal infant, was without doubt a sad and painful
necessity: but reasons of State, and responsibility for
order, imperiously prescribed these last measures.
This was the determination of Louis-Philippe's
Government.

Would any other sovereign have acted differently

in similar circumstances, just when the fires of civil war were scarce extinct, in presence of the enthusiasm of the revolutionary party, before Europe threatening or ill-disposed?

The *Journal of Blaye* commences 3rd of February, 1833, with a report to Marshal Soult, President of Council and Minister of War. After preliminary report we find:—

Colonel Chousserie wrote to the Duchess to inquire if she would receive me. She sent him the following answer:—

'Colonel, I have received your information with great vexation. It is a fresh annoyance from the Government. I have already told you, sir, that I would do anything in my power to impede them. Thus I will not receive General Bugeaud, nor the persons whom he probably brings with him. If necessary, I will shut myself up entirely in my own rooms. But the Ministers will have to answer to Europe for what a daughter of Henri IV. and of Maria Theresa* has had to suffer. She will know how to die in fetters rather than yield to tyranny. This is my determination. I hope I shall see you, sir; be sure I shall never forget your kindness to me.'

I caused a short answer to be sent her that no tyranny was involved in the change of Governor, far from it; that the King had himself enjoined upon me to treat her with the utmost respect and attention, that she might be convinced by the actual words he had desired me to report to her, and that if any harshness had been contemplated in my mission I should not have accepted it. My position as a French officer, and a selected representative of the country, is a warranty.

The following letter from General Bugeaud to his friend M. Gardère, at Paris, gives some curious particulars as to General Bugeaud's first interview with the Duchess de Berry:—

Château de Blaye, 3rd Feb., 1833.

My dear Friend,—I arrived safe and sound, and immediately assumed the command, and I already know my men and my post as

* The Duchess was daughter to the King of the two Sicilies, a Bourbon descended from Louis XIV., and his sister was Marie-Amelie, Queen of Louis-Philippe. The King's mother Caroline was daughter of Maria Theresa, Empress of Austria.--ED.

well as my own pocket. I am well lodged, well fed, well warmed, well lighted both with lamps and candles. When my wife comes, I shall be very well able to endure my prison.

The Duchess would not see me. She declared it was a fresh annoyance from the Government, and that she would not bear it. I did not insist, and as an experiment on the female character, I simply announced that I had a verbal communication to make from the King; and I would only present myself when she wished to hear it.

Remembering that it is good tactics with the fair to sometimes seem indifferent, I told Mme. d'Hautefort that the manner in which I had been received when I went to examine the place had taken from me any wish for admittance ; and that, though not a descendant of Henri IV. and of Maria Theresa, an expression of the lady's, I also had my pride, which was founded on my personal antecedents. This ruse seemed to have succeeded. Mme. d'Hautefort came and told my aide-de-camp that she thought Madame would ask to see me to-morrow.

(Signed)　　BUGEAUD.

(The General was compelled by his duty to visit the Duchess's apartments, though she would not receive him.)

To the Marshal (Soult).
5th February, 1833.

Sir,—There is nothing fresh to report as to the Duchess. Her state of health is the same. She walked to-day in the garden with her companions in captivity. She has expressed no wish to see me, and I have avoided being in her presence. I only visit her lodging at night, so as to excite her desire to see me. If she persists in her refusal, I will see her in a few days as she walks in the garden, to observe her state of health. In justice to Colonel Chousserie, I should say that the military arrangements were so well considered, that I have very few changes to make.

*　　*　　*　　*　　*　　*　　*

I have the honour, &c.

On February 18th there is a report to the Minister of a second interview with the Duchess, and on the same day was written a letter to a friend, M. Mourgues, prefect of La Dordogne, with an interesting account of the first interview.

*　　*　　*　　*　　*　　*　　*

' You know, I think, that I was very ill received by the Duchess de Berry, who at first refused to admit me on any other terms than as a gaoler making an inspection. I used language to her that was approved by the Government, and abstained from seeing her. I had excited her curiosity by sending her information that I had been desired by the King to convey his own words to her, and that when she wished to hear me I would wait upon her.

This method, so powerful with the fair sex, was not successful, and another had to be tried. Some days afterwards, having requested an audience of Mme. d'Hautefort, I told her, ' Madame, I do not insist on being admitted to the presence of the Duchess de Berry; the manner of my reception prevents me from wishing for it. Without being descended from Henri IV. and Maria Theresa, I also have my pride, grounded upon my whole life. However, as I should not like the Duchess's health to suffer from our want of inter-course, I make her the offer of sending an officer with her whenever she wishes to walk out.'

The Duchess answered that she would not be so rude as to walk out with anyone but myself; that what she had done was not the least personal; it was a lesson she had chosen to give the Govern-ment. Then she several times expressed to my aide-de-camp an intention of seeing me. I allowed myself to be wanted for some days at last, yesterday I paid her a visit and was very well received.

She was remarkably cheerful. She talked about farming, bees, poetry, war, and diplomacy. Twice she tried to touch on the politics of the day, and I turned the conversation. She turned sharply to Mme. d'Hautefort the first time, and said to her, ' How cleverly he whips off the hounds !' The second time, ' He has tact.' We parted the best of friends. Her cheerfulness surprises and defeats me ; her health is excellent.

*　　*　　*　　*　　*　　*　　*

The following letter is important as giving General Bugeaud's strong remonstrance against measures which the Government proposed to carry out in order to put an end to the state of suspense.

To the Ministers of War and the Interior.

22nd February, 1833.

Gentlemen,—I have received your despatches of the 19th and
the two instructions appended to them. These instructions, like
all that are prepared at a distance from the spot where they are to
be carried into execution, are susceptible of great modification, unless
there is an absolute determination to relinquish every sort of reserve
with the Duchess. Being entirely convinced that such a determination would not be to the advantage, either of the King or country,
I would request you to entrust the application of extreme measures
to another person. As the prescribed measures are not urgent, I
take the liberty of suspending the performance of them, even in
matters that I consider possible, until I receive your reply to the
following observations and the analysis of your instructions, paragraph by paragraph, that I forward.

If it is true that the Duchess de Berry is in the supposed
condition (and it is my opinion that she is), it is at the most six
months gone. Therefore there is no necessity for haste in using
your power to impose Doctor Ménière and the nurse upon her.
There is more advantage in temporising, and obtaining by confidence, and a careful watch, the same result that might be expected
from the presence of the two above-named personages. But even
suppose that they were quartered, by authority, within her house,
that would not advance matters. The Duchess, who is of a very
decided character, would withdraw into her room, would not see the
doctor or nurse, and if they came near her, I am convinced that she
would proceed to extremities, she would tear their eyes out. In any
case she would have nervous attacks that might be very dangerous. If
after all these scenes, which could not fail to become known to the
public sooner or later, she did not prove to be in the condition
supposed, or if these vigorous measures should cause an accident,
either by determining a premature confinement, or injuring her
health, it is easy to foresee that great inconvenience would result to
the Government. The press of all colours, and honourable men of
all parties, would throw stones at us. The hatred to the King in a
certain class would be redoubled in intensity, and he would lose in
the estimation of his friends.

But is the object of sufficient importance to cause the risk to be
run of encountering such things, and could it not be attained by
other means? I do not hesitate to say, No! the object is not great
enough, and there are besides other means of attaining it. These
methods are for the most part adopted, and I propose to establish
them all in succession, but with tact and reserve, for it is the only
way that seems to me to be good, *the only one I could adopt.*

In this way of proceeding I do not hesitate to include the perfect openness you advise towards d'Hautefort. It was already part of my plans. I will wait to be better acquainted with her, for I have only seen her four times as yet. Your despatches and instructions decide me upon speaking to her this very day, at 9 or 10 o'clock, so as to be able to communicate the result to you. Meanwhile this is the actual state of things.

I have applied to General Janin for a corporal of gendarmerie, so I have three men of that force, and I put one of them every night to watch in the apartment immediately below that of the Duchess. From this point the smallest sound is audible. Another sub-officer is on guard above, and at the side of the corridor leading to the apartments there is also an officer. One of them will always be on the watch near the wicket, whence everything can be seen and heard. Movements can only be observed until the hour when the persons detained retire to bed, for then they are isolated by curtains noiselessly placed at their door, and similarly removed early in the morning. M. de Brissac, the Duchess, and Mme. Hansler, can communicate, for they are in the same set of rooms; M. de Brissac on the left of the entrance to the parlour, the Duchess on the right, and Mme. Hansler, by the side of her mistress in a little room.

I should be far from wishing to separate M. de Brissac from the rest. I believe he has so honourable a mind that he would be incapable of lending himself to a crime. So his presence seems to me a security. His letters and his wife's have convinced me that this couple are very good people. I am good friends with M. de Brissac. I reckon upon speaking to him also. He has served in our ranks, he loves soldiers, and he is not ill-disposed.

I expect to gain much assistance by watchfulness. On the smallest unusual noise the sub-officer under the room will communicate with the officer on guard by means of a sentry posted before the lower window. I have had iron bars fitted to this ground-floor. The officer off duty, and the two sub-officers, one of whom is orderly on watch under that room, are shut up at nine in the evening. The same sentry will desire the relief porter to call me at the smallest sound, as well as the military commandant, and the civil commissioner, whose lodging is near the walls. Doctor Ménière, who is also two paces off, will be warned. The nurse sleeps close to the tower and can enter at any moment, but not go out freely again.

I see the Duchess every day.

My aide-de-camp, M. de Saint-Arnaud, on one excuse or another, sees her two or three times. He is clever and observant. The officer on duty and the sub-officer see her all day. It would be very difficult for them to miss seeing any event, or the smallest derangement of health.

*   *   *   *   *   *   *

The respect and esteem displayed towards the Duchess by her companions, and her own perpetual cheerfulness, which we are certain of, by observations that we make unknown to her, all convince me that if she is in the condition supposed, there is, at the same time, a cloak prepared to save her reputation, that is to say, a secret or pretended marriage. Supposing this to be true, there is no doubt she will declare it when the fatal moment approaches. A proof that this moment is not near is that she does not desire Mme. d'Hautefort to sleep in her room, and that her habits are unchanged. And my conviction is finally confirmed because she takes no pains to conceal her condition. Twice Mme. d'Hautefort, noticing that I was making observations, came between her and me.

I detain my despatch until I have seen Mme. d'Hautefort, I am going to examine the instructions on other sheets.

22nd February, 1833, *3 p.m.*

The thrust has been made. Things will go better than I thought, or dared to hope. I asked for Mme. d'Hautefort, and said, ' Madame, the moment is come to be perfectly open with you. In good souls openness arouses reciprocity, and I count upon that. The government desires to be released from the existing state of uncertainty, and desires to make sure that the event that should be the consequence of the condition supposed, or rather that they almost certainly know to exist, may not be concealed from them. They give me orders to take measures that may either be amicably received, or else imposed by force. I will not apply this last method, as you shall see by the first page of my reply. But another man would employ it. It is for you, madam, to judge if it is more desirable for you to persuade Madame de Berry to take a noble course. There are two, the avowal of her pregnancy, if it is the case, the establishment of the fact if it be otherwise. In this last case, it ought to be important enough to Mme. de Berry to put an end to the reports current among friends and foes throughout France, and to reappear in all her glory before the eyes of her partisans. If she is in that condition, perhaps there is a secret marriage, and the same interest should make her acknowledge it. If there is no marriage, there is the object of putting a stop to a number of little measures which she would call vexatious, but which would become the duty of the government towards the country interested in the authentication of the event. See, madam, whether you feel strong enough and attached enough to the Duchess as to open the question. I think it should be done most frankly; show her the government despatch and the two first pages of my reply. She will know what I think. She will judge whether she ought to keep me near her by an avowal of her condition, or by having it authenticated, or by bearing amicably all the measures ordered by the ministers.'

Mme. d'Hautefort listened attentively to my speech, though her face visibly changed. She answered,

'General, I swear upon my honour that Mme. de Berry has never made any communication as to her condition to me, nor has she to Mme. Hausler. *Like all the world, we have our suspicions, and can see her visible increase of size.* M. de Brissac and I have talked about it, and to provoke the Duchess's confidence the other day we said to her, Madam, in your position you should not look on us as gentleman and lady-in-waiting, but rather as friends to whom to communicate all your troubles, that they may help you to bear them. This language was ineffectual, we know nothing.'

Thereupon Mme. d'Hautefort read your despatch and part of mine, and said, ' Nothing, General, could be more honourable than your sentiments, your frankness challenges mine, your confidence challenges mine. I will do everything to keep you near us, but let us take counsel with M. de Brissac.'

M. de Brissac spoke like Mme. d'Hautefort. He swore several times that he knew nothing, but suspected. He was more excited than Mme. d'Hautefort. After a long silence I spoke again: ' Take courage, a course must be decided on. Which of you two will undertake to tell the Duchess everything?' Long silence. I went on, ' It seems to me more proper for Mme. d'Hautefort.'— ' Yes, indeed.' said M. de Brissac; ' as for me, I could not do it.' Mme. d'Hautefort said she would devote herself. ' Will, madame,' I answered, ' take the Minister's letter, this sheet of my reply, pages one and two, and try to remember the reasons I have given why Madame should take a decided step.'

Mme. d'Hautefort came back a moment after. She was in such trouble that she had forgotten all the reasons to be urged. I saw they must be written down, and added this consideration, that the Duchess de Berry should be induced to give evidence of her condition by the wish she has to regain her freedom speedily. If it be ascertained that there is no pregnancy, it is probable that she will be free, and the disarmament arranged with Europe, and that without delay.

Mme. d'Hautefort came back in an hour's time looking strangely, and said to me, ' General, I have told Madame everything. She has read the Minister's letter and yours. She is much affected by your behaviour and feelings. She cried a great deal, but confessed nothing.'—' Well, madame, what shall we do? What shall I write to the Government?　Must I tell them to send me a successor?'—'General, give us a few days, I beg.'—'Madame, I can only give you till Sunday, at five in the evening. If a course is not decided on by that time, or I am not permitted to put in force all the measures ordered by the Minister, I shall request to be relieved.'—'General, we will do all we can.'

The expression of Mme. d'Hautefort's face gives me hopes of a speedy solution.

I suspend the execution of your orders, so necessary to the country, from love of the King. I have always thought it the duty of a general, at a distance from his chiefs, to take upon himself to change or modify his orders, according to the circumstances, and as far as his power extends. I am confident we shall attain our object by honourable means. Depend upon my patriotism.

Your respectful servant,

BUGEAUD.

5.30 p.m.

P.S.—I have just been summoned to the Duchess. She almost threw herself into my arms, weeping. She pressed my hand and confessed that she was secretly married in Italy, that she is pregnant, and she thinks it her duty to her children, to her friends, to herself, to acknowledge it. I congratulated her heartily, and asked for a written declaration. She hesitated a little, but at last consented. I wait for it to add to this second despatch.

My heart is lighter by three hundredweight; I am happy the object is gained. The honour of the King and the country is saved. Everything is favourable to the throne of July.

Declaration of Marie-Caroline, Duchess de Berry.

Under the pressure of circumstances and the measures ordered by the Government, though I had most important reasons for keeping my marriage concealed, I think it my duty to myself as well as to my children to declare myself to have made a secret marriage during my residence in Italy.

At the citadel of Blaye, 22nd February, 1833

MARIE-CAROLINE.*

---

* A recent letter from General Count Trobriand contains a most complete justification of General Bugeaud's proceedings, as it comes from the Duchess de Berry herself.

GENERAL TROBRIAND TO MADAME X——.

New Orleans, 5th April, 1878.

DEAR MADAM,—The incident referred to in your letter of 12th March last is perfectly correct. My remembrance is very accurate. It was in 1846. I was

There is also a curious little letter of the General's to his friend the Prefect.

Blaye, 27th February, 1833.

MY DEAR SIR,—When you receive this letter, the newspapers will already have informed you of the Duchess de Berry's confession, and the Carlists will be crushed and indignant. We shall very soon be obliged to protect the Duchess de Berry against them, ' the heroic prisoner, the new Joan of Arc, Maria Theresa, &c., &c.'

Certain it is that I have become interested in her since she has been in the depths of misfortune ; she calls me *son ami*, she almost has cause to do so, and I fully intend to offer her my services for the future, if perchance she should obtain permission to remain in France (not very dangerous now). I would persuade her to buy a property in Périgord, and place at her disposal my agricultural experience, and all my neighbourly good offices.

I thought that I was very far from a diplomatist. But I have performed a bit of diplomacy ; it is true it has been frank, open, and bold, the tricks of Metternichs or Talleyrands would perhaps not have been so successful. Sometimes the simple take one in more than the cleverest. I have managed to obtain an acknowledgment that will simplify my duties and those of the Government. It has not been without difficulty.

BUGEAUD.

living at Venice, and had the honour to be frequently admitted to the company of the Duchess de Berry at Vendramin Palace. One evening there were a few of us together, and mention was made of the captivity at Blaye, and one of the visitors thought fit to speak harshly of the proceedings generally laid to the credit of General Bugeaud when he was governor of that fortress.

Then the Princess said, ' I see you share in the general error, but I assure you that General Bugeaud was not at all as he has been usually represented. In reality the Marshal is a kind man, who had a difficult task to perform, and did it as best he could, trying to reconcile his duty as a soldier with the consideration due to me. So I had no real ground of complaint against him. He was an honest man, and we remained friends when we parted.' I was much struck with her words ; she was the last person from whom I should have expected a defence of him who was governor of Blaye when she was a prisoner there. The account of the matter completely reversed the generally received ideas, and those that I had myself conceived on authorities that I thought incontestable.

You will thus understand, dear madam, how the incident impressed itself so clearly upon my memory, so that, after so many years, I can produce almost exactly the language that the Duchess de Berry used on the occasion.

(Signed)   R. DE TROBRIAND.

The General received a letter from M. d'Argout expressing his great satisfaction.

However, though the Duchess had stated the fact of her marriage, she refused to divulge the circumstances or the name of her husband, though pressed to do so by the General and her own attendants, Madame d'Hautefort and M. de Brissac.

'Madame,' said the General, 'take a friend's advice, if I may call myself one, and tell us the circumstances of the marriage.'

'General,' with extreme vivacity, 'do not say another word to me about it, I will never write anything more. The Government are wretches! They long for my death! They will have it!'

With these words she rushed into her room and banged the door in his face, a moment afterwards reappeared and said,—

'My anger is not with the General; I have only to praise him, but with the Government.'

Then she went back again.

The General's letter to the Minister, Marshal Soult, concludes, ' I continue to think that by the end of the month her condition will be much more clearly visible, and that then the Duchess might be set at liberty without risk, notwithstanding the bad faith of the Carlist party. She will have no more political influence, for even those who now deny are convinced in their hearts. If she crosses France by short days' journeys there will not remain the least doubt. Even the fact of her being set at liberty will be the best of proofs. In my opinion this measure would be magnanimous and merciful. Besides, it will have the advantage of relieving the Government from the danger attending possible accidents that might ensue upon a confinement taking place under painful moral circumstances. I should give this advice with my conscience in my hand if I was summoned to the Ministers' Council.'

On March 20th, 1833. the General reports that the Duchess seems to make herself out before him worse than she really is, and that he had asked M. de Brissac and Madame d'Hautefort if they would be ready to give a written attestation of the expected event when it occurred. but they refused. He had therefore pointed out that in consequence of their refusal it would be necessary for the Government to take more stringent measures to verify the event.

There are in existence three manuscripts of a treatise on Street Fighting, the germ of which is given in the following letter to M. d'Argout :—

CONFIDENTIAL.

22nd March, 1833.

MY DEAR M. D'ARGOUT.—This letter is not official, and is not intended to address you on the subject of my present duty. However I must tell you, by the way, that the Duchess de Berry, whatever she says, is not very ill. As a proof I send you a note of her dinner yesterday and breakfast this morning. I have reason to believe that the Duchess went to bed yesterday on purpose to receive me.

Now I come to the real object of my letter. The Bergeron trial has revealed to us the power of the Society for the Rights of Man. I think it is dangerous, and that precautions must be multiplied against its probable attempts. No doubt the attention of the Government is awakened to it. I do not presume to sound the first alarm, but I know that men, very much occupied, do not always think of everything ; and I thought it only my duty to my country to give you an idea on this matter. Excess of good cannot be an injury.

What seems superfluous may be very useful. A military author writing about sieges, when he came to the opening of the trenches put, 'The earth is to be thrown on the side towards the fortress.' One of his friends said it was useless to put that in. 'Leave it,' said he, 'if it does no good it will do no harm.' Some time afterwards, at the siege of Philipsburg, the trenches were opened and the earth thrown towards the camp!

You may be surprised that I do not rather write to the War Minister than to you. You will easily understand that military reserve to superiors, and the great distance between the Marshal and me, both in respect of rank, experience, and service, does not very well permit of my giving him advice; and any qualifications I might make use of in expressing my opinion would not prevent the appearance of it.

My eyes not being quite cured, I continue through my aide-de-camp.

I think that the Government in Paris should act as if it was at the advanced posts, and should take the following precautions.

Fortify and battlement the chief guard-houses; put a small store of cartridges in them with biscuits and wine for two or three days, all calculated on the number of men that would rally there and defend themselves to extremity.

The Maire's offices ought also to be provided with cartridges. I know that means have been taken to arrange for the assembly of the National Guard.

Cartridges should be issued to the chiefs of the line regiments, who will only distribute a portion to the soldiers, and put the rest in the barrack magazine.

Issue to them also, to be kept in barracks, axes, crowbars, and handspikes. They should be responsible for these stores, and hand them over to the troops who relieve them.

Ascertain that the higher officers of the line regiments have a sufficiently exact knowledge of Paris, and especially of the places where they would have to act, and the points they would have to defend.

Let as many as possible understand the plans for the defence of the city of Paris.

Transfer the bakeries from Paris to Vincennes, Courbevoie, and the Ecole Militaire; keep them always well filled, and have small stores of biscuit in two or three safe places. It is to be remembered that the King's guards had no food, and this was one cause of their defeat.

It is not prudent to have all the artillery at Vincennes, or at the Ecole Militaire. I should like to place two batteries at Courbevoie.

Always have a corps of twelve thousand infantry and artillery, and two thousand horse, within one day's march of Paris, with the two-fold object of answering for the instruction of the princes, general and superior officers, and restraining the factious of the capital.

Proclaim the object of these measures, in order to reassure good citizens, and to put a stop to the malicious interpretations of the press. I would frankly say that these measures are taken to protect liberty from the attacks of secret societies, such as the Society for the Rights of Man, the Friends of the People, &c.

The same or similar measures should be taken with respect to Lyons, or other cities where there may be fermentation and secret societies.

There should immediately be issued instructions to all the commandants of military divisions and subdivisions, in case of insurrection, which might by wonderful chance be successful in Paris. They should have orders to obey no order coming to them by any other authority than the King's, either by telegraph or messenger.* They should always be provided with ammunition.

A proclamation ready prepared for such an event should be sent to them, so that in case of necessity the same ideas and principles might be made public throughout France. This proclamation should appeal to the love of real liberty, to the material interests of commerce and wealth, to patriotism, to the honour of all good citizens and of the army.

The generals should have orders to mobilize a portion of the National Guard. A scheme should be prepared beforehand for this purpose, so as only to put the safest men under arms.

Wherever local peace is secure the general should march his troops to Paris without waiting for orders.

The prefects should receive orders to support all these arrangements, the instructions to be secret.

Only men of spirit and energy should be left at the head of the divisions and subdivisions.

Unless all these precautions are taken beforehand, it is certain that feeble and irresolute men will be found at the head of divisions and departments, who will allow themselves to be drawn into the popular movement for want of a line of conduct previously marked out.

Most men have need to be directed by instructions that must provide as much as possible for eventualities.

Foreseen events lose three-quarters of their moral influence, and instructions given by means of that foresight prevent all irresolu-

---

* It may be interesting to note that a telegraphic despatch (semaphore) sent from Paris at 3 p.m. reached Blaye at 12.—ED.

tion and divergence in the actions of the diverse instruments of
government.

The measures relating to Paris, to great cities, and the camp,
will not alarm public opinion if their object is openly avowed and
announced by a well-drawn proclamation declaring that these precautions are only directed against the same seditious persons who
have stained the capital with blood, while it is reassuring in the
interests of liberty.

*   *   *   *   *   *   *   *

Receive, my dear M. d'Argout, &c.

28th March. 1833.

*   *   *   *   *   *   *   *

CHAPTER XV.

LEGITIMIST TACTICS (1833).

Journal of Blaye — Legitimist Tactics — Precautions for Verification — Instructions —Comte de Choulot — Bugeaud persuades the Government to be contented with Witnesses' Certificate.

I HAVE already reproached the Duchess de Berry, Madame d'Hautefort, and M. de Brissac, with having had illicit communications outside the walls, and have made them sensible of the dangers for them. They gave but a clumsy denial. I will return to this.

*   *   *   *   *   *   *

I perceived by several conversations with the Duchess or her suite that she was desirous either of making propositions to the Government, or that the Government should make them to her. I also thought I saw that they were in some difficulty about the proposals and how to formulate them ; and this determined me to write a letter, enclosed. I had no reason to be sorry for this when it brought me the reply. also enclosed, allowing me to keep Deneux, a man so necessary to the verification of the event we expect.

MADAME LA DUCHESS DE BERRY TO GENERAL BUGEAUD.
Citadel of Blaye, 27th *March*, 1833.

I can only be very thankful to you, my dear General, for the motives that prompted the proposals you submitted to me. When I first read them I was determined to give a negative reply, and have not changed my views on reflection, and I will decidedly not make any advance to the Government. If they think it necessary to impose conditions on a liberty so necessary to my *completely ruined* health, let them inform me in writing. If they are compatible with my dignity, I will consider if I can accept them. In any event, General, I cannot forget that you have known how to combine the respect and regard due to the unfortunate with the duties laid upon you. I am glad to express my thankfulness to you.

(Signed)   MARIE-CAROLINE.

P.S.—I have just heard that M. Ménière is going away, and that M. Deneux is forbidden to see me without Doctor Dubois.

declare that under no circumstances will I admit M. Dubois to come near me,* though I cannot but observe with great sorrow the distrust the Government entertain for M. Deneux. I do not oppose his remaining, but I will not make any request in that respect.

5 April, 1833.

* * * * * * *

I think it will be prudent by the end of the month to make Ménière sleep in the room close to the Duchess's apartments. Independently of that I shall leave the key of the door of the corridor leading to the apartments with the officer on duty, and he will go and listen five or six times in the night.

Besides, I do not the least suppose that they will conceal this event. The Duchess talks more openly of her condition than would a Paris shopkeeper very lawfully married. She shows a wish to nurse the child herself; she is also surrounded by five or six persons who would have to be induced to transgress orders, and that is impossible. If it be suggested that the infant might be conveyed away under the tower, that is still more impossible, because there is only one exit, and it is guarded by two sentries, a trusty officer, and sub-officer. Do not therefore be the least uneasy on these two heads; the only reasonable one in which I agree with you is the Duchess's health after her confinement.

* * * * * * *

To Monsieur d'Argout.

12 April.

Sir,—I have the honour to forward to you a letter from Madame de Brissac to her husband, containing an inclosure that seems to me to be worthy of your attention. I have underlined it, and doubly the part that seems to mean that a state of pregnancy is feigned in order to be set at liberty, or at any rate that M. de Brissac had given his wife to understand this to be the case. These would be a new kind of deceitful tactics.

This discovery might well make us less amenable to any propositions that the Duchess might make, and the admission of the counsellors she asks for.

It is evident that the party are prepared to represent the pregnancy as a subterfuge for the purpose of getting set at liberty. As to me I think her condition is very real, for a man must be blind

---

* The Duchess's dislike to Dubois arose from his having attended her husband when he was assassinated, and she thought him unfeeling. She complained very much that the King knew this, and yet wished to impose him on her as medical attendant.

not to believe in it, and must think that MM. Gintrac and Deneux are two rogues or quite ignorant. The only thing that seems clear to me is that they want to take advantage of our kindness and mercy to play us a trick, to obtain her liberty, and then to laugh at us.

Extract from Madame de Brissac's letter.

M. de Sémonville said yesterday to some one, who told me, that his government had quite decided upon setting madame at liberty after her confinement. That does not do us much good, we who do not believe that she is pregnant.

Notwithstanding even Deneux's letters, what an inconceivable method this would be to select, compromising what is a thousand times more precious than life, for the attainment of anything in the world. My poor friend, I am always thinking of you. I am feeling all that your noble heart and pure mind must experience in all possible cases.

To Monsieur d'Argout.

15 April.

Sir,—I did not intend to mention to you a little, almost unimportant event, because I was a little mystified, and one does not care to acknowledge that. But the sub-prefect having told me that he had said something about it to you, and that you expected particulars from me, I think it my duty to inform you.

A certain Count de Choulot, having travelled from Prague, and brought with him the portraits of the Duchess de Berry's two children, asked me for an audience, that he might present the two miniatures. I did so. The conversation promised frankness; he several times told me that he had no doubt that the Duchess de Berry was married, and pregnant: that most of the Legitimists believed the same as he did; that the denial of the press injured the Duchess much: adding that, if he could see her, he would tell her not to listen to the bad advice from all around her, but assent to all the verifications and guarantees the Government wanted for setting her at liberty. He stated to me that Monsieur de Brissac and Madame d'Hautefort were not sensible persons, and would only give the Duchess very bad advice. He repeated these things many times, begging me to let him see the Duchess for a moment. I consented to allow him ten minutes private conversation with her, on condition he would allow himself to be rigorously searched. He complied with the condition, and he conversed with the Duchess for ten minutes, watch in hand. I was in the room close by. When he came away I took him to my house, and put the following questions to him. ' Well, have you seen whether the Duchess de Berry is pregnant? Has she told you? And what shall you say in public?' 'Why, I cannot say that she is pregnant, only that she is married, for she told me so.' 'What, sir, you did not see her condition? did she manage to conceal her size?' 'But, General, she remained seated, so I could not tell.' 'Sir,' indignantly, ' you had no doubts before you saw her, and you have doubts now; it is infamous.'

Thereupon my aide-de-camp, M. de Saint-Arnaud, spoke to him in most insulting terms, telling him he was a man without faith or honour. I told him, ' Saint-Arnaud, go to the Duchess and ask her from me if it is true that she did not rise before this gentleman, and if she did not tell him she was married and pregnant; we will see if the gentleman is as much of a liar as he is treacherous.'

Saint-Arnaud went like lightning, and came back the same, with an indignant face. ' The gentleman is a cowardly impostor,' said he, ' unworthy of your kindness for him, unworthy of the decoration he wears at his button-hole. The Duchess told me that she walked about before him, and had positively told him that she was married and pregnant; and she offers, General, to tell him so again in your presence.'

Thereupon we treated the wretch as he deserved, and he cannot have the shadow of honour about him, when he has not required satisfaction for the abuse. Lastly, I turned him out in disgrace, but not without a keen desire to make him jump out of the window, or spend one or two days in a casemate. It took all the influence of our modern manners to deter me from doing this.

This is, as you see, a specimen of the good faith of that party. I know them now, they shall not catch me again.

If you wish for information as to this Monsieur de Choulot, inquire of a Monsieur Darmand, table de hôte, rue de Rivoli, No. 10.

It is a proof of Monsieur de Choulot's interview having no important effect, that three days afterwards the Duchess wrote me the letter I have forwarded.

There certainly is no occasion to publish an account of the Comte de Choulot. As for me, I told him that if he published anything in the papers at variance with the truth, I would not only expose his infamous conduct, but break his head wherever I met him.

It seems that these threats were not quite sufficient, for M. d'Argout writes on 17th April : —

*   *   *   *   *   *   *

I asked you yesterday for information as to Count Choulot's proceedings at Blaye. You will see in the *Quotidienne* an article announcing that he had seen the Duchess. I know that he boasts of having obtained from her lips some information as to the moral constraint exercised upon her when she wrote the famous declaration that appeared in the *Moniteur*.

M. de Choulot has prepared a protest containing the Princess's alleged words, and has lodged it with a notary. This man, as I have told you, is a very dangerous intriguer; I shall be very impatient to receive your reply, that I may be able to answer any questions put to me, and to advise a remedy for this unfortunate occurrence. However, it is not important. The Carlists have their theme, and will not relinquish it : as a general rule not a word they say is to be believed, none of their promises, none of their oaths. Nothing binds them, and nothing ever has bound them ; they are past masters in the art of perfidy.

Heartily yours, dear General,   C. D'ARGOUT.

To THE MARSHAL PRESIDENT OF COUNCIL.

16 *April.*

*   *   *   *   *   *   *

The refusal to send her Messieurs Chateaubriand and Hennequin has greatly exasperated the Duchess, she launched out into invectives against the Government. I let her run on, so as not to provoke a scene injurious to her health ; but M. de Brissac and Madame d'Hautefort having joined chorus with her, I lost patience, and spoke to them as they deserved. ' It is you and your party who are the Duchess de Berry's real enemies, it is you who sacrifice her to party spirit. You make it impossible to really set her at liberty by your bad faith, your Machiavellic denials, the abuse and calumny of every kind you fling on the Government. While Madame authorised Monsieur Deneux to say that she was pregnant, this is what Madame de Brissac wrote to her husband' (and I read the sentences you know).

' You see, madame, that from these words it is plain that M. de Brissac has never told his wife of madame's state, but has, perhaps, led her to suppose that the condition is pretended in order to obtain liberty. Judge now if you are not the victim of party spirit. You should have consulted no one but yourself.'

M. de Brissac was at first quite stupefied, but he cried out that he had said nothing to his wife, because he chose to say nothing, and would never say anything : that there was an attempt to make him play a part in politics, but he would not play it, he did not care to have himself in print all alive.

I answered: 'Sir, there is no question of playing a part in politics, but only to act in the same manner as the Duchess did when she made Doctor Deneux speak. By that you would have prevented the denials and calumnies that hinder the Government from carrying out their good intention of setting the Duchess de Berry at liberty. With people who have taken the course of denying everything, it is necessary to adopt the course of awaiting the last and strongest of proofs.'

Madame d'Hautefort said, 'Ought madame's condition to be made public for the satisfaction of the *juste milieu?* General, you will have enough to do: you will never convert me.' 'Madame,' said I, 'be quite convinced that I do not wish to convert you, that there is no question of the *juste milieu* here, but only of the Duchess de Berry. If *juste milieu* wins its stake in six weeks, it will convince the most incredulous, and present them with a baby.' 'No, General,' cried the Duchess de Berry, 'you will not convince any one, they will poke their noses into it: they will see me and my child only to deny it again! Instead of that I wanted to make proposals to the Government, if MM. de Chateaubriand and Hennequin had advised me, that would have been better for them than the confinement.'

'It is very unfortunate, madame, that your Highness has chosen to rely upon party spirit. These gentlemen, according to their manners, would have given you no advice unless conformably to their own interest. Disinterested advisers, like me for instance, would have been preferable.' 'Sir,' cried M. de Brissac, 'your Government is ruining itself: if anything happens to the Duchess de Berry, it is lost.' 'Sir, the immense majority of the Chambers and of the nation think with the Government on the question of the Duchess de Berry.'

Several unsuitable expressions of M. de Brissac had drawn this apostrophe upon him. The conversation continued long enough in this tone. The Duchess de Berry several times repeated to me that the plan she wished to propose was very favourable to the Government, and better for them than any verification. I insisted upon knowing this plan, and the Duchess de Berry seemed for a moment disposed to communicate it to me, but M. de Brissac opposed it. In this particular that person and Madame d'Hautefort departed from their usual practice. In the course of talk there slipped from M. de Brissac and Madame d'Hautefort an expression that I was trying to make proselytes, but should never win them over to the *juste milieu.*

'Be quite convinced,' I said to them forcibly, 'that the *juste milieu* has no need of you : it fears you not, and your support would be but a trifle, if, indeed, it were not hurtful, for you have spoilt almost all the causes you were devoted to. At this moment you are forwarding republicanism with all your power, and outraging the Government that protects you, and is even discredited in the eyes of our party by protecting you. If the republic came, it would be sure to avenge us. Look at the declaration of the Society of the Rights of Man' (*Journal des Debats of the 12th*).

The Duchess de Berry declared several times that she would do nothing, and propose nothing, unless she was allowed to see some advisers of her own choosing, but that it seemed quite clear the Government wanted to kill her.

'No, madame, no, the Government is far from desiring your death, but it desires some surety; and there was no dependence in the men who, having in the way of Machiavel taken to the plan of denying everything, would have taken advantage of the visits to Blaye to confirm the Legitimist public in the notion that you are not pregnant.' 'I am sure they could not have done so, for I should have told them to make known my condition, and the statement of such important persons would have convinced every one, while the other means the Government will adopt will convince no one.'

I have faithfully conveyed to you, sir, this curious conversation. You can draw the deductions. If I were allowed to express my opinion to the Council, I would say that I cannot see much danger in the visit of MM. de Chateaubriand and Hennequin, under necessary conditions. It is quite certain that the publication of the Duchess's condition by M. de Chateaubriand would have dispelled all doubt; and I can hardly believe that such a man as he is would have refused to say what Deneux has published. He would have found it a subject for writing some fine pages of romance, and we know very well that he never lets slip the chance of a godsend of that kind. To take another point, we are coming much nearer to the event, and perhaps it would be better to wait till it occurs than enter upon a negotiation, the issue of which cannot be foreseen. In this last course we also run the risks of illness, and accidents ensuing upon the confinement.

To the Count d'Argout.

19 April.

. . . . . Fresh useless attempts to prevail upon the Duchess to consent to verification. Ménière persuaded her to tell him her plan. I consider it is insufficient. I wrote to her upon it, and she replied in the letter, copy enclosed.

There is nothing more to hope. She must be confined here, and the verification of the birth by witnesses must be official.

The conditions judged necessary were that MM. de Chateaubriand and Hennequin should come to receive from the Duchess and five witnesses the declaration of her marriage and condition, upon their undertaking, before they came, to publish the declaration; the Government undertaking to set the Duchess at liberty as soon as this was done. The Duchess refused, stating that she could not bind her friends.

Telegraphic Despatch to the President of Council.

The Duchess asked for two advisers. The Government refused, and sent four doctors. Her Royal Highness refused to see them. Before consenting to admit them, Madame wishes for a promise that MM. de Chateaubriand and Hennequin may come, without any condition imposed on them, to give her the advice they think most useful to her, and for this purpose may be permitted to converse with the Duchess as long as necessary without witnesses.

As it is of consequence to lose no time; if this proposal is accepted, the Government should immediately invite MM. de Chateaubriand and Hennequin to proceed to Blaye, and they would receive a letter from Madame, requesting them to wait upon her before they enter the citadel.

I advise you to allow these gentlemen to come; but we are too near the event to set the Duchess at liberty without all the security desirable. All her changes of front are caused by the wish to obtain her freedom, and leave a door open behind her for the passions of her party. Remember there is not more than a month left, and that her health is as good as ever; but do not incur the evident reproach of having refused her advisers, when there cannot be any danger in it. If you permit the coming of the Legitimists, precede them by instructions to conclude the matter or renounce it definitely. This ought to be the last negotiation.

The doctors are very impatient to return to Paris. Answer immediately.

Telegraphic Despatch to COUNT D'ARGOUT.

22 April.

The Duchess de Berry persisted in refusing to see the four doctors, yet Drs. Deneux and Ménière had almost overcome her by their reasoning. She asked for a few minutes to consider, and in two hours sent me the following letter :—

'*Citadel of Blaye, 22 April*, 1833.

'GENERAL,—As the Government refuses me any sort of advice, and does not even give me a single pledge that I shall be set at liberty after the verification, I cannot receive MM. Orfila and Auvity. I request you to express my regret to them.

'I will continue to receive the careful attendance of MM. Deneux, Gintrac, and Ménière, with whom I am especially pleased. I will not give any ground for accusation that I am not doing everything that depends on me to secure a mother to her children.

'I eagerly take advantage, General, of any opportunity to do justice to your heart and intentions.

'MARIE-CAROLINE.'

This is matter to make a good newspaper article, to give assurance that you have taken all possible precautions for her health, and also that she is not very ill, as she has refused the advice of four distinguished physicians.

Telegraphic Despatch to the Minister of War and the Interior.

3 *May.*

As the event draws near, the difficulties become more apparent. Everything possible will be done to keep the confinement from our knowledge. Whether they succeed or not, or whatever we do to verify it, they will deny it.

The *Guyenne* has already foreseen the confinement as the end of the play they are acting. After these considerations, I address you the following questions, and request you to reply to them categorically. I attach more importance to the ' civil register,' for which I am sure there will be Deneux's declaration, than to any sort of verification. Do you agree with me ?

This being answered affirmatively, ought we to disregard considerations of humanity, of danger, and even of decency ?

I very decidedly think not. Do you agree with me ?

Will not the verification be a superfluity to the civil register, and not rather act in contradiction than in support ?

Will it not be worth more to have Deneux's declaration simply certified by witnesses appointed at the time, as well as by the maire, and make them all sign the civil register ?

This is my opinion. Besides that, this would enable you to dispense with odious and dangerous means, which would bring you little advantage, this register could never be suspected of being forged ;

any writers who impeached it might be prosecuted. Can you tell me whether you would release Madame if the verification takes place? I could make use of it.*

Reply if you please as soon as possible.

BUGEAUD.

*General Bugeaud's advice prevailed. Thanks to his persistence with the ministers the Duchess de Berry was spared the painful trial of verification.

The Duchess was either more simple or more cunning than her friends and attendants: their object seems to have been to save the credit of the royal cause; she wished to avoid personal annoyances at the moment. While on the voyage to Palermo, she adopted some of her friends' tactics; in later times, however, again doing justice to Bugeaud.— ED.

CHAPTER XVI.

THE BIRTH (1833).

To the Count d'Argout.

3 May.

THE more I think of it the more am I convinced of the inutility
and danger of a verification. Whatever you do it will be treated as
null. If you had a hundred witnesses who had seen . . . . . the
Legitimist papers would none the less say it was false. Thus we
should be taking harsh precautionary measures to no use, and at the
moment of the perils of childbirth exposing the Princess to the
dangers of too great excitement. The deed of verification is not
protected by law. It is vulnerable on every side. Far from being
a useful assistance, it will serve as a conductor to all the blows
aimed at the civil register. The latter, if alone, would rule: any
one who impeached it could be prosecuted. With the breastplate of
the deed of verification it would be a thousand times pierced through
and through. These advantages must not be given to our enemies.
Let us leave the sword of the law hanging over their heads by only
having the civil registration. Easily without any violence we will
surround it with all the solemnity you wish. All the witnesses
named to verify the fact of the birth may be witnesses to the declaration that MM. Deneux and Ménière will make before the maire,
and sign the civil register. We will gather them together in the
Duchess's parlour as soon as we know that she is taken ill.

This seems to me incontestably the wisest course, especially
under the consideration that, according to all appearances, we shall
have but an imperfect verification. I know the tactics they propose
to employ; they are these :—they will accept nothing freely. This
is a settled plan ; they will oppose everything, and have the answer
ready, ' What you intend to do is atrocious, but you have the power.'
They will keep her in pain as long as possible, and then call Deneux,
and he will say that the presence of any persons besides the accou-

cheurs and two women would be dangerous to the Duchess. Suppose we came in time we should be obliged to remain in the parlour, or else be barbarians; and what could we say or do that would be worth as much as the declaration that Deneux will make before us and the maire? I could be sure of a hundred votes in the council for the civil registration alone. It is the safest course, the simplest, easiest, and the most honourable.

*   *   *   *   *   *   *

Thus the General returns again and again to the inutility of a preliminary verification of the Duchess's condition. The Government at Paris, not considering the dangers and cruelty of this measure, strongly insisted upon its taking place. Being an influential deputy, and personally responsible for the grave interests entrusted to him, General Bugeaud gave the ministers to understand that he would not undertake to execute their orders, if ever these orders appeared to him to exceed certain limits.*

At last came the end.

To the President of the Council.

10 *May*.

Our uncertainties and fears are ended! Everything has gone

---

* No doubt the historian who has given the most circumstantial account of this event is M. Louis Blanc, then deputy of the department of the Seine. His *Histoire de Dix Ans* is a remarkable book, though stamped with partiality. How much I prefer it to M. Thiers'!

The chapter on the captivity of Blaye is especially curious. It proves the close alliance that then united the republicans and pure Legitimists. The author expatiates with complaisance upon the martyrdom inflicted upon the Princess, endeavouring to throw the odium more upon the King's government than upon the King himself. As to General Bugeaud, the portrait Louis Blanc draws of him is most curious. One feels that the writer is striving between his conscience, love of truth, and political passion. 'This was a soldier, endued for such an one, with eminent qualities, possessing in certain things some solid knowledge, remarkable for grotesque common sense. (Do you see the grotesque common sense?) Not so wicked as strange, even sensible by fits, but angry, stupid, tactless, impatient of the restraint of delicate proceedings, and animated with a subaltern's zeal, hardly able to elevate its humility by his arrogance, his freedom, and swaggering airs. The arrival of such a man was a thunderstroke to the prisoner. She had no difficulty in seeing what he was, through the respect in which he sincerely tried to train himself: she was afraid of him.'

satisfactorily. and I hope the Government and the country will be satisfied.

I remained with the Duchess de Berry from two o'clock in the afternoon till her dinner-time. I saw her sit down to table. Drs. Ménière and Deneux spent the evening with her till ten o'clock. Nothing announced so speedy an event.

At three, the lieutenant of gendarmerie. Solabel. on watch below, came and knocked at my door. At the same moment Madame Hansler came out into the passage to call the doctors. and they entered the room. I immediately ordered the three guns to be fired to call my witnesses. and they came. M. Dubois was a witness of the birth; he was in the room, the military commandant and I at the door.

As soon as the child was born the Duchess asked for me, and I went to her bedside. She held out her hand ; I pressed it, and she returned the grasp. I read her your telegraphic despatch of yesterday, assuring her of her release in case the verification was properly carried out. ' General, I hold to all I promised you.'

The official report tells you the rest.

To THE PRESIDENT OF THE COUNCIL.

10 May.

*   *   *   *   *   *   *

The verification will take place as agreed between the Duchess and myself. She will herself present the infant, and declare that it is hers.

*   *   *   *   *   *   *

When he signed his declaration, M. Deneux added. ' I have delivered of a child the Duchess de Berry, wife by legal marriage of Count Hector Lucchesi Palli, of the princes of Campo-Franco. gentleman of the bed-chamber to the King of the Two Sicilies. domiciled at Palermo.' *

---

* The Duchess de Berry, Maria Caroline Ferdinande Louise. born at Naples, 5th November, 1798, was daughter of François Joseph Xavier, then hereditary prince of the two Sicilies, Francis I., king of the Two Sicilies, and the Archduchess of Austria, Maria Clementina. She died in April, 1870.

She married, 17 June, 1817, Charles Ferdinand d'Artois, Duke de Berry, a son of France, son of Prince Charles Philippe of France, Count d'Artois, Monsieur, the King's brother. The Duke de Berry died by hand of an assassin at Paris 13 February, 1820.

By this marriage she had one daughter, Louise Maria Theresa, born 21st September, 1819, who became Duchess of Parma, and a posthumous son, Henry Charles Ferdinand Marie Dieudonné, Duke de Bordeaux, Comte de Chambord, born 29th September, 1820, at Paris. Died 1883 at Frohsdorf. The Duchess de Berry was therefore thirty-one years of age when she brought into the world, in the citadel of Blaye, the infant born of her second marriage with Count Lucchesi Palli, a Sicilian gentleman, chargé d'affaires of the King of Naples at the Hague.

GENERAL BUGEAUD TO M. GARDERE, at Paris.

Blaye, 11th May, 1833.

You will have been glad to learn, my friend, that I have happily ended my mission, for I consider it terminated. In all this I have been labouring to reconcile very different interests, and have the satisfaction of thinking that I have been completely successful.

The Government has all the sureties desirable. There is no reason for detaining the Duchess any longer, and she will be immediately set at liberty.

As for me, I expect and wish for nothing more out of this business than to spend five or six months with my oxen and my clover.

The Duchess looks upon me as one of her best friends. She pressed my hands most affectionately yesterday. She esteems me because she perceives that I have been a faithful servant to my Government and country, and have also paid due respect to a woman in her position.

Write to me at once, and at length, of the talk of Paris about this business; and matters in general, the look of Paris, parties, the National Guard, &c.

Your sincere friend,

BUGEAUD.

TO THE PRESIDENT OF COUNCIL.

13th May.

I am completely rewarded by the King's approbation you have been desired to convey to me. I desire nothing else, and as I wish to avoid the unpleasantness of a refusal to Government, in case you should have the idea of giving me any recompense, I beg of you to do nothing. If I might be allowed to mention a wish to you, it would be to be free till the month of October, and at that time I should be glad to receive a command at Paris.

Then follow letters recommending officers for valuable services, &c., at Blaye, and arrangements for the Duchess leaving Blaye by water for her voyage to Palermo, which was likely to take place about the 3rd or 5th of June.

*

There is no doubt, sir, that the press and caricatures have a bad effect upon the soldiers. Several anecdotes that have come to me

have shown me this. As the army is one of the most powerful
guarantees of order, we must take care not to allow it to be corrupted
by the Anarchists.

As it is inevitable for the troops to read newspapers, I should wish
some to be prepared for them, to give them just notions on politics
and affection for the King's government, as well as mention of military matters. I think they ought not to be delivered over to the
factions without an antidote. In the same strain of ideas, I have
long been wishing that honest men of independent means, who are
interested in good order, would form companies for encountering
the evil-disposed press with the press, since this is the only weapon
suitable. We should soon have conquered that cruel enemy to
peace and to the country, if men would put a little real desire into
it. What an advantage we should have over the journalists if we
set up newspapers without idea of speculation, but only to make the
truth triumph! We could give our sheets very cheap, often gratis,
for the shareholders would not hesitate in taking their shares to consecrate their capital to the triumph of the principles of a wise liberty,
without expecting interest; ready, on the contrary, to lose their
shares if necessary.

To the Count d'Argout and Marshal Soult.

4th June.

Gentlemen.—I have received this moment the instructions for
departure that you addressed to me on the 2nd. There is no difficulty in their punctual execution. The embarkation at Blaye will
take place about eleven in the morning of the 8th, ceremoniously, but
without too great a crowd. Neither the Maire nor the Sub-Prefect
will issue proclamations: but the officers of the National Guard, with
whom I am on good terms, will mix beforehand in the crowd to
induce the citizens to keep silence. I think I can assure you that
everything will pass off with propriety. You shall have an official
report of the embarkation, signed by all the signatories of the certificate of birth and several officers of the National Guard. I will take
two or three Legitimists, high-crested folk, in the steam-vessel as far as
the *Agathe.* At this moment there are very few persons who doubt.

M. Hennequin came here yesterday. He saw the Duchess to-day,
and dined with her. I asked him to dinner yesterday. His conversation is witty and lively. He is pleased to talk of current affairs,
and especially his pleadings at Rennes, which he thinks ought to
hand him down to posterity. He maintained the contrary to us on
many of the questions that were raised there, and, clever as he is,

was sometimes defeated. He praised the genius, or rather the ability, of the King, for, according to him, his genius may be contested, supposing he did not let drop the happy words, that are remembered, as they contain one or many thoughts. I answered him, 'He has done better than that, he has let off many discourses stamped with reason and great political scope. He has done better still, he has known how to judge of his position, resist evil counsels, and follow the good; compare that with the sharp speeches of Charles X.' Otherwise, M. Hennequin has a very reasonable tone, and shows me a good deal of respect.

TO THE MARSHAL, WAR MINISTER.

5th June.

*　　*　　*　　*　　*　　*　　*

The Duchess flew into a violent rage when she heard that the Government required from her a letter declaring that her health and her daughter's are quite good enough for a sea voyage, with a request to go to Palermo, and list of the persons to accompany her. Vociferations against the Government, the Ministers, &c. She retired in a rage: came back quieter. I went away, telling her to consider.

I am sure she will write, but without mentioning her daughter. The report of the embarkation, and four or five thousand witnesses, will destroy this remnant of obstinacy.

Thus concludes the Journal of Blaye. General Bugeaud accompanied the Princess to Sicily; and we shall relate the consequences which so unjustly weighed upon the life of the Governor of Blaye, and soon after caused the death of Deputy Dulong.

The event was hardly accomplished, and the birth of the Duchess's daughter duly verified, when there broke forth from all sides, in the Legitimist and Republican press, most odious imputations and grotesque calumnies against the King's Ministers, and especially against the Governor of Blaye. This anonymous abuse, these ridiculous stories, to which men of sense did not attach any importance, inflicted cruel wounds upon the victim. We find confirmation of this in letters written at this time by General Bugeaud to the Prefect of La Dordogne, for whom he had great affection.

GENERAL BUGEAUD TO M. MOURGUES, PREFECT AT PERIGUEUX.

Blaye, 2nd June, 1833.

I think I am more independent than those who proclaim their independence in their writings and speeches. Independent, and even insolent, towards power, they grovel before the people in the streets.

I never flatter any one, neither kings, nor prefects, nor people. I ask for nothing, want nothing. I desire to be nothing but what I am; I can be so without the Ministers: I have won my position without them, and I shall be able, at need, to gain promotion without the Ministers or my position in the Chamber.

In a word, they are in want of men like me, and I am in no need of them. This, I think, is complete independence; but it will not make me unjust, for my mind and soul are not independent of my reason.

* * * * * * *

While the *Agathe* was sailing towards the coasts of Sicily, Mdme. Bugeaud was delighted to leave the citadel of Blaye, and return to Excideuil with her children. Though the letter below is of a private character, we think it worthy of publication. It shows something of the state of feeling at this time, and the strong love his family entertained for the General.

MADAME BUGEAUD TO GENERAL BUGEAUD.

Excideuil, 15th June, 1833.

MY DEAR.—We have just arrived in good health, but very sorry to be here without you. I cannot tell you how sorry I am at your going: I have the ship that took you away from us always before my eyes. How sorry I was when my short sight prevented my making you out upon the deck: I was paralysed, and neither heard nor saw; in this state I returned to the citadel, to the house you had just left; but when I arrived there I awaked from this kind of sleep. Then all the dangers I dread for you presented themselves to my mind. How often did I wish to be alone! I had not even that mournful pleasure. It was necessary to receive the adieus and compliments of a crowd of persons, who seemed not to have a notion how it all tormented me. At last we went off; I was suffering a good deal: my malady was supposed to be from the heat; I was very glad to let it be supposed so, to avoid the consolations that your good sister, who went with us, would not have failed to give me. I wanted none of them. I wanted to be free to think of you, and give free course to my ideas. How painful they were! We stopped at Saint Mer; the children wanted to rest there, and I consented. On our arrival I heard a bell ringing, and was told it was for the benediction, so hastened thither. And if God will grant my sincere prayers and vows, your voyage will be fortunate: for, my love, I prayed for you, and never, I think, were prayers so heartfelt. I was so unhappy, and I love you so much. Next day we arrived at X., where I was overwhelmed with visits and inquiries for your health and your return: at Excideuil, the same thing over again. Your sister, Fanny, Ambroise, their children, and Gustave came at once. They dined with us, and are quite well.

18th. The children are well, they have resumed their old occupations, and would be quite contented if dear papa was come back.

The journey had tired me; but now I do not feel it any more. I am taking pills, and am strictly dieted. I hope you will not tell me that I do not choose to be cured.

I receive a quantity of visits. All ask for tidings of you, when you will return, the road you come, &c., &c. These continually reiterated questions, that I cannot answer, are a real punishment to me. Several Carlists have displayed a great wish to come and see me; they seem to wish to make us amends for the infamies of their *Gazette*, which is frightful. The honest men, the *Memorial*, and even the *Echo*, have done full and entire justice in the matter. All say that an honest man neither can nor ought to pay attention to it: many subscribers have given it up. Thus, my love, we must shut our eyes and ears upon it: contempt is the only answer: but it is too much to tell you of this; to come to the fountain:* your disinterestedness is considered sublime: you are loved and admired, there never was a man comparable to you, and your devotion to your country.

23rd.—I am come from La Durantie; the corn is splendid, even the spring corn, but there is some rotten in the last. They are beginning to mow: there is not much grass in the poor meadows: the trefoil is a little light.

---

* After the Mission to Blaye, the King offered 20,000 francs to General Bugeaud, who refused them and asked that they might be applied to the use of the town of Excideuil. So a fountain was erected in the park of Excideuil, of which mention is made in the next letter.

The timber frame of Saint Pantaly will be set up to-morrow; a beginning has been made in paving the yard at Excidenil, but it will still be a long time before everything is finished. M. Lestang has nothing to do; the workmen are not very speedy. However, I hope that it will be advanced when you come.

I have received a letter from your sister, who gives me an account of your voyage as far as the frigate. Poor Thomas! you were sick already, what will you be in the open sea! How I long to see you come back. Till then I shall be always in terror of your meeting with an accident.

Adieu! my love, travel as quickly as possible, I am so uneasy, I long to embrace you. Marie wants to say a little word. Adieu! adieu!

(Signed)   C. B.

Though of a previous date to a letter just given, we think it very desirable to insert here the following letter written to General Bugeaud, during his residence at Blaye, by a prominent inhabitant of Excideuil, Doctor Chavoix.*

DOCTOR CHAVOIX TO GENERAL BUGEAUD.

Excideuil, 26 *May*, 1833.

We have received to-day, General, the notification of the useful edifice that your disinterested generosity has conferred upon the town of Excideuil. I make haste to express to you, as friend and citizen of Excideuil, but specially as very devoted friend, all the admiration that I feel for such noble conduct as yours. I have been so much touched by this noble and patriotic action, as this very day to have proposed to several members of the municipal council,—not knowing how to express to you all the recognition you deserve,—I have proposed, I say, first, to give you a public vote of thanks, and then to place upon the monument that will be raised, under your auspices, a simple and modest inscription that will commemorate at once the

---

* Doctor Chavoix, now the very Republican Deputy of the Department of La Dordogne, will, no doubt, forgive us for exhuming the interesting letter that he addressed, forty-seven years ago, to his friend, the General Deputy of Excideuil. If M. Chavoix has rather changed his opinions by 1881 who shall dare to throw the first stone at him! Anyway, the noble and patriotic feelings expressed by the honourable doctor and friend of the Bugeaud family belong to all time, and we are certain that M. Chavoix would not hesitate to repeat them to-day.

patriotic disinterestedness of a citizen, and the gratitude of his compatriots. On a slab of black marble will be placed these words :—

To GENERAL BUGEAUD

THE GRATEFUL TOWN OF EXCIDEUIL.

So far my project has only met with approval. I hope that by power of patriotism we shall compel the grumblers to be silent, or at least to chatter in the shade. The native *bousingots* have not yet dared, as far as I know, to make any outcry against this immense improvement to beauty and utility in our city. No doubt they cannot venture to say that it is the sweat of the people devoted to this fancy ; for such a foundation is for the people's good, if I am not mistaken. Besides, they seem little enough pleased at the turn their business is taking. I think, like the *Courrier Français*, as it was obliged to confess the other day, that the republic has lost ground by the very efforts of its partisans. It is a very curious thing, and instructive at the same time, to see these gentlemen throw off the mask one after the other. After the trial of the Society for the Rights of Man, here comes that of the *Aviso* of Toulon which surpasses, in audacity and wickedness, even the maxims of that society. It even has positively stated, as no doubt you have read, that it is necessary to plunder the tradesmen, the capitalists, the bankers, the manufacturers, &c., &c., because they are idle and make the most of the people, growing fat upon their sweat. If the jury do not condemn such *loups-garous*, we must draw up the ladder and prepare to be firing guns very soon. I think that the Government ought to put a very sharp bridle upon these curs ; to forbid their balls, their banquets, &c., &c., and if they think fit again to treat an honourable man to a charivari, to give them such a worrying as to make them lose the wish to do it again. This is the general desire. I flatter myself that the publication of such extravagancies will bring back to us some trustworthy men ; I should augur very ill of any that lean upon such maniacs.

The other day I was at Hautefort ; there was much talk of the Duchess. There was a gentleman there come to spend some days at the castle, called the Marquis de la Fare. A man over sixty, well educated, formerly a soldier, who had seen you in Spain when you were fighting there : he lives at Marseilles. He is one of the most reasonable Legitimists that I have met. Some surprise was expressed at your having accepted the command at Blaye. 'But,' said I, 'I suppose a soldier ought to obey his chief, when there is nothing dishonourable in the order he receives.' 'You are right,' said he ; 'it should be so.' Then they asked me several questions with regard to Blaye. I satisfied their curiosity with such information as I was authorised to give them. 'But,' said Mdme. de Damas, 'how is it that the commissary of police, Joly, whom M. Chousserie had declined to receive, had the entry of the citadel as soon as General Bugeaud took the command?' I answered, 'That is a tale of your newspapers; nothing is falser than the story of M. Joly's empire in the citadel of Blaye. I know that General Bugeaud would not have allowed it, and, besides, I refer to the Marquis de la Fare, who has been a soldier. Is it not true that soldiers dislike the police?' 'It is very true,' answered he; 'there is not the shadow of probability that General Bugeaud, who has the reputation of being a strict soldier, would have chosen to let in a commissary of police to watch him.'

Further, neither M. de Damas, nor the abbé, nor any one else, deny the fact of the pregnancy and birth. The abbé even went further; he converted, as he told me, the unbelievers of his party that they might not be exposed to the ridicule that attaches to the denial of evidence. ' I am very glad that it is a daughter,' said he, 'because when people speak of the two princes, there will be no question which.'

Really there are none but case-hardened Legitimists that still deny the birth. The abbé told me that there was anger among them against those who believed.*

I went twice to La Durantie as I passed. It is magnificent, admirable to see such cultivation. Your oats are the finest, almost the only ones I have seen.

---

* The maddest legends are often the most difficult to destroy. No one could imagine the stories told at the time about the Duchess de Berry's captivity. The unfortunate political necessity that had compelled Louis-Philippe to arrest his niece, in order to put an end to an attempt at civil war, was the subject of the most odious comments. As to the poor Princess, whose resolution, spirit, and goodness have become traditional, she was cruelly punished by the consequences of her heroic imprudence.

The person who had most to suffer from these fables was General Bugeaud. Many years after the drama of Blaye, the Legitimists, especially in the country, only mentioned the name of the savage gaoler with shuddering. The Comtesse de Feray told us that in 1867, General Feray having taken over the command of the corps d'armée at Toulouse, on Marshal Niel's giving it up, she was at the beginning of her stay in that city the object of a studied reserve and coldness on the part of the Legitimist society. The nobility of the country rancorously persecuted in her the daughter of the Governor of Blaye.

It was not till some time afterwards, when the unbelievers were convinced by irresistible testimony coming from the Duchess de Berry herself, that the Legitimist society of Toulouse altered their former manner. It must be said that it became quite lavish of unequivocal marks of esteem and sympathy to the innocent victim of political passion.

I will give you a bit of news that will please you.   The other day
I met the commissioners of the Lanouaille Society for the inspection
of trefoil.   They told me they had found some much finer fields
than last year, and that next year there would be still finer and
more of them.   You will be expected at the agricultural fêtes of
Lanouaille.

The Excideuil Society had a meeting to choose a young man
to send to the model farm at Grignan, to enjoy the advantage you
procure for him, as well as for our country.   The choice fell on a
son of Martel, who seems intelligent and capable of profiting by it.

I beg of you to convey my respects to Mdme. Bugeaud, and the
assurance of my unlimited devotion.

CHAVOIX.

The *Agathe* left Bordeaux on the 8th June, but
did not reach Palermo till July 5.   The following is
General Bugeaud's despatch, written on board the
vessel, and giving Marshal Soult an account of
his mission.

GENERAL BUGEAUD TO THE PRESIDENT OF COUNCIL, &c.

Roads of Palermo, 5 *July*, 1833.

SIR,—I write to you before landing.   A brig is reported making
sail, believed to be French.   I wish to take the chance, intending to
send you a report of the landing and anything I learn in another
letter or the end of this one.

Our passage was much hindered by contrary winds or calms.

The Duchess de Berry was in perfect health ; the terrible,
frightful chest disease talked of did not make her cough once : her
daughter improved a good deal.

As soon as she was in the ship the Duchess's manners to me, my
aide-de-camp, and M. Ménière, changed completely.   She put us
aside with an affectation savouring of childishness, and implying
pettiness of spirit.   She forgot our care and respect while she was
a captive at Blaye, and behaved to us almost as if we had been
cruel gaolers.   For the sake of opposition, and in order to make us
the more feel the sting of her conduct, she was excessively polite
to all the naval men, and even went so far as to take the arm of
a simple midshipman.   And she has just given a gratuity of twenty
days' pay to the whole crew.

Seeing her formal intention of mortifying me, I retired upon my own dignity, and contented myself with asking her how she did once a-day.

The captain of the French brig, M. Nolette, corvette captain, which lay in the roads yesterday, has come on board. He informs us that the governors of Naples and Palermo have not been warned of the arrival of the Duchess de Berry; that the French consul is equally ignorant, and nothing is prepared for the Princess's reception. Count Lucchesi only reached Palermo last night.

As the brig is immediately starting for Toulon, I close my letter without being able to give you any further information.

Receive, sir, &c.

Bugeaud.

At the same time as he wrote to Paris, General Bugeaud addressed a letter to the French consul, desiring him to obtain a report of the Princess's landing from the Neapolitan authorities.

*   *   *   *   *   *   *

' It is my duty to procure a document from the Sicilian authorities, attesting the landing of the Duchess de Berry and her infant at Palermo. No doubt the minister, as well as myself, counts upon your amicable relations with them to obtain it. But, I think, the utmost expedition will also be required. If we let the Duchess land before we demand the acknowledgment, before the paper is prepared, and even signed, we shall not get it. The Duchess has a great dread of giving the smallest paper that the Government might make advantageous use of. Thus, in my opinion, this request must immediately be made to the proper quarter; and, if assented to, the document must be prepared and signatures procured, so that it may be handed to me at the moment of landing.

In the excitement of the moment a thing will not be refused, that they might make difficulties about afterwards.'

It appears that the request was complied with, as there is a formal letter to the General from the Prince of Campo Formio, dated 5th July, and reporting the landing of the Duchess and her infant on that day in good health.

General Bugeaud did not stay long at Palermo. and was delighted to begin his return journey to France. Doctor Ménière, one of the persons named by the Duchess de Berry herself, to accompany her to Palermo, remained some time in Sicily. There is a very curious letter written to the General by the doctor, giving some remarkable information not hitherto made public, as to the attitude of the court of Naples towards the Princess.

DOCTOR MÉNIÈRE TO GENERAL BUGEAUD, AT EXCIDEUIL.

Naples, 27th July, 1833.

MY DEAR GENERAL,—Perhaps you will think I have been rather slow in keeping my promise, but hear my story and you will forgive me.

Almost as soon as I had landed I found that it would be difficult for me to leave the country as soon as I had intended. The feast of Saint Rosalie was to commence on the 11th and last five days; the steamer's arrangements were only for leaving Palermo on the 19th or 20th, and I found myself fixed in Sicily for a fortnight. That did not please me at all. Having settled myself as well as I could in this country of savages, in four or five days' time I went to pay a visit to M. Deneux, who, as well as the abbé, was quartered in the Butera Palace with the Duchess. I found the doctor not much enchanted with his habitation; his little almost unfurnished room was contiguous to that of the women, and the dear man sighed. It is true that he had the honour of eating at the table of the Countess Lucchesi, and he might have been gratified with this especial favour if the cookery of Palermo had been as good as that of Blaye or the *Agathe*, but he could not eat any of their infernal ragouts, and was not long before he became ill. While I was conversing with him Madame Hansler came to say that the Princess wished to see me. I passed into the room of the two ladies of the bedchamber, and in a few moments the Duchess came in, skipping as usual, half dressed, and in a very good humour. She asked me twenty questions at once, where I was living, if I liked Palermo, &c. She told me of her daughter and M. Lucchesi. All this seemed to be natural enough. When I took leave of her I made my adieus, but she told me that she greatly hoped that I should not go away without coming to see her again. This is the historical side. Now for the chapter of gossip.

At home the Princess is only a countess, and everything is arranged on the footing of a private person. At the Viceroy's palace she has a small set of rooms as a Royal Highness, but this subtle distinction was only established after a long negotiation. There was a gala at the court on the occurrence of the queen-mother's fête. It was on this occasion that the masters of the ceremonies were embarrassed, and many personages did not choose to attend the kissing of hands. The fact is that the public voice is against the marriage. In the great world they find it hard to swallow. The Duchess goes out a great deal; she takes exercise most evenings upon the Marina, a beautiful promenade on the sea-shore. She has beside her Madame de Beaufremont, and on the front of the carriage is her husband, flanked by MM. de Ménars and de Beaufremont. An outrider precedes the equipage. I have seen her rooms, they are nice; the gentleman's are next, but to say the truth communication is possible. *Nota bene,* the bolts are on her side. In fine, the husband always looks cold, as you saw him on board the *Agathe.*

On consideration of departure there were a number of different opinions. Every day there was a different arrangement. So M. Deneux, the abbé, and I had engaged our three places in the steam-boat. Next day these gentlemen engaged a fourth for Madame Hansler; another day they countermanded this place, as Madame Hansler was to stay till the end of the month. Later, Madame Hansler and the little girl's nurse were to come with us; even the she-goat was put on board. Next day this plan was quite given up. The fact is that the Duchess wanted to go to Naples, then to Rome, and then to Prague, passing through northern Italy. I should tell you that at the steam-boat office the nurse had been described as 'Madame Portier, nurse, and her child.' A passport was wanted for the child as it is a Sicilian, and then came the difficulties. It seems that the Duchess had been told that she could not go to Naples, nor into Italy. It is even stated that the Court of Austria refused to allow her to travel to her father-in-law, King Charles X.

On the 19th I went to pay my adieus to the Princess. Madame de Ménars announced me, introduced me to Madame, and I had quite a solemn audience. I found all the faces long, M. Deneux quite red, Madame Hansler crying with sorrow at not going, &c., &c. As I passed the nurse I caressed little Anna, nursed her in my arms and kissed her, telling her that I loved her almost as much as if I was her father. The nurse told me, ' She would be very happy to have a father like you, poor *petita!*'

This, my dear General, is all I can tell you about this interesting matter. My stay in Palermo has been long, but I have gained some good by it. I have seen many people. I have been called in consultation by people of the first flight. I have been asked many questions, and it was not difficult to see the feeling that pervaded this curiosity. The unbelievers are numerous. I have had to give the lie to many absurd reports. For instance, it is said that the Duchess had shown on her wrists the print of the fetters she had worn at Blaye. I was very sorry for the haste of your departure. You could have remained here without the least inconvenience. When things are observed from far, curious judgments are made. The General, the Deputy, would have eclipsed all the little court of Butera, and the public would have been on your side. I have been received in several great houses by personages who had refused to go to the palace. Ladies did not choose to meet our princess, who seems to me not to have gained much by her change of condition. If she is obliged to remain here, I think that she will find means to escape.

Adieu, my dear General, I cannot form wishes for you, what do you want at Excideuil or La Durantie? Keep a kind recollection of me, for you owe me this for the real attachment that I have for you. Forget my freaks, contradictions, and ill-humour. All that is outside; the structure I can venture to say is better, and I hope you thought so. Allow me to present my respects to Madame Bugeaud, and to wish her good health. I send a most affectionate embrace to my comrade Marie and the dear Drondron. Be good enough to remember me to your sisters, and generally to your whole family and friends, whom I have had the advantage of knowing at Blaye.

I do not forget dear Saint-Arnaud.

Believe me always your devoted servant,

MÉNIÈRE.

I have not sent to M. Argout the gossip I forward you. If you have anything to tell me, write to Florence, *poste restante*.

CHAPTER XVII.

POLITICS—DUEL (1833-4).

General Bugeaud's Return—Confidences to friends on the Paris and Country Press—Session of 1833—The Deputy of Excideuil, his Aversion for Journalists—The Duel with Dulong—The Newspapers—Insurrections in Paris and Lyons, 1834—Story of the Rue Transnonnain—Bugeaud's Generosity—Letter to the Minister, Colonel Charras.

GENERAL BUGEAUD, on leaving Palermo, went direct to Paris, where he had to give the King's Government an account of the delicate and difficult duty that had been entrusted to him. A few days afterwards he returned to his dear Périgord, where his family and friends were impatiently expecting him. A letter to his friend Gardère shows how sensitive he was to the attacks of the press.

GENERAL BUGEAUD TO M. GARDÈRE, AT BORDEAUX.

Excideuil, 3rd August, 1833.

The information you give me, my dear Gardère, about the fêtes at Paris has pleased me much. I have learnt to distrust the odious press so much that I only believe what an honest man says, who is no journalist. I even distrust the Ministerial press. If only every Frenchman thought the same as I do about journalists, they would no longer be dangerous, and soon obliged to change their manners. What a horrible despotism is that of the pamphleteers! Was that of the barons, kings, and Jesuits, ever comparable with it? Did they ever possess this horrible power of vilification and perpetual calumny? Did they order the post of the kingdom every day to carry out the poison of sophistry and falsehood all over France? The press first makes you mad and savage, then makes you slaves and wretched. And yet how is this hydra to be fought?

We could not seek to return to censorship without great risk. All the world has not yet seen the monster's horns and claws. To forbid attacks upon the principles of government would be a worthless palliative.

I only see two remedies: the vote without deliberation for the jury, and the press itself to fight the press. This last method, to be effectual, ought to be made use of by the citizens and not by the Government. Besides that, it has not money enough to do the business, all its writings are considered tainted by the men who ought to be attracted. It is for rich men, friends of order, to associate themselves for the extension of the press in all cities, in all the provinces, and most of all in Paris, where newspapers can be compiled better than anywhere, and distributed all over France. Would it be difficult to get together ten societies of this kind in Paris, composed of fifty or sixty members, who would dedicate a capital to this, and find its interest and liquidation in the improvement of public thought, and the greater movement of business?

These societies should flood France with cheap papers, well composed and interesting on all subjects. There should be attempts by all possible means to gain, and especially to buy, the good writers of the factions. This would be a double victory, for war would be carried on by means of the enemy's soldiers.

I beg you, my friend, to think seriously of this, and speak to your acquaintances of it. Is it not better to devote money to such an enterprise, and to take some trouble, than to be perpetually exposed to having to go out into the streets and fire shots.

I do not tell you about my voyage, it would take too long. At last everything went well. I handed over the Duchess and her daughter at Palermo in good health, and I got a receipt given me by M. de Campo Formio, father of Count Lucchesi. The King sent me his compliments through his Ministers of the Interior and War. And they performed their duty in the most flattering manner.

My fellow-citizens were preparing at Excideuil to come out in cavalcade to meet me, but I surprised them by coming a day too soon. Disappointed in this plan, they gave me a serenade and some improvised fireworks. All the *juste milieu* and all the people were there, with some Republicans, naturally not a single Carlist. That party holds me in detestation, and I return it, though less blind and better grounded in my hate.

Adieu, my dear Gardère, &c.

BUGEAUD.

The General's confidences to his prefect, M.

Mourgues, are not less interesting. From the year 1831, General Bugeaud had been deputy and member of the general council of Excideuil. The interests of his department lay very close to his heart, and the prefect M. Mourgues had become a friend of his. The young editor of the official newspaper of the prefecture alluded to in this letter was no other than the great writer, Louis Veuillot, who afterwards went with the General into Africa as his secretary.

GENERAL BUGEAUD TO THE PREFECT DE LA DORDOGNE.

Excideuil, 2 October, 1833.

It is still me, my dear M. Mourgues. You will take me for the greatest beggar in France ; but in reality what else is a deputy, who has the great reputation of having a little credit ? Must he not devote his whole life to begging ?

We have destroyed the proceedings of the old court, the titled minions, the favourites, the ruling courtesans, the confessor's power. But when intrigue and ambition left the Tuileries and Versailles, they split into innumerable bits and invaded towns and country.

Well, considering this, we are wrong to fear a republic. for the smallest post will have a thousand candidates. The love of place and selfishness rule almost all actions ; they preside at the election of a deputy, form the opposition, and swell the majority.

It was well worth forty years of declamation against the corruption of courts to succeed in spreading it over the whole social body ! Formerly it was located like a distemper ; now it is universal like the cholera. It is no doubt a tool of government, and perhaps the establishment of ours is so difficult, in consequence of the medley of virtue and corruption to be observed in our parliament.

A large corrupt majority under a dexterous minister could do the work of the country well. It is cruel to say it, but it is a fact.

*　　*　　*　　*　　*　　*　　*

I hope that our newspaper will make a good success ; I have procured a good number of subscriptions for it. It seems to me to be a want in the political moral force of the department. One is so weary of exaggeration, falsehood, and calumny. I advise our editor to make extracts from the best papers, mentioning the source, which he does not do, and some of the maddest articles of the *Courrier, National, Tribune,* and *Corsair,* with a little commentary.

Of the gods whom we serve behold the difference

The *Figaro* is a paper little known in the department, there are sometimes very sharp articles that might enliven the *Memorial*.

Your affectionate and devoted

BUGEAUD.

The General returned to Paris at the end of autumn, 1833, for the session of the Chambers, and, as usual with him, took an active part in parliamentary work. All the questions that closely or distantly touched upon the army were handled by him. As he had a perfect knowledge of all the things he discussed, the Chamber always listened to him, and never failed to form a clearer opinion from his words. Utopias of government, and revolutionary theories, found a passionate opponent in him. His frankness, his good sense, the boldness of his notions and opinions exasperated the opposition journals.

A biographer of the Marshal, M. Bezancenetz, wrote in 1851, "to one and another he spoke his thoughts with a distinctness and sometimes roughness of speech, that very speedily placed him under the ban of that liberal press, falsely so called, but which he so truly characterised, pleasantly calling them " the aristocracy of the inkbottle." Even before the General's actions had caused him to be outlawed by the opposition journalists, they, perceiving that they had to meet an adversary who would make neither peace nor truce with them, declared against him one of those infuriated wars of public writers against politicians, in which it is very rare that the latter escape defeat. The heavy guns and the light artillery of the opposition press were directed against him. His life was scrutinised to discover ground for calumny, his words were travestied, his intentions were incriminated : the rallying word was sent all round, and they hoped to get the better of him by ridicule, intimidation. or calumny. This time the journalists' calculations turned out wrong. They had attacked a man who did not respect the fourth power of the state, and who was but little affected by their attacks.' (In this we think the biographer mistaken.) 'The deputy of Excideuil let the papers talk, and marched none the less firmly along the straight path he had entered upon, not seeking but not avoiding occasions of expressing his whole thoughts upon the tyranny that some men claim to exercise over the whole country in the name of liberty.'

On the 25th of January in a discussion of the war estimates, one of the most outrageous opposition deputies, M. Dulong, having insolently addressed General Bugeaud, he took notice of the words. A retraction made in the beginning having been withdrawn, a meeting took place. The event was fatal, the General's adversary received a ball full in his face. This event caused an immense amount of exasperation, especially as M. Dulong was a natural son of M. Dupont de l'Eure, one of the venerated chiefs of the opposition.

We have extracted some significant particulars from the papers of the time. However, the most precious document, certainly. is the letter given below, written by the General to one of his old comrades, M. Fayant. commandant of the veterans in the country.

This letter, begun before the meeting and finished the day after the duel, gives an account of the unlucky adventure. This simple narrative, without boasting or passion, but also without hypocritical regrets or false sentiment, well displays the General's character.

GENERAL BUGEAUD TO CAPTAIN FAYANT.

Paris, 28 *January*, 1834.

MY DEAR FAYANT.—The minister has given me a formal promise that you shall be in the first list of nominations to the Legion of Honour as an officer. General Schneyder has told me that the papers are ready.

I regret very much that you have got your head stuck among these veterans; it was your own choice, otherwise you would have been chef-de-bataillon more than a year ago. But I advise you to take your retirement soon; it will be almost as good as that of a chef-de-bataillon, and then, perhaps, we have to fear a modification of the law of 11th April, 1831.

You have had disagreeables, troubles, and annoyances, in your position. Well! I can tell you my position is not pleasant. I have no time to eat or drink. I am assailed everywhere by millions of petitioners: besides, there is the Chamber, and that alone is work enough to do; then my brigade, and you may judge how I am engaged.

30th January.—I have just had an affair. In the sitting of the 25th. I said from my place to Larabit, ‘We obey first, and remonstrate afterwards.’　M. Dulong shouted to me from his place, ‘ Does obedience go so far as to make you turn gaoler?’

I went to him to demand satisfaction for this affront. He excused himself, but imperfectly. I said to him ‘To-morrow.’ Next day he consented to write a letter to the *Journal des Débats*, the only paper that had reported the outrage. Next day the letter did not appear, I learnt that he had withdrawn it. A fresh explanation was indispensable. I very soon understood that the *bousingots* had persuaded him to withdraw his explanation, and stirred him up to fight. I insisted on the letter or a meeting. They would not make any concession; I took their hour and chose the sword. Dulong’s seconds would not accept it at all. ‘ Well, gentlemen, we will each fire a pistol-shot, and take the sword if there is no result.’ The same obstinate refusal. I proposed successively two pistol-shots and the sword, the sabre, the musket, and on their refusal of everything, in derision, the cudgel. At last wearied with such a long discussion, I said, ‘ Well, gentlemen, since the offended party must make all the concessions, I will fight with the pistol till one or other falls.’

Yesterday at ten in the morning we met in the Bois de Boulogne ; we were placed at thirty paces, with liberty to advance upon one another up to twenty. I aimed at him twice to draw his fire, but without result ; on reaching the barrier I thought it prudent to take the first shot, having a very good weapon.   When I had lowered my pistol in the line of his nose as far as his cravat, I fired, before I intended, and hit him in the head.   He fell straight down, and breathed till this morning at six o'clock.

The unhappy man was the most insolent one of the left.   If that was fate, it was better it should fall there than elsewhere.   The gods have been just ; you see how he insulted me!

I had expressly asked for an increase of salary for your son and the little Desramières : I am informed that Desramières alone has obtained it on account of his good notes.   I shall urge it again for you.

Your friend,

BUGEAUD.

The *Messager* of the 30th January, 1834, thus reports the occurrence:

'A fatal meeting took place this morning in the Bois de Boulogne, at the Rond-point du Cèdre, between M. Dulong, deputy, and his colleague, General Bugeaud.   The weapon arranged was the pistol.

'The seconds of M. Dulong were MM. Georges Lafayette and Colonel César Bacot.   Those of M. Bugeaud were General de Rumigny and Colonel Lamy.

'The two adversaries were placed at forty paces.   They advanced upon one another, both holding their pistols presented.   They had not taken more than about a couple of steps each, when General Bugeaud fired.   M. Dulong fell at the shot, the ball having struck the brim of M. Dulong's hat above the left eyebrow, entered the head, and not come out again.

'M. Dulong was bled upon the spot by M. Jules Cloquet, and conveyed to his home, rue Castiglione, in a carriage by M. Georges Lafayette.   At two o'clock he was again bled more copiously, but the severity of his wound left little hope.

'All friends and colleagues of M. Dulong who had been informed of this deplorable event, made a point of meeting by his bed of suffering.   Arrangements were made to send information by express to M. Dupont de l'Eure, the relation and best friend of M. Dulong, and to send him a letter, written by the latter, under a presentiment of the unhappy event.'

The cause of the duel arose from the circumstances thus given in the *Journal des Débats:*

Marshal Soult.—A soldier must obey.

M. Larabit.—The President of the Council reminds me of the duty of obedience; I recognise it; but when a man is in the right, and attempts are made to make him recede from it, gentlemen, he should renounce his obedience.

Many Voices.—Never, never.

General Bugeaud.—Obedience first.

M. Dulong, through the noise.—Is obedience to go so far as to make a man to become a gaoler? (Disturbance.) So far as ignominy? (Noise, disturbance.)

In consequence of the explanations to which this inaccurate report had given rise, M. Dulong had written a letter intended for insertion in the *Journal des Débats*, but on the Monday evening the *Bulletin Ministériel* gave the following account:

'The *Journal des Débats* reported yesterday an insulting expression addressed by M. Dulong to the honourable General Bugeaud. To-day it was said in the Chamber that the General had demanded satisfaction, and required M. Dulong to write a letter to appear to-morrow in the *Journal des Débats*.

'The manner in which M. Dulong's proceeding was represented in this note induced the Honourable Deputy to recall his letter to General Bugeaud, and place himself at his disposition. Thus this note had caused a resumption of the quarrel.

'However, yesterday again General Bugeaud had stated that he would accept any explanation agreed upon by the seconds. Unfortunately, it appears that there was a determination to make this discussion a party matter.

'At two o'clock MM. Lafayette and Bacot proceeded to the Tuileries, to withdraw the letter, that M. Dulong had at first written, from the hands of M. de Rumigny. But that gentleman there declared to them that the letter had been burnt by him in the King's presence. The written statement of the destruction of the letter was signed by M. Bugeaud.

'The deplorable issue of this encounter gives prominence to the senselessness of parliamentary duels, and the odium attaching to the conduct of those who added venom to the affair.

'What, indeed, does this blood, shed for the honour of M. Bugeaud, prove? Was he any the less the agent in command of the guard of an illegal captivity? The name of gaoler was not correct, that is true, but why? Because this name is that which the law gives to the legal custodians of prisoners, because it is inapplicable to the man who undertook functions, that being illegal have no name in any language. The blood of M. Dulong does not wash away anything.'

All the republican journals, the *Tribune*, the *National*, and others, whose articles had conduced to this fatal meeting, had endeavoured, with such sincerity as is their universal characteristic, to embitter the quarrel, and make the Tuileries play an odious part. One of them, namely, the *Tribune*, thus concluded its article:—

Thus all hangs in one system. Between citizens, civil war; between private persons, duels. Do you not see blood everywhere?

You wear a general's uniform, you stain it by a gaoler's work. There will come a day when you will be reproached for the stain, and then you will fight and kill or be killed; and that nothing may be wanting, your journals will stimulate, the aides-de-camp will serve for seconds, and the chief of the state will be the depository of the documents, and will burn them.

And all this was done *à propos* to the one question where the law was broken beforehand, where its whole artillery has been insulted by a minister's caprice.

Is this infamy enough? There is a court ball to-night.

*   *   *   *   *   *   *

The obsequies of M. Dulong have been performed to-day, and will be for ever remarkable for the generous sympathy and the display of wisdom exhibited by the population of Paris on the occasion.

From daybreak the capital presented the appearance of a vast camp along the whole line, from the Champs Elysées to Père La Chaise. The whole crowd was on foot. The rues de Rivoli and Castiglione were full of municipal guards and town police in squads, and of those persons, known by their appearance and their bearing, who make up the brigades of the secret police. Some pieces of artillery had been marched along the streets and boulevards; it was known that they were loaded with grape, and the lighted matches carried with them showed plainly enough the determination to make use of them.

All this parade of force did not intimidate anyone, and happily did not also give rise to the exasperation that is often caused by the useless di-play of hostile forces. The admirable population of the capital (it is admirable to all eternity, that population), filled all the dist-ict around the house of death, and all roads the company were to traverse. Cries of ' Vive Lafayette' could be heard all along the line.

MM. de Salverte, Cabet, Tardieu, Langlois, Carrel, and Dupont, mad- patriotic and affecting speeches over the grave of the representative of the people.

Tribune, 3rd February, 1834.

The Duke de Broglie and the Count d'Argout having left the Ministry in the month of February, M. Thiers resumed the portfolio of the Interior.

A short time afterwards (April, 1834) the terrible insurrection of Lyons broke out, only preceding by a few days a fresh armed rising at Paris. It seems to us desirable, when recalling these events, to bring in the testimony of a historian who cannot possibly be accused of partiality for the Monarchy of July, we mean M. Louis Blanc.

Without doubt we are far from wishing to excuse the melancholy events that attended the repression of the disturbance in these unholy days, when the soldiers, fired upon from the windows, took upon themselves to make terrible reprisals. But, alas! is it not principally upon the men who had publicly enunciated this maxim, ' Insurrection is the most holy of duties,' that history should lay the responsibility of the blood shed, the massacres of the Cordeliers of Lyons, of the Faubourg Vaise, and the house, No. 12, rue Transnonnain?

This is the commencement of the cynical account of those terrible days, the 13th and 14th of April, 1834, ingenuously given by M. Louis Blanc :—

However, orders were given (by the Committee of the Society of the Rights of Man) to several of the sectionaries to go into the public ways, to remain there a moment in a discreet attitude, and then to disappear. They were told, ' It is not intended to *commence* the attack, it is intended to pervade the air with an agitation that will show what is the disposition of the people.' This order was ill understood or ill executed. On Sunday, the 13th, in the rues Beaubourg, Geoffroy-Langevin, Aubry-le-Boucher, aux Ours, Transnonnain, Maubuée, Grenier-Saint-Lazare, barricades were built by a handful of excited men, whose ardour, it seems certain, was perfidiously stimulated by police agents. (A matter of course.)

Everywhere prevailed the noise and preparation of arms, the monotonous beat of the assembly, the cautious promenades of patrols, horsemen hastening through the city bearing redoubtable messages. For the Government thought it their duty to marshal all their resources; it was with an army of nearly forty thousand men, it was with the assistance of the National Guard of the suburbs mustered, it was with thirty-six pieces of cannon, pointed on different sides, that Generals Torton, Bugeaud, Rumigny, and De Lascours, prepared to sustain the conflict.

The attack began about seven in the evening, and with it the mourning of so many families. A staff-officer of the National Guards, M. Baillot, fils, was carrying orders to the mayor's office of the 12th arrondissement, and four chasseurs were with him; a ball wounded him mortally. M. Chapuis, colonel of the 4th legion, received a severe wound in the arm. Soldiers and insurgents fell never to rise again; at least the strife was short. At nine o'clock the fire died away, and the now inevitable capture of the barricades that still cut off the rues Transnonnain, Beaubourg, and Montmorency, was deferred to the next day.'

Louis Blanc, Histoire de Dix Ans.

Here we find in the private notes of the Countess Feray some important revelations on a fact which has remained obscure, and which we think it right now to completely clear up :—

What were our terrors during the risings of April, 1834! After a long day, my father, who was in barracks at the Ecole Militaire, came home, broken down with weariness and sorrow. He was in despair at this struggle between Frenchmen. He had served as the especial target of the rioters, who saw from afar his lofty stature and brave white head. M. Thiers, curious to study on the spot the military manœuvres he has afterwards so cleverly described, had never left him, though pressed by him to do so. My father every moment feared to see him struck by the balls that rained about them.

In 1871 M. Thiers, President of the Republic, again told me the history of that day.

Next day my father was shocked to read the abominable account of the affair in the rue Transnonnain, where he was called, the sharpshooter, and murderer of women and children. His eyes filled with tears, and he said, 'Why this is dreadful; I, the best friend of the lowly and the brave people!' My mother answered, 'An immediate protest must be made, this accusation must not be left upon your memory.' 'I cannot do it, I should appear to be accusing my comrade. General de Lascours, commanding in that quarter, unhappily, could not prevent his soldiers, when assassinated through the loopholes of the cellars and the garret windows, from firing at the houses whence came the shots. He will be sure to tell what took place, and to exculpate me. You may be sure he will do so; it is his duty; he need scarcely expect attack, as he is not like me, the object of the journalists' dislike.'

General Lascours kept silence. And so, when my father saw my mother and his sisters weeping at these cowardly insults, he serenely said to them, 'My dears, I beg of you be calmer; do you think I do not suffer? God was misunderstood, abused, covered with ingratitude upon this earth. Have I the right to complain?' When I think that this melancholy history is still made use of by the fanatics of the Legitimist party, and the republicans, I think my father was very generous.

Heaven guard us from wishing to disturb the calm of history by sad and inopportune reminiscences; but it may be allowable here to point out that in the most serious events of his life Marshal Bugeaud had to suffer cruelly, because he had been by the chances of politics and discipline several times placed under the orders, or by the side, of M. Thiers. Not to mention the furious attacks and incessant abuse to which the Marshal was exposed during his whole life, in consequence of certain facts, how many persons now still actually tack to his name the epithets of gaoler of Blaye, executor of summary justice, execu-

tioner of Transnonnain !   Now it is upon M. Thiers,
as Minister of the Interior, that rests the whole responsibility of these two political actions, the arrest and
imprisonment of the Duchess de Berry, and the
repression of the rising of 1834.   By a singular mis-
conception, it is upon General Bugeaud alone that
the unpopularity has hitherto always pressed.

During the continuance of the reign of King
Louis-Philippe, Marshal Bugeaud abstained from
any recrimination, and disdained to justify himself in
respect of the conduct attributed to him in such an
undeserved fashion.   It would have cost him much
to disclose an historical fact, that certainly had
nothing dishonourable about it in his eyes, but
was nevertheless painful to the General, under
whom it took place.

At last, when the revolution of 1848 had given
rise to the establishment of a new government, and
the incessant attacks began to be still heavier against
the supposed murderer of the rue Transnonnain, the
patience and resignation of the old Marshal of France
were exhausted.   This eternal part of scape-goat was
burdensome to him, and for the first time he thought
it his duty to put an end to an odious and lying tale.

In these proud and indignant terms did the old
corporal of Austerlitz write to the War Minister of
the French Republic, who chanced to be Colonel
Charras :—

MARSHAL BUGEAUD TO THE WAR MINISTER, COLONEL CHARRAS.

Paris, 28 *March*, 1848.

CITIZEN MINISTER,—You are my natural refuge against a
calumny which grieves me and terrifies my family, for it appears in
newspapers, in motions at club meetings, in anonymous letters.   It

is evident there is a desire to devote me to the rage of the people
of Paris, by the accusation that I ordered the massacre of the
rue Transnonnain in April, 1831! Well, sir, I did not go into that
street, nor did any fraction of the troops under my command. I
had under my orders the 32nd of the line, Colonel Duvivier, now a
general of division, and the 9th legion, Colonel Boutarel. It is easy
to institute an inquiry, and I request that it may be instantly set
on foot in order to put a stop to reports that revolt me. Yes, I was
willing to defend the laws of the country from attacks by violence;
but to give orders for the slaying of old men, women, and children,
the very thought of it would have shocked me.

The man who has often felt the pure enthusiasm of a victory
over the foes of France could not descend to order barbarities. The
inquiry will prove that, far from showing ferocity, I delivered a
crowd of prisoners from ill-treatment. The National Guards of the
9th legion, who were in front of the Hôtel-de-Ville, can attest this,
and among others M. Gabis, captain and deputy.

After a long career of entire devotion to my country, after
having reduced the Arabs of the whole of Algeria to submission, I
was far from expecting to be attacked with so much violence and
injustice by men who make a profession of elevated patriotism.

Receive, &c.,

Thomas Bugeaud,

Marshal of France.

A ministerial crisis ensued upon the risings in
Paris and Lyons, and general elections took place in
the month of June, 1834. The events in which the
deputy for Excideuil had been engaged had caused
him to incur most ferocious hatred. However, he
came off victorious in the contest, and tells his friend
Gardère about it in the following terms :—

General Bugeaud to M. Gardère, at Paris.

Excideuil, 27 July, 1834.

I ought to have informed you instantly of my victory, my dear
Gardère; but I acknowledge that, amid the chaos of visits, of
congratulations, of dinners and breakfasts, I forgot it. You already
know that I defeated the two parties united against me with

wonderful determination and unity. All means, even the most vile, have been tried to get rid of me.

To what a degree of political depravity has the press brought us! Men most opposite in principles and manners united with the object of overturning France, and casting her into the gulf of revolution. This is shocking! But the two oppositions, and especially the Republican, are well punished. Almost everywhere are they beaten. The Chamber will be excellent, and we can hope for better days.

BUGEAUD.

This life of political and parliamentary strife, in which this powerful organization and sturdy temperament was engaged, shortly came to a pause, and we shall very soon find General Bugeaud in his proper sphere, before the enemy, in Africa.

CHAPTER XVIII.

LANDING IN AFRICA (1836).

General Bugeaud in 1836—His portrait by Armand Marrast—Start for Africa—
State of the Colony—Disaster of Macta, 1835—Marshal Clauzel—Landing—
Bugeaud's commencement—Campaigning—Difficulties of the Road—Mustapha
Ben Ismael.

STREET-FIGHTING, the passionate struggles of Parliament, and the cowardly attacks of a disloyal press, were far from wearying or crushing General Bugeaud's energy, and had only steeled his determined soul. And so in 1836, when he was summoned as a soldier to take the command of a brigade in Africa, he displayed on this new theatre—really his own—all his peculiar powers. He was fifty years old, his mind as strong as his body. He is thus described by one of his secretaries :—' He was tall in stature, squarely built, and uncommonly powerful; his face was plump, and full of muscle, slightly marked with the smallpox ; highly coloured, eye light grey ; piercing glance, but softened in ordinary life by the expression of kindly sympathy ; nose slightly aquiline, mouth rather large, lip thin and smiling. When his expression, with its frank and simple character, was suddenly animated by the sudden passing of a thought, genius lighted up his large and powerful forehead, crowned with a very few hairs that rose in silvered spires. Everything in him breathed the habit of command, and the imperious carriage of a will sure of securing obedience. It was an iron nature, greedy of fatigue, inaccessible to the infirmities of age, that should only have vanished in the clouds of a field of battle.'

His enemies — his political adversaries — and certainly they were numerous, did him justice. The republican, Armand Marrast, President of the Assembly of 1848, in a biography full of gall and abuse of Deputy Bugeaud in his character of politician, does not fail to judge impartially of the soldier. He says, ' An active man, prompt at a blow, fashioned in Spain by the Guerilla Wars, careful of the soldier, watchful for his well-doing, popular with the troops thanks to his barrack fellowship, savouring of the old campaigner ; brave also, and unsparing of himself, Bugeaud, by the very speed of his movements, showed he was better than any one at this nomade-hunting.

' However, we ought in justice to say that Bugeaud, by his system of war, by his frequently rash expeditions, always fortunate, by the intrepidity of his actions, and, to use the expression, by the mobility of his courage, consolidated our power in Algeria, pacified several of its provinces, chased the Arabs to the confines of the desert, gave some rude shocks to the prestige Abdel-Kader enjoyed, and prepared for the future the germs of a serious and productive colonization.'

When General Bugeaud received orders from the War Minister to proceed to Algeria, the French possessions in the north of Africa were placed under the government of Marshal Clauzel, who had for the second time been invested with that high office on 8 July, 1835.

Public opinion, or rather public malice, then loudly imputed to the King and his Government a secret intention of relinquishing the new conquests, in despair of holding them with profit.

The country and the Chambers were divided between two systems : the one consisted in giving violent shocks to the Arab mind by successive expeditions, and giving up such half-measures as paralyse or ruin all enterprises ; the other lay in erecting fortifications and powerful establishments in certain selected places of the territory, ruling and pacifying at the same time.

The honour of planting the banner of France on the soil of Africa belongs to the Restoration. General de Bourmont had landed at Sidi-Feruch on 14th of June, 1830. Algiers capitulated on the 5th of July, and the Dey of Algiers received permission to relinquish his states. Some days afterwards King Louis-Philippe succeeded King Charles X., and so the Orleans dynasty found itself beneficial heir to the last victories of the elder house of the Bourbons. In spite of the jealousy and discontent of England, the new government did not hesitate to keep this glorious conquest of the Restoration—not, however, without serious difficulties, and the opposition of a notable portion of the nation. The destinies of Algeria were long uncertain. The advantages and importance of this magnificent possession were little understood in France. The most various, the most contradictory, the most strange opinions were uttered in the Chambers. The partisans of limited occupation, and even of relinquishment, were numerous.

On another side the French Cabinet were prevented by anxieties arising from the state of Europe and domestic troubles from receiving much benefit through this important colony.

The first years of the French dominion in Algeria were both painful and barren, and the selection of generals deplorable. The five or six years succeeding the conquest comprised a period of experiment. Opinion in France, and even in the nascent colony, was undecided. There were doubts between total or restricted occupation, between peace or war, between conquest by arms or by ideas, by the influence of civilization! There had been a moment's thought of granting the Algerian provinces to the son of the Bey of Tunis to rule under one suzerainty. Native beys had been tried without success.

The Duke of Rovigo,* formerly Police Minister under Napoleon, almost the only one among the earlier governors who gave indications of initiative, and of energetic qualities, had died suddenly. Under General Voirol, who succeeded in 1833 to the temporary Governor d'Avizard, General Desmichels, commanding the province of Oran, had signed a treaty with Abdel-Kader on the 26th February, 1834,† the spirit

---

* Savary.

† Some months ago, having reached the African period in the life of Marshal Bugeaud, I conceived the notion of making application to the Emir, Abdel-Kader, and asking him his opinion of his illustrious conqueror. My letter to the Emir and his reply were these :—

Most Valiant Emir,—I have collected some precious documents, hitherto almost unknown, concerning Marshal Bugeaud, he who was your illustrious adversary, against whom you fought so long and so gloriously.

I have given the account of his youth and employment under the great chief the Emperor Napoleon I. There now remain to be made known his doings in Africa, his numerous combats with the children of the desert and of the mountain.

Therefore I address a request to you. I ask you to describe, in a few words, your whole and sincere opinion of the great soldier by whom it was the will of God that you should be conquered, and who has long been slumbering in the tomb.

If you grant me this peculiar favour, I shall be thankful to you, for your words are true and your judgments equitable. I shall be thankful to you, for the words that issue from your mouth will have a great authority with the men of to-day and those who live to-morrow.

I send you the salutations and respect due to those who have spent many years on the earth, and have performed glorious actions.

HENRY D'IDEVILLE.

Paris, 6th October, 1881.

of which was to substitute for the Turkish rule, that
had formerly embraced the whole country, an Arab

To his Lordship the noble character the Honourable Count HENRY D'IDEVILLE.

Praise to God, &c.—Having presented to you our salutations, we inform you
that on receipt of your letter it was exceedingly agreeable to us to learn that you
have undertaken to publish all the facts relating to the life of our friend, General
Bugeaud, who made war upon us with such remarkable courage and perseverance.
It was especially when we met him face to face at the Tafna that we were able to
appreciate his political ability, as well as his military qualities. On that occasion
we recognised all the genius and kindness that was in him. He was a worthy
representative of the great nation. Submissive to the decrees of God, we have
surrendered our sabre to that nation, after a lengthened strife upon the fields of
battle. We are happy to do justice to Marshal Bugeaud, and congratulate you on
the subject of the book you have undertaken to write, also conveying to you our
especial esteem.

The sincere friend,

ABDEL-KADER EL HUSSEIN.

Damascus, 8 Techerine-Tani (November, 1881).

The most redoubtable adversary that France encountered in Algeria, the man
who, for sixteen years of heroic conflicts, fought for his faith and the independence
of his country, Abdel-Kader is undoubtedly the most remarkable and important
personage that has arisen for a century among the Mussulman populations.

Marshal Soult said in 1843, ' There are now only three men in the world who
may legitimately be called great, and all these belong to Islam. They are Abdel-
Kader, Mehemet Ali, and Schamyl.'

The life of our illustrious enemy is little known in France.

. Lui, le Sultan né sous les palmes,

Le compagnon des lions roux,

Le Hadji farouche aux yeux calmes,

L'Emir pensif, féroce et doux !

Abdel-Kader was born about the end of the year 1806, at the Ghetna of Sidi-
Mahiddin, near Mascara, in the territory of Hachem, province of Oran. Gifted
with remarkable energy, an eloquence and power of attraction that it was difficult
to resist, he had only to come upon the scene to subjugate wills and conquer
hearts. He was small in stature, well proportioned, and excelled in all exercises
of the body. His glance, piercing and gentle, was hard to bear.

Abdel-Kader's father, the Marabout Mahiddin, of the tribe of Hachem, was
greatly reverenced by the Arabs, and, as a Marabout, enjoyed a great reputation for sanctity. When the tribes round Mascara desired in 1832 to recognise him
as supreme chief, he refused that honour, and offered the place to his young son
Abdel-Kader. Having inherited his father's popularity, he was accepted. Old
Mahiddin on this occasion related that, being on pilgrimage to Mecca some years
before with his eldest son and Abdel-Kader, one day that he was out walking with
the first he met an old fakir, who gave him three apples, telling him, ' That is for
you, that is for your son here, and the third is for the Sultan.' ' Who is the
Sultan ?' asked Mahiddin. ' He,' answered the fakir, ' whom you left at home when
you came to walk here.'

This legend, most religiously believed in by the partisans of Abdel-Kader, contributed to the consolidation of his power and fortune.

Thenceforward the life of Abdel-Kader is identified with the history of the conquest of Algeria. During those long years he alone held our troops in check ; pro-

kingdom in the interior, and a French occupation of a certain number of ' presides ' on the coasts.

---

phet and warrior, by turns he preached a holy war and fought step by step against the invaders.

We omit all the events of the war—the capture of the Smalah in 1843, and the numerous campaigns, to come to the fatal conclusion. Having surrendered himself into the hands of General Lamoricière, the 22nd of December, 1847, the Emir was conducted to the Duke d'Aumale, and spoke thus: 'I should have desired to do sooner what I am doing to-day; I awaited the hour appointed by God. The General has pledged me a word that I trust. I have no fear that it will be violated by the son of a great monarch like the King of the French.'

Next day, as the prince was returning from a review, the ex-Sultan presented himself on horseback, and, surrounded by his principal chiefs, dismounted a few paces from the Duke d'Aumale.

'I offer you,' said he, 'this horse, the last I have ridden ; it is an evidence of my gratitude, and I hope it may bring you happiness.'

The prince replied, 'I accept it, in the name of France, whose protection shall for the future cover you, as a mark of oblivion of the past.'

The 25th of December, 1847, the Emir, his family, and some servants, were embarked in the frigate Asmodée, and conveyed to Toulon.

The convention made with General Lamoricière, ratified by the Duke d'Aumale, according to which the Emir was to be taken to Saint Jean d'Acre or to Alexandria, was about to be put in execution when the miserable revolution of February destroyed the throne of Louis-Philippe.

The Emir understood that mischief was to be apprehended. He said to Colonel Daumas, attached to his person and interned with him in Fort Lamalgue, 'Here is a Sultan, announced to be powerful, who had contracted alliances with many other sovereigns, who had a numerous family, who was quoted for his experience ! Three days have been enough to dethrone him. And you do not wish me to be convinced that there is no other power, no other truth than that of God ! Believe me, the earth is but carrion, dogs only can fight for it.'

It was in vain that the Emir caused a warm and pressing address claiming the liberty promised him by the generals and the son of the King to be forwarded to the members of the Provisional Government. The Republic kept him prisoner at Pau and Amboise, contrary to the promise of the King's government. The Prince-President restored his liberty in 1852. He sailed for Broussa, and is now in retirement at Damascus. It was there in the month of June, 1860, he nobly seconded the proceedings of Christian France by actively engaging in the defence of the Maronites against the Druses. Abdel-Kader came to France at the time of the exhibition of 1867, and has not since quitted Syria, where he is surrounded with the respect and reverence of all Mussulmans and all Christians.

Abdel-Kader stimulated fanaticism, but was always free from it himself, and the best proof is in his action at Damascus. I myself consider that a remarkable point in his character, not yet sufficiently brought into prominence, is his admirable resignation when conquered, and his impregnable fidelity to his word and oath, his keeping faith. Notwithstanding favourable opportunities, and the incessant instigations from his co-believers, for more than thirty years the Emir has refused to resume the contest against France. God not having allowed him to be victor, the Mussulman has broken his sword, the faithful believer has bent head and knee before the fatal decree.

By this treaty the Emir Abdel-Kader had obtained the right to appoint residential agents in Oran and Mostaganem, they remaining French cities; reciprocally, a French officer was to reside in the Arab capital, Mascara. Arzew remained to the Emir. There was freedom of trade, even in powder and arms. The contracting parties promised protection to European travellers into the interior, and to Mahometans in the coast towns.

General Drouet d'Erlon became Governor-General on the 22nd July, 1834. Born in 1765, this veteran of the wars in Spain and of Waterloo, being very old, was supported by General Rapatel in the command of the army.

The new Governor began by disavowing the policy of concession, that came to a climax with the shameful treaty of Desmichels. He recalled the negotiator, and replaced him by General Trézel, a partisan of conquest. Abdel-Kader, uneasy at this change, accredited to the Governor Drouet d'Erlon, at Algiers, Ben Durand, a Jew of Oran, formerly dragoman to Hussein Dey, and secret instigator of the treaty of Desmichels.

Although the Chélif was not named as a boundary in the treaty of 1834, it was accepted by common accord. Abdel-Kader, no doubt wishing to show that he had no intention of receding before the change to be apprehended in the French system, crossed the river and came to Milianah, where the Mahometans received him enthusiastically.

He installed there Bey Ben Allah Sidi Embarek, a distinguished warrior, of a great family of the Sahel of Algiers, who had for a moment been in our service. He also established an arsenal and a cannon-foundry in that town.

Though he constantly applied, General Trézel did not receive any instructions from the old Governor, who was tricked, perhaps, by Ben Durand. It was then that Trézel assumed the offensive, considering the situation too serious, for the encroachment upon Milianah was not an isolated fact. He advanced beyond Oran on the valley of the Sig. The commencement of hostilities was not delayed. In the first day Colonel Oudinot, commandant of the French cavalry of the advanced guard, was killed. General Trézel, at the head of the rear-guard, renewed the attack; but his troops manœuvred badly, and became clubbed; the confusion was great; there was want of discipline; the baggage was pillaged, and the barrels of wine staved by our own troops.

The enemy's numbers hourly increased. The second day Trézel determined to retreat fighting, with his convoy between the two bodies of troops. As the direct road to Arzew seemed to be held by the enemy, the French general thought he should do right to return to the coast by the gorges and marshes of the Macta. But the Emir perceived the movement, and seized the defile before him. Our rear-guard, fearing to be cut off, broke up and joined the advanced guard. Seized with a panic, the drivers of the convoy cut the traces, and fled with their horses, leaving the stores and wounded upon the ground. The Arabs rushed upon the waggons with terrible shouts, cut the throats of the sick and previous day's wounded, and rushed upon the broken battalions, brandishing severed heads upon the ends of their guns. Meanwhile, a knot of energetic men had taken up a position on a height, singing the ' Marseillaise ' as a rallying cry. The knot became a battalion, and would not be broken. The brave little band re-entered Arzew, keeping the enemy at a distance, but several hundred Frenchmen had perished.*

The Governor, Drouet d'Erlon, who had neither ordered nor forbidden the expedition, disavowed it when he heard of the disaster; General Trézel was replaced by General d'Arlanges, and he, on the 8th of August, 1835, handed over the duty to Marshal Clauzel.†

Marshal Clauzel proceeded in person to the province of Oran to avenge the disaster of the Macta. This expedition, in which the Duke of Orleans was engaged, concluded with the brilliant combat of Habra, 1st of December, 1835; the burning of Mascara, 7th of December, 1835; and a speedy retreat to Mostaganem. Tlemcen was occupied in January and February, 1836. But these were only military promenades followed by retreats, and did not weaken Abdel-Kader's influence. Indeed, Tlemcen was blockaded as soon as it was occupied.

---

* The number of 800 is given by M. Galibert, *L'Algérie ancienne et moderne.* The *Annales Algériennes* say only 300 killed, 200 wounded, and almost all the stores.

* Bertrand Clauzel, Count and Marshal of France, was born in 1772, at Mirepoix, in Ariége, and died in 1842. Enlisted as a volunteer he made the campaigns of 1794 and 1795 with the army of the Pyrenees, commanded a brigade in Italy in 1799, accompanied General Leclerc to San Domingo, then assisted Rochambeau to bring the remains of the army back to France. Promoted to the rank of general of division, he served from 1805 to 1809 in the north, in Italy, in Dalmatia, and in Illyria, distinguished himself especially in the war in Spain under Junot and Massena, and directed in 1812 the retreat from Portugal that was compared to Ney's in Russia. Louis XVIII. had appointed him inspector of infantry during the first restoration, but banished him by the ordinance of 1815 for having joined Napoleon on his return from the island of Elba. Clauzel retired to the United States, and did not return till after the amnesty of 1820. Deputy of Rethel in 1827, he was a member of the Liberal opposition. Appointed Governor-general of Algeria after the revolution of 1830, he defeated the Bey of Titery at the Col de Tenia, occupied Medeah and Blidah, and endeavoured to colonise the plain of Mitidjah. Recalled in 1831 because he wished to cede the provinces of Oran and Constantine to some Tunisian princes, yet the King appointed him Marshal soon after, and in 1835 again entrusted him with the government of Algeria. He took Mascara, but failed before Constantine, and was a second time relieved. From that time till his death he lived in retirement.

General d'Arlanges. taking up a position in camp at the estuary of the Tafna. on the side nearest to the besieged place. soon found himself almost blockaded. Endeavouring to penetrate to Tlemcen. he engaged in a combat that was at least undecided. in which he was himself wounded. as well as his chief of the staff, Colonel de Maussion. and which cost us three hundred men. Whatever were the losses inflicted at the same time upon the Arabs, a combat in Africa. where three hundred men are lost, is singularly like a check.

During this time, incursions. more insolent than ever. reached the very gates of Algiers. The Arabs captured some cattle at Point Pescade. killed soldiers at Dely Brahim, and at the Emperor Fort. They even reached Bouzaréa.

It was under these eminently critical circumstances that General Bugeaud was sent with three regiments to relieve the camp of the Tafna. The province of Oran. that had just been the scene of the disaster of the Macta and the checks of the Tafna. was the theatre where our discouraged troops had most need of a victory. It was necessary to restore confidence : this was the new General's work.

'A French column.' says General Trochu, 'important by the valour of officers and men, after difficult operations in the province of Oran. was driven into a corner by the sea in the sandy delta formed by the mouths of the Tafna. It was surrounded by the whole levy of the country in arms, attacked every day in its hardly defensible position, driven to continual efforts and painful sacrifices ; its moral condition, like its material. bordered upon disarray. The situation was serious. The Government and public opinion were excited. An immediate despatch of troops, starting directly from the Mediterranean ports, was resolved on. The command was given to General Bugeaud.'

The six battalions of infantry, designed for the camp at the Tafna, formed an effective force of 4500 men. The King, wishing to put an officer at the head of these troops on whose vigour he could reckon, had cast his eyes upon General Bugeaud, who alone seemed capable of contending with Abdel-Kader. The Minister of War, in the end of May 1836, instructed him to proceed to Toulon, and thence to the mouths of the Tafna, and take the command, secure the post on the Tafna, march upon Tlemcen, and examine if it was tenable. He was also to report to General Rapatel, the interim Governor-General.

The reinforcement, partly embarked at Port Vendres, partly at Marseilles, reached the mouths of the Tafna between the 4th and 6th of June, and General Bugeaud, who landed at the same time as the troops, caused them to encamp on both sides of the Tafna.

General Rapatel, advised of the speedy arrival of General Bugeaud, had exerted himself to arrange the organization of all the various services required by the troops to be assembled on the banks of the Tafna. The director of artillery and the military-intendant had proceeded to Oran, while merchant-vessels conveyed thither six field-guns, thirty-six mules, and the ammunition and provisions necessary for the troops, as well as a reinforcement of 112 gunners. General d'Arlanges had embarked to return to Oran and resume the command of his division.

As soon as General Bugeaud landed, he took all

the measures necessary for the organization of the expeditionary column, leaving the protection of the entrenched camp to a battalion of African light infantry, with the addition of some companies composed of all the exhausted and ailing men of every regiment, the military artificers, and three hundred men drawn from the garrison of the island of Rachgoun. This collection, added to some coast-guard gunners, made up an effective force of twelve hundred men, the command being entrusted to the engineer chef-de-bataillon, Perraud, who was to complete the fortifications.

When General Bugeaud reached the mouths of the Tafna the situation was very serious, and on landing he saw it to be so at the first glance. Then, for the first time, did he put in practice his views as to the way to fight the Arabs, and he applied the firmness and decision that he used in all the actions of his life to his modifications and radical changes in the former methods of warfare. Having come to take the command, and pursue the military operations directed against the Emir, he lost no time in calling together the colonels and chiefs of corps the very next day, and harangued them in a way that could not fail to astonish them.

'Gentlemen,' he said, 'I am fresh to Africa; but in my opinion the method of pursuing the Arabs hitherto employed is defective. I was long campaigning in Spain; now the war that you are carrying on here presents a great deal of analogy with that we undertook in 1812 against the guerillas. You will allow me to utilise the experience that I then acquired. I am, therefore, of opinion that strong columns should be absolutely broken up, and we should disencumber ourselves of the artillery and heavy baggage that impede our march, and hinder us in pursuing or surprising the enemy. Our soldiers, like the soldiers of Rome, should be free in their movements and unencumbered: at any cost, the weight that burdens them must be lightened. Our mules and horses must carry the food and ammunition, and the tents answer the purpose of pack-saddles and bags. Then we shall be in a condition to cross mountains and torrents without leaving our baggage behind us.

'Finally, gentlemen,' said the General in conclusion. 'I shall be very glad to converse with you individually, and receive your observations and advice. So you will gratify me much whenever any one of you will come and converse with me, and ask me for, or give me, any explanations.'

The General was hardly gone, when the colonels and chiefs of corps looked at each other in amazement, and shrugged their shoulders, considering the new comer to be senseless and presumptuous. Colonel Combes,* an excellent soldier, very brave, but violent and rather narrow, was the most angry and most bitter at the meeting. Besides, all the rest agreed with him.

---

* Michael Combes, born at Feurs, Loire, in 1788, died before Constantine, 15th October, 1837, distinguished for his gallantry during all the campaigns of the empire, fought at Waterloo, left the country, and did not return till after the revolution of 1830. Ordered to occupy Ancona at the head of the 66th of the line, he seized the citadel by a daring attempt, that was disavowed by the Government. Deprived of his command, and then sent to Africa, he was successively colonel of the 1st Foreign Legion, then colonel of the 47th of the line, and commander of the Legion of Honour after the battle of the Sickack. He was engaged in the expedition to Constantine. Mortally wounded just as he was leading the second column up the breach to the assault, he encouraged the soldiers while hiding the severity of the wound, and before he died desired to report the success of the operation he had been charged with to the general. After his death, General Bugeaud most energetically urged the Chamber to grant a pension to his widow.

'As the General authorises us to speak openly to him, and tell him what we think, I will go to him to-morrow, and in your name, gentlemen, present him with our opinion.'

In fact, next day Colonel Combes did wait upon his General, and informed him of the impression his yesterday's speech had produced upon the officers. 'Our soldiers,' said he, 'will lose confidence without artillery, and will not march. It is cannon alone that sustains their courage ; to dispense with it would be disastrous. General, it is impossible for you to persist in your plan ; I am charged in the name of all my colleagues to convey our opinion to you faithfully as you authorised us.' The General replied to the Colonel that all these objections had already been presented to him, and that, in spite of the opinion of the chiefs of corps, he persisted in doing as he had decided. When Colonel Combes tried to raise his voice, the General confined himself to telling him, 'Sir, I certainly requested every one of you to come and give me his observations and advice. But at my discretion, if you please, to attend to them at my pleasure. With this, Colonel, I thank you, and request you to retire.' The new commandant's orders were executed, the guns and waggons were embarked, and all was ready to commence the campaign.

This was General Bugeaud's beginning. 'Thus,' said M. Guizot afterwards, 'did he immediately give the war a character of bold initiative, unfettered and unforeseen mobility, and swift and indefatigable activity.' He applied himself to pursue Abdel-Kader at all points of the Arab territory, to forestall him, to reach and conquer him or to baffle him, that is to say the Arab nation personified in its hero.

Just as General Bugeaud landed on the banks of the Tafna there occurred a little characteristic event that for once covered the superintendents of victuals and contractors for the troops with confusion. This is the story told us by one present. It is not from yesterday that the old quarrel between the army and the commissariat bears date. There were complaints in the time of the Romans of sacks of corn filled with earth.

Several times had our poor soldiers, worn out with weariness, and undermined by fever, complained, and not unreasonably, of the bad quality of the drink served out to them under the name of wine. This production no doubt cost the Government dear enough, but was not the less execrable. The contractors took mighty oaths that our men, as usual, were making unfounded complaints, and that this wine was as pure as their inmost hearts. Just at this time some terrible storms and hurricanes ravaged the coast, the sea rose in fury and rushed inland, throwing back the waters of the Tafna to a considerable distance. Our men's camp was placed not far from where the river enters the sea. One morning, what was the general astonishment when, at the issue of rations at meal time, all our soldiers, from the general to the simple private, putting their glasses to their lips, found a distinct taste of salt in their wine. The thing was simple enough ; the sea water had been mixed by the tempest with the water of the Tafna, so it had become salt since the disturbance. This was an irrefragable proof that our soldiers' wine was regularly baptized with river water.

On the 10th of June General Bugeaud was ready for a start. Having received information that Abdel-

Kader had sent troops in the direction of Oran to burn our allies' harvests. and that his camp was at Oued-Sinan, he first of all proceeded towards Oran. instead of marching upon Tlemcen. He started at night, for the enemy was near, and it was necessary to avoid attack when traversing a dangerous country. Yet the difficulty of a night march in an unknown country full of obstacles, covered with brushwood, would soon have thrown the columns into disorder. Scarcely a league had been made, when the General was obliged to halt and wait for day. As soon as it broke the columns were reformed, and pursued their march on the broken ground that inter-venes between the sea and the road followed in the previous April. Thus the worst places were crossed without hindrance. About nine o'clock, as the heads of the columns were coming out upon the flats, they met the first horsemen of the Emir, who had started very early from his camp at Oued-Sinan to attack us. Twelve or fifteen hundred horsemen, whom he had posted on heights, rushed upon the right flank, and the rear of the columns, and also the centre where the baggage was. The attack was repulsed by a battalion of the 62nd of the line, and a squadron of the Chasseurs d'Afrique.

General Bugeaud halted the heads of the columns to concentrate them, as they had lengthened out on the march, then he took the offensive. But the Arabs, finding our troops marching resolutely against them, did not keep their ground, and retreated after firing a few shots. Mustapha,* the chief of our auxiliaries,

---

* Mustapha Ben Ismaël, one of our most faithful and useful allies, chief of the Douairs and Smélas, in Algeria, was born at Mascara, in what year is not very well known, as the Mahometans take but small count of their age. He was between 65

charged with great impetuosity at the right moment, and throwing himself upon the Kabyles brought back a number of heads. General Bugeaud writes that he was shocked at the sight, but, nevertheless, could

---

and 70 in 1838 when he came to France to appear before the court-martial on General de Brossard.

At the time of the conquest of Algeria, Mustapha was aga of the Donairs and the Smélas, two tribes composing the Maghzen of the Bey of Oran.

When Marshal Clauzel's expedition to Oran took place, Mustapha received at the same time the General's propositions and those of the Emperor of Morocco. Both of them made him an offer of succeeding Hassan, the former Bey of Oran. Mustapha, despising the overtures of Muley-Ali, the emperor's lieutenant, refused to go to Tlemcen to receive investiture. His property was laid waste, he was taken prisoner, and did not obtain his liberty until France had established the non-interference of the Emperor of Morocco in the affairs of the regency.

Abdel-Kader, having treated with General Desmichels, Mustapha entered upon an open conflict with the Emir, whom he called ' the Shepherd's son,' in contempt. After several fights, Mustapha retired to the citadel of Tlemcen, to the Turks and Couloglis. On the arrival of the French in January, 1836, Mustapha went to Marshal Clauzel, and said, ' In six years I have received more than a hundred letters from generals, and have not ventured to trust them. Your reputation and conduct give me so much confidence that I am come to put myself into your hands.' A few days afterwards he fought in our ranks, and never left them again. The success of General Perregaux's expedition, on his return from Tlemcen, in the east of the province of Oran, was in great part due to Mustapha. On the 30th of April, 1837, he was made officer of the Legion of Honour, and promoted to the rank of marechal-de-camp (major-general). At the combat of the Sickack, Mustapha was wounded in the hand, and remained crippled, without losing any of his activity.

In 1838 he came to France, and, after giving evidence in the Brossard court-martial, spent several days at La Durantie with General Bugeaud. The Countess Feray tells us, ' It was at our house of Excideuil that Mustapha was received with his family and suite. When my father introduced him to my mother, he said, " You have four wives in your country, I have only one that I love like four." Mustapha gravely answered, " My four wives are not worth your one." ' In 1841 he again distinguished himself in the expedition against Tackdempt and Mascara. In the end of 1841, with Colonel Tempoure, he opened negotiations with Sidi-Chigi, a respected Marabout, who joined our party against Abdel-Kader, and thus induced the submission of the tribes near Tlemcen. This glorious campaign and noble conduct gained him in February, 1842, the cross of commander.

In 1843, after the capture of Abdel-Kader's smalah, General Lamoriciere sent forward the cavalry towards the sources of the Chelif, and Mustapha was to catch a flying tribe. On his return to Oran with his maghzen, loaded with the booty of the razzia, General Mustapha was attacked by an ambuscade in a wood at El Biada, near Kerroucha, and received a ball point blank that killed him on the spot. His troopers, numbering 500, were seized with a panic and fled, leaving his body in the hands of the enemy. Abdel-Kader is said to have caused the corpse of old Mustapha to be mutilated, the man who used to say, ' I have only two enemies in the world, Satan and the son of Mahiddin.' The command of the goum of the Donairs and Smelas, forming the maghzen of Oran, was given to his nephew, El Mezari, who was his first aga. The mutilation was afterwards contradicted.

not refrain from praising the intrepidity of his warriors.

General Bugeaud then marched against the Arabs and dispersed them with the same facility. When the Emir's infantry. hidden in a fold of the ground, saw their cavalry in flight, they speedily disappeared. We lost five men ; the loss of the Arabs was not great, but there were some persons of importance among the dead.

After that the enemy did not show themselves. The General continued his march, and in the evening reached Oued-Ghazer. where he established his bivouac. The regiments lately come to Africa behaved with bravery, though they suffered most from fatigue, and abandoned muskets, packs, and camp equipage. Many men would have lagged behind, and been massacred but for the active care of the rear-guard and the ambulance. Some committed suicide. and demoralisation even made its appearance among the officers, to whom General Bugeaud addressed some sharp language.

On the 13th of June, the troops started early, and encamped for the evening at Oued-Sinan. On the 14th, the camp was on the Oued-Amria ; and on the 15th, at Misserghin. General Bugeaud made over the command to the colonel of the 24th of the line, and continued his progress to Oran with all the cavalry. This five days' march from the Tafna to Oran caused the reappearance of our Arab allies upon the marches of Oran, who had been kept away by the fear of Abdel-Kader.

General Bugeaud on June 16 addressed the following despatch to the Minister, being very much impressed with the behaviour of our troops :—

GENERAL BUGEAUD TO MARSHAL MAISON, MINISTER OF WAR.

For the command in Africa there must be men of vigorous mould both morally and physically. Colonels and chefs de bataillon who are a little aged, whose vigour of heart and mind is not sustained by physical power, ought to be recalled to France, where they could be either retired or take garrison commands. Their presence here is much more injurious than beneficial. Also, to carry on this war successfully, there must be brigades of mules with military organization, so as not to depend upon the inhabitants of the country. We must have the power of proceeding in any direction with activity, so as to be able to pursue the enemy to any point where he may retire, and not load the soldiers, as is done, so as to make them unable to perform the severe duty that falls upon them in such a rough country and burning climate. There is actual barbarity, I might even call it treason to the nation in loading them with seven or eight days' provisions, sixty rounds, shirts, shoes, kettles, &c. Many sink under such a weight, and the strongest must be marched so slowly that it is impossible to make the rapid movements that are the only means of securing success. Mules under military organization seem to me to be the best base of operations in Africa. I have made a calculation that there ought to be eighty to each thousand men. They would carry ten thousand rations, and the soldiers have in little bags a reserve for four days. This would give a supply for fourteen days, and that is quite long enough for the campaigns that can be made in this country. They must be short to avoid losing all the soldiers. With the country transport, if an affair is at all sharp, there is a risk of losing the provisions and wounded. On the 12th, when my transport was attacked, many of the camel and mule drivers at once threw down their loads, and it took a great deal of energy and activity to make them pick them up again. Things must be done liberally, as that will be economy in men and money. *We must be strong or be off.** Especially it is necessary only to send strong soldiers, and these men must be commanded by young and energetic officers. If I had three thousand of the soldiers of Spain, with mules to carry their provisions, I could overrun the whole province of Oran and be master of it. The regiments that have been two or three years in Africa begin to be good, but also their effective strength is much reduced. The three fine regiments I have brought will also become good, but this will be when they have lost two or three hundred men, weak in both mind and body. Humanity, economy, and prudence in war, all require that only selected men should be sent to Algeria.

---

* Il faut être forts ou s'en aller.

The authority and precision with which this general of brigade speaks to the Minister is remarkable. It was really the personal position of General Bugeaud, an influential deputy, and much appreciated by the King, that enabled him to express himself thus.

CHAPTER XIX.

THE SICKACK (1836).

AFTER resting his troops ten days, the General resumed the campaign to convoy a body of troops to Tlemcen. On the 19th he bivouacked at Misserghin, and the 20th on the Rio Salado. On that day three hundred men were unable to continue their march from heat and fatigue. He sent them back to Oran under the escort of the native cavalry, and himself reached Tlemcen on the 24th.

Here follows the very curious and faithful report that General Bugeaud addressed to Marshal Clauzel, Governor-general of Algeria. The sure and rapid judgment with which he had in a moment measured our position in Africa is remarkable:—

Tlemcen, 24th June, 1836.

SIR,—I have reached Tlemcen after five days on the road. They would be short days' marches for Europe; they are long enough for Africa with its heat. The march from the Tafna to Oran had taught me that the troops must be most prudently led in order not to lose, in five or six days on the road, as many men as in a battle. I therefore took all imaginable and possible precautions at Oran in the matter of provisions and transport. I halted frequently; wherever there was water I stayed two hours or spent the night, and, notwithstanding this, at two days from Oran I had to send back nearly three hundred men who could march no further from one cause or another. After that, my litters and camels were again covered with soldiers and officers. The new regiments are detestable for this sort of fighting. They only become good after being purged of near half of their force. The —— light is a specimen; it came to Africa seven months ago with 1600 and some men; it has not 900 in the ranks, but these 900 are good. It must be allowed that apprenticeship costs rather too dear.

Among the new regiments the —— is the one I have been most displeased with. It was very much demoralised, almost in despair; four men committed suicide in a march of four leagues, and it furnished as many to the litters and camels as all the rest put together. This mischief came from the top. The body of officers were discontented at having been re-embarked immediately after their return from Corsica. They loudly gave vent to their complaints, lamented over the soldier's fate, and pretended that they had never seen troops driven so hard, while in the other regiments it was agreed that they never had been marched with so much care and plenty. They said, 'Compare with this the expedition to Mascara, where we were without food for five days' (that was only a brigade, the others only wanted for two or three days).

The Colonel and Lieutenant-Colonel are but little fitted for this war. The latter is a bully and a grumbler. Young men are wanted with ardour, and a future. I have been obliged to take serious notice of the *morale* of the ——. I called up the officers, and harangued them before the soldiers. I discussed their complaints aloud. I showed them that there was no foundation for any of them, that they had water and food in abundance, that there had been a halt after every hour's march, that the regiments had taken turns to lead, to be in the middle, and rear of the column, &c. Then, changing the tone of the discussion, I told them that their complaints of the soldier's fate were but a bad cover for the lowering of their *morale*, and the soldiers would not have made complaints but for their example.

The Lieutenant-Colonel was stupid enough to blame me for the fatigues of the 12th, when there was fighting. This was fine sport to me. I answered him as he deserved, and my reply produced a good effect. If such a thing was to occur again I should relieve the two highest in rank of their commands, and I told them so in strict privacy.

I have told you all this, sir, to confirm you in the opinion that you, no doubt, already hold, that is to say, that Africa requires troops especially selected for it, and especially commanded by young leaders, ardent and vigorous. Some young men have distinguished themselves in Africa; if you keep this unfortunate conquest, they must be promoted, and given the command first of regiments, and afterwards of columns.

Perhaps I have been rather long in coming to my report of military matters. We saw no enemy for the first five days, but to-day Abdel-Kader's cavalry attacked my rear-guard in the broken ground that separates the Amiguier from the Safsaf. At first I did not take much notice of the slight firing that had commenced, but seeing that it became more serious, I halted the heads of columns, and proceeded to the rear of the centre one, intending to give the pursuers a lesson, who have, I think, been allowed to take up the delightful habit of harassing us with impunity. I caused all the tirailleurs to turn back behind a hillock, and formed three echelons of cavalry and two of infantry. When I was giving orders to the first echelon to allow the enemy to adventure largely before charging them, the leader thought I was ordering a charge and went off at a gallop. He received at short range the fire of a much larger number of cavalry, six men were wounded, four horses killed, and the charge abortive. I advanced with the second echelon and flung the whole upon the enemy. At this moment Mustapha, whom I had sent for, and was as usual hunting wild boars with his Douairs upon my left flank, arrived most opportunely upon the enemy's flanks as we were pressing him in front. His rout was complete. The worst mounted fell by the sword, and their heads were cut off. Among them was an aga of Abdel-Kader's, and one of his chaoushes. I gave orders for the pursuit to be continued till all were dispersed. This took us back as far as the Amiguier, but it was not lost time. The lesson was valuable. It taught the Arabs that it was not good to come snuffing so near us : it showed our soldiers that when one wants to act lion, one makes one's tail respected. It was the more necessary because before the charge several officers assured me that it would not succeed, that we should weary our horses, and that when we went about we should be harassed again. We did not see a single man again, and this vigorous proceeding probably saved us 100 or 150 wounded that we should have had by the firing on the rear-guard, probably continuing all the way to the Safsaf. Besides, it is disgraceful for 6000 men to let themselves be thus mocked by a handful of men, although it must be allowed that they are very dexterous horsemen. I had six men killed and thirteen wounded. I will report the names of the military men who distinguished themselves in my order of the day. After this combat I halted two hours upon the Safsaf, one league from Tlemcen. It was then that Cavaignac, the Bey, and the chiefs of the Moors and Jews, came to meet me. They have been almost always blockaded. Abdel-Kader was there yesterday with five or six thousand men, and 120,000 head of cattle, he destroyed the scanty harvest round Tlemcen. They say he has retired towards the Empire of Morocco; I saw the marks of two guns that he took with him; others say that he is awaiting me at the meeting of the Isser and the Tafna. I shall know soon, giving my troops one day's rest and then marching upon him.

Besides my desire to catch Abdel-Kader, I am compelled to march upon the Tafna, for there is no means of living here without trenching on the little store of the garrison. I should tell you that this much-vaunted land is a small oasis, that it is pleasant to find after crossing thirty leagues of barren and uncultivable desert that divides it from Oran; but at the same time, it is very surprising to see anything so little like the Oriental description given us. Tlemcen is a heap of wretched ruins; it was a collection of little square huts, with nothing left but the four walls in a greater or less state of dilapidation; a small portion is still standing, and is not more beautiful. It contains four or five thousand Jews, Moors, or Coulouglis,* who seem very miserable, and are very wretched in consequence of the blockade and stoppage of all trade. Such a state of things cannot continue; if we do not destroy Abdel-Kader's power, and occupy the country in force, the inhabitants of this miserable town must submit to the Emir, or we must carry them to some other place. The contribution commenced their ruin, the blockade contributed much to it, and as they make nothing, their little purse must be exhausted.

The geographical position of this town is agreeable. Beautiful streams coming down from the neighbouring hills cross it, and these go to water gardens and an olive wood that I had expected to be larger from the pompous language of an African enthusiast. I fancy I am liberal in putting the produce of the olives of Tlemcen at 200,000 francs (8000*l.*). After this wood there are some indifferent fields; some bits of barley that have escaped Abdel-Kader show that the harvest was very poor; not an ear of wheat. To find any it is said to be necessary to go to a distance of six leagues in the hills; and even that is not certain, but it is quite clear that there would have to be a fight with the Kabyles before it was harvested. It would take two days to bring back a little corn; during those two days we should eat as much as we gathered, and the troops would be harassed; so we must give up harvesting, at least, for the moment. When I return, if the people of Tlemcen can furnish me with three days' provisions, I will take them harvesting with me. I have to leave three hundred foot-sore at Tlemcen, and take instead two hundred

---

* The Coulougli is the child of a Turk and an Arab woman.

men of the garrison, and three hundred Coulouglis, under the command of Cavaignac.

As I can only send this despatch from Rachgoun, I will finish it there.

Rachgoun, 29th June, 1836.

The enemy did not dispute the crossing of the Isser with me, nor that of Mount Talgonat, which is, however, very difficult. Reaching the Isser at ten in the morning, I pushed the heads of my columns towards the road that leads by the Tafna. I allowed the troops to rest till three in the afternoon, then changed flank to the right and took the road leading over the hills. All the Arabs agreed in saying it is better than the lower road by the Tafna. The engineer officers declared the contrary by induction. I took the side of the eye-witnesses, and I did well. Over the hill, though there is an ascent of 500 metres (1650 feet), a good road for wheel-carriages might be made in a day or a day and a half's work. The difficulty for a large column is that there are only two insignificant springs: but it is easy to protect a convoy everywhere. The road on both slopes passes along a spine, flanked by enormous ravines, making a natural fortification, but the neck must be held with a strong portion of the column as a preliminary. A column takes three hours to cross this mountain.

I slept on the hill the 27th, and 28th at the foot of the northern slope, towards the banks of the Tafna, four leagues from Rachgoun. I had two objects in halting there: to pasture my cavalry upon some small fields of barley, so few of which are to be found in this promised land, and to reconnoitre the lower road. At four o'clock I marched upon this road with four battalions and the cavalry. The infantry was placed in succession in echelon on commanding points, then the cavalry, and with the allied Douairs I went just within sight of my camp on the banks of the Isser. We found several bad places; but there is one where six hundred men might stop an army. Two perpendicular mountains contract the valley, narrow enough before, and the Tafna closes it from one mountain to the other with a ravine forty or fifty metres (150 feet) deep, with perpendicular sides. The engineers were obliged to allow that the Arabs were right; if there was a proposal to make a road from Rachgoun to Tlemcen in time of peace, it ought to be made on the lower line, but in time of war, and with the work we do in the worst places, the higher line must be taken, as it is the safest. But I will make neither the one nor the other: the lower one does not suit me at all, and as the higher is waterless, I cannot remain there two days in this heat. Besides, only having six bad waggons with bad teams at Rachgoun, it is not worth the trouble we should take; in two days' work we should consume the loads of food, and the stores of Tlemcen would not be increased. So I shall confine myself to loading my four or five hundred camels and mules. I expect that they will carry ten days' food for the column and two months' for the garrison of Tlemcen, and that will give them provisions for about six months. I hope to find some cattle at Tlemcen. As soon as Abdel-Kader's camp was broken up, some Arabs came to market. I caused the Bey to write to all the tribes in the neighbourhood, to induce them to submit, and come to trade at Tlemcen.

I shall only remain at Rachgoun long enough to organize my convoy. I cannot maintain my cavalry there and my numerous transport without going far to forage, and great precautions have to be taken to prevent accident.

Neither can I live at Tlemcen; therefore it is an absolute necessity to return to Oran; I propose to cross the mountains of the Beni Hamer to chastise those rebellious tribes. On our return to Oran the troops will require some rest during the greatest heat. Thus I shall have nothing to do for some time, and it will be a chance to leave the command to General de l'Etang, who will, no doubt, have to come, and visit Algiers, so as to have the power of telling the Government and the Chambers my opinion of the colony, with a knowledge of it.

Recognising the necessity of leaving the man, who had begun the business pending at Oran, to complete it, so as to give continuity, I have begged General d'Arlanges to continue, and I leave him in the enjoyment of the indemnities attached. You, sir, will judge whether you should allow me the expenses of entertainment. Meanwhile I do my duty in entertaining, and shall be quite satisfied whatever you decide.

It seems that Abdel-Kader has retired towards Morocco, because the tribes responded but badly to his appeal. They see that we are quite determined to fight, that they have nothing to get but blows, and this disgusts them. They are also generally very miserable. Obliged to fly with their herds, they are massed towards Trava and Madroma, and there they are ill-treated, and only just allowed to stay. So they are much disgusted with the war, and I expect some overtures. A Kabyle Marabout has requested an interview with Mustapha on a hill where a fire is to be lighted: we shall see. I am quite convinced that the country might be conquered, for a time at least, with a good deal of exertion and expense; but I do not consider that there would be a sufficient recompense for the cost and the blood-shed. I will develope this another time. I will conclude with two words on the posts of Tafna and Tlemcen. Time presses, the vessel must start to fetch us what we want; I shall not have time to make a copy of my despatch, and request you to keep one for me.

I think that now with the forces we have, it is well to continue the occupation of Tlemcen, and to manœuvre round it as much as possible, but for that there must be magazines: this is the difficulty.

I continue to think that the post of Tafna is not at all so necessary as that of Tlemcen. Far from facilitating operations, it impedes them: and the harbour is so abominable all the year round, so impracticable for seven or eight months, that nothing can be built upon it. I should much prefer an entrenched post upon the Sinan, half way between Oran and Tlemcen. It would be easily provisioned with waggons and mules, and the movable columns would find it a central post to renew their supplies of food and ammunition; and this would be much more advantageous for work than going to the Tafna outside the circle of operations. It is further from Tlemcen to the Tafna than it is to the Sinan. From there the troops could penetrate anywhere, after getting ten or twelve days' provisions. The post at the Tafna is in a blind-alley among the Kabyle mountains; the river has to be ascended for operations round Tlemcen. From that point of the Tafna there are at least three days' march, or about sixteen leagues. So, to take three days in going for food, three days in returning to the centre of operations, is very troublesome and paralysing. If there was force enough both might be done, but for choice I should give the preference to the post of the Sinan; I allow that it is more difficult to make a permanent establishment there than at the Tafna, on account of the difficulty of transporting wood, lime, &c.

With a good transport system both might be dispensed with. It would be less costly, more secure, and more convenient for operations than the Tafna. Tlemcen might be provisioned with twelve waggons, and the column with eight mules per thousand men.

I will not conclude, sir, without saying a word about our allies, the Douairs. I am exceedingly pleased with them, they are intrepid and skilful horsemen. They are clearly superior to our cavalry for reconnoitring, skirmishing, and fighting in difficult ground. Mustapha, their chief, is a worthy man, and very sensible. There are other chiefs highly to be commended for their bravery and intelligence. It would be just, sir, and politic, to give a good salary to these men, who serve our cause so well. I earnestly invite you to adopt this view, and to call upon the general who is to command at Oran for a report on this matter. It will be more beneficial than the fortifications that are sometimes injudiciously multiplied.

Receive, sir, &c.,

BUGEAUD.

Tlemcen, the ancient capital of the kingdom of Tlemcen, which contained the towns of Vedrona, Oran, Arzew, Mazagran, Mostaganem, and Djijilli, had encountered many vicissitudes. Attacked, taken and re-taken, now by the Turks, now by the Moors, now by the Spaniards, the town, with superb ramparts and great minarets, had by the last century become nothing but a focus of insurrection, and half thrown down. The Emperor of Morocco had seized it in 1830, but soon had to relinquish it. The Coulouglis, led by Mustapha Ben Israel, who defended the Méchouar, or citadel, passed into the service of France. Marshal Clauzel had taken possession of the town in the month of January of this same year, 1836, and had left a garrison there under the orders of Captain Cavaignac,* the same whom General Bugeaud found on his arrival.

---

* Cavaignac, Louis Eugene, born at Paris in 1802, died in 1857, educated at the Ecole Polytechnique, was appointed to the 2nd Regiment of Engineers in 1824. In 1828 he made the campaign in the Morea as Captain. At the time of the Revolution of 1830 he was in garrison at Arras. He was the first officer of his regiment to declare for the new state of things. Soon after, he was placed on the unattached list for having signed at Metz a protest against the system of peace at any price attributed to Louis-Philippe. Restored to the active list in 1832, he was sent to Africa, after having declared that he would not fight against the republicans on the occasion of a rising. Courage for anything and eminent services soon dissipated the repugnance that his opinions and avowed spirit of independence had excited in his chiefs. He was distinguished in the expeditions of Medeah, Bouffarik, and Cherchell, in the combats of Ouara, the pass of Mouzaia and Affroun. He was appointed chef-de-bataillon in the Zouaves in 1840, then in the light infantry of Africa, and assisted the same year at the taking of Cherchell, and afterwards defended it successfully against an attack of the Arabs. Being made Lieutenant-Colonel of the Zouaves for this brilliant exploit, he took part in the expedition against Medeah, and fought the Beni Menad with credit, at the passage of the Shaba-el-Kessa. He again attracted notice in 1841 before Tackdempt, and succeeded Lamoricière as Colonel of Zouaves. In 1842 he took an important part in the combat of El Harbour against the Beni Rachel. He passed into the 32nd Regiment of the line a short time before the battle of Isly, in 1844, where he commanded the advanced guard, gained the rank of Marechal-de-camp (Major-General), and received the chief command of the province of Oran.

After the Revolution of 1848, the Republic gave him the rank of General of

The fortification of Tlemcen was well protected; but our troops were isolated, as if blockaded in an island in the midst of generally hostile populations, and were in want of food. Bugeaud provisioned the place, and then leaving his foot-sore men, returned to the camp at the Tafna, where he stayed several days. On the 4th of July he again marched for Tlemcen, and on the 6th met the Emir, who came at last to stop his road.

It was the first encounter of these two great champions, who were destined for so many more

---

Division, and made him Governor-General of Algeria. Deputy of Lot at the Constituent Assembly, Cavaignac reached Paris two days after the 15th of May, when the national representation had been violated by a rising, and received the post of War-Minister from the executive commission. A month afterwards, on the occasion of the formidable insurrection of June, the Assembly unanimously entrusted him with the duty of defending Paris and the Republic. According to the General's opponents there might have been calculation on his part in the avoidance of immediate vigorous action, in allowing the danger to become aggravated, the number of assailants to increase, in abandoning several divisions of the city to them, so as to induce the representatives to confer a dictatorship upon him. His friends on the contrary assert, and with more probability, that he acted with great wisdom by first completing the preparations for attack and defence necessitated by the greatness of the danger, by not exposing an army numerically insufficient, and perhaps demoralised, to the chance of a check, by calling up all the disposable forces near Paris so as to strike the insurrection on all sides with the certainty of success. In fact the repression was vigorous and complete, and when, after the victory, Cavaignac came to restore to the Assembly the discretionary powers that it had given him, he was named by acclamation responsible chief of the executive power, and it was declared that he had deserved well of his country.

When the election of President of the Republic came, Cavaignac's disinterested patriotism was not a sufficient warranty for the re-establishment of order and security in the opinion of France, as, being absolute master of power, he had surrounded himself with men already supposed to be compromised, or manifestly unqualified. On the 20th December, 1848, Cavaignac made a dignified descent from power. Thenceforward, considering himself as responsible for his political friends, from whom everything was slipping, he kept up an opposition to the President of the Republic that may possibly have been attributed to disappointment, and even induced him to approach the men whom he had fought against in the days of June. At the coup-d'état of the 2nd of December, 1851, he was arrested as a precautionary measure and taken to Ham. Released a few days afterwards, he took his retirement and went into private life. Elected deputy for Paris in 1852, he refused to take the oath, and was declared to have vacated his seat by a vote of the legislative body. He had just received a fresh nomination at the elections of 1857 when he was removed by death.

years to be rivals in daring, cleverness, and intrepidity. Alone, perhaps, of all the Arab chiefs and French officers, who were on the 6th of July, 1836, upon the banks of the Sickack, the Emir Abdel-Kader is still surviving.* This was, besides, the only set battle in which the great chief engaged the French. He soon understood with his marvellous intelligence that the struggle against the invaders was impossible, if continued under the same conditions, and from that very day he adopted the method of harassing, laying ambuscades, and retreating, that nothing but General Bugeaud's genius could conquer.

It seems to us useless to give our own account of that day, in presence of the authentic documents emanating from the General himself, and therefore will leave him the work.

This is the telegraphic despatch that General Bugeaud addressed to the Minister, Marshal Maison, to announce to him the victory of the Sickack :—

Tlemcen, 7 July, 1836.

Abdel-Kader had for four days been awaiting my great convoy at the crossing of the Tolgoat, upon the banks of the Tafna. Not having any advantage if fighting there, I made a feint, and crossed elsewhere at night.

Next day, the 6th, he attacked me with all the forces he had collected in a fortnight, at the moment my convoy was crossing the ravine, excavated by the Sickack. I made the convoy march upon Tlemcen with a portion of my forces; with the rest I took the defensive, and Abdel-Kader experienced a complete defeat. His infantry, especially, was destroyed. I saved a hundred and thirty from the carnage ; and am going to send them to Marseilles. It was in the ravine of the Isser, where I threw them, that the greatest destruction took place, that is to say, at four leagues from the spot

---

* This volume of the French work was published in 1882.—ED.

where the fight began. He left all his wounded, and four standards, one of them being that of his regular infantry.

Bugeaud.

Two days later the conquering General sent to the Minister his report, hastily written on the field of battle, reflecting the original boldness and grandeur that distinguished this true man of war :—

Tlemcen, 8 July, 1836.

Sir,—My telegraphic despatch has informed you in short of our success of the 6th. As you have often been victor, you, better than others, will estimate the happiness that I have in reporting to you a combat that was my ambition, only excepting that Abdel-Kader was neither killed nor taken; his own horse remained upon the field of battle.

Without exaggeration, the affair of the Sickack may be called a battle, because all the forces that my adversary could command were present.

He had called up all the assistance he could, to prevent my victualling Tlemcen, and for four days had been posted on the Tolgoat, near the Tafna. A reconnoissance I had pushed thither, with the object of examining the road for another occasion, and giving him the change, had made him think that I meant to go that way, while I never had occasion to do so.

My convoy was likely to be coveted by him, and I counted upon it to make him come to a serious engagement, that I might probably have sought for in vain by other manœuvres. To invite an attack is the best way with such an enemy upon such a field; but it was necessary to fight in a favourable spot; and that was the only thing I was anxious about.

I started from Rachgoun (Haârch-Goon) on the 4th, at four in the afternoon. I pushed on three battalions, under the orders of Colonel Combes, on the road to Tolgoat, and I encamped some distance behind him with my convoy of five hundred camels, and three hundred mules. At two in the morning Combes noiselessly quitted his camp, by a path to the left, he was to occupy the col of Sab-Chiouli in two hours and a half's time. One hour later the convoy and the rest of the division proceeded thither. The col was not guarded, but four or five hundred men of the Beni Hamer were just coming there by the other slope. It was too late; by seven o'clock all my convoy had passed, and we were descending towards the Isser. Abdel-Kader was too distant to oppose our march. The river was crossed without interruption, and I encamped upon the left bank, well pleased to have crossed the chain of hills without fighting.

Abdel-Kader was drawing near me, having heard of my march. At three in the afternoon, fifteen hundred or two thousand horse, under the orders of his lieutenant, Bou-Koom, defiled in sight of my camp on the right bank of the Isser, and came to encamp a league upon my right. I judged that this manœuvre was intended to surround me next day in the deep ravine of the Sickack, that I had to pass twice on my road to Tlemcen. I made a reconnoissance in search of another road, but all presented difficulties, either for the fight or for the convoy.

I decided upon crossing the Sickack, and left my camp at three in the morning, with the two-fold object of passing the first ravine, and of being nearer Tlemcen before being attacked, so as to throw my convoy into it, and to resume the offensive as soon as I should be freed from this vast encumbrance. I announced this resolution to the troops: ' You will be attacked to-morrow on your march; you will know how to bear the enemy's insults for a time, and content yourselves with restraining him. But as soon as I can throw the convoy into Tlemcen, you shall take your revenge; you shall march upon them, and throw them into the ravines of the Isser, the Sickack, or the Tafna.'

This was verified with unheard-of good fortune. Notwithstanding my diligence I was attacked by the camp on my left at half-past four in the morning, when only half of my convoy had crossed the first ravine of the Sickack; I caused them to be stopped by the Douairs, a battalion of the 24th, and a squadron of the 2nd Chasseurs.

When Colonel Combes had crossed the Sickack, he had cleverly taken up a position protecting the convoy.

Suspecting that Abdel-Kader's column would not be long in appearing on the plateaux of the left bank, I made haste to arrive there with the head of the centre column and my left column.

Abdel-Kader was just entering with about three thousand horse, three thousand Kabyles on foot, and his regular battalion of a thousand or eleven hundred men. I deployed the 62nd and half of an African battalion parallel to the Sickack, but behind the crest so as not to be seen by the enemy following us. I formed up the 23rd and half an African battalion at right angles to the left of the 62nd. In front of the 23rd and parallel to it, I formed double columns echeloned on the centre battalion of the three battalions of Colonel

Combes, and I threw forward, on the left flank of the 62nd, two picked companies as skirmishers, and the Spahis of the 2nd Chasseurs. The second Chasseurs as a body had been recalled, and placed in column of squadrons opposite one of the intervals of Combes' battalions. The convoy was placed in the angle formed by the line parallel and the line perpendicular to the Sickack. It was guarded by two hundred men of the battalion of Tlemcen and the Coulouglis. I recalled the Douairs and skirmishers who were keeping the Arabs back from the right bank of the Sickack, in order to encourage them to cross to the left bank. The Douairs were slow in assembling, and could not take their post in the line of battle because the events moved too quickly. I know no other fault in this intrepid cavalry, than throwing themselves so recklessly into the fight that they can hardly be made use of any more for subsequent events. But as soon as they see that their presence is necessary on any point where the combat is becoming serious, they come up of themselves. And they did so successfully during this day.

It is evident by the disposition described, that I was going to engage in a double combat in square formation.

Against European armies this disposition might appear vicious, the apex of the angle might be thought weak, as liable to be enveloped and crushed. But, here, this inconvenience was redeemed by the circumstance that one of the lines was covered by the ravine, and that the other rested its right upon the same obstacle. Besides, no order can be bad with Arabs, provided only one has firmness and resolution. I also could not have selected, in the whole country, a battle-field more advantageous than that offered to me by chance. Abdel-Kader had a plain behind him, easy for cavalry, from two to three leagues in extent, and surrounded on three sides by the Sickack, the Isser, and the Tafna; so that I was almost sure, when I put him to flight, of driving him upon a ravine where he must experience loss provided the pursuit was vigorous.

I wanted ten minutes more to finish my dispositions and distribute the duties with precision. It was also necessary to give the enemy time to cross the Sickack, in order to throw him into it. The Emir did not choose to give these ten minutes. He drove in my Spahis and skirmishers upon me, and advanced in great unformed masses with frightful shouts. I judged that it was the moment to take the offensive in my turn, and that a retrograde movement might compromise everything. After firing shell and grape upon this vast confusion, all the troops moved simultaneously at my command, and very freely attacked the enemy.

The combat on the plateau was the most important; Colonel

Combes' three battalions, one of the 47th, two of the 17th light, acted with a resolution and rapidity remarkable for troops so weary with marching and heat. The Arab horsemen were so numerous, that the firing with which they saluted us resembled the fire of two ranks of our infantry. They gave way but slowly. I thought the moment favourable to throw the second chasseurs upon them. I ordered this regiment to charge home, and it was quite successful at first. The Arabs opposite to it were overthrown, and a part of the Kabyle infantry was sabred. But the right wing of the Arabs having attacked the left flank of the chasseurs, while on another side their infantry, issuing from the ravine, fired upon their right flank, they retired with some loss and betook themselves to the protection of the battalions that I brought up to their succour, almost at racing speed. The artillery, under the orders of the brave Colonel Tournemine, conformed to these rapid movements, although it seemed before to be impossible with the mountain equipment.

The Arabs gave way a second time; again I sent my cavalry at them. The four hundred Douairs had rejoined me. Unhappily their Aga Mustapha had bee nwounded, by a ball in the hand. Though deprived of this excellent chief, they did me great service; they and the chasseurs covered themselves with glory. Everything was overthrown; and the Arab cavalry, embarrassed by its very numbers, lost many men, horses, and arms; its killed and wounded remained in our power.

Abdel-Kader, himself, whose standard we had seen in the rear in the midst of his regular infantry, advanced with that reserve and the cavalry he had managed to bring back. This is said to be the first time that the Arabs have been seen to make use of a reserve, or bring it up so appropriately. This last attempt could not stop us a moment; we flung ourselves upon this body, and it, notwithstanding a well-sustained fire, was broken and thrown in perfect confusion upon the most difficult spot in the ravine of the Isser. A rapid descent terminated in a rock almost perpendicularly cut from thirty to forty feet above the ravine's edge. There began a horrible carnage that I was unable to stop, do all I could. To escape certain death, these unfortunates flung themselves from the rock; and broke their necks or crippled themselves horribly. Soon they were deprived of this miserable resource; our chasseurs and light troops found a passage and made their way into the bed of the river; the enemy were hemmed in on all sides, and the Douairs were able to gratify their horrible passion for cutting off heads. At last by shouting and striking with the flat of the sword, I succeeded in saving a hundred and thirty men of the regular infantry. I am going to send them into France. I think it is entering upon a good road. Humanity and policy will alike be satisfied. These Arabs will get notions in France that may bear fruit in Africa.

A large number of muskets given to Abdel-Kader, when he was an ally, remained in our possession. Besides the weapons of the killed and wounded, many of the soldiers had thrown away their arms in order to make their way among the rocks, where they had need of both hands. Our Douairs were, every one of them, carrying two or three heads and three or four muskets. I gave them all the money I had, but I told them that it was for the prisoners and not for the heads, and for the future I would not pay any one.

The Arab cavalry had, like cowards, abandoned their infantry and fled towards the Tafna. I saw them making an attempt at a rally on the edge of the plateau, before going down to the river. I marched against them with the 17th light, the 47th, the 23rd and the artillery; leaving the cavalry to pursue the remains of the infantry and the Kabyles. This cavalry (the Emir's) did not await me; it crossed the Tafna, and I halted upon the right bank, my troops being much tired and the heat excessive.

To return to the first field of battle where the 62nd and half an African battalion had to charge the enemy who had attacked the convoy, and part of whom only had crossed the Sickack at the moment when I was obliged to take the offensive. This portion was flung into the ravine, and fired upon at very close quarters; it experienced very great loss in men and horses killed. After this victorious charge the 62nd, relieved from the enemy in front, came to support my successful movement.

As soon as the victory was pretty well decided, I caused the convoy to proceed towards Tlemcen. Although without my herd of bullocks and all the officers' stores, I determined to sleep upon the field of battle the better to establish my victory.

Receive, &c.,

BUGEAUD.

After this combat, the General halted two hours upon the Sessas. There Captain Cavaignac, the Bey of Tlemcen, and the chiefs of the Moors and Jews, came to meet him. Abdel-Kader had been blockading them for a long time with five or six thousand men, and had the country round ravaged by twenty thousand head of cattle. He had started the evening before, some said, in the direction of Morocco; others, to Mount Tolgoat. Bugeaud encamped his troops under the walls of Tlemcen; gave them a day's rest, and departed for the camp on the Tafna, in order not to diminish the garrison's supply of food.

In a memoir on the war in the province of Oran, and the means of bringing it to a conclusion, by General Bugeaud, July 1836, he thus sums up the ideas he had conceived from this short campaign. His persistence in modifying the system of war shows how much importance he attached to these innovations that he applied, afterwards, when he was appointed to the Governor-generalship of Algeria :—

The expedition to the Tafna lasted from the 12th of June, 1836, to the 19th of July; but if we fall into inaction we shall draw but little advantage from the success already obtained. The system of active columns must be persevered in; scouring the country and fighting the enemy whenever he appears; leaving him no security nor rest; no safe place for the women, children, and cattle. But for that is required, in the province of Oran, an effective strength of fifteen thousand men at least. And more. these troops must be composed of picked men and vigorous volunteers if possible; the officers must be young men, with a future; no old superior officers near their retirement: no old disgusted captains.

The system of transport hitherto in use, being the hiring of camels and mules from the tribes under our hand, must be given up. Besides being expensive, it has the inconvenience of delaying the march and rendering secresy impossible in operating; the convoy occupies a very large space, and nothing is so difficult as keeping order. At the least danger they throw down their loads and fly: and then the loss is irreparable. If this is the means of carrying the sick and wounded, they are often ill-treated and abandoned by the Arab drivers; lastly, a large number of troops must be sacrificed to baggage guard, and the column thus weakened.

There ought to be eighty to a hundred mules per thousand soldiers, with military organization, and driven by a sufficient number of soldiers of the train; and they being armed would only require a very small number of men to assist them to protect the convoy. The general would no longer be paralyzed by his provisions; could change his route, and on occasion pursue the enemy. Thus, carts must be given up and artillery on wheels, for which roads have to be made.

The expeditionary columns ought not to be less than six thousand men strong, of whom twelve hundred should be cavalry. The fortified posts should not be too much multiplied, as they diminish the disposable force of men, are expensive and difficult to revictual, and give chances of surprise in which the Arabs excel.

This is the language of congratulation from the Duke of Orleans to General Bugeaud on his victory:

H.R.H. THE DUKE OF ORLEANS TO GENERAL BUGEAUD.

The Tuileries, 3rd August, 1836.

I have been too much delighted, my dear General, at the brilliant success you have just gained, not to hasten to add my congratulations to the evidences you receive of the King's approval and the general satisfaction. To the joy that I shall always experience at the victories of the French arms is added, in this instance, the remembrance I have brought back of the province of Oran, having traversed it with a portion of the troops under your command. I know most of the military men whose names appear with praise in your report, and request you, my dear General, to be my interpreter to them. Be kind enough to tell them that I bitterly regret that I was not among them during this campaign, and that I shall be happy, if it is necessary, to interest myself here in procuring the grant of the reasonable requests you have made to the Minister in their favour.

Adieu, my dear General. I know we shall meet soon; and I renew the assurance of all the feeling with which I am your affectionate

FERDINAND-PHILIPPE D'ORLEANS.*

---

* The Duke of Orleans, Ferdinand-Philippe, born in 1810, died in 1842, eldest son of King Louis-Philippe, had made his first essay of arms in Belgium at the siege of Antwerp, before he learnt war on a large scale in Africa. He arrived there in 1835, just when Abdel-Kader had won a victory at the Macta, and took the command of the expedition to Mascara, which he occupied after having received a wound at the combat of the Habrah. The King, in 1837, sent him into Prussia, to Vienna, and into Italy; in 1839 he returned to Africa under Marshal Valée. As soon as he arrived he received the command of one of the divisions ordered to force the Iron

After this letter we think it will be interesting to produce a passage from a book of the Prince's own, *The Campaigns of the Army in Africa*, 1835 *to* 1839. In this remarkable work, a monument of affection that the descendants of the Duke of Orleans have raised to their father's memory, the eldest son of King Louis-Philippe shows himself to be a writer of high class, a great thinker, and a real soldier :—

The combat of the Sickack was not only the most brilliant success obtained in the open country ; it was the most legitimately won victory ; for it was the one with which chance had least to do, and the General had done the most by combinations well adapted to the qualities of his soldiers and the faults of his enemies.

The Emir had lost his regular infantry : 700 muskets, six standards, and 130 prisoners, now soiled by contact with Christians, and so more to be regretted than the 12,000 Mahometans killed under arms in the civil war.

This vigorous action had only cost the French thirty-two killed and seventy wounded. It was a great check to Abdel-Kader, but it came two years too late. The Emir's power had already roots enough to resist a passing storm. . . . . .*

The Arab army was broken up, but the people remained possessed of all that formed their power, their union, their spirit, their unseizeableness.

It would have been necessary to conquer him ; General Bugeaud had neither the means, nor the will, nor the orders. Having no further plan to execute, he endeavoured to diminish the burthen of the chain

---

Gates, and he passed this defile notwithstanding the rocks, the torrents, and the efforts of the Khalifa, Ben Salem. A short time afterwards, at the head of his troops, he penetrated into the 'Maison Carrée.' The next year, the army hailed him as its chief for the expedition directed against the old Arab province of Titery, after the heroic resistance of Mazagran. It was in this campaign that the Duke of Orleans crossed the Col of Mouzaia, defended by Abdel-Kader in person, captured Medeah and Milianah, and thus secured possession of the right bank of the central Chelif. Such were then the leisures of our princes !

* In the *Quarterly Review*, Oct. 1883, the passage is continued, 'He transported far away from the territory entire tribes whose fidelity he suspected, and beheaded the chiefs who showed signs of faintheartedness. Throughout, the Arabs obeyed a prince whose confidence in himself and in the final triumph of his cause seemed to increase with adversity.'

that bound the division of Oran to the garrison of Tlemcen, by increasing the store of provisions in the Méchouar with the corn gathered in the neighbourhood; but his troops consumed more than they could harvest without implements, and he returned to Oran on the 19th of July, scouring the province, doing damage, weakening the Arabs, but without subduing the tribes who awaited the moment when the French should pause after their victory.

General Bugeaud had gloriously discharged the commission he had received to raise the blockade of the Tafna, to revictual Tlemcen for three months, and to beat Abdel-Kader. He had even found the means to bring the modern Jugurtha to a pitched battle, by taking for the base of his combinations his enemy's self-love, cupidity, and ambition, as well as military science and art.

He made over the command of a division, inured to war and well taught, to General De l'Etang, and returned to France, having received a telegraphic summons, as the events on the frontier of Spain hastened his return.

Before he went to France, General Bugeaud was able to be present at the *fêtes* given at Oran, on the 28th and 29th of July, to celebrate the sixth anniversary of the accession of the chief of the Orleans family to the throne. Advantage was taken of this solemnity to sing a *Te Deum* in the Christian church as a thanksgiving for the preservation of the King's life on the occasion of Alibaud's attempt on the 25th of June. The *Moniteur Algérien* of the 13th August, 1836, adds: 'The various authorities having joined Generals Bugeaud and De l'Etang at the new castle, proceeded in a body to the church. Public prayers were offered up in the mosques and the synagogues at the same time. Distribution of alms in money to the poor of all nations was also made. In the afternoon there were horse-races, followed by races on foot between private soldiers equipped and armed carrying their packs. In the evening six military bands united. These various sights were beheld by an

excited crowd, in which the natives were to be noticed
expressing their joy with piercing cries.'

General Bugeaud embarked for Algiers on the
30th July, and from thence returned to France. He
left the province of Oran quiet, and the markets well
enough provided both with cattle and with commodities of all sorts. Several chiefs of the Beni
Hamer had begun to negotiate with our faithful ally
Mustapha with a view to their submission.

As to Abdel-Kader, he was near Mascara with the
remnants of his regular infantry. His authority with
the tribes had received a wonderful shock. and but for
help from Morocco, his financial position would have
been very precarious, but his energy and activity did
not at all fail him. He drew the fugitives from
Tlemcen to Nédrouma, and proceeded to manufacture
arms and clothing for his soldiers. Then, to avoid
the French attacks, he went and took up his quarters
at Takdempt, and speedily raised from its ruins this
old Roman town, lying thirty leagues from Mascara,
placing the seat of government there.

On the 2nd of August. after this short and brilliant
campaign, Maréchal-de-camp (general of brigade)
Bugeaud was promoted to lieutenant-general (general
of division). His colonel's commission went as far
back as the month of June 1814, that of general to
1831. It must be allowed that this promotion was
neither speedy nor undeserved.

However. this was not the opinion of the opposition journalists. A spiteful Republican sheet, the
Messager, having published some comments upon this
appointment, drew the following reply from the
General :—

To the Editor of the Messager.

You have said that I entered the Chamber as a colonel, and am now lieutenant-general, after having held *the most lucrative commands*. This assertion contains two errors, to employ the most polite language.

It was on 2nd April, 1831, that I was made maréchal-de-camp, after eighteen years of colonel's rank, after having commanded the advanced guard of the army of the Alps in 1815, and waged three successful combats at the head of this advanced guard. The last took place at l'Hôpital in Savoy, six days after Waterloo. With these antecedents, a man may be made maréchal-de-camp without favour. My election as deputy took place in August 1831.

You know the reason of my last promotion. Perhaps the army will not attribute it, as you do, to a complaisant vote.

The lucrative employments that I have held, according to you, remain to be noticed. During the first year I was of the legislature, I was unemployed. A brigade in Paris was given me, when the rising was imminent, and I had the honour of defending the laws and the throne. Like my comrades who were employed, I got nothing but my simple pay.

I request, and, if need be, I require you to publish my letter in your first number.

BUGEAUD,
Lieutenant-general.

Excideuil, 30th October, 1836.

CHAPTER XX.

THE TREATY OF THE TAFNA (1837).

Critical Situation in Algeria—General Damrémont Governor—Bugeaud sent to Oran April, 1837—Instructions—Competition of Powers with the Governor—Letter to Count Molé—Signature of the Treaty of the Tafna.

MARSHAL CLAUZEL'S recall had been decided on after the check to the first expedition to Constantine, that took place November 1836, a few months after General Bugeaud's short campaign in Africa.

The situation in Algeria was critical ; seven years after the capture of Algiers there had been no sensible advance since the first days. The forts were occupied, and nothing, or almost nothing, beyond. It was now necessary to concentrate all forces on one point and strike a certain blow, under the penalty of having to divert the whole of the French army and the greatest part of the budget to a simultaneous conquest at all points of the colony, a resolution difficult and dangerous in the face of the parliamentary complications of the government of July.

Marshal Clauzel's successor, General de Damrémont,* appointed Governor-general on the 12th of

---

* Charles-Marie Denys, Count de Damrémont, born at Chaumont, Haute Marne, in 1783, died before Constantine in 1837. Leaving the military school then held at Fontainebleau in 1804, his first fights were at Austerlitz, at Jena, and Friedland, then he went to fight in Dalmatia and in Germany, 1807-1809, in Spain and Portugal, 1811-1812. Recalled to the Grand Army in 1813, he was at Lutzen, where Napoleon made him colonel on the field of battle. The following year he

February, 1837, reaching Algiers only on the 3rd of April, was not a stranger to Africa. He had taken a distinguished part in Marshal de Bourmont's expedition, and was much valued by the troops. Revenge for the retreat from Constantine was necessarily the object of the French cabinet, and the principal task of the Governor-general. But to avoid dividing his forces at the moment of the attack upon Constantine, it was necessary as a preliminary to make peace in the west.

Thus it was necessary to choose a soldier who should also be a negotiator; General Bugeaud was naturally selected for this mission.

Just as General de Damrémont was arriving at Algiers, April 1837, General Bugeaud was landing at Oran, with a rather undefined authority, making him in effect independent of the Governor-general, who took it rather ill. There was written from Toulon on the 14th April, 1837 :—

The steamboat *Sphinx* anchored to-day in the roads of Lazaret. This vessel brings us intelligence from Oran to date of the 8th of April.

General Bugeaud arrived on the 5th by the *Sphinx*, having embarked at Port Vendres. The General had with him his aides-de-

---

was distinguished at Brienne, at Champ Aubert, at Vauchamp, at Etoges, at Montmirail, and at Meaux. First aide-de-camp to Marshal Marmont, he was soon afterwards appointed negotiator of the armistice that preceded the capitulation of Paris in 1814. Maréchal-de-camp in 1821, he made the campaign in Spain in 1823 with credit. In 1830, being entrusted with the command of one of the brigades of the army of operations against Algiers, he gained fresh repute at the siege of that town, and was sent for his good service to take Bôna. The rank of lieutenant-general was the recompense of his services. He then returned to France, and in 1832 was appointed to the command of the 8th military division at Marseilles. Dexterous and vigorous, he was able to save this place from the civil war that threatened it. Being selected in 1837 to be governor of the French possessions in the north of Africa, he had the direction of the second attack on Constantine. A breach had been made, Damremont went to reconnoitre it, when he was mortally wounded by a bullet. He had been created a peer of France in 1835.

camp and Colonel Combes, colonel-commandant of the 47th, in all eight persons.

As soon as he arrived M. Bugeaud had interviews with the principal Arab chiefs, especially with Ismaël, whom he knew well. On the 6th the General received the visits of the officers of the garrison; immediately afterwards the organization of the army of operations was commenced, and all is now ready for campaigning.

The active division does not exceed 12,000 men; it is made up of the 1st, 23rd, 24th, 47th, and 62nd regiments of the infantry of the line, the 2nd Chasseurs d'Afrique, the 3rd battalion d'Afrique, Spahis and Arab auxiliaries. The expeditionary corps was divided into three brigades, commanded by Generals Rulhières and Laidet and Colonel Combes.

General Brossard, commandant of the Oran division, will not go on the campaign; but he will have some troops of the line, the engineers and the artillery, under his orders at the divisional head-quarters.

It is in the general orders for the active army that the soldiers are to be in their great-coats, and only carry in their packs one pair of shoes, shirts, and the little necessaries required for the repair of their effects. The report of the evacuation of the camp at the Tafna that was already spreading has gained consistence since General Bugeaud's arrival, but it seems for the moment that the garrison will only be reduced.

All presages well, the army is in the best of spirits.

General Bugeaud was one of the youngest generals of division, but, to tell the truth, he was honoured with the King's personal confidence. Besides, he was a deputy, and in these parliamentary days, this gave him a sort of exceptional independence of senior general officers, such as the Governor-general de Damrémont. It has often been said that, at the business of the Tafna, the General had a commission to renew the war against Abdel-Kader if he could not induce him to make peace, and for the moment relieve the French Government and army from any care for the provinces of the centre and west.

Such was the secret thought and real aim of the

King's Government; and what proved it was the ratification of the Treaty of Tafna, notwithstanding the very serious objections of General de Damrémont and the French opposition in the press and Parliament. General Bugeaud, who, according to his formal instructions, was to quarter the Emir beyond the Chélif, and make him pay tribute, excused him from the tribute, and granted him on the north of the Chélif the district of Cherchell, bordering on the Mediterranean. The treaty was nevertheless ratified.

The principal blame attaching to the French Government in this matter was for leaving the two Generals de Damrémont and Bugeaud in ignorance of their respective powers. General Bugeaud, while not much relishing the Governor, his regular superior, acted with his usual loyalty in writing to him on May 25, 1837:—

'Nowhere, in my instructions, am I told that you are to sanction the peace I am to make, and that I am only to prepare the treaty, as appears from the expression in your letter of the 14th of May. If the Government has told you otherwise, if you have powers that have been kept concealed from me, the mistakes and inconveniences that have arisen are neither your fault nor mine; they arise from the Government not having established the division of power in a plain and well-defined manner. The blame must be thrown where it is due.'

As soon as General Bugeaud arrived, he launched a threatening manifesto against the tribes that showed hostility to France.* At the same time he caused Abdel-Kader to be sounded. The chief did not show himself averse to peace, but at first seemed to think

---

* The original text of this proclamation to the Arabs cannot be found.

that he would have to meet two French negotiators, General de Damrémont for the Titery, and General Bugeaud for Oran. In this uncertainty as to the powers of the newcomer, he did not hasten himself, but even got out of the way, going into the heart of the province of Algeria. Indeed, at this time, the Emir installed his own brother as Bey of Milianah, arrested eighty influential Coulouglis, and received a deputation from the town of Blidah, still French, and destined so to remain, but terrified at the neighbourhood of the powerful Emir.

The presence of Abdel-Kader in the centre of the Titery stirred up an insurrection of the Issers to the east of the Mitidjah, and obliged the Governor-general and his lieutenant, General Perregaux, to make an expedition to the Isser, and to occupy Blidah. In this campaign a combat, glorious to our arms, was fought at Boudouaou the 25th of May, 1837.

The temporary disappearance of the Emir left General Bugeaud without reply to the first propositions which he had made through the mediation of the Jew of Oran, Ben Durand, whom we shall come to again. The General was vexed, and entered upon a campaign, although desirous of making peace according to his instructions. He started from Oran at the head of 9000 men, and went to Tlemcen. He completed the re-victualling of it, then advanced upon the Tafna, reaching it upon the 23rd of May. All these marches were effected without any incident but the exchange of a few shots with the tribes, in the absence of the Emir.

The Emir rapidly returned when he heard of these incursions. The negotiations were renewed through the channel of Ben Durand. Abdel-Kader, always hesitating about Bugeaud's competence to dispose of the Titery, decided on entering upon negotiations in consequence of the unexpected conditions that he found offered.

By this treaty the Arab sultan was recognised as an independent sovereign. He obtained the cession of the whole interior of the provinces of Oran and the Titery, and even the district and port of Cherchell, giving access to the sea. Besides, a very important clause in a religious point of view was conceded to him, the relinquishment of the tribute.

The following letter commenting on the treaties gives some very interesting explanations on the particulars of these negotiations, and brings into prominence General Bugeaud's qualities:—

GENERAL BUGEAUD TO COUNT MOLÉ, MINISTER OF FOREIGN
AFFAIRS.

Camp on the Tafna, 29th May, 1837.

SIR,—I have always thought that in grave circumstances a general or statesman ought to be ready to assume a great responsibility, when he has a conviction that he is serving his country well. I have just been applying this principle, long established in my mind. I thought it my duty as a good Frenchman, as a faithful and devoted subject of the King, to negotiate with Abdel-Kader, although the limits of territory were different from those pointed out to me by the War Minister.

I said to myself that the Minister and his clerks could not judge of the shades of the question as I could, knowing the places, and facing the difficulties. I also perceived by the despatch of the War Minister of the 18th that ideas were still ruling in Paris that might have been just a year or eighteen months ago, but are at present no longer in correspondence with the circumstances.

I have given you to understand by my despatch of the 27th, sent through Spain, the small importance that I attach to limiting Abdel-Kader to only some special portion of territory; that I even consider it advantageous to give him more, because he gives us a better warrant of safety, and more commercial advantages than the uninfluential beys it was proposed to establish between the Emir and us. It was this line of ideas that determined me to exceed my instructions. For all the rest, the conditions are equal or superior to those that were approved by the War Minister.

I reserve to France Mostaganem and its territory, so as not to relinquish any point on the coast, and yet the instructions authorised me to confine myself to the marshes of the Macta.

I acquire on the coast a new important trade post at the estuary of the Rio-Salado, better than that of the Tafna. Lastly, I obtain a war indemnity in stores that will maintain ten thousand men and one thousand horses at Oran for more than a year.

There is only the one point, therefore, of boundaries on which I have exceeded the directions. I hope that the Government will not consider that this point alone ought to frustrate a treaty that will immediately give us easy and safe intercourse over the chief part of the regency; that will establish security for agriculture in the plain of Mitidjah and the zone of Oran; that will stop the effusion of our soldiers' blood; in a word, will render it possible to establish something in the shape of colonisation, tending to our firm establishment upon the soil of Africa, and close the door upon the pecuniary sacrifices that are the subject of keen discussion every year in the Chambers.

I hope that a reduction in the price of commodities will allow the troops kept in the regency to be supplied more economically than in France; and the customs, revenue, and commercial gains will from this year begin to remunerate us for the expenses we have laid out.

I expect I shall be asked if these are not delusions, and what security is there for Abdel-Kader's sincerity, or assurance that he will properly comply with the terms of the treaty, and give you commercial and agricultural security in your territory and his own.

My answer would be that the knowledge I have obtained of the Emir's religious and sincere character, as well as his power over the Arabs, gives me an earnest conviction that all the conditions will be perfectly complied with. I make myself the Emir's security, and I prove the faith I have in his word by the great responsibility I take upon my own head.

Yet I will avow that one thought alone has caused me to hesitate. I said to myself three weeks or a month must pass before this treaty can be authorised by my Government. This period of time is the most suitable for fighting against the Arabs; this will be half a campaign missed; what shall I be thought of as a soldier? Thus did I overcome these scruples. First I considered how barbarous and harrowing to the feelings it would be to burn the harvest of a people whose principal desire is to treat, and with whom I have been treating. And further I have considered that the campaign would be still more profitable in July, as that will this year be the real time of the wheat harvest : that in June I should find the barley gathered into silos, and that if the campaign begins later it may continue longer, because we keep our cavalry, our transport, and the health of our soldiers untouched until the 1st of July.

But if it was necessary to lose the whole campaign, would this still be a consideration sufficient to forbid our trying a new state of things, that in my opinion may give us all the advantages I have enumerated? If the treaty is badly carried out, and does not fulfil our hopes, could we not do next year what we intended to do this year? The Arabs will dread it, for they have a perfect comprehension of all the destructive power of a column organized like mine. They said aloud, even Abdel-Kader's envoys themselves, that they knew very well that they could not resist me, or prevent my burning their harvest : but that they would fly to the desert, where they had reserves of provisions, and come back when fatigue compelled us to return to our towns.

Perhaps I shall be asked how it is that, with such advantages, Abdel-Kader could not be restricted to the province of Oran. Notwithstanding the opinion I have already given, I did everything in human possibility to attain this object, and if Abdel-Kader had been left to himself I should have obtained some concessions. But the other chiefs and the marabouts several times cried out that they would sooner die than yield up any more. It was necessary to dispute with them a long time to gain article 4, which establishes that the Mahometans living in our territory shall not be subjects of the Emir. This point touched upon the religion to which these men are quite fanatically attached. Just as much debating was requisite to obtain the cession of some portions of territory belonging to the devoted tribes who first raised up Abdel-Kader upon the scene. Lastly, there is hardly an article that has not been keenly disputed.

I made a strong demand for Tenès and Cherchell, but Abdel-Kader explained that these two ports were surrounded by Kabyles over whom he had no religious influence, that this population was so savage and independent that if we were to go and establish ourselves there we should be, as at Bougie, always at war with them ; but he thought he could warrant the obtaining free use of these two little ports for our commerce. It was necessary to be content with these reasons, and, besides, I think them true from the information I have obtained.

I have the honour to point out to you that if we give up Tlemcen, which was onerous to us, we acquire two towns that we have never seriously occupied—Blidah and Coleah. I am firmly persuaded that it was impossible to gain more, unless we had gone through a long war full of successes, but possibly of reverses.

What do we risk by making trial of a rule founded upon the arrangement that I have just made ? Even from the first we shall have a great diminution in the current expenses, and the losses of all kinds that war implies, of men, horses, mules, clothing, equipage, ammunition, excessive price of commodities, &c., &c.

The Oran division will cost nothing for food during this year of trial, and there will be time for preparation, in every point, to recommence the war in the month of April next if we fail in our attempt.

Meanwhile, the camp of the Tafna, that troublesome post, is evacuated, and the buildings are sold for more than three hundred thousand francs, according to the goods given me in exchange.

The more I examine the considerations I have laid before you, the more am I convinced that there is wisdom in this determination. The last discussion in the Chambers on the supplementary credits for Algeria supports me most especially. My treaty satisfies all the opinions given ; and M. Thiers himself, who formerly posed as the warmest partisan of absolute conquest, but now confines himself to advocacy of a certain zone around our fortified towns, and amicable intercourse with the Arabs. Thus everything sanctions my treaty, except one passage in the War Minister's instructions. This is it :—' You are then to insist absolutely, as you have expressed your intentions, on reserving the zone you have indicated round Oran, and keeping Abdel-Kader restricted to the province of Oran. Absolutely you must require a boundary, if not the Foddah, at least the Chélif, and not leave to Abdel-Kader either Milianah or Cherchell.'

And below, ' The three essential points, that you are not to depart from, are the sovereignty of France ; the confinement of Abdel-Kader within the province of Oran, bounded at least by the Chélif, that is to say, leaving outside it Cherchell and Milianah ; and the reservation of the zone you have pointed out from the Habra to the Rio-Salado.'

That which has emboldened me to exceed these orders is, that the first idea of this limitation seems to have been derived from my correspondence with the Minister, and so these are in some ways my own ideas that I myself alter.

In three or four days I am going to leave the Tafna and return to Oran. If you approve of my plan, I request to be allowed to remain a month or two to settle the basis of our establishment in the zone reserved, and lay the foundations of one or two military colonies in it. I will send the War Minister a detailed report of everything that seems to me useful to be done. At the present time I mention the salt-works of Arzew, and its excellent harbour, near which we ought to make establishments for a traffic that may become considerable. The salt-works also might afford a good revenue. The Russians of the Black Sea and other people who import iron into Spain, and return with cargoes of salt, would prefer to come to Arzew, because the iron would find a ready market; there is salt there, it is nearer than the coast of Spain, and the anchorage safer than at Valencia, where these vessels generally go.

If you do not approve of my treaty, I still request to remain to make the campaign of July, August, and September. This is no small sacrifice for the sake of the decision that I thought it my duty to make. I really felt that in the advantage of seeing my family again there would be a compensation for the annoyances I have experienced, wrongly no doubt, at the commencement of my negotiations, and my recall would have procured it for me. But if, unhappily, there is war to be made, it would be disgraceful for me to return to France without having once more given proof that I am far from dreading it.

I am with respect, &c.,

BUGEAUD.

P.S.—I have given information to the generals and superior officers of my division as to the clauses of the treaty. They were unanimously satisfied, and declared it would not be wise to refuse such conditions. However, they were all very desirous of fighting.

The same day that General Bugeaud despatched the above letter to Paris for the Minister of Foreign Affairs, he addressed the following to the Governor-General Count de Damrémont, whom he rather suspected of having endeavoured to open negotiations with Abdel-Kader at the same time that he did so himself:—

To the Governor-General Count de Damrémont.

From the Camp on the Tafna, 29 *May,* 1837.

General,—I owe you some reparation, and will freely pay it. Abdel-Kader assures me that you have never made proposals of peace to him.

So I was deceived by Durand, who was playing a double game to obtain concessions from both contracting parties by lying to both of them.   He was labouring chiefly to make his own fortune; he is a sordid man.   I have not made use of him in these last negotiations; I have treated directly.

Accept my excuses, General.   Efface from your mind the impression that my unfounded reproaches must have left.

Receive, &c., &c.,

BUGEAUD.

The text of the Treaty of the Tafna, signed the 30th of May, 1837, was this :—

Between Lieut.-General Bugeaud, commanding the French troops in the province of Oran, and the Emir Abdel-Kader, has been agreed as follows :—

Art. 1. The Emir Abdel-Kader recognises the sovereignty of the French in Africa.

Art. 2. France reserves in the province of Oran, Mostaganem, Mazagran, and their territories, Oran, Arzew; also a territory thus bounded: on the east by the river Macta and the marsh from which it issues : on the south by a line starting from the above-mentioned marsh, passing by the southern shore of Lake Sebkha, and reaching as far as the Oued-Malah, Rio-Salado, in the direction of Sidi-Saïd, and from that river to the sea, so that all the land contained within this circumference shall be French territory.

In the province of Algeria, Algiers, the Sahel, the plain of the Mitidjah.extending on the east as far as the Oued-Khadra and beyond; on the south by the first crest of the first chain of the Little Atlas, by the Chiffa, as far as the angle of Mazagran, and thence by a straight line to the sea, enclosing Coleah and its territory, so that all the land contained within this circumference shall be French territory.

Art. 3. The Emir shall administer the province of Oran. that of the Titery, and the portion of that of Algiers that is not comprised on the west within the limits pointed out in Art. 2.   He shall not penetrate into any other portion of the Regency.

Art. 4. The Emir shall have no authority over the Mahometans that choose to dwell in the territory reserved to France, but they shall remain free to go and live on the territory administered by the Emir, as the inhabitants of the Emir's territory shall be able to come and take up their abode on the French territory.

Art. 5. The Arabs living on the French territory shall freely exercise their religion.   They shall be able to build mosques there, and follow their religious discipline in every respect under the authority of their spiritual chiefs.

Art. 6. The Emir shall give to the French army 30,000 fanègues * of wheat, 30,000 fanègues of barley, and 5000 bullocks.

The delivery of these commodities shall take place at Oran by thirds; the first to take place between the 1st and 13th of September, 1837, and the other two at intervals of two months.

Art. 7. The Emir shall purchase in France the powder, the sulphur, and the arms that he requires.

Art. 8. The Coulouglis who desire to remain at Tlemcen or elsewhere shall freely hold their properties there, and be treated like the Hadars; those who desire to retire into French territory may freely sell or let their properties.

Art. 9. France cedes to the Emir Rachgoun, Tlemcen, the Mechouar, and the cannon that were formerly in that citadel. The Emir undertakes to provide carriage to Oran for all the effects, as well as the warlike stores and provisions of the garrison of Tlemcen.

Art. 10. Trade shall be free between the Arabs and the French, and they may establish themselves upon either territory.

Art. 11. The French shall be respected among the Arabs as the Arabs among the French. The farms and properties that French subjects have acquired, or shall acquire, in the Arab territory shall be secured to them. They shall have free enjoyment, and the Emir engages to recompense them for any damages the Arabs may inflict upon them.

Art. 12. The criminals of both territories shall be reciprocally given up.

Art. 13. The Emir engages not to give any spot upon the coast to any power without the authorisation of France.

Art. 14. The trade of the Regency can only be carried on through the ports occupied by France.

Art 15. France shall be able to keep agents with the Emir and in the towns under his administration, to serve as intermediaries with him for the French subjects in trade disputes, or any others that they may have with the Arabs. The Emir shall enjoy the same power in the French towns and ports.

---

* The fanegue is a Spanish measure of capacity for dry substances, nearly equivalent to sixty litres (a bushel and three-quarters).

CHAPTER XXI.

ABDEL-KADER.

The General's Interview with Abdel-Kader—Description of Abdel-Kader—The Emir's Letter to the Governor-general—Cessation of Hostilities—Pacification.

GENERAL BUGEAUD was very desirous to be acquainted with the Marabout warrior, the chief who had held the French armies in check for seven years. As soon as the signature of Abdel-Kader had been placed upon the instrument of the Treaty, the General caused proposals for an interview in a spot selected between the two camps to be made to the Emir. The Arab accepted them, and the account of this memorable interview is given in a confidential letter addressed by General Bugeaud to Count Molé, the Minister of Foreign Affairs :—

To COUNT MOLE, MINISTER OF FOREIGN AFFAIRS.

From the camp of the Tafna, 2nd of June, 1837.

Since I forwarded to you through Spain the treaty that I believed I had concluded with Abdel-Kader, and the account of the reasons that had decided me, I have met with a thousand difficulties, and several times thought that I should be obliged to send you a war bulletin instead of the original of the treaty that I had announced to you with too much precipitation in order to lose no time.

I suppose there is nothing in the world so difficult as negotiation with the Arabs. It is much easier to conquer them in action. All the articles have been discussed anew with a truly Arab tenacity: on my side I stiffened myself, and did not yield on any point but the annual tribute, because that was a matter of religion : and to hold to it, was to break everything. In compensation I obtained a great tribute paid at once, and Mostaganem, that I had yielded at first. At last, after much going and coming between Abdel-Kader's camp and mine, the treaty was brought to me invested with the Emir's signature or his seal, for an Arab never signs.

I proposed to him an interview for the next day, at three leagues from my camp, and six or seven from his. He accepted it, and at nine I was on the spot with six battalions, my artillery, and cavalry. I remained there till two in the afternoon without hearing of the Emir. At last some Arab chiefs, with whom I had been in communication the previous day, came successively bringing me dilatory excuses: one said that the Emir had been ill, and only started late from his camp; another added that the Emir would probably request me to defer the interview till the next day, but that nevertheless he was approaching; a third came and said ' he is quite near, but he has stopped:' a fourth told us he was soon coming, and that I could go forward a bit; it was then five in the afternoon.

Wishing to take my troops back to camp, and make a definite end of it, I determined to go forward with my staff. I was in a gorge, broken by hills: I proceeded more than an hour without seeing anything: at last I saw the Emir's army at the end of a valley, taking post upon some hillocks so as to make a great show. At this moment the chief of the tribe of the Oulasias, Bou-Hamedy, came to meet me, and said, ' The Emir is advancing towards this hillock: come, and I will guide you to him.' I was then among the enemy's advanced posts: to retreat would have been to show timidity, and perhaps disarrange all the business, so I followed him, after telling him that I thought it unmannerly of his chief to make me wait so long. The Kabyle, thinking that I was hesitating, told me to be easy and not afraid. I told him, ' I have no fear of anything, and am used to the sight of you, but I think it unbecoming in your chief to make me wait so long and come so far.' ' He is there: you will see him directly.'

However, we still went a long way before we met him. Some apprehension was manifested among my staff: an officer of high rank called out that we were quite far enough. I answered, ' It is no time now to give advice; we must not show weakness before these barbarians.' And I went forward. At last I saw the Emir's escort advancing towards me. The appearance of it was really imposing: there were 150 or 200 chief marabouts, remarkably fine men, still more imposing from the slowness of their movement. They were riding splendid horses, and making them paw the ground and rear with great elegance and dexterity.

Abdel-Kader was some paces in advance, riding a fine black horse, which he managed with great skill. Sometimes he made

him bound with all four feet in the air, and again rear upon his two
hind feet; several Arabs of his household held the stirrups, the
skirts of his burnous, and, I think, his horse's tail. To avoid the
ceremonial slowness, and show him that I had no apprehension, I
came up to him at a gallop, and, after asking if Abdel-Kader was
there, I cavalierly offered him my hand, which he took, and pressed
it twice. He then asked me how I was. I returned the compliment, and, to shorten the time that the Arabs generally take up in
these preliminaries, I invited him to dismount, so as to talk more con-
veniently. He dismounted and sat down, without inviting me to be
seated. I sat down by him. The band, entirely composed of shrill
hautbois, began to play so as to prevent conversation; I made signs
to them to be silent, and they were quiet.

Before entering into conversation, I examined for a moment his
appearance and costume, not differing at all from those of the lowest
Arabs. He is pale, and a good deal resembles the portrait often
given of Jesus Christ. His eyes and beard are of a dark chestnut, his
brain well developed, mouth large, teeth irregular and white; his entire
appearance is that of a devotee. Except at the first address, he keeps
his eyes turned down, and never looks up: all his clothes were dirty,
coarse, and three-parts worn out; an affectation of strictness and
simplicity is perceptible.

I said to him, 'There are not many generals who would have
ventured to make the treaty I have concluded with you, for it is
partly contrary to my King's instructions' (they do not understand
what a government is). 'It was considered that you would be sufficiently powerful without coming beyond the province of Oran: I
did not fear to further increase your power, because I am confident
that you will not use the power given you by the treaty otherwise
than to ameliorate the life of the Arab nation, and keep it in peace
and intercourse with France.'

'I thank you for your kind feelings towards me,' he answered. 'If
God wills it, I will make the happiness of the Arabs, and if the
peace is ever broken it shall not be my fault.'

'In this point I have made myself your surety to the King of
the French.'

'You run no risk by so doing; we have a religion and customs
that oblige us to keep our word; I shall keep it better than the
French; I have never broken it.'

'I count upon it, and therefore I offer you my private friendship.'

'I accept your friendship. I will keep my word; but let the
French take care they do not listen to plotters, as General Trézel
did.'

'The French do not let themselves be led by any one, and it will not be any private acts done by individuals that can break the peace; it would be the non-performance of the treaty. or a great act of hostility. As for the culpable acts of private persons, we will inform one another, and reciprocally punish them.'

'That is very well, you need only inform me, and the guilty shall be punished.'

'I recommend to you the Coulouglis, who remain at Tlemcen.'

'You may be easy, they shall be treated like faithful allies. But you have promised me to place the Douairs in the country of Hafra' (a part of the mountains between the sea and the Lake Zegba).

'Perhaps the country of Hafra will not be enough, but they shall be so placed as not to be able to break the peace.'

'That is well.' A moment's silence.

I resumed. 'Have you given orders to resume trade relations at Algiers and around all our towns?'

'No; but I will do so as soon as you have given up Tlemcen to me.'

'You know that I can only give it over when the treaty has been approved by my King.'

'What! have you not power to treat?'

'Yes, but the treaty must be approved. This is necessary to security, for if the treaty was made by me alone; another general who relieved me might undo it; when being approved by the King, my successor will be obliged to keep it.'

'If you do not give up Tlemcen, as you promise me in the treaty. I do not see the necessity of making peace; it will only be a truce.'

'That is true, it can only be a truce. But in this truce you will be the gainer, for I shall not destroy the harvests while it lasts.'

'You can destroy them, it does not matter much to us; and now that we have the peace, I will give you a written authority to destroy anything that you can. You could only destroy a small portion, and the Arabs do not want corn.'

'I believe that the Arabs do not think like you, for I see they are very anxious for peace, and some have thanked me for having spared the harvests from the Sickack until now, as I had promised Hamadis Sacal.'

Here he smiled with a scornful air, as much as to say that he cared very little for the loss of the harvests, and, changing the conversation, he asked me,

'How long is it before notice of the French King's approval can arrive?'

'It will take three weeks.'

'That is very long.'

'But what do you risk by the delay?   It is I that lose.'

At this moment his Kalifa, Bénarach, who had drawn near, interrupted, and said,

'It is too long, three weeks; it cannot be waited for more than ten or fifteen days.'

I answered, 'Are you lord of the sea?'

'Well! in this case,' answered Abdel-Kader, 'we will only re-establish trade relations when the approval has come and the peace is definitive.'

'You will do most harm to the men of your faith, for we receive everything we want by sea, and you will deprive them of trade.'

I thought I could not insist any more, and asked him if a detachment left at Tlemcen, with some stores, might come in safety to join me at Oran, where I expected to be by the 8th or 9th.   He answered me that it might go in perfect security.   Then I rose, but he remained seated; I thought I perceived an intention of leaving me standing before him; I told him that it was proper for him to rise when I rose myself, and then took him by the hand with a smile, and raised him up.   He smiled, and did not appear offended at this liberty, great in the eyes of the Arabs.*   His hand, which is pretty,

---

* At the Chamber of Deputies, in the sitting of June 8, 1838, General Bugeaud, replying to a question as to the consequences of the Treaty of the Tafna, gave this picturesque account of it, and was much applauded : 'I had made peace ; I did not choose to be contented with the signature or seal of a chief.   I wished to have it sanctioned by the Arab people, and so I demanded an interview with Abdel-Kader.   He at once consented, and we fixed the meeting-place on the banks of the Tafna, at a spot called El Zubeecka.   It is not a village, only a ravine (laughter). It was four leagues from my camp, nine from Abdel-Kader's.

'He came five leagues more than I did to the meeting-place.   I do not see that there is any reflection on the national dignity in that. (Applause from the centre.)

'It was natural for me to arrive before him.   He was very late, and I afterwards learnt why ; it was because he wished to collect as many people as possible. He marched very slowly, because detachments were reaching him from all sides.

'It was four in the afternoon when an army appeared at the end of the valley. This valley is especially tortuous and full of hillocks.   There is no long view in it. Impatient at having waited so long, and desirous of bringing my soldiers back to camp, for they had brought none of the materials required for making soup—and I care very much for my soldiers having their soup to eat (laughter)—I determined to enter the valley myself with thirty of my officers.

'All at once I found myself surrounded by Abdel-Kader's scouts : I had them before and behind, they came from everywhere. (Laughter.)   My chief of the staff M. de Maussion, said to me, "We are in danger, let us get back as quick as possible."   I answered, "No, it is too late ; on the contrary, we must show them a noble confidence, must go to them;" and I started at a gallop.'

These words, spoken sharply by the General while he snapped his fingers, brought some approving laughter from the Chamber.

seemed to me to be weak: I felt that I could have crushed it in mine.

This physical weakness gives a still greater proof among the Arabs than with us, how much moral force is superior to physical, for the less civilised people have a greater appreciation for bodily strength. We made our mutual adieus, and mounted our horses. He was re-conducted towards his army with the same ceremonial as he had come. When the Arabs, who had kept silence religiously during the whole interview, saw that we had parted, they burst out into shouts of joy that echoed majestically among the hills. At this moment a clap of thunder, that was very long drawn out, came to add to the magnificent character of the scene. My suite were quite thrilled, and all shouted at once, 'It is splendid, it is imposing, it is admirable. I shall never forget it as long as I live!' I stopped a moment on the scene of the conference: I endeavoured to count the army before me, and I think I am moderate in laying it at ten thousand horse. It was massed to a great depth upon a line of more than half-a-league, over some hillocks shaped like sugar-loaves; the horsemen were crowded from base to summit.

'Happily,' said I to the officers around me, 'the number of this multitude is no advantage in action; they are only individuals, there is no power of unity. The six battalions behind us could march through the middle of them, and soon break up this sort of order that has been established with so much difficulty, and is, no doubt, one of the reasons why the Emir was so late.' The officers thought as I did.

While the scene I have just described to you was in progress, my little army was in a state of great anxiety. They thought me very imprudent to have ventured thus to place myself in the hands of these barbarians, and were considering if it would not be well to march up to me and support me in case of accident.

In fact, I was at a distance of more than a league, and with my company of thirty-six persons, among whom were the commissary,

---

'I reached Abdel-Kader, who was himself advancing to the appointed place. We met, and I proposed to him to dismount. He did so, and sat down upon the grass; I sat by his side. I can declare to you here that it was I who always played the first in the conversation. I interrogated him, I asked him questions; he answered me in monosyllables, for the Arabs are small speakers, and have not the ⸺ench fault. (Laughter.)

'This conversation lasted about forty minutes. When I had said to Abdel-Kader all I had to say to him, I rose. Abdel-Kader remained seated. I fancied I saw in this act a certain notion of superiority, and so I made my interpreter tell him. "When a French general rises before you, you should also rise;" and while my interpreter was translating my words, I took Abdel-Kader by the hand and lifted him up; he is not very heavy.' (General laugh.)

two surgeons, two Neapolitan officers, and M. de Dinaizaine, a Danish officer,—a very honourable company, but not formidable in fight—there was no resistance possible : it was a matter of confidence.

I give you, sir, a rather theatrical account, so that you can, if you like, make a newspaper article of it. I have been a faithful historian, so you have only to give the facts to a good painter. I should suppose that several accounts of this really picturesque scene have been forwarded to the papers by some of those present.

Receive, sir, &c.,

BUGEAUD.

A few days later General Bugeaud gave his personal opinion of the treaty in a private letter:—

To M. GARDÈRE, AT PARIS.

Arzew, 15 *June*, 1837.

DEAR GARDÈRE,—I take advantage of an hour's rest, during the greatest heat, to answer your letter of the 1st of May. You judge me too much with the eyes of your great affection, and you see everything that I do or say in a good light. Unfortunately, the public does not see as you do. You confirm what I had already heard, that the press have bitterly censured my proclamation to the Arabs. I have read nothing ; I have not had time. How could I have read these wretches? Are they worth the trouble of sacrificing to them an hour of the country's time ?

You expected war bulletins, and so did I, though my proclamations invited peace or war. After many difficulties and objections, peace has won the day. When Abdel-Kader saw me on a campaign, when the tribes had the sight of my easy and imposing march from Tlemcen and the Tafna, they sent me more reasonable propositions, and after long debates I have concluded a treaty, that is at the moment submitted for the acceptance of the Government. I am sure this treaty will be condemned as much or more than my proclamations ; but wise men will approve it, and that is all I want.

In order to conclude it I had to go against the instructions I had long unsuccessfully requested from the Government, and obtained at last, when everything was spoiled by the indirect proceedings of General Damrémont. But I had especially to struggle with myself. It cost me a great deal to put an end to everything, and return the sword to the scabbard without fighting, when the zeal, confidence, and perfect devotion of my division promised me some glorious combats.

I regretted it most of all, when at our interview the Emir displayed before me 12,000 horse, and I learnt that 3000 horse and 4000 foot had come to him from the frontiers of Morocco.

I then had proof that he was preparing for a great battle; and then you would have had the bulletin you expected, though I had only 8500 men.

I sacrificed all these certainties to what seemed to me conformable to the real interests of the country. I calculated that some successful combats would not advance the question, for we were not prepared to occupy and subdue the country; that after two or three months of laborious marching, after burning a quantity of crops, throwing 1200 or 1500 men into hospital, it would be necessary to go back and make new overtures for a treaty, and be contented with a peace uncommonly like one I could make before these labours.

It is less glorious, but wiser. I know I shall not be thanked for it, and in that lies some merit of the action.

Besides, the war is not compromised if the treaty is not adopted. I hold myself ready to march to the East, being relieved of the post on the Tafna, and of all anxiety about Tlemcen, as I have provisioned it for more than a year.

Meanwhile I am studying the country reserved to us, and am preparing to compose a memoir as to what can be serviceably done there towards the foundation of anything advantageous and durable. You will observe that my peace satisfies all the opinions spoken from the Tribune by M. Thiers himself, and especially the excellent speech of M. Busson.

To you,

BUGEAUD.

Although the General had executed the orders of his Government when he signed the treaty of the Tafna, public opinion at the first moment was far from ratifying it. The press and the parliament did not spare the General either criticism or blame, and it was not till later that the policy of France was understood, and obliged to disembarrass itself from Abdel-Kader, so as to be free to repair the check met with in the first expedition to Constantine.

The *Moniteur Algérien* of the 21st of June thus announced the signature of the treaty of peace in its official portion :—

'The Governor-general hastens to inform the inhabitants of the French possessions in the north of Africa, that his majesty the King of the French, on the 15th of this month, gave his approval to the treaty concluded by General Bugeaud with Abdel-Kader.'

There is a very interesting letter written by M. Léon Roches* in 1837, from Abdel-Kader's camp, then our ally. It gives the best description of our irreconcilable enemy, and the organization of his forces that we are acquainted with. It exhibits this chief of savage peoples, fanatic and ignorant :—

Camp of Sour el-Ghozlan, near the Ouennogha, entrance of Kabylie, 19 December, 1837.

You have, no doubt, stared at a lithograph in all the print-shops, representing a mulatto with a cruel face and bloodthirsty look, covered with rich garments and splendid arms, and read below Abdel-Kader; and from this you and I, and all France, have taken our ideas of the appearance of this Arab chief. Imagine my surprise, therefore, from the portrait I am going to draw you of the Emir, to whom I have been presented, and whom I have seen every day for a month.

His complexion is fair, of a dull white; his forehead large and high: narrow black eyebrows, much arched, over two large blue eyes fringed with black lashes, and full of the moisture that gives the eye so much brilliancy and softness.

His nose is well made and slightly aquiline, his lips thin but

---

* M. Léon Roches, an adventurous spirit, full of courage and bravery, who afterwards, as chief interpreter of the army in Africa, became one of the most valued instruments and most devoted friends of Marshal Bugeaud, was twenty-five when, through some romantic adventures, he became attached to Abdel-Kader in 1837. A remarkable intimacy founded on mutual esteem sprung up between the Emir and the young Frenchman. We shall see afterwards how useful the relations of M. Roches with Abdel-Kader were to France.

not pinched, his beard black, full, without being thick, short, and ending in a point, his face oval.

A little tattoo mark between the two eyebrows blemishes the fairness of his forehead, his hands are small and thin, and remarkably white, one of them is almost always resting on his foot, which is not the least inferior to it in its proportions or whiteness; his stature is not above five feet and some lines, but he is strongly built.

Some turns of a small cord of camel's hair fixing a haik of fine white wool upon his head, a cotton shirt, a tunic of the same stuff, a white burnous and a brown burnous, this is all his dress.

He always holds a little black rosary in his right hand, and is rapidly telling over the beads; when he listens, his mouth is always pronouncing the words of prayers applicable to the occasion.

If an artist wanted to paint one of the monks of the middle ages, who were animated by sublime ideas of religion, and by the courage that often made them take up arms for the defence of that religion, he could not find a better model.

There is as much ignorance about his mental qualities as about his physical.

He is educated; he is merciful, though Mahometan policy sometimes compels him to have recourse to bloody executions; he has stirred up the Arabs in the name of religion, that powerful motive that shakes empires; he wishes to bring the Mahometans back to Mahomet's institutions, his government to the form of the old government of the Kalifs, the conquerors of Africa. His code and his charter is the Koran.

For three years Abdel-Kader had been waging an unequal war with France. The last campaign, when General Bugeaud had pursued and beaten him with unwearied activity, had brought him to extremity: his treasure was exhausted, his regular army decimated and demoralised, his dominion considerably restricted, a large number of the tribes had revolted. The kabla (south), and all the cherg (east), refused his rule. His only supporters were the tribes of the province of Oran, and even some of them were hesitating; no taxes found their way to his coffers, his position was becoming more critical from day to day. He felt this, and did everything to secure the peace that the French government were driven to make by the force of circumstances; the treaty of the Tafna is signed, and Abdel-Kader looks forward to a brilliant future.

We French, enlightened and civilised, get no advantage from this treaty; we trust to the good faith of the Arabs; and we shut ourselves up in the greatest security within the boundaries, that we do not even seek to know.

He, the ignorant and barbarous Arab, does not lose a moment, and only looks upon this peace as a truce, during which he ought to make better preparations for war.

He is very careful not to make the Arabs acquainted with the tenor of the treaty ; he only lets them learn what may be of service to him in the execution of his plans.

He has divided the country, of which we have granted him the sovereignty into eight provinces : he has chosen in each province, among his nobles, the most intelligent and ambitious man, appointed him chief of this province, and given him the title of Khalifa, lieutenant.

He has divided each Khalifate into three, four, or five agalics, each agalic is composed of a number of tribes, varying according to their importance.   Each tribe is commanded by a Kaid.

The taxes are received by both the Agas and Kaids, to be poured into the Khalifa's chests.   Every six months he lays before the Emir an account of his receipts and payments.   The surplus is paid over to the treasury to provide for the pay of the regular army, and the state expenses.

Abdel-Kader assumes the following titles. Emir El-Moum_inin, Nadhyr Bit El-Mel, El-Moudjehed, Fi Sebil illa, Khalifa Moulai, Abdel Rahman, Sultan El-Gharb : Prince of the believers, Inspector of the State treasure, Warrior in the way of the Lord, Khalifa of Moulai, Abdel Rahman, Emperor of the West.

Do you want an idea of his policy ? Listen. He increases his treasure with the arrears of taxes that he has paid up by the tribes that remained under him. He recruits his army of foot and horse ; he calls all his auxiliaries friends : and goes with them to punish the tribes of the kabla (south). His first success decides in his favour all that are wavering : and makes all that have revolted submit through fear. Some he generously pardons : others are punished with death ; some receive gifts ; others are drawn by the attractions of ambition. The further he goes the more formidable become his forces : six months have hardly elapsed since the treaty of the Tafna ; and here his dominion is recognised from the frontiers of Morocco to the frontiers of the province of Constantine.

But where is he going eastwards with his 12,000 auxiliary horse, his 3000 foot, and 400 Khielas, regular horse, and his artillery ?

He is going, first, to establish a Khalifa in the provinces of Hamza and Sabaou : who is to unite under his rule the Kabyles and Arabs who inhabit the whole country extending from the first southern chain of the Mitidja, as far as the province of Medjana. Because, although the French did not intend to abandon this great extent of country to him, they did not reserve it to themselves by any clause: and that which belongs to no one, belongs *primo occupanti.* Now the Emir chooses to be the first occupant.

He goes, secondly, to support, by his approach, the Khalifa who has just been appointed by him in the province of Medjana; because in the treaty there was no more mention of the province of Constantine; and if the French have seized the town, they are not for that masters of the whole province.

Besides, there is a report among the Arabs that the French will soon do with Constantine as they have done with Tlemcen; that they only took it to give it over to the Emir who is for the future to reign alone all over Africa. The French still keep the coast for a time: but as soon as Abdel-Kader has confirmed his power and replenished his coffers, he will buy Algiers, and the Christians return home.

What do you think of this policy? For there is no need to tell you that all these reports are spread by the Emir's orders.

I confess to you that I am dejected; all my illusions are vanishing one by one. Instead of an open peace during which I hoped to work with an ignorant but sincere chief at the civilisation of the Arabs, I see an armistice that will be injurious to my country.

If ever, in the future of time, France again should have to make a treaty with an Arab chief, may she well remember that the Arabs are still the Numidians who fought the Romans two thousand years ago: that their enmity is still further augmented by all the hatred that difference of religion stirs up in them; may she carefully read the clear and laconic treaties that the Romans made, when they gave peace to a barbarous nation; and may she distrust Punic faith grafted upon Mahometan faith.'

After the peace was signed, and the interview with General Bugeaud over, Abdel-Kader had sent the following message to General de Damrémont, through Captain Pellissier, lately appointed director of Arab affairs, in place of the Aga of the Arabs, whose functions had been suppressed. It will be noticed that there were still some doubts remaining in the Emir's mind on the validity of Plenipotentiary Bugeaud's powers, and he addressed himself to the Governor-general for the removal of his scruples.

PRAISE TO GOD ALONE.

THE EMIR OF THE FAITHFUL, SI-EL-HADJI, ABDEL-KADER TO
THE VERY ILLUSTRIOUS GOVERNOR DAMRÉMONT, CHIEF
OF THE FRENCH TROOPS AT ALGIERS.

May the favour and blessing of God, as well as his mercy be upon him who follows the path of justice.

You should not be ignorant of the peace that we have made with General Bugeaud. We should have desired the peace to be concluded through you; because you are a wise man, gentle and accustomed to the usages of the cabinets of kings; but the General at Oran having written to say that he had the King's sign manual for negotiation, as was the case, in consideration of his proximity we have prepared with him an authentic act, as you have been perfectly informed. I am therefore now on a footing of confidence, and depending on the treaty that has passed between us and the French nation. Calm yourself, therefore, on your side; expect that everything will turn to good and according to your wishes. You shall not experience damage from anything that the Arabs of the countries placed under my command can do, on this side of Bouffarik, of the Mitidjah and around.

In a short time, if it please God, I will come over to your side: I will cause disorder to cease; I will clear up all business with you as well as with others, so that nothing shall remain out of harmony with reason. If you have need of anything that is in our power, we will satisfy you and not remain in debt. It should be the same with you to us. When your letters reach us with demands for anything you want, as has been and always will be the habit of friendly princes, I also will write to you everything concerning the affairs of this world.

Written the Friday evening of the 1st of the month, Rabi-el-Tami, in the year of the Hegira, 1253, by order of our lord the Emir of the believers; he who makes religion victorious, whom may God protect and deliverance come by him! So may it be.'

Letters from Algiers, at this time, say that as soon as the knowledge of the suspension of hostilities had spread among the tribes, the plain became quite quiet. The tribes of the east alone appeared undecided as to what they have to do. The Governor-general had caused the camp of Boudouaou to be occupied, so as by this demonstration to encourage the party desirous of peace; and several chiefs had requested interviews with the officers of the direction of Arab affairs.

General Bugeaud had gone, on the 14th of June, from Oran to visit Arzew and Mostaganem. As for Abdel-Kader, he went to Medeah in his province of Titery.

The *Moniteur Algérien*, of the 12th of August, 1837, published this note in its official portion. Although the Governor-General de Damrémont had disapproved of the treaty of the Tafna, he recognised its results:—

In spite of the violent declamations of which the treaty of the Tafna may have been the subject, it does not the less remain an established fact that the peace it arranged commences to bear fruit. Indeed every day sees increasing importance in the trade relations with the interior, and quieting of our intercourse with the natives; safety of roads; respect for property and person; more numerous arrivals; this is already the first effect of the stipulations it contains. We no longer have to notice those treacherous kidnappings and bold strokes that were almost incessantly sending families into mourning, and putting difficulties in the way of business.

Notwithstanding the pacific assurances of the Count de Damrémont, minds were still far from being pacified, and the tribe of the Hadjoutes had not abandoned its habits of incursions and brigandage.

It was at the beginning of the month of October, that the Governor-General de Damrémont undertook the siege of Constantine. The city was taken on the 13th of October, but the Governor-general met with his death there. General Bugeaud was detained at Oran, as inspector of the troops placed under his command, and did not join in this expedition. His mission being ended he returned to France by the Minister's order.

In a letter to M. Louis Veuillot at Paris, dated 20th of July, General Bugeaud gives the reason why he did not share in the expedition to Constantine:—

It only depended upon me to be entrusted with the negotiations and demonstrations at Constantine. M. Delarue came to make me the offer of it, and M. Molé told me, confidentially, that there was no one but me to develop the pacific system that I had founded in Algeria. I replied that I was flattered by the confidence shown me by the Government; and that in return I ought frankly to tell them what seemed to me to be for the interest of all. This is the exact passage in my letter.

I sincerely think that it would be better to entrust this business to the Governor-general. He is intended to remain long in Africa, and perform a great and difficult duty there. Now, to order the execution of two great operations close to him, without his participation in them, would be to lower him far too much. And there would be another danger in so doing, namely, that not having had any share in the negotiation of these treaties, he would not be equally zealous in their maintenance. Even unknown to himself he might allow himself to fall into practices and views that would be but little favourable to the system you desire to maintain. It is unhappily the tendency of the human mind . . . . .

I assure you, my dear Veuillot, that greatness is not all roses, and especially in Africa. I find it impossible to keep up my correspondence, or to write a memoir begun a month ago; I am so bothered with the thousand delays of organization. . . . . . Ah! how I long to return to Périgord. And at the end of all this to be attacked, calumniated, abused; it is too much.

Your friend,

BUGEAUD.

After the treaty of the Tafna, Bugeaud had been employed by the Minister's order, of 22nd July, 1837, as inspector of the troops placed under his command, that is to say, in the province of Oran; though the

Government had no intention of keeping him in Algeria. While Governor-general de Damrémont was making preparations for the second expedition to Constantine, Bugeaud was confined to his post at Oran.

We are able to give a letter, curious in many respects, from General Bugeaud to M. Louis Veuillot about the siege of Constantine, that cost us so much blood on the 13th of October, 1837. The General had known the great writer at Périgueux, about the year 1832. Veuillot was the editor of the *Memorial de la Dordogne*, and the relations between the soldier and the journalist soon became cordial; indeed intimate. We shall have occasion to refer to this again.

GENERAL BUGEAUD TO M. LOUIS VEUILLOT, AT PARIS.

Oran, the 1st of November.

MY DEAR VEUILLOT,—I am still here, and God knows when I shall get away from Africa. Constantine is taken; but the Governor is killed and many brave men with him; among them the brave Colonel Combes, my friend. A reverse, frightful for the little army and humiliating for France, only hung by a thread. They were come to their last day's provisions; and some very bad weather had frozen the men and destroyed a great number of horses. If the town had not been carried it would have been necessary to retire; leave all the material, and perhaps die of hunger on the road. So I had very good cause for insisting that this siege should only be undertaken in the month of May. At last the town is taken. A fine feat of arms has redeemed the honour of the French flag. God and our brave men be praised! Valour has repaired the faults of policy, and of the general combinations of the war. The ministry have in it a fine vehicle for the elections. You will allow that it would be melancholy for so many brave men to have shed their blood as an election vehicle; for it was that which caused the expedition at the present season, and then Garnier Pagès' infamous committee would have won. Do you think we should have been bound to bow the head under such an infamous yoke?

Your friend,
BUGEAUD.

General Bugeaud's expectations regarding his stay in Africa were not to be realised. He received orders to leave it, and returned to France on the 12th of December, 1837.

CHAPTER XXII.

THE BROSSARD TRIAL (1838-1839).

THERE is a painful event in General Bugeaud's life that we should have liked to omit for evident reasons. Yet this incident attracted so much notice at the time when it took place, and the great soldier's enemies made so many attempts to make use of it against him, that we feel compelled to give it considerable space in this recital.

We hasten to say that our hero personally had nothing to expect from the prosecution brought against General de Brossard; but it will be understood how painful it was to General Bugeaud, not for his own exculpation or justification, but for the explanation of the facts, to reveal certain acts of indecorum of which his colleague, General the Marquis de Brossard, was accused.

The treaty of the Tafna had given rise to some severe criticism. The concession to Abdel-Kader of sovereignty over almost the whole of the provinces of Oran and Algiers, while only reserving the ports and a sufficiently shabby zone for colonisation, was a renunciation of the fine conquest made by the Government of the Restoration in its last hours. It was reducing it to the small proportions of the barbaric settlements. within which, since the time of Charles V., the Spanish Government had always found its few colonists blockaded, without being able to draw any benefit from their possessions, though so near the metropolis.

General Bugeaud saw the defects of his work so clearly that he thought it well to justify his conduct in the letter he addressed to the President of the Council of the Ministers on the 29th of May, 1837, given above.

The treaty of the Tafna contained a secret article, by the terms of which the Emir was to make over to General Bugeaud 100,000 boudjous, about 180,000 francs (some 7200*l.*), the General having a right as plenipotentiary to what is called, in official language, 'a sealing present.' The Count de Molé, Minister of Foreign Affairs, had duly authorised the General to receive this sum. which he destined to be used upon 'the vicinal roads of his department, and to reward the officers concerned.' The French Government. however, refused to accept this clause. So General Bugeaud left the Emir his 100,000 boudjous. and in this way paid him for the goods furnished by the Arabs when Tlemcen was revictualled.

The existence of this clause, though never executed. was a cause of complaint against General Bugeaud in the prosecution brought against General de Brossard.

On the 13th of January, 1837, General de Brossard* had taken command of the province of Oran, relieving General de l'Etang, who returned to France. The very name, 'province of Oran,' was a much-exaggerated expression at the time. The French, indeed, only occupied, besides the town of Oran and its suburbs, a few spots closely blockaded by the Arabs, among them Tlemcen and the Tafna.

If General Bugeaud's powers as plenipotentiary were ill-defined as regards the Governor-general Danrémont, they were not much better, if we may believe General de Brossard, as regards himself. According to the pamphlet the latter published, headed, '*On the Morality of the Accusation brought by General Bugeaud against General de Brossard,*' before he appeared before the court-martial at Perpignan, Bugeaud's mission had been limited by the King with the description, 'commanding the active division.' 'Bugeaud,' says General de Brossard, 'has by an official falsehood usurped the command of the Oran division.' Perhaps this was a first cause of dispute between the two generals, of whom Brossard was the senior.

One of the means employed by Abdel-Kader to discourage the French before the treaty of the Tafna was to starve them. The military administration, being in considerable difficulties how to feed the troops, as too often happens, accepted the tolerably leonine offers of two Jewish brothers named Durand,

---

* Brossard (Amédée Hippolyte, Marquis de), born in 1784 at Folléay (Seine Inférieure), served in 1796 among the Vendéens, then in Condé's army. Returning to France in 1806, he was in the expedition to Portugal, then all the campaigns of the Grand Army. Chief of the staff of the first division of the expedition to Algiers in 1830; maréchal-de-camp in 1833, he was commanding the subdivision of the Drôme when he was sent to Algeria. He died in 1845.

or, according to the nomenclature in use by the Arabs, who like to refer every man to his father's name, Ben Durand,* that is, 'the son of Durand.'

The French administration contracted to receive at specified prices, highly advantageous to these Israelites, supplies of meat and grain, if they could procure such, and this not under bond. Now, the brothers Ben Durand proceeded to Algiers itself to obtain a ratification of this very exceptional contract by the Governor-general himself, General Rapatel being then a temporary governor. The Jews Ben Durand had an idea that Abdel-Kader himself might furnish them with these supplies, in this way :—

If the French were in want of bread and meat, especially for the garrison of Tlemcen, where Commandant Cavaignac was closely blockaded, Abdel-Kader wanted ammunition, powder, iron, and steel. The brothers Durand obtained a permission for this contraband of war to be delivered to the Emir. It was even forwarded to him in the French artillery waggons.

It was thus that the ingenious Israelites, being too well supported, played a double game, and made the French believe that the plan was to deliver to Abdel-Kader, in exchange for cattle and corn :—

---

* Judas-Léon Durand, called Ben Durand, appeared at Perpignan as a witness before the court-martial. The *Gazette des Tribunaux* of September 2, 1838, thus describes him :—' Forty-five years of age, of a very stuffy appearance ; a turban, an Arab dolman, large pantaloons. By the wretched material of his great sleeves, mended in several places, it was hard to divine one of the richest merchants in Africa.'

It is probable that this African Israelite, like many of his co-religionists, even in Europe, called himself by the name of the town where he was born, Oran, by the Arabs pronounced *Ouaan*. The first French that landed may have made Durand of this.

1. Munitions of war.

2. Arab prisoners, taken at the battle on the Sickack, detained at Marseilles, it being a duty imposed upon the Emir by religion to deliver them as soon as he could.

3. A sum of money agreed, for the provisioning of Tlemcen, of 41,000 francs (1750*l.*); according to General de Brossard, 36,806 (1460*l.*) only.

But, in their negotiations with Abdel-Kader, the brothers Ben Durand made no mention of the remittance of the French money ; they only demanded from the Emir cattle and corn, especially for the provisioning of Tlemcen, in return for munitions of war and the rest'tution of prisoners.

On the other hand, the bargain ostensibly made between Durand and the commissary at Oran only mentions the price, nature, and quality of the matters to be furnished ; there is no mention of prisoners, or of the Arab Emir.

Thus, Abdel-Kader supposed he had ransomed the prisoners for goods ; the French authorities thought they had bought the goods for ready-money, and freed the prisoners as a measure of policy and generosity. As for Ben Durand, he congratulated himself on appearing to render a service to both sides, and kept the French money. It is even probable that he obtained payment also from the Emir as a reward for his good offices.

When a demand for the return of some French prisoners, captured in the province of Algiers was made, and the Emir seemed disposed to assent, as soon as the treaty was signed, one of his intimates said to him publicly, 'What! you restore the French

their prisoners for nothing, when they made you pay
roundly for your men.'*

This speech was reported to the French authorities, and roused the suspicions of honest General
Bugeaud. Orderly-officer Allegro, sent by him to
Mascara, learnt the truth from the Emir, although
Abdel-Kader was very discreet. General Bugeaud
personally questioned Ben Durand. The Israelite
boldly answered, 'My business is to make money.
I have faithfully performed my contract with the
commissariat. What matter to you the profits that I
have been able to make, and the way in which I have
made them?'

Ben Durand had, in reality, alone appeared in the
bargain; he had caused the goods agreed upon to be
delivered at Tlemcen; he had been paid the price.
The return of prisoners was only an accessory measure, not inserted in the contract, and consented to by
the French authorities to facilitate the negotiations.

Ben Durand added, 'Again, though I have no

---

* Extract from the indictment laid against General de Brossard :—

'These reports having come to General Bugeaud, he desired to know the truth,
and sent his aide-de-camp, M. Rouvray, to Abdel-Kader, when the Emir answered
that he did not know what they were talking about. Then in August, 1847,
General Bugeaud sent M. Louis Allegro, lieutenant in the Spahis of Bona. He saw
that he could only get a reply from Abdel-Kader by stratagem. In his interview,
which had for its principal object to obtain the freedom of some prisoners made
from the Douairs, he first reminded the Emir in pompous terms of all that France
had done for him : after which he came to the promise made to General Bugeaud
to give up the Douairs prisoners, seeing that the General had *made him a present* of
the prisoners taken at the Sickack.

Abdel-Kader, annoyed at this expression, called out that it was no present made
him by France, as he had ransomed them by re-victualling Tlemcen.

'I know quite well that you speak the truth,' answered Allegro ; 'but that
should not prevent your restoring the Douairs prisoners.'

Though Allegro had been very careful not to allow any appearance of satisfaction
at having surprised Abdel-Kader's secret to be visible, the Emir saw he had let
slip a word he should not, and said, 'Allegro, I tell you all this, and rely upon
your discretion.'

account to give of my profits, my conscience is quite easy, as I shared them with General de Brossard. Besides, in consideration of the sum of 200,000 francs paid down, and 50,000 francs a-year secured to his family, the General has engaged to arrange with the Emir to make the French leave Algeria.'

A portion of this confession unfortunately agreed with certain information, otherwise obtained, as to the peculiar perquisites allowed to General de Brossard on the purchase of provisions.

General Bugeaud, after a very animated conversation with his colleague, De Brossard, placed him under close arrest. This being done, he informed the War Minister of the charges that had arisen against M. de Brossard, and announced his being sent to France for trial.

However, he soon repented of his severity. In a second letter he conjured the Minister not to prosecute judicially upon his former report, and to permit M. de Brossard to go and finish his career in the Portuguese service. General Bugeaud on this occasion also claimed the King's indulgence. In fact, General de Brossard's family had gone to Oran to beg the General's mercy, and he felt the influence of pity. It was too late; these grave facts had already become public, and justice must take notice of it.

GENERAL BUGEAUD TO HIS MAJESTY KING LOUIS PHILIPPE.

Oran, July, 1837.

SIRE,—General de Brossard has acted very wrongly towards your Majesty, towards the country, and towards me. I have been obliged to deprive him of his command.

He has requested me to allow him to proceed to Paris to submit himself to your august tribunal. He wishes, he tells me, to confess everything to your Majesty.

I beseech your Majesty to forgive him, as I have forgiven him in what concerns me. Misfortune, and the painful situation of his family, have betrayed him into these errors. Your Majesty will pity his wife and three children.

As to him, Sire, if I might be permitted to give any advice, I should propose to send him to Portugal, and arrange for him the means of entering into the service of that country. He has ability, he speaks English and Portuguese, he is insinuating, and he might be useful, for he has tact.

Be good enough, &c.,
Bugeaud.

General de Brossard refused to go and take service in Portugal; and although landed in Spain, where he might soon have placed himself beyond the reach of French power, he went in person to demand a trial before the 1st Court Martial of the 2nd military division, sitting at Perpignan under the presidency of the Maréchal-de-camp Thilorier, August, 1838.

A confidential letter of General Bugeaud to the War Minister, dated 6th of September, 1837. was given in the indictment. The following passage is most remarkable :—

Thus has General de Brossard unworthily compromised the dignity of France. France believed it was generously releasing its prisoners: they were sold! You will see the result. As the Emir paid for these prisoners, he thought there was no duty of reciprocity. He certainly released nineteen French prisoners to me, but he always evaded the return of the women and children.

General Bugeaud wrote this second letter to the War Minister, General Bernard :—

Oran, 21 September, 1837.

Two days ago I wished to have an explanation with General de Brossard. I had marked the passages in my record of correspondence, commending him so much to you. I read them to him in succession, and during the reading he often thanked me. When I had done I said to him, 'What would you think of a man who having been thus treated had only laboured to injure his benefactor?' 'He would be a wretch.' 'Well, General, it is you yourself that you have described.' He was struck as if by a thunderbolt.

Then I enumerated my own personal grievances, being also those of the State; and I added, 'But what are your wrongs towards me? Nothing! These are your crimes towards the King, the country, and the army.' Then I told him all I knew, and concluded thus: 'You understand that you can no longer remain here; therefore, make ready to depart by the first steamer; I will have sick leave given you.'

He denied it a moment, but he soon threw himself on my mercy, confessing a great part of the actions of which I had accused him. His wrong-doing towards me he almost entirely admitted. He confessed his proposals to Ben Durand for passing over into Abdel-Kader's service; but he said there was nothing serious in it, and the extravagance of the proposal was enough in itself to prove the impossibility of it. As to the facts about the money, he acknowledged them, but he alleged that he had not known of the bargain about the prisoners till afterwards.

After these confessions, he gave me a touching description of the situation of his family, and said with a sigh that was what had led him astray, and destroyed him.

*　　*　　*　　*　　*　　*　　*

The incident of the secret article of the treaty of the Tafna, served as an argument for General de Brossard and his counsel for his defence. General Bugeaud, who appeared as a witness in the end of August, 1838, before the court-martial at Perpignan, showed great annoyance at these suggestions. Several times in the course of the proceedings he lost the coolness so necessary to all men who feel they are without reproach. Without suspecting it he defended himself with the keenness of an accused person, adopting the position that the counsel was far from attributing to him. These various outbursts of anger are so characteristic, that we think it well to give some of them.

The counsel for the defence, Me. Boinvilliers, having asked in the sitting of 28 August,—*

'Will General Bugeaud give some information as to a sum of 180,000 francs that had been promised by the Emir?'

General Bugeaud: 'I was quite desirous of making known my correspondence relating to these 100,000 boudjous that the Emir had actually promised, and I intended for the vicinal roads of my department (commotion). The 100,000 boudjous (the boudjou is worth 1 franc 80 c.) were left to the Emir, whose letter is here :—

' " If it never was your intention to sell me my prisoners, and if you delivered them to me gratuitously, you must then have sent me money for the barley, the wheat, and the cattle I provided you with for Tlemcen, and for which I have not received a centime (23rd of September, 1837)."

' I wrote back to him—

' " If any one asks you on my account for the 100,000 boudjous that you promised me, answer him that I renounce them. This will answer for the price of the goods you have sent to Tlemcen. It may then be said that the prisoners were given you gratuitously, and you will not hesitate to return to me the women and children of the Donairs."

' Thus you see I returned the Emir his present of 100,000 boudjous ; this does not concern the trial, but it does concern my reputation.

' I had only asked for this sum for my department, and I only did so after consultation with M. Molé, Minister of Foreign Affairs. I had requested the sanction of the Government : it was refused me, and so I took this indirect way of really paying Abdel-Kader for the provisioning of Tlemcen, by renouncing the 100,000 boudjous that I had intended partly for the vicinal roads of my department, partly to give to the officers with me.'

And further on in the same sitting in reply to General de Brossard—

' I had asked for 180,000 francs for the vicinal roads of my department.'

On some commotion among the audience, the General stood up and said :

There is nothing but what is very honourable in that, gentlemen! I communicated it to M. Molé, who answered me, ‘When the time comes I will be your advocate in the Council.’ When M. de Brossard knew that I had only asked the Emir for 100,000 boudjous, he said to me, ‘Have you forgotten the officers who have served with you?’ I answered him, ‘I shall have 100,000 francs for the vicinal roads of my department ; the 80,000 francs remaining will be divided by me among the officers and soldiers who have behaved best. I have put your name in the list for a share of 10,000 francs.’ He answered, ‘What is 10,000 francs? That would not set my affairs straight, and I should be thought to be paid with those 10,000 francs. I will not have it.’

Thus on the question of these 100,000 boudjous, such a mark of disapproval as was manifested by a simple movement among the audience found General Bugeaud remarkably irritable.

It is certain that General Bugeaud had gone back to recollections and examples in the wars of the First Empire. At that time the military chest of the extra-ordinary territory, augmented by the tribute from the enemy imposed by Napoleon I., was continually open to make benevolences, both in favour of officers and of works of public utility. But Bugeaud was not Napoleon, and times had changed. The system of order, and control of the Government of July, in the military and financial point of view, was no longer that of the Consulate and the Empire.

At the last hearing (that of the 30th of August, 1838) General Bugeaud's replies were very sharp. He requested to speak at the beginning.

‘I demand a correction in a personal matter. The reporter, in taking down Ben Durand's deposition, made him say that, when I

heard of De Brossard's wish to go over to Abdel-Kader, I said, " The
dastard." * I expressed my indignation strongly enough, but I did
not use the word dastard.'

Reporter Robert: ' Durand said that when General Bugeaud
learnt the fact he cried out, " The scoundrel." I put " dastard." '

The President: ' So you said " scoundrel." '

Thus General Bugeaud does not deny having
really applied the term ' scoundrel ' to a French
general, but he protested when he was stated to have
called him ' dastard.' This is entirely a military
distinction.

Then came the defence by General de Brossard's
counsel, Me. Boinvilliers.† Every one knows the
latitude of speech permitted to advocates, especially in
criminal cases, with the object of saving the accused.
These liberties of speech were not to General
Bugeaud's taste, when he thought himself ever so
little attacked.

' Four days afterwards,' said Me. Boinvilliers, in the course of his
argument, ' appeared General Bugeaud's denunciation.'

M. Bugeaud, rising: ' Mr. President, I cannot allow such an
expression; it concerns my honour!'

The President: ' Do not interrupt.'

M. Bugeaud: ' I cannot suffer any outrage upon it! A chief who
makes a report does not make a denunciation.'

The President: ' You have not the right of speech. I am
obliged to keep order in the hearing. The defender must not be
interrupted.'

M. Bugeaud: ' The defendant must not outrage my honour; he
must not call me an informer.' (Disturbance among the spectators;
cries of ' Order, order.')

The President: ' General, you must not interrupt; you were not
interrupted.'

---

* ' Lâche,' afterwards ' Gredin.'

† Afterwards Deputy at the National Assembly of 1849, then President of
Section in the Council of State, and lastly, Senator of the Empire.

M. Bugeaud : 'If the court will not make me respected, there is nothing left to me but to make myself respected.' (More disturbance, fresh cries of 'Order.') 'I cannot admit the word informer.'

The President : 'General, you shall have the right of speech on personal matters after the defence.'

M. Bugeaud : 'It would be too harsh a regulation if a chief could never be severe, could never make a report, and, if it were allowable to throw the name of informer in his face.'

The President : 'General, I repeat you shall have full scope for a reply on personal matters.'

M. Bugeaud : 'I am silent.'

On another occasion, Bugeaud, having again interfered with the course of the defence, Me. Boinvilliers said, 'I shall not reply any more to the interruptions for which the witness's excitement is the only excuse.'

M. Bugeaud : 'I am not the least excited.'

Me. Boinvilliers : 'Then you are inexcusable for continually interrupting the defence.'

During all the speeches of counsel, Bugeaud had notes taken by Colonel Marey, sitting next him. When Me. Boinvilliers had done speaking, General Bugeaud advanced to the bar, and placed himself opposite the seat of the defence, saying that he did so in order to be heard by as many persons as possible.

'Then,' he said, 'the positions are changed. It is I the witness, who am the subject of a violent attack by the counsel for the defence; attacked in my honour, in the same honour that he has so well defended for General de Brossard. I shall demand from the Government a serious and exhaustive court of inquiry on all the matters that took place at Oran. I shall myself demand to be brought before a court-martial, and I shall choose Me. Boinvilliers to defend me, for I admire his fine abilities.'

Then he again recited the facts. The counsel for the defence, Boinvilliers and la Fabrègue, objected to reopening the discussion, but General Bugeaud would not stop for such a trifle. The advocates objected again.

Bugeaud: 'But it is generosity in the defence, when it has over-stepped all recognised limits (murmurs from the audience), when it has exceeded all these limits,' resumed the General, raising his voice, 'to allow a deputy, a general, the father of a family—for I, too, have a wife and children—to come and invoke all those feelings that you for the defence have invoked for another person. You wish to drive me off into newspaper controversy, and you do not wish me to reply before this audience who have heard the attack.'

Then General Bugeaud pertinaciously returned to the discussion of those incidents with which his name was mixed up. As he spoke, he fascinated the defender with his look. The President seeing it, requested him to address himself to the Court.

M. Bugeaud.—'I have turned towards the defender! I have my eyes upon him : and therefore I am addressing him.'
The President.—' General, you must not.'
M. Bugeaud, excitedly, slapping his thigh violently.—'Then I cannot explain.'
The President.—' Give your explanation, General, but to the Court.'

Bugeaud continued to pursue the subject. For the third time he came to the 100,000 boudjous, and said in the 80,000 francs intended for the officers, there were presents for all, there was one for General de Brossard, there was one for Ben Durand.

Me. Boinvilliers.—'No doubt the General does not understand in what a false position he has at this moment placed himself, as regards the pleadings.'
M. Bugeaud.—' What, then, can I not speak ?'
Me. Boinvilliers.—' You put yourself in the most false position possible, by continuing this discussion.'
M. Bugeaud.—' I have just done, I have only one fact more.
The President.—' I request you to be brief.'

M. Bugeaud.—'I tell you that I should have done long ago if you had not interrupted me.'

There were murmurs and exclamations among the audience. After this disturbance, having several times protested against it, General Bugeaud cried out, 'I should have a good deal more to say, but you stop my mouth.'

The court-martial dismissed the accusation against General de Brossard on all counts, except that of having been engaged in business incompatible with his position as commandant of Oran. General de Brossard was in consequence condemned to six months' imprisonment, and a fine of 800 francs (32*l.*): he was besides declared incapable of undertaking public duties.

General de Brossard entered an appeal. Of the six grounds for quashing the conviction brought forward by the defence, the witness Bugeaud alone had furnished three by his excitement at the examination.

The result of this trial of General de Brossard was different. The judgment of the first court-martial having been quashed for error of form, the second court-martial also sitting at Perpignan under the presidency of Maréchal-de-camp Pailhan, gave a verdict of acquittal, after seven consecutive sittings, commencing on June 21st, 1839. General Bugeaud this time abstained from appearing as a witness.

The *Moniteur* of the 4th of July, 1839, mentions that General de Brossard, who had long been wanted at the suit of some of his creditors, was immediately transferred from the citadel to the house of detention for debt.

We must add that General Bugeaud having thought himself insulted by Me. Boinvilliers, the counsel for General de Brossard's defence, during the hearing, wrote him the following letter :—

GENERAL BUGEAUD TO M. L'AVOCAT BOINVILLIERS.*

SIR,—You have exceeded the bounds of a legitimate defence as affecting me. You were not contented with rebutting the accusations made against your client; you made personal attacks upon me unjustly, and so as to wound. If you had no intention of insulting me, I hope you will not refuse to give me a declaration to that effect, which you will understand I need.

I have the honour, &c.,

Lieutenant-General BUGEAUD.

Me. Boinvilliers replied :—

GENERAL,—I am sure I kept within the bounds of my right, and even within the strict observance of conventionalities as regards you; what I said was nothing but the accurate repetition of facts that you yourself had publicly declared, or documents that you had written: it would be my duty, and I should perform it with regret, to say the same things in the same way if the occasion again occurred.

As to any intention of insulting you personally, it would have been contrary to my duty, it was foreign to my mind.

Receive, &c.,

BOINVILLIERS.

Being attacked by the Ministerial papers, General Bugeaud, as usual, bore very impatiently what he called the injustice of the Government towards him. The angry letter he wrote from Excideuil to his friend Gardère displays these feelings :—

GENERAL BUGEAUD TO M. GARDÉRE AT PARIS.

Excideuil, 20 *September*, 1838.

I had read the article that has so justly irritated you, and you

----

* *Moniteur*, 6th of September, 1838.

may suppose that I have been excessively angered. I have just written to M. de Bussy, and told him that I depend upon his friendship to show it to M. Molé, so that he may understand my feelings. I promise you that there is a warm description of my annoyance.

If we were not so near the opening of the Chambers, I should follow your advice, at least partially, for I should not choose to show my memoir to the Minister. But I have stated that I shall give an explanation before the Chambers: I must wait for that time, and apparently I shall not wait to be challenged before I speak.

What then is to be done now is to procure the insertion of a note to the publisher of the article in the *Commerce* and one or two other papers that have published the article you send me, signed by you or by Ambroise, and thus expressed :—

'Sir,—I had called General Bugeaud's attention to the unjustifiable article referring to him in the *Débats* of the 17th, and I, as well as several of his friends in Paris, requested him immediately to publish a memoir, explanatory of the proceedings at Perpignan, because the Ministerial journals seem, to a certain point, to sanction the attacks of the opposition press. The General replied that he knew very well how to appreciate the conduct of the Ministerial journals in this matter, as well as the efforts that those of the opposition will make to cause him to break silence, but that he had expressed his intention of giving an explanation before the Chambers, and had determined to say nothing before that time.

'I think it my duty, sir, as the General's friend, to make this resolution known, so that the public may not put a bad interpretation upon the General's silence.'

I have had a report from Marseilles of a very flattering expression of M. Thiers about me. He was describing my services, and when he came to Blaye, said that 'millions were at the gate, and plots besieging the citadel. General Bugeaud accepted the command, and we were secure. It is a shame to abandon a man who has done so much service, and can do so much more.'

I am every day receiving equally flattering letters from Africa, and it is only in the Ministerial newspapers that I am supposed to find other sentiments.

Do not lose a moment in publishing the letter if you approve it.

Yours,

BUGEAUD.

After his mission to the Tafna, General Bugeaud

did not return to France till the end of December, 1837. Indeed, we have seen that his duties as Inspector of the Infantry, under his command for the year 1837, had kept him in Africa until that date.

For the whole of the year 1838 he remained unattached. His parliamentary work, and still more his agricultural occupations at La Durantie, absorbed him till January, 1839.

European events then occupied the Cabinet of the Tuileries so much, that there were thoughts of massing troops upon the frontier. On the 22nd of January, 1839, the negotiator of the Tafna was called from his retirement, and appointed command-ant of the 4th infantry division of the corps assembling on the northern frontier. A few months afterwards, this corps being disbanded. the General again became unattached on the 25th of May of the same year.

Thus his stay at Lille was very short. We see by the following letter to M. Gardère. that the press did not cease to occupy itself with him, and that. as usual, he bore the discomforts of notoriety very impatiently.

GENERAL BUGEAUD TO M. GARDÈRE, AT PARIS.

Lille, 10 *February*, 1839.

I received your little word with great pleasure. I should be still better pleased if your business took you to Lille whilst I am condemned to remain in this frozen country, where. however. I was warmly received by the troops. Whatever the *National* has said, they have great confidence in me. This is shown in a thousand ways. from the private soldier up to the lieutenant-general. who commands the 16th military division. You will feel that this flatters me, not with an empty pride, but with the thought that

these currents of opinion will probably be one day the best element
in the services I can render to the country.

This has not prevented the Republican journal of Arras from
attacking me, and blaming me for the murder of Dulong, and the
homicides of the rue Transnonnain. A Périgord man, living at
Arras, sent it an energetic reply; and it put the letter in without
remark. The Republican journals of Belgium are also excited
about my coming to Lille, but in their attacks they allow their
respect for my military qualities to show through. These people
seem to undertake the task of making me a celebrity. I should
hardly be known but for their hatred. Like you, I felt much
annoyance when I heard of the dismissal of Persil; but it subsided
when I reflected that this ex-minister had made the mint a kind
of radical club against the Government, that as chairman of a
committee he had himself threatened the officials with dismissal if
they voted for the 221 who are the majority faithful to the principles
of the 13th of March and the 11th of October. Persil was
punished by the law of retaliation.

My annoyance also subsided when I reflected on all the mischief
that has been done, and will still be done, by this unworthy
coalition, that has divided and dissolved a good Chamber, that
has awakened all the hopes and all the furies of the Republicans
and Legitimists, so as to create a real danger. I think it would
have been better not to dissolve the Chamber, and that a coalition
Ministry should first have been tried (I do not mean a coalition
pure), that would have fairly represented the factions of centre left,
centre, and centre right. At least, there would have been the gain
of dissolving the coalition through the jealousy of the men who would
not have had a place in the combination, or who would not have
found the satisfaction of their theories in it.

However it may be, my friend, I applaud you very much for voting
for the men who will be preservers of order at home, and peace
abroad, and not for those fools who wish to throw their country
into trouble. If war came upon us to-day through the follies of
your demagogues, who are attacking Belgium in newspapers, and
speeches, and plots of all kinds, how will you carry it on, with
50,000 men in Africa, 20,000 at Paris, 8000 at Lyons, 12,000 in
la Vendée, 6000 in the South,—all points that cannot be stripped
without imprudence? Add to this, that our cavalry regiments can
hardly make up three squadrons, that our fortified places are not provisioned, &c. In a word, nothing is ready, and they wish to throw
themselves upon Europe, having given it warning to prepare: for
such is the advice given it every day by our journalists and tribunes.

The Chamber having been dissolved on the 2nd of February, 1839, the general election took place in the following month. The electors of Excideuil again selected General Bugeaud as their deputy. The coalition, composed of Thiers, Guizot, Berryer, and Garnier Pagès, left centre and theorists joined to the antidynastic opposition, having won in these elections, the Minister Molé-Barthe-Montalivet-Salvandy had to retire on the 31st of March, 1839.

This is the language in which the newly elected deputy of Excideuil relates his success to his friend Gardère. The re-election or defeat of Republican deputies alone interests him: —

GENERAL BUGEAUD TO M. GARDÈRE, AT PARIS.

Excideuil, 8 March, 1839.

You have heard of my triumph, my dear Gardère; it has been complete and incontestable. The small number of dissentients, when they voted against me said it was not against the man, but for the principles. Never was it seen so quiet. A stranger would not have suspected that there was an election at Excideuil.

The result of the elections shows plainly enough that, with but little exception. the Chamber will meet again just the same as it was before. The difficulty will not be obviated; so a Ministry will have to be tried. representing the various shades of Conservatives, as an attempt to rally them. The struggle cannot be recommenced without great danger. All the passions are roused. The Republic is audaciously lifting its head. They will talk of a rising, as if it was a hunting-party. It is time for union, if we do not wish to be overwhelmed and surrounded. A truce to the struggles of ambition and vanity; the storm groans: To the helm! To the cables! Furl the sails! No more talk of shades, for the sun is obscured by a great shade.

Around me four Republicans have been elected; one in the Dordogne, three in the Haute-Vienne.

My letter is for you and for Odiot. I have no time to write two. My house has been full for a week, and they give me plenty to do. I have sent my election address to the *Débats* and the

Presse. Have you read my little pamphlet, *A Letter from a Lieutenant, &c. ?*

All the world loves you here. I shall be at Paris about the 24th. Adieu, adieu.

Your old Friend,

BUGEAUD.

The General returned to Périgord at the end of the month of May, being relieved of his command of the division at Lille in consequence of political circumstances, that is to say, the cessation of anxieties from without. The next letter to M. Gardère that we give is particularly interesting. It gives the General's views with respect to Algeria. In fact, he had hoped that the Government would have selected him to accompany the Duke of Orleans when the Prince went to our possessions in Africa. But the General himself suggests that he had given umbrage to the Ministry, and General Schneider, who then held the portfolio of War Minister, was but little disposed to put forward such a man as General Bugeaud.

The Duke of Orleans, contrary to General Bugeaud's expectation, made a point of communicating with him, and condescended to give him some information about his journey. This letter and the two following ones, preserved as a great treasure in Bugeaud's family, do as much honour to the royal Prince as to his correspondent. The great warmth, intelligence, and tact with which the heir of the throne concerned himself about Algeria is remarkable in them. The touching confidence and affection that he displayed towards the old soldier of the Empire are a title to glory for both of them.

It is not without a sinking of heart that we recur

to those days, and think how much these two men have been wanted, and, especially at the present day, are wanting, to France.

GENERAL BUGEAUD TO M. GARDÈRE, AT PARIS.

Excideuil, 18th September, 1839.

I have neglected you very much, my dear Gardère; but I had desired Ambroise to give you news of me, and ask about you. On the 7th and 8th I had attacks of fever that have left me rather weak, and have made me neglect my friends. Then, business in heaps, journeys to visit relations. and to be present at agricultural meetings; this is enough to make you excuse me. I have a great deal to do in arranging all the affairs of my properties, so that an absence of eighteen months or two years may not be too troublesome, and I assure you it is not a little business.

It is quite settled that we are to go and establish ourselves at Paris in November. I have already desired Claire to hire an abode for us as arranged with the Clonard family. I would not give you this trouble knowing how busy you are. I wanted not to be far from the Chamber, nor from the Clonard family.

Here is Don Carlos gone quite to the bottom. The fact shows that the King seems to have had good reason for unwillingness to intervene. and the ministers are going to brag of their success, because they have sent a few more brigs to the coast. In reality. it is all owing to two men. Maroto and Espartero. The first had placed himself in a terrible situation by his cruelty, and the second cleverly made use of it.

You ask me what the Duke of Orleans is going to do in Africa; I absolutely know nothing. It seems there is to be an advance along the main road as far as Sétif. that Collo, Dellys, and perhaps some other points, will be occupied: and this will increase the dispersion, the difficulties as to provisions and administration, without any advantage in return. Why am I not there? I am perfectly ignorant; not a word has been said to me. A newspaper to-day asserts that the Prince is not to command that he will join the expedition as an amateur. On another side I know how jealous and ready to take offence Marshal Valée is. Perhaps that is the reason why they have not chosen to take me.

But. was not a word of explanation due to me? Have I lost credit since the King's very flattering conversation that I told you of? Have not I given fresh proofs of devotion? I confess to you that I am a little hurt at these proceedings. I have just showed it to the

Prince in a letter full of dignity and reserve, but that he will feel
very well. It will find him probably at Port-Vendres. I will tell
you what he answers if he does send me a reply.

BUGEAUD.

The Duke of Orleans, contrary to the General's
expectation, made haste to answer him. We give
this first letter, and also the two written by the
Prince on his return from Africa, which we have
alluded to above :—

H.R.H. THE DUKE OF ORLEANS TO GENERAL BUGEAUD.

Algiers, the 28th September, 1839.

I have not forgotten, my dear General, the conversation you
remind me of, and I have not changed my manner of looking at it.
Be kind enough to believe this. But I am not come here to make
war, but really only to see the army in Africa, the establishments
that have been founded now four years, and the province of Constantine, that I do not know. That is the sole object of my voyage.
And if there was to be a rupture with Abdel-Kader, no one but
myself should have informed you.

I thank you for proposing to send me your speeches. I had
read them at Perpignan, in the *Journal de Débats,* and they
interested me much. Being myself a member of a society, and one
of the founders of it, and being proud of having received medals for
some colts of my stud, decreed by secret vote, I can follow all your
excellent advice, and share in the teaching your words convey.
Excuse, my dear General, the desultoriness of this note, written in
haste, as I arrived here, where I found your letter, on returning
from Oran, and believe all the sentiments with which

I am,

Your affectionate

FERDINAND-PHILIPPE OF ORLEANS.

H.R.H. THE DUKE OF ORLEANS TO GENERAL BUGEAUD.

The Tuileries, 1st *of December,* 1839.

The last news from Africa, my dear General, of events you had
foreseen long ago, makes me desirous of a conversation with you when
you return to Paris; and when you come here you will see that I have

not forgotten the conversations that we have previously had on the subject.

Receive, my dear General, the fresh assurance of all my sentiments.

Your affectionate

FERDINAND-PHILIPPE OF ORLEANS.

H.R.H. THE DUKE OF ORLEANS TO GENERAL BUGEAUD,
AT EXCIDEUIL.

The Tuileries, 9th of December, 1839.

I received this morning, my dear General, your letter of the 5th, and I make a point of thanking you by return of post. I keenly regret not being able to converse with you, not only because all the phases of so complex a question as that of Africa cannot be examined by letter; but also because in what I have to say to you there are things that I cannot determine to put on paper. But I will try to find a way to inform you of some of them.

I have read again and again, with the greatest care, the excellent advice that your letter contains, as to the measures to be immediately taken in Africa, and the preparations for the war which is kindling at this moment. I have been long 'convinced,' as you know, of the excellence of your system of war in Africa, and the experience that I had of it in the very miniature command that I have just held in Algeria, has convinced me, though all was on a very small scale, that it is the sole means of avoiding the misfortunes inevitable to any other mode of action, and the only chance that we can have of getting satisfactory results, always with great difficulty.

Unhappily, my voice here is *vox clamantis in deserto;* and though at first, even before the receipt of your letter, I had persuaded the Council of Ministers to adopt some measures, that are very similar to those which you propose, for the operations, for the reinforcements of cavalry, for the supply of mules, and the organization of the infantry and cavalry; yet, all the tenacity that, in the public interest, I could oppose to *the ill-will of the subordinates* was not strong enough to conquer the obstacles that you know as well and better than I do.

My ardent zeal for the future of French Africa, my deep attachment to an army truly worthy of its mission, and the conviction that, like you, I am in the right of it, will make me still redouble my efforts; but to move this inert world, which opposes continual carelessness, like Archimedes, I must have a lever; and it is the want of my natural fulcrum that makes my chief difficulty. This is painful; but I am not a person to be easily discouraged, or daunted, when it is a question of the advantage of the State. I shall persevere.

Adieu, my dear General. I am much grieved to hear that you continue ill. Believe, I beg of you, in the assurance of all sentiments from

Your affectionate

FERDINAND-PHILIPPE DE ORLEANS.*

---

* This fine letter of the Duke of Orleans involuntarily induces us to make a comparison between the proceedings in 1839 and in the present day. It shows how very respectful the Princes of the royal family were to the laws and constitution of the State, and how their conduct differed from that of the little Republican despots. If a royal prince, an accomplished soldier, gives up the idea of putting the wisest and most practical ideas into execution, and bows to the decisions of the cabinet, meeting the ill-will and ignorance of the subalterns;—what are we to think when we see in our day the jaunty bearing with which our ministers and their ringleaders treat the country, and even its representatives; enforcing their will upon them, and drawing France into mad and costly adventures, safe to get the measures taken, and the accomplished facts obediently ratified by a subsequent vote!

CHAPTER XXIII.

SYSTEM OF WAR IN AFRICA (1840).

THOUGH General Bugeaud had gained the rank of lieutenant-general by his campaign on the Sickack, after his return he was far from professing much enthusiasm on the subject of Algeria.

When there was a vote upon the address, 19th January, 1837, in which a sentence referred to the recent disaster of the first expedition to Constantine, the General spoke. While he explained, in matters of colonisation, his preference for certain departments repudiated by the metropolis,* turning to Africa, he avowed that there was no mean between conquest and retreat, and that conquest required an effective military force beyond anything hitherto thought of :—

This country is described as admirable, and having a most brilliant future. Cotton, cochineal, indigo, gold-dust, ostrich-feathers (laughter), ornament the speeches of the patrons of Africa. Others will tell you, with long details, and more reason, as I think, that it would probably be better to employ your treasures, and your soldiers' arms, in cultivating your downs, making canals and roads. There must be a speedy decision; the interest of this country, per-

---

* Probably referring to his scheme of cultivating waste lands by military villages.—ED.

haps its safety, demands this, for it is no trifling matter to have 30,000 or 40,000 men engaged beyond sea; the interest of the colonists, attracted to that country by hopes, exaggerated, as I think; lastly, the interest and glory of an army that has lavished its blood for six years. It has not yet been supplied with the means necessary for conquest, or getting a decisive success.

There is no middle path. The mixed system talked of, lying in clemency, in good conduct, in justice, does not exist. It is good to use in time of peace. War cannot be made by halves. There must be peace, or war with all its consequences.

Some say they will not have a retreat; then it is necessary to arrange for victory. To obtain a good result, the expedition to Constantine must not be an isolated fact; it must be combined with a general plan: you must show yourselves strong everywhere at once to influence the Arab mind.

It is useless to try treating with the Arabs, unless we are victorious; they would laugh in our faces. The Arabs respect and honour no one but the victorious enemy. And do not go and believe that a little force of 20,000 or 30,000 men is enough for that.

A Voice.—How many?

General Bugeaud.—At least 45,000 men (prolonged movement). I was the first in 1831 to demand peace, when everyone was asking for war. I am not fond of war, but I speak of the Arabs: and with the Arabs a man must know how to wage war, and to do it quickly, if he is not to have to do it for a long time.

M. de Rancé.—It is the only way to have peace.

General Bugeaud.—Men say that the Restoration conquered Africa, and that the Government of July neither knows how to keep it, nor how to administer it. Gentlemen, the conquest was never made; it is still to make.

The General's second visit to Africa and his treaty of the Tafna gave him fresh authority in parliament. In the sitting of the 7th of June, 1838, he thanked the speakers of the current session for their courtesy, saying that he had not been so well treated the previous year. Next day he spoke at length upon the very treaty of the Tafna, 8th of June.

He said he considered the convention of the Tafna as the ministers' work, as they had given him instructions to make peace, and had ratified it. The war, as Thiers said, was badly done, because the means were generally insufficient. Flying expeditions destroyed property, but when winter came men had to be in quarters, and the pacification of the country had not advanced one step. Counting on the influence of the campaign of 1836, he thought he could offer Abdel-Kader peace, and did so by a proclamation, also threatening the Arabs with fire to their crops. This seems barbarous, but it is the only way to touch the Arabs. When ready for the campaign, a communication was received from Abdel-Kader that he accepted the ultimatum. Were the harvests to be burnt, some 3000 or 4000 soldiers doomed to perish, five or six millions to be spent, when everything was obtainable that war would give us? So peace was made and ratified, and he thought it well for the business of Africa.

I put a stop to the heavy war expenses. I gained time for making establishments. I gained time for considering the question. For public opinion has still much to learn. *You have not yet got a system.*

Territory was abandoned to Abdel-Kader, but he had got it already. Indeed, he had Coleah and the plain of the Mitidjah as well, and they were secured to France by the treaty.

If the warlike spirits within this Chamber or without wish to renew the war, nothing is easier. Come here to the tribune, and call upon the Government to renew the war. Well, gentlemen! treaties have never bound nations when they were not conformable to their interests. The Emir will supply plenty of occasions for breaking this, without our having need to violate it ourselves. He has supplied them already, if my information is correct.

Then, the war will be renewed: but it must be carried on better than you have hitherto done, or it had better be let alone.

It is not that the Arabs are unconquerable. I believe that France will conquer them when she chooses. But that will take 100,000 men, well handled. They must be in large divisions, strong enough to maintain themselves, and then the Arabs may be told, ' You shall neither plough nor sow, nor gather your harvests without my permission.' And then there must be 300,000 colonists behind them.

Another way would be to have light moveable columns to burn the harvests and retreat; that would make an end at last, but it would be a very long time first, by tiring out the Arabs.

It was on this occasion that the General gave his description of the interview with Abdel - Kader, inserted above.

Again, on the 15th of January, 1840, do we find the General justifying the treaty of the Tafna. The same day, in the debate upon the draft of an address to the King containing this sentence—

After victory we do not doubt that your Government will, in concert with the two Chambers, occupy itself in searching for definite means of securing the safety and stability of the establishments that France desires to keep in Algeria;

the General moved to strike out the words, ' after victory ;' and explained his system of war in Africa.

I should never be in doubt of victory with French soldiers, but I cannot approve of such a want of practical mind. I should be tempted to apply the speech of Francis I.'s jester, who said, ' Sire, your councillors are greater fools than I am; for they are quite convinced that you can get into Italy, but have not said how you are to get out of it.'

*   *   *   *   *   *   *

I shall not be suspected when I say that restricted occupation seems to me to be chimerical. And yet it was with that idea that the treaty of the Tafna was made. You desired to keep the little zone in the province of Algiers, and spent a great deal to do so. And now the moment war has broken out our entrenched posts are past; the Arabs have overrun the plain of the Mitidjah, and destroyed the shadow of colonisation that we had so laboriously established in it.

Gentlemen, there are only three plans to adopt: abandonment, maritime occupation, and absolute conquest.

Abandonment, official France will not have it; the writers, that is, to say, the aristocracy of the inkbottle, will not have it (laughter). The fathers of families who see their children perish in Africa may think otherwise; but they neither talk nor write; they work and are not consulted.

Maritime occupation would be good if we could have some Gibraltars on the coast that could be guarded by 1200 or 1500 men and supplied by sea. But that is impossible, you have considerable populations to feed: 35,000 souls at Algiers; 12,000 to 15,000 at Oran; 8000 at Bôna, &c. You could not suffocate these large populations between four walls; they must each have a zone for their requirements, and for the safety of these zones 25,000 or 30,000 men would be wanted.

*　　*　　*　　*　　*　　*　　*

There only remains absolute domination, and the subjugation of the country.

I think that great nations, like great men, ought to make their mistakes with greatness. Yes, in my opinion, the possession of Algiers is a mistake; but as you choose to commit it, as it is impossible for you not to commit it, you must commit it grandly, for that is the only means of getting any profit out of it. Therefore the country must be conquered, and Abdel-Kader's power destroyed. If I did not fear to weary the Chamber, I would describe my own system (Speak, speak).

In Europe we make war against interests as well as armies. When we have beaten the armies we seize the centres of population, of trade, of industry, the custom-houses, the archives, and these interests are soon forced to capitulate.

There is only one interest to seize in Africa—the agricultural interest; it is more difficult to seize there than elsewhere, for there are no villages nor farms. I have reflected long upon it, rising up and lying down; and I have not been able to discover any other way of subduing the country than seizing upon this interest. As near as possible to the desert there must be established columns powerful enough to leave the indispensably necessary guard at the quarters, at the stores and the hospital. I have made a calculation that a column of 7000 men, well led, would be enough to beat the largest possible collection of Arabs; for in tumultuous gatherings, and the Arabs are nothing but tumultuous gatherings, numbers have nothing to do with the business: they are a multitude of very brave individuals without power of union. Beyond a certain limit the number is nothing, provided the soldiers are thoroughly convinced of this truth, that their *morale* may not be affected by the sight of the multitude.

I should wish the columns to be made up to 10,000 men; so as always to have 7000 disposable, and 2000 or 3000 non-effective or as indispensable guardians of the depôt. I would establish one column at Tlemcen, one at Mascara, one at Medeah. I would give the commanders orders not to pursue the Arabs, as it is useless; but to prevent them from sowing, reaping their harvests, or pasturing their cattle. (Hear, and commotion.)

These murmurs seem to say that the Chamber finds this method too barbarous. Gentlemen, war is not made philanthropically; he who wills the end wills the means.

In fact, the Arabs cannot live without Algeria. In the desert there is no corn and but little pasture; only enough for sheep. The dates and wool of the desert are exchanged for the corn of Algeria.

The Arabs can fly from your columns into the desert; but they cannot remain there, they must capitulate.

*   *   *   *   *   *   *

You want military colonists* (murmurs), or civil if you like it: the name matters little, but they must be under military organization, for the colonists must be great warriors in such a country.

The War Minister, General Schneider, refused to enter into particulars; he even thought it dangerous, whatever the previous speaker said, to publish the Government plan. In general terms he rendered homage to the army of Africa, an imposing force, without any trenching upon the forces on home service.

General Bugeaud could not be satisfied with such generalities, and spoke again.

The extreme right and the extreme left applauded

---

* This was the first time General Bugeaud said the words, 'Military Colonization.' Though his words were received with murmurs, it will be seen afterwards that when Marshal Bugeaud had become Governor of Algeria, he never, for a moment, gave up this notion, as he thought it not only salutary and productive, but also vital to the colony. Even to the last day of his command, he persisted in urging the application of it upon the Government, with an energy and obstinacy that was the real cause of his final recall.

General Bugeaud, their declared opponent, whom they persecuted so determinately in the press and upon the tribune.

After this speech, King Louis-Philippe understood that the ministers had no system, but that General Bugeaud had one capable of accomplishing the conquest of Algeria in a few years. After this speech Lieutenant - General Bugeaud was virtually the Governor of Algeria. He was so in reality six months afterwards.

In the month of May, of the same year, the discussion on Algeria came again before the Chamber; a new minister had replaced the old, and General Schneider had given place to General Despans-Cubières. General Bugeaud asked the new cabinet if there was a plan :—

I asked the last ministry what was their system; they could not explain it : I doubt if there was one at all (laughter).

I have reason to believe that the new ministry has not got one any more. (More laughter.) When war is going on : when there are 60,000 men employed it is necessary to have a system. It is unexampled in the *fasti* of nations, for a war to be commenced with a great army and no object. Perhaps the ministry have a plan; but a good one they have not. (Laughter and murmurs.)

* * * * * * *

Gentlemen, as you are irrevocably condemned to remain in Africa, something must be done : there must be a grand invasion like those which the Franks made : like those which the Goths made; otherwise you will come to nothing. (Exclamations.)

The truth must be told without dissimulation. I had rather frighten you than deceive you. There must be a great military invasion; but before that colonists must be got together. There must be a persuasive appeal made to them : for without it you will get none. Wherever there is good water and fertile land : at Tlemcen, at Mascara, the colonists must be placed without finding out to whom the lands belong; they must be distributed with full possession.

* * * * * * *

Marshal Clauzel, a former governor - general, answered General Bugeaud, and while defending his own actions, said something in encouragement of the new notions.

The President of Council, M. Thiers, just contrary to his predecessor's speech in January, gave his general approbation to Bugeaud's system; but neither was he sparing of eulogiums on the system of General Rogniat, lately dead, which consisted in raising a continuous obstacle along the Mitidjah.

General Bugeaud reascended the tribune.

The President of the Council has said that I was a peremptory spirit (laughter). I do not reject this epithet: for it is with a peremptory spirit, when it is right, that great difficulties are conquered. (Very good.)

I was wrong. The cabinet has a system: that which is established at Constantine. It is not in opposition to mine; and I should like things left as they are in that province.

But that system is in opposition to the one I have described for the other provinces. (Marks of impatience.) Gentlemen, policy and diplomacy have been tried upon the Arabs, and have had but very poor success. The beys placed in different spots had not influence enough over the country.

When the Arab colonisation, spoken of by the President of Council, is tried at some points, I should wish military colonisation on a large scale to be tried at other spots.

Yes. Abdel-Kader must be conquered: he must be destroyed, for without that you will not come to anything. Marshal Clauzel has just told you that Abdel-Kader's character is little known. I certainly think that African is not known well enough. His capacity, his subtility, his duplicity, make him very dangerous, and so we must wage war against him with determination. But for that there must be large forces, and a great deal of perseverance. It is then certain that a peremptory spirit is needed.

In the correspondence exchanged between the General-deputy and his friend M. Gardère, we find traces of his anxious thoughts about the events passing in Algeria. It can be seen that, from this moment, the General expected to be appointed Governor-general of our colony.

La Durantie, 7 August, 1840.

My Dear Gardère,—I have to repair a long silence to you. I have been so busy, and running about so much, that you must excuse me.

I have just been visiting almost all my electoral district. I have been well received everywhere, though a small number of electors have deserted my banner for that of M. Chavoix; but as at the same time twenty-five new electors have taken up their abode at Excideuil as my supporters, I do not fear my opponent. Other electors also are inclined to get themselves transferred to Excideuil.

I have been a widower since the 29th of last month. My wife, my daughters, and my son are gone to the waters of Castera (Gers) with my two sisters.

What do you say to the pompous report of Marshal Valée and his Napoleonic proclamation?

It has succeeded in throwing dust into the eyes of the Government. They think he has done well, and that he must go on.

They are really blind not to see what the junior sub-lieutenant in the army sees very plainly, and that is, that he has done nothing. that the only result of the campaign is that two garrisons have been thrown ten leagues forward, and blockaded by the Arabs; the army diminished in strength and means of all sorts.

Has a serious victory been won? Has a single one of Abdel-Kader's battalions been destroyed? Have any prisoners been made? Have any submissions been made? Has Abdel-Kader asked for peace? Have we safety around us? Not a bit of it all.

I looked at things thus before I received letters from Africa. I have received several that confirmed my suppositions. Lastly. I have just read in the *Débats* that the tranquillity enjoyed, just round Algiers, was only temporary; that several detachments have been attacked between Bouffarik and the capital, near the model farm, &c. However, to listen to Marshal Valée. the war was almost at an end. He told his soldiers, You will have the glory of terminating a war that has lasted six years, and of giving France a vast and beautiful colony.

It would be hard to laugh more audaciously at France and the Government. And the Government is pleased, and the press does not say anything! Oh, how that teaches me what a simpleton I have been to speak the truth, and try to make my country avoid the scourge of the conquest of Africa. Official France chooses to be deceived. If you do not flatter her passions to serve her, she overwhelms you with abuse.

What do you think of the reports of war? these mountain-cleaving airs that the ministerial press is putting on? As for me I do not believe in it; it will exhale in smoke. Our situation in Africa has given courage to defy us. It will make us come to a settlement, if they will make us ever so few concessions.

However, it is possible that a war may be the result, and then we shall have to make prodigious efforts. Then we shall see if our warlike writers, our terrible disturbers, will enlist to go and deliver peoples oppressed by kings!

Ambroise and his family are well. Madame de Puissegency (his sister Phillis) alone is in bad health. She writes that the waters are doing her some good.

I am at last sending you the lion skin I had promised. Write to me and tell me what Paris thinks of the war and the ministry.

Friendship, &c.

BUGEAUD.

The following letter, also addressed to M. Gardère, was written a few days before General Bugeaud's official nomination to the government of Algeria. His military programme had caused a great sensation in the Chambers and the country. The King and the ministers could not avoid yielding to the pressure of public opinion, and giving Marshal Valée a successor.

GENERAL BUGEAUD TO M. GARDÈRE AT PARIS.

Paris, 17 October, 1840.

MY DEAR GARDÈRE.—My being sent to Africa is still a pressing question, and I really think it is settled, but not to be published yet. I have anticipated your advice; I have not stirred at all. Though I am not Achilles, they may come and fetch me from my tent.

No doubt the soldiers of Mazagran would think a little pension worth more than a monument; but such things are put up for posterity, and to multiply fine actions by preserving the remembrance of them. The pension would not have the same effect.

A thousand loves, amigo,

BUGEAUD.

CHAPTER XXIV.

POLITICAL ORATOR (1831–40).

In order to give a more complete knowledge of the man, it seems well before following Governor-general Bugeaud, the conqueror and pacificator of Algeria, into Africa, to study his character in parliamentary discussions. There, as in all the events of his life, we shall find him the same, with his somewhat cynical frankness, his originality, his quick intelligence, and the admirable good sense that has a traditional reputation. His abrupt and rather rough eloquence, the precision of his language, the vivacity of his repartees, the warmth of his patriotism, fixed the attention of all; and we do not believe that, since his time, an orator of his mould and temperament has raised his voice on the tribune in the Palais Bourbon.

General Bugeaud was first elected deputy at the elections in August, 1831. For the entire duration of the July monarchy the electors of Excideuil, Dordogne, continued to give him their confidence.

He had been raised to the rank of General of Brigade, or rather, in the style of the times, Maréchal-de-camp, on the 2nd of April of that same year. He received Lieutenant-general's epaulettes five years afterwards in consequence of the victory of the Sickack. So it was not to his votes as a ministerial deputy that he owed his rank, the reproach that was cast upon him by his adversaries of the right opposition after Blaye, and of the left opposition after the death of Dulong and the disturbances in the rue Transnonnain. Besides, this imputation was roundly denied by Bugeaud himself in a letter he addressed to the *Messager* newspaper.

Bugeaud was not a dumb deputy : quite the contrary. He was not one of those deputies, of whom there are many in the Chambers, and especially in the centres, who content themselves with voting, approving, and, on exceptional days, venturing an interruption, taking sides in committee-rooms, or on commissions, and, when wanted, making a valuable report upon any question. Bugeaud was not dumb, Bugeaud was not calm. He was quite ready to mount the tribune, and even to speak in public. He was glad to speak to his colleagues in the Chamber and to his peasants at Excideuil ; and at need he would go down into the street to harangue the hot heads of Périgord, who were preparing a charivari for him in 1832.

He was an orator. and a French orator in the fullest sense of the word, in his vivacity, his animation, and his patriotism. There are few of his speeches that do not contain original traits, exciting the sympathy, or provoking the hilarity. of his colleagues. An expression that might slip out in his hasty speech was sometimes rather vulgar, but the orator would explain it, and return to the charge to develop his thoughts, even at an interval of several years. Such was the famous 'peck of oats' for which he was so much blamed.

Bugeaud had presented himself to his electors as a partisan of the monarchy of July. But he did not intend to be a revolutionary, far from it. On the 8th of May, 1839, he explained from the tribune why he did not take his seat upon the opposition benches :—

M. Garnier Pagès has said that I announced to my constituents in a circular that I was going to sit by the side of MM. Laffitte and Dupont de l'Eure.

That is not perfectly accurate. (Hear.) I only said I should sit by the side of General Lamarque. Indeed, my place was there, and it was there that I took my place at first.

Why did I leave it? I will frankly say, because I found opinions there quite contrary to what I expected to find. It is because I found there such extraordinary opinions (laughs from the centre) as to the direction to be given to the revolution of July, and our conduct abroad, that I found it impossible to bend my reason to my promise. I loyally informed my constituents, and explained my reasons in several letters. They entirely approved, and the proof is that I am still here. (Laughter.)

How could I, a warrior, who think I know something of war, have remained in a division of the Chamber that wanted to make war upon all Europe without having organized a single battalion? (Exclamations on the left.)

Well, gentlemen, this was the effect of all your debates of that time, and was the opinion your writers published every day. They said, it is not necessary to have organized troops for making war upon Europe. They wanted immediately to go to war upon the Rhine, and announce to Europe that the revolution of July was not to go any further.

M. de Lafayette, if it be allowable to make the dead speak, said one day, We have not to engage in a war of tactics and strategy, but a war of proselyting and liberty. I think I answered him then: The war of proselyting and liberty resolves itself into battles, and to win battles there must be battalions, squadrons, and batteries, all well organized. (Applause from the centre.)

They counted much upon the sympathy of the peoples, and turned that to account. I who have experienced what the sympathy of the peoples is, in the different countries where I have fought, I had not much faith in that.

Thus General Bugeaud became resolutely ministerial, because of the consequences that the sequel to the revolution of July might have produced, by an inconsiderate declaration of war against Europe. As soon as he entered the Chamber, he declared this, though he was quite independent of the ministry and the ministers, and chosen deputy without their influence, perhaps against their wishes.

On the 13th of August, 1831, he proclaimed from the tribune his adhesion to the peace policy desired by the country.

The great subject of national anxiety at that time to Bugeaud, as well as to all sensible men, was the possibility of an armed intervention in favour of Poland, which was demanded by the left, and the short-sighted patriots.

Bugeaud showed that he had been the comrade in arms of all the Polish heroes of 1807, and yet he repulsed with all his might the folly of an armed intervention on the Vistula after 1830.

Notably on the 22nd of September, 1831, in the debate upon Poland, Bugeaud combated the favourite idea of the left, namely, their desire to attack Europe with the National Guards :—

An army cannot dispense with communications to its country. To send an army into Poland, it would be necessary to protect the communications against the confederation and against Austria; then it would be necessary to have an army upon the

Rhine as a base of operations, an army of observation upon the Pyrenees, and forces in the interior to repress the factions, and that would take not less than 800,000 men.

In fact, it is very certain that in a battle the troops not engaged, but holding an enemy's corps in check, are no less necessary than the troops that fight. Just the same in politics; a people can be protected just as well by threats of war as by actually making it. Well, that is the part we have played with regard to Poland; we have told Austria and Prussia that they shall not make war on Poland. This threat has prevented the conclusion of the struggle in a few weeks.

Three years afterwards, on the 6th of January, 1834, on the discussion of the address, he resumes the same theme:—

I was much troubled at the pertinacious attempts in the discussion on the address in 1832, to procure adoption of a sentence that I thought dangerous, it was this: 'We are assured that Polish nationality shall not perish.' A great nation should never proclaim what it can do; for if it makes an announcement that is not realised it is accused of weakness. (True, from the left.)

*   *   *   *   *   *   *

More than that. The first gun fired upon the Rhine would have been the signal for the fall of Poland; 15,000 men starting from the duchy of Posen, and 15,000 from Gallicia, would have finished Poland in a week. After that, the enemy's armies would have advanced from Poland upon the Rhine for a much greater war.

There is no use in always saying we have let Poland perish. We have done for her much more by peace than we could have by war. By keeping the peace, we have kept all Europe in check. If you had fired a single gun upon the Rhine, Europe would no longer have had to consider you, she would have crushed Poland, a week's work.

The General-deputy was very ready to speak. He even sometimes attacked subjects for which his knowledge and experience were, perhaps, insufficient, such as the supply of stamps for registration, and the monopoly of tobacco. But most of his speeches can be reduced to three favourite themes:—First, the encouragement of agriculture ; second, the maintenance of the honour and prerogatives of the army ; third, war against the rioters, republicans, opposition journalists, members of secret societies : to sum up, all the people whom he described with a picturesque appellation, ' the aristocracy of the ink-bottle.'

The analysis of all these speeches would not be a good way of making Bugeaud's parliamentary work known. It will be our duty to make quotations from these statements, so full of humour and good nature, and now so completely forgotten.*

The old Colonel of the army in Spain, having become passionately fond of farming, during his fifteen years on the unattached list, as soon as he became a deputy, claimed to be a representative of the popular type of soldier labourer. He desired that the army, in time of peace, should be employed in agricultural work.

On the 21st of April, 1832, he said, I am only a soldier labourer. Make agriculture flourish ; turn in that direction a large proportion of the financial and intellectual power of the nation ; encourage agricultural enterprise ; stir up the great and public functionaries to occupy themselves with it. Make agriculture become a profession, an opening for abilities, that for want of a

---

* The very first day he made his appearance on the tribune the Deputy Bugeaud excited the hilarity of the Chambers by a humorous sally. Having to report the election of Count du Châtel, President by age,' Deputy of Jonzac, the Deputy of Excideuil used this expression, ' I move the admission of our venerable " dean in years," though he has not produced his certificate of birth.'

Bugeaud was then so unknown in parliamentary circles that the official newspaper gave his name as M. Buffant, *Moniteur Universel*, August, 1831, page 1265.

career, are used to the injury of the country, in composing bad writings, Saint Simonism,* and a thousand other follies.

Let Algeria be colonised. That is all very well, but it would be much more interesting to colonise our great moors of Brittany and Bordeaux. A portion of the army might work at that; and villages be built there, not in form of a camp, but on a commodious plan for the pursuit of agriculture. Soldiers would occupy them, with the object of being taught the art of war, and of bringing the surrounding lands into cultivation. When this result was obtained, these villages and their dependencies would be sold or let. Thus the army could produce a portion of its cost, and make a considerable contribution to the nation's prosperity.

At every debate on the budget, on every address, he is anxious to claim advances of credit, favours, and honours for agriculture. It is in the creation of agricultural societies, that he sees the remedy for the general indifference of the political world to agriculture. On the 28th of February, 1832, he moved for a credit, enormous at the time, of two millions of francs, with the object of establishing a society in every canton. It may be said that General Bugeaud was the real creator of agricultural societies in France, by his persistent exhortations.

'Of all the means of improving agriculture,' said he, 'the most efficacious, and most speedy, is the establishment of agricultural societies; that is my " Delenda est Carthago."'

Two years later, in the sitting of the 6th of May, 1834, he thus expresses himself upon the same subject :—

There has just been a vote, and there has every year been a vote, of a considerable sum for trade, for art, for music, for the theatre; and nothing is done, absolutely nothing, for the encourage-

---

* St. Simon, born 1760, died 1825; his doctrines were advanced Socialism, touching equalisation of property, marriage, &c. A sect was formed on his principles after his death.—Ed.

ment of agriculture. It is not that we expect to be encouraged by strokes of the budget (laughter), for it would take ten budgets like ours to encourage agriculture.

We have not public spirit enough left in France, especially in the country, to establish agricultural societies, if we do not get an impulse from the Government. The 200,000 francs that I move for, will only be a trifle; we do not want great money votes, but a life-giving institution.

*　　*　　*　　*　　*　　*　　*

We ask the King himself, the Princes, and the public functionaries, to attend to agriculture, and give it the impulse that is so necessary.

I especially demand that the Minister of Commerce, for the words are more important than might be supposed, will be good enough to take the additional title of Minister of Agriculture, and head his letters 'Ministry of Commerce and Agriculture.'* (Marks of assent.)

Every member of the society is anxious to produce on his property some specimens of the cultivation that he extols and rewards. A peasant cannot go to mass, to a fair, or a market, without finding along the road some specimens of the cultivation, for which instructions and rewards are given.

The agricultural society should only embrace one canton. I am very glad to say so from this tribune, for it is very generally supposed that it would be desirable for the society to embrace an arrondissement. This extent is too large. There would not be zeal enough available if a whole arrondissement had to be inspected. The commissioners would be engaged for several days in visiting the crops, and zeal does not go so far as to sleep out. If you hold agricultural feasts in the head-quarters of departments, very few peasants will go there; if you hold them in the cantons, all the peasants will go.

Eight years after the commencement of this interesting campaign, just before his parliamentary career was closed in order to go and conquer Africa, General Bugeaud on the 5th of June, 1840, joyfully attests the progress effected, the success obtained :

Allow me to cast a glance at the agricultural societies. They

---

* This wish of Deputy Bugeaud's was accomplished; some years afterwards the Ministry of Commerce and Agriculture was created.

have been very seriously taken up. They have been so multiplied, there are, I believe, 600, that the Minister of Agriculture, I am sure he will not contradict me, finds the sum for their encouragement insufficient.

It certainly is an admirable institution ; there cannot be a better or more popular; it unites the poor with the rich : it compels the rich to draw near to the poor for the encouragement of agriculture. I do not hesitate to say that it is the most progressive of all our institutions ; and that it alone is worth more than all the political reform so noisily demanded.

Among the means of encouraging these useful establishments, one of the best is the distribution of honourable and other rewards; I should like crosses of the legion of honour for the men who have most distinguished themselves in the proceedings of societies ; and I should like some bursaries arranged for their children in our royal colleges.

General Bugeaud often spoke at the meetings of the agricultural societies at Excideuil. We will only give extracts from two speeches that he made there, on the 1st of September, 1839, in the two years interval of rest, when the conqueror of the Sickack, and negotiator of the Tafna, a second time interrupted his active military life, before resuming the sword that was to subdue Algeria.

To the members of the society the General made a speech in French, containing the following remarkable passage :—

*   *   *   *   *   *   *

To those who dream of the extension of political rights I should say : How can you expect men to value these rights, and make use of them, as long as they are in a state of wretchedness? The first need of the twenty-four millions of cultivators, and the six millions of workmen, is not electoral reform, but a better material existence, a necessary preliminary to a better moral position. There is no one, even these venerable churchmen, who have honoured our meeting with their presence, that is not interested in the progress we pursue. Their special care is the improvement of morality. Well, nothing could be a more powerful assistance to their holy mission than easy circumstances in the country.

Do not suppose, gentlemen, that I seek to gain popularity by holding this language. I have never flattered the people's passions; I have told them the truth, and run the risk of their displeasure. I have never chosen to feed them with chimerical and dangerous notions, as some do; I have served them, and will serve them again, in their real interests; in their evil passions, never!

As for the peasants, he harangued them in *patois*, placing himself within their range, both in language and ideas, with delightful kindness :—

My friends, more than ten years ago, the gentlemen of this canton, who love you and look upon you as brethren, afflicted at seeing how badly your painful toil was recompensed, united to teach you a more intelligent system of work. Yet the greatest progress hitherto obtained, is that you no longer resist our teaching in words. You no longer say, It is better to do as our fathers did. You even are ready to agree that the cultivation of forage crops and roots, as well as the lessons given about vines, are good things. Unfortunately, your actions do not answer to your words; the force of habit holds you back, and you make no progress.

At considerable distances there are to be found some small squares of trifolium, sainfoin, and lucerne, but they are not much bigger than the sheets of your beds. You are not bold enough to quit your old routine: you do not know how to come to a decision. You act as if you had a thousand years to live; and you march at a snail's pace.

My friends, life is short; you must not leave everything for your children and grandchildren to do. Whatever you do, there will remain plenty for them to do. Forward then, march! Increase the cultivation of roots, for nothing considerable can be done in the way of cattle without roots. I will not tell you to give up the cultivation of maize; it is useful, especially in the years when there is a dearth of wheat; but I would tell you to reduce it; by reducing the space it is not certain that you will reduce the quantity of the harvest, for you may treat it better. Try to mix maize with roots of all kinds. You may plant the rows of maize at ten or twelve feet apart, and grow beetroots, potatoes, and turnips in the interval.

Do not be afraid, my friends, of multiplying cattle; they are the source of all other progress. I have heard some say that if a number of them were bred, there would be no sale to be found. That is a great crime. France draws from the foreigner some fifty or sixty millions (of francs) worth of cattle, or the produce of them. Why should we leave this profit to foreigners? I can also say that the consumption of meat is daily increasing in France, as the people become a little more easy in their circumstances. You yourselves, my friends, if you follow our lessons, you will not confine youselves to eating it on carnival and holidays.

When you have made a good sale in the town of the goods you produce more than you need, you may come back with a leg of mutton, and eat it with all your little family.

Then he gives them advice about their plough, telling them it was almost as bad as that of the Bedouins in Africa. Then he speaks to the peasants of the unfortunate tendency of their sons to go into the towns. a tendency that the progress of agriculture would arrest.

* * * * * * *

General Bugeaud was ready to speak on questions of customs' duties, when they were connected with agriculture. He was a protectionist by temperament and conviction. There were many such speeches ; we give an extract from one on the 18th of April, 1840, on presenting a report to the Chamber about the enactments on sugars : it displays the General's protectionist ideas :—

It is not very becoming to the other industries to blame the beetroot sugar for the involuntary protection (the Continental system), that encouraged its growth. All of them have been born, and have only grown, under the shade of protection ; some of them are still protected by prohibition.

Without the protectionist system of the Empire, should we have the cotton trade and many others? Is not our shipping interest protected by all our customs laws, and do we not still give enormous premiums to the deep-sea fisheries? So beetroot has done nothing but profit by the principles common to all her sister industries. . . . It is certain that beetroot feeds a greater number of cattle with its pulp, as it can be kept the year round in silos. If it is true that our cattle are increased in price, it is a fresh proof of the prosperity that this industry has spread abroad, because it is clear that consumption has made a greater advance than production. . . . This is one of the fine victories of modern agriculture. It spreads work and prosperity over our country. It finds a use for the feeble arms of old men, women, and children, both in the fine season and the dead. It is a powerful means of abolishing pauperism.

Thus, General Bugeaud, in his energetic defence of the sugar industry, and his endeavour to obtain protective legislation for it, was prophetic of the future. In fact, this agricultural industry has become a source of wealth for France, and of comfort in the country.

By continual pressure, General Bugeaud had founded the agricultural societies. On the 18th of April, 1840, he proposed a central institution, a superior council of agriculture. This council was in existence under the Second Empire, and is again one of the felicitous ideas realised, thanks to him.

When it was a question of agriculture, Bugeaud did not make payment in words alone, he paid with his purse. It has been previously shown that he had presented the gratuity of 20,000 francs, given to him after his mission to Blaye, to his canton for the establishment of fountains there. We have also seen that he ran some risk of compromising himself by asking Abdel-Kader at the Tafna for 100,000 francs for the vicinal roads of La Dordogne.

In reply to some attacks, one of his friends published an account of General Bugeaud's gifts to works of public utility in La Dordogne. This account is contained in a letter dated Excideuil, the 9th of September, 1838, to the *Courrier Français* signed 'Langlade.'

A half-pay colonel for fifteen years, having no interest with the Government, General Bugeaud, by trouble and sacrifice of every kind, managed to secure some important roads for Excideuil, when it had no communications or trade. His name is to be found at the head of every subscription for the public benefit. He regularly sacrificed a portion of his income for works of public utility, though he had then no election favours to expect, nor such popularity as would serve objects of ambition.

This is a list of the sums he spent upon roads alone; and no doubt some are omitted :—

Road from Excideuil to Périgueux	. . .	1200 fr.
„ No. 6	. . . . . .	500
„ from Thenon	. . . . .	600
„ from Excideuil to Brives	. . .	600
„ from la Nouaille to Thiviers	. .	1200
„ from Excideuil to Jumilhac	. .	1200
„ from Angoulême to Aurillac	. .	3000
„ from Jumilhac	. . . .	2000
„ from Excideuil to Montignac	. .	2000
„ from Saint-Pierre de Chignac	. .	2000

A portion of these sums was liberally subscribed by M. Bugeaud when he had only his small half-pay and but little private fortune.

He devoted the 20,000 francs given him for his command at Blaye to the construction of fountains at Excideuil and La Nouaille.

With his habitual soldierly frankness, living without concealment, without calculation, and with open heart, he had not omitted to tell some intimate friends, before he started for Africa, that he hoped to obtain these 100,000 boudjous, that such a noise has been made about, and that he intended them for the roads.

General Bugeaud's laudable passion for vicinal roads and material interests was not his only object. The founder of agricultural societies also endeavoured to enlighten the peasants as to their duties and their rights by the establishment of elementary schools. Being convinced that the country gains little benefit from knowledge as long as it is poor, he taught the cultivators of the soil to enrich themselves, and gave them leisure to draw their first useful learning from the village schools.

Different from most of the governmental deputies, Bugeaud never feared a debate. He was quite ready to challenge or attack from the tribune the men who, he had a prophetic feeling, would be the destroyers of the monarchy of July—the Aragos, the Garnier-Pagès, the Lamartines. He only once was called to order during his parliamentary career, on the 20th of March, 1834, and that was for a sharp speech against Berryer, who was not sparing of him after the business of Blaye.

So the republican opposition, according to their usual tactics against those few adversaries who opposed them with a vivacity comparable to their own, accused him of assuming a tone of provocation (sitting of March 24. 1834).

They disparaged him unworthily, and one of the hard heads of the party, Armand-Marrast, described him thus: ' An undistinguished appearance, a corporal's language, and that sort of self-possession peculiar to the private soldier that puts orders in place of any feeling or any thought.'

To other than dishonest opponents, Bugeaud's characteristic as a political orator was his admirable good sense. It was thus that he opposed the right of association in the army claimed after 1830, which not unnaturally seemed to him likely to disorganize it :—

The petitioners have made a mistake in supposing that there can be any association but that of the National Guard. (Dissent on the Left.)

There ought to be no association in the army but that of duty. Men must be disposable at any hour, at any moment. An officer cannot do anything without requesting his colonel's permission. I was commanding the 56th Regiment when associations first made their appearance. The officers came and asked me if they might join an association. 'Why do you want to do it?' I asked. 'For the defence of the State, and to oppose the return of the older branch of the Bourbons.' 'Have you not got an association? Have not you taken oaths to Louis-Philippe and the charter? Why, you are at the outposts, you will be the first to fire a shot. You will be in the front of the fight, and you want to put yourselves at the tail of an association.' They all understood this reasoning, and not one joined the association.

General Demarçay, who answered him, shouted out, 'The honourable speaker's doctrine is, that when a citizen enters the military service, he should completely surrender himself, both physically and morally.' Bugeaud made no answer, for that was most certainly his opinion.

He also opposed the throwing open of the general councils* on the ground that the members, being principally men more conversant with the fields than with public speaking, would be shy, and the whole deliberation would fall into the hands of a few advocates, if spectators were present.

He was an energetic opponent of the extension of the franchise, and especially of universal suffrage, an institution that Europe may envy us, but is careful not to adopt. He was right in thinking this extension to be dangerous to the nation's peace.

Especially, on the 15th of January, 1833, he thus expressed himself:—

It is a great mistake to suppose that there is an increase of liberty by extending the franchise. Is the elector more free than the citizen who has not a vote? Certainly not; he exercises a duty and a mission; his mission accomplished, he returns into the crowd, and is ruled by the same laws as the other citizens.

---

* Of elected members for regulating the affairs of departments.

On the 6th of January, 1834, he shows that it is impossible for universal suffrage to be in any way a remedy for the people's misery.

On the 7th of February, 1835, he said on the famous question of the addition of the *capacities* :—

I admit that in 1830 and 1831 I should have voted for the addition of the capacities; but after that, the capacities showed me they knew too well what they were about. (General laughter.) They showed me that poor capacities wish to become rich capacities. These are the capacities that have created the bad newspapers, and inundated us with so many detestable principles. It is they that have brought upon us Saint Simonism, associations, and risings. These are the capacities that have organized the Society of the Rights of Man. Give me Big Jack, give me Big Peter, I like them better than capacities without fortunes. (General laugh.) It is because a man has capacity that, if he is poor, I should mistrust him. He will wish to put forward his capacity, make it come to the top, not of what it is in reality, but of what he thinks it is: he will turn the country upside down till he has attained his object.*

On the discussion of the address of 1834, in the sitting of the 6th of January, he draws an interesting comparison of the people in town and country :—

As for the misery of the people, what people is it that is meant? Certainly not the country people, who are attached to their work. They are but little susceptible to club oratory. So it is the town population that is meant! One of our honourable colleagues has justly described them by the name of 'the aristocracy of workmen.' Yes, the aristocracy of workmen, for they earn as much as three and four francs a-day, while the country people only earn twenty sous for the season round, and twenty to twenty-five in the finest months of the year. (Commotion.)

I know no other means of improving the condition of either of the peoples I have mentioned than the development of trade and in-

---

* When the deputy of Excideuil spoke these prophetic words, would it not seem as if in 1834 he was prophesying the accession of the capacities, a new social stratum, out of which came the Chambers of 1876 and others, that the republicans themselves, anticipating history, already designate by a grotesque appellation that will remain popular?

dustry. That speaker sought his remedy in universal suffrage. It is in the material improvement of the people that true liberty is to be found; it is not in the barren advantage of going to drop ballots into an urn fifty or sixty times a-year.

Whenever the riots that ensanguined the first years of Louis-Philippe's reign became directly or indirectly the object of a discussion from the tribune, General Bugeaud did not hesitate to combat the insurgent enemies of his country with his tongue, as he had done with his sword.

In the sitting of the 1st of February. 1832. on the matter of the decorations given to the army after the riots at Lyons :—

The Government is continually blamed for having given decorations to the soldiers, who have fought to make the laws respected. And why is there not equal surprise at those so profusely given to the conquerors of July?

Why, then, should not they be similarly rewarded? I will say more: the conquerors of July have been rewarded more than the winners of ten battles. No objection ought to be made to the soldiers, who have made the laws and order respected at Lyons, being rewarded.

Gentlemen, there is a saying that French bayonets only thirst for the blood of the stranger. That is true, in the sense that they only desire to fight against the enemies of France. but also they are always ready to fight the factions. (In the Centre, ' Bravo!')

They wish to make resounding speeches heard; we also will make some to be heard. Yes, we will fight the factions. (' Bravo, bravo!') We wish all Frenchmen to rally round the throne of July; and as to the factions. we shall always be ready to fight them under whatever colour they appear.*

---

* The outbreak of the wrath of demagogues depended upon most secret causes. In 1830 the revolutionists again supposed that they had finally seized upon the Government. It slipped from them by that mercy of God towards France that has often disarmed the enemies of its rest at the very moment of their triumph.

Open or mysterious associations were everywhere exercising their baneful rule. When the severe commercial and industrial crisis was weighing upon the whole of France, some serious insurrections at Lyons and Grenoble, in 1831, revealed the

In many of the quotations that have been made, the speaker's sentiments with regard to the press are very evident, and yet Bugeaud said he was not systematically hostile to the press. He said so with a certain precision at the beginning and the end of his parliamentary career, in 1831 and in 1840. In 1831 the question was of a grant to a journal named the *Stenograph*, intended to publish the exact words of political orators.

'I attach a great deal of importance,' said Bugeaud, 'to the truth being known. It is a fresh public means of disseminating a faithful account of our speeches, and of supplying the provincial press.'

On the 30th November, 1840, immediately before his departure to take up the Governor-generalship of Algeria, he said :—

It would be wrong to suppose that I am opposed to the liberty of the press. At bottom I am only opposed to its errors. I have not the least desire in the world to see its liberty suppressed. I wish that all sensible men would restore it to a better path, by reprobation of its misdeeds.

*   *   *   *   *   *   *

Our discussions are entirely transformed; they are not on what we have seen and heard, but something totally different. If the press would return to the language of truth, it would be useful to the country, and I declare I would love it exceedingly.

In 1834, in the discussion of the address, he said :—

An advanced, a very advanced, orator has told us of persecutions of the press, the misery of the people, and universal suffrage.

---

mournful bondage that enslaved the peaceful and sensible workmen, who allowed themselves to be drawn into actions and crimes, that they soon abhorred.—GUIZOT, *Histoire de la France.*

Persecutions of the press! But, in truth, that makes every one smile. Is it not, on the contrary, the press that is essentially a persecutor, that persecutes all honest men, all patriots, all those who have consecrated their lives to working for their kind, and precisely for the very people it pretends to protect? It is the press that persecutes, with lies and calumny, disparaging every action, every man. It is, in a word, the greatest despotism that we have yet laboured under.

Again he said upon the same subject, the 23rd of May, 1835—

Thus, for instance, when I let slip the words, ' a peck of oats,' (general hilarity), the newspaper, *Temps*, so distorted my views that it made me say things most improper for a soldier. The result was that a chef-de-bataillon of the department of the Lozère wrote me an insulting letter. He told me that I was a vile man. I answered him, ' I see plainly that you are a vile slave of the press (laughter) ; I will, however, descend to your level, and teach you to read newspapers. I will give you a meeting half-way, and we will fight it out to the death.' (Commotion.)

'The chef-de-bataillon replied, ' I have since read other journals, among them the *Débats*, and I see that your views were misrepresented. I hasten to make my excuses to you, and withdraw my subscription to the *Temps*. (Prolonged laughter.)

'This is the sort of thing brought about by the press. It has caused much bloodshed, and will cause more.

We here conclude our extracts from General Bugeaud's speeches upon general policy, agriculture, and political economy ; and will devote a special study to General Bugeaud as a military orator, that is to say, to Deputy Bugeaud taking part in parliamentary discussions on the army.

CHAPTER XXV.

BUGEAUD, MILITARY ORATOR.

MARSHAL BUGEAUD was famed for his care of the soldier on campaign, and this was equally displayed by him in parliament upon all questions relating to the position of officers, and especially to that of non-commissioned officers.

General Bugeaud was rich for the time when he lived. The competence he enjoyed as a country gentleman, during the fifteen years that he was un-attached, the happiest time in his life, was sufficient for his needs and tastes. So he often declares that his pleading is not for himself, but for his comrades.

Indeed, on considering the great improvements that the Second Empire and the third Republic have introduced into the position of officers and soldiers, alike in pensions, pay, and accessory advantages of all kinds,* it is easy to see that in 1830, under a new-born government, encountering great financial diffi-

---

* The Second Empire, besides considerable increase of pay, restored the pay of the members of the Legion of Honour, organised military messes, gave the army the right of travelling for quarter fares, tobacco at reduced price, &c. The third Republic doubled pensions; under the Government of July the army, in all these respects, was under the general rules.

culties, just after the half-pay time of the Restoration, the pecuniary position of officers was far from enviable.

Deputy Bugeaud therefore seized upon every chance of promoting the pecuniary interest of the soldier, and claiming increase. In the sitting of the 13th of December, 1831, in the budget debate he observes that civil pay had been frequently increased since the time of the Empire. A colonel commanding 3000 men and 100 officers only receives 8000 francs, when some heads of offices get 20,000. The army saves nothing, even the soldier spends more than he gets ; for there is not a man that does not write to his mother for money when he goes into hospital.*

Next year on the 13th of March, 1832, he spoke strongly against Mangin's amendment to reduce military pay. On the 17th of February, 1834, he moved an amendment in favour of officers returning

---

* The pay of officers has been wonderfully increased since the Regulation Law of the 25th of December, 1837. We give a comparative table of the infantry pay in 1837 and 1882.

Pay.	In 1837.	In 1882.	Increase.
Colonel	7600	9756	2156
Lieutenant-Colonel	5020	6084	1064
Chef-de-bataillon	4240	5004	764
Captain, 1st class	2724	3420	696
Captain, 2nd class	2324	3168	844
Lieutenant	1666	2448	782
Sub-Lieutenant	1416	2268	852

In the cavalry each rank receives about 200 francs more than in the infantry. In the artillery these differences are less marked.

Captain, 1st class	2924	3600	676
Lieutenant	2116	2628	512
Sub-Lieutenant	1916	2556	640

The pay of Generals of Division has not been much increased. It was 26,400 francs in 1837, it is 26,910 francs now. It is the General of Brigade, Maréchal-de-camp, that has benefited most by the new regulations; he received 13,600 francs under King Louis-Philippe, he receives 15,948 francs under the Second Republic, that is to say, 2348 francs more.

home as released prisoners. The picture he draws of
their situation is melancholy :—

No persons can be more unfortunate than officers returning from
captivity. They are always plundered of all they possessed. Their
watches are taken, their money, their clothes, and often their boots.
I have often seen officers return barefooted from captivity! While
they are prisoners they lose their promotion; when they return they
are unattached, their place is taken.

Certainly, it is to be hoped that not many French officers will be
captured; but it is often the bravest that are made prisoners, as they
hold their ground longest, as they expose themselves oftenest, and go
nearest to the enemy as skirmishers.

In the debate on the regulation of the numbers of
the staff in 1834, General Bugeaud had raised a kind
of parliamentary tumult by comparing the promotion
expected by deserving officers to ' a peck of oats.'

' It is an expression borrowed from our most celebrated fabulist,'* said the orator, a good deal surprised
at the disturbance raised by his familiar expression.
In the discussion of 1835 the General repeated his
expression, and this time, as he surrounded it with
some oratorical precautions, it passed without contradiction.

' First, I will call attention to the fact,' said he, in the sitting of
the 14th of May, 1835. ' that of all European armies the French is
that which has proportionally the fewest generals, and pays them the
least.

' In time of peace an army cannot do without promotion; there
must be emulation. Unhappily men are so created. They do not
like to remain in the same position.

' When the colonel has done good service he must be made a
general officer. And this is the reason why the list of general officers
should be proportioned to the strength of the army. There is a
general need of keeping up this salutary emulation. I will not say that
it is necessary to have " the peck of oats," since it causes laughter, though

---

* La Fontaine's Book 1, Table iv. *Les Deux Mulets.*

One was very proud of carrying a load of money, but when thieves stole the
money and wounded him, the other said, ' If you had been doing the humble duty
of carrying oats like me, you would not have suffered.'— ED.

the expression was certainly very applicable. (Laughter on the left.) I ought not to hesitate to make use of the words of one of our best poets, but I will say that emulation is as necessary to soldiers as to civilians. A substitute wishes to become procureur-du-roi, a sub-prefect wishes to become prefect. It is human nature. What would you do with the colonels if you had not a list of general officers?'

In June, 1838, he moved for the establishment of an African bounty, extra pay. He had seen the situation himself in the campaigns of the Sickack and the Tafna. The suppression of the African bounty in 1834 had made a great change in the position of the officers and men. The duty in Africa was very severe, and expenses were great, the cost of living in camp very high, clothes often worn out. A bounty was indispensable to repay the extraordinary expenses men were compelled to incur in keeping up the dignity of their rank.

After some expressions of approval from the Chamber, the amendment was opposed by Government, and was at last rejected.

In the case of especially distinguished officers, he moved for rewards intended to serve as an encouragement for future generations of soldiers. The amount of pension he demanded in 1834 for the widows of generals, such as Decaen, Gérard, Daumesnil, would seem moderate enough to-day. ' Such great examples must not be lost. They are so many patterns to hold up for imitation by the army. By recompensing these illustrious generals in the persons of their widows, you will sow so as to reap. Such payments are pro-ductive of a rich future.'*

---

* Marshal Jourdan's widow, 12,000 francs, 6000 of them being from the Pension Warrant of 1831 ; Decaen, 3000, of which 1500, &c., and the others like-wise.

His pleading for a pension to the widow of Colonel Combes, his old comrade, who fell at Constantine, is still more touching. The proposal had been opposed by the Finance Minister :—

The Finance Minister has performed his duty as guardian of the financial interests of this country. I have another to fulfil, that of guardian of the military honour, which is also a treasure to the country.

Alas! perhaps I was the cause of Colonel Combes' death, of that death which was really so glorious, and one of those no soldier can regret.

Combes was discouraged, and wished to retire: he thought he had reason to complain of a denial of justice: he thought he had deserved the rank of maréchal-de-camp, and it had not been given him. I met him at Perpignan, and told him, 'Colonel, there is still some good to be done; and for men like you, when there is still something to be done, it is no time for repose. Will you go with me to Africa?' He consented; but circumstances did not answer to his ardour. The expedition to Constantine came just as he had written a fresh application for retirement. I made him tear up his letter, he went to Constantine, and what he did is well known.

He made his way into the town, and encouraged the soldiers after the horrible explosion that had caused some hesitation in the ranks. He received the fatal blow just as he was making sure of victory. When he saw it was safe, he went back to the breach and met the general-in-chief and the Duke de Nemours. He told them what he had done so quietly, that they only saw that he was wounded when he turned away. Then they saw the hole where the ball had gone through his lungs and his shoulder-blade. 'Happy,' said he, 'will they be who survive this victory!' Next day he was dead. You need not be afraid of disordering our finances by making a noble exception in the case of Colonel Combes. Such characters will not be too common. If your decision should succeed in multiplying them, there would be nothing in it but cause for rejoicing (10th February, 1838).

When military honour seemed in question he was still more eager than on questions of money.

In the sitting of the 15th of September, 1831, General Bugeaud proposed and carried an amendment confirming the decorations granted between the 4th of February and the 7th of July, 1815, both by the Emperor and also by the commanders of corps.

A few days afterwards he also moved the confirmation of ranks given by the Imperial Government at the same time.

On March 10, 1832, there was a debate on a bill brought in for the conveyance to the Pantheon of the remains of citizens Foy, La Rochefoucauld-Liancourt, Manuel, and Benjamin Constant.

Marshal Clauzel having proposed to add Marshal Ney, and place him first in the list, General Bugeaud proposed to add to the five names those of Dugommier, Masséna, Hoche, Kléber, Desaix, and La Tour-d'Auvergne.

M. Odilon Barrot, in reply, having called the persons put forward by Bugeaud 'honourable,' the General cried out, 'Sir, they are more than honourable, they are illustrious.'

In 1831 there was a debate on the revision of the charter as regards the persons eligible for nomination as peers of France. It was proposed that they should be chosen among the citizens who had served six years in elective civil offices, members of the chambers of commerce and of general councils, paying 3000 francs in direct taxes. General Bugeaud made a claim in favour of the army.

When the desirability of employing General Deputies upon active service was contested in the Chamber, General Bugeaud made a lively defence of his rights.

Certain debates in the Chamber gave General Bugeaud cause for entering upon the principles of strategy, the qualities of a soldier, the greater or smaller advantage of fortifications, and the discussion of principles. It is sad to say that his opinion was much more appreciated abroad, especially in Germany, being insufficiently valued in France.

On the 20th of March, 1832, when there was a debate on the maintenance to be granted to the old armies of the West, he gave an interesting explanation of the war of ambuscade, as he understood it.

' In Spain,' said he, ' for six years we had guerillas, or bands, in the midst of our armies. Certainly we did not spare them. They were not Carlists, and we could seldom destroy any of them. The minister ought not then to be blamed because he has not put a stop to these disorders, it really is not in his power.'

M. Odilon Barrot.—You cannot compare France, even La Vendée, to Spain. It is an insult to the country.

M. Bugeaud.—To which country?

M. Odilon Barrot.—It is an insult to La Vendée and to Britanny, which are also inhabited by patriotic populations.

M. Bugeaud.—I do not know how any insult to La Vendée can be found in what I say. I compare the chouans to guerillas, and there is a perfect identity between these subjects of comparison. Bands are not to be destroyed by theories; there must be muskets, activity, perseverance, courage, and especially legs.

In general, it is better not to pursue them: it is a bad plan. This war is like a wolf-hunt, and must be worked by surrounding and ambuscades. When there is information that a band has appeared in such or such a village, it is no use to go there in a straight line; detachments must be directed upon the points of retreat, and time given them to arrive before advancing upon the village. Ambuscades at the crossings of rivers and intersections of roads must sometimes succeed if they are varied and well concealed. In summer, I consider, this method will be less wearisome, and more useful than the continual expeditions that are made. The officer in each cantonment ought to have a perfect knowledge of the roads, the paths, ravines, and streams in the circle that lies between him and the neighbouring cantonments. The cantonments ought to communicate by signal. The duty of each detachment must be drawn out beforehand, so that where notice is given of a band, every one can go and take up the appointed post without losing time.

If this system is well organized, it seems to me likely to give good results : my brothers in arms will judge of it : but the best way of all is order within.　　If you wish to put an end to chouannerie, for the Government to be strong against the Carlists, cease, yourselves, to make violent attacks upon it, and tie its legs and arms, and then tell it 'to be strong.'　(Great disturbance at the extremities : a voice, 'Whom are you speaking of?'　'Order.')

On the 11th of May, 1835, he describes what he thinks the way to make a good soldier :—

Some think that teaching a man drill is enough to make him a good soldier : that is a mistake.　Drill is the last thing in a soldier's education.　A man is not a soldier till he has got over his home-sickness : when the regimental colours are like the village church tower : when he loves his colours : when he is ready to take sword in hand whenever the honour of his number is attacked : when he has confidence in his chiefs, in his right hand and left hand man ; when they have eaten their soup a long time together, as the Emperor used to say.　This, gentlemen, is what makes the real soldier.

Why does the law of enlistment require seven years'* service ? Because it considers that it takes seven years to make a good soldier. A man becomes a soldier in the first three years of service ; but he will never make one if he thinks he shall only stay three years with the colours.

Now comes a real prophecy of the dangers with which the war of 1870 threatened us :—

Empires are only defended or invaded by battles.　War goes

---

* We are very far from seven years' service now.　Reduced in 1868 to five years, that are in reality cut down to four, if the ideas that prevail at present are carried out, the term of military service will soon be no more than three years. Under these conditions the army is nothing but a school, that all the young citizens fit to bear arms, pass through as quickly as possible, so as to get a more or less complete military education, and rejoin it in the hour of danger ; but this cadre must have a very solid and energetic constitution to supplement the deficiencies of military education in these young soldiers ; and to receive, without cracking or breaking down, the immense flood of humanity that will come in twice or thrice twenty-four hours, and triple the strength of the army on its peace footing.　All lies in this ; not to reduce the length of service until the cadres, especially the lower cadres of the troops, that is to say, the non-commissioned officers, are very perfect.

very fast, and if peace was broken, you would not have time to organize troops, as you had at the beginning of the French revolution. I repeat it, war travels very fast now, and from the very commencement it is necessary to be in a state to give battle with a chance of victory. A battle won gives the victorious army immense advantages; it usually wins a square of eighty leagues a side.

The bringing in of a bill on recruiting for the army is due to deputy Bugeaud. The question was the employment of a bounty on re-engagement, instead of military substitution.* The plan adopted under the Second Empire.

In 1836 we find these words, alluding to the fortifications of Paris :—

Believe that with the modern system war travels fast, and the first battles decide the fate of the campaign. A battle won gives the victor a square of some sixty or eighty leagues the side. Paris is within this square. An ever-to-be-deplored spirit of opposition has prevented you from fortifying Paris; fortify the whole of France, by accepting my propositions about the army.

In 1838, speaking of the great objection to a multiplication of fortified places, he attacks the question of the fortifications of Paris :—

The events of 1814 and 1815 have not passed unnoted through my mind. Now I consider the abuse of strong places as the greatest danger that threatens the country.

When fortresses are too numerous, and in my opinion they are so now, they absorb the greatest part of the active forces. Now these are the army that defends the territories; the army that makes conquests and keeps them. I do not mean to say that all fortresses are to be abolished; but I say there must be a good

---

* Military substitution, a person drawn as a conscript for military service finding a man to act as his substitute. The plan, under the Second Empire, was for such persons to pay a sum to the Government office, when the money received was used to provide bounties to induce old soldiers, who had served their time, to re-enlist. In 1872 the permission to find substitutes was abolished.—ED.

selection of those that may be serviceable, if too numerous they may be the ruin of the country.

The engineer officers say, if we had not got them we would not build them; but as we have them, let us keep them. The same reasoning as in the case of Africa.

Gentlemen, if these fortresses could keep themselves without danger, like the superfluity of monuments in our towns, I should say keep them, even at the cost of some millions. But there is great danger in keeping what is useless. When war comes, it will be necessary to put garrisons into these strong places; they must not be allowed to fall into the enemy's power.

But it is said, when you are in front, a few veterans and some national guards will be enough. When we are in front that is well, but when we retire it is different. Why? because a battle is lost and we are too weak. It is at the moment when the army needs reinforcement, when the army is not in condition to hold the country, that it is necessary to garrison fortresses.

What happens then? Why the fortresses fall one after the other, because there is no army at large to protect them. I remember that in 1836 I came to Algiers; I inquired the strength of the army, it was 12,000 men. At this moment something took place at Bougie. The commandant was murdered. That town was supposed to be threatened, and it was proposed to send a reinforcement of 800 men. The General commanding in Algiers *could not find 350 men*, though he had 12,000. And why? Because there had been such a multiplication of camps and block-houses in the Sahel and the Mitidjah, that the 12,000 men were all absorbed. Though I wish some fortresses to be abolished, I certainly could not mention those to be destroyed. I should wish at the same time to have some built in the interior, upon the Loire for instance, so as not to have all our military establishments upon the frontier.

But especially I desire to see this great question of the fortifications of Paris resumed.

Because the question has been some time unpopular, that is not a reason against its resumption. I hold to popularity as much as another, but I hold still more to the safety, the dignity, and independence of my country as regards the foreigner, and I have a most firm conviction that as long as we have not fortified Paris, we shall not have as much weight as we ought to have in Europe.

Do you know who it was that rejoiced at seeing this question given up? It was the foreigner!

I do not decide upon the system of fortification, but in my present opinion detached forts are preferable.

Again in January, 1841, after Bugeaud had been appointed Governor-general of Algeria, he once more spoke in the Chamber, advocating the fortification of Paris, a national question above all others in his eyes.

We see what fundamental importance Bugeaud attached to the fortification of Paris. It may be supposed he made a considerable contribution to the settlement of the question ; for the advice of a general, just selected from among the youngest to be made Governor of Algeria, must have had considerable influence upon the councils of the July Government.

The fortifications of Paris did not prevent the final catastrophe of the war of 1870. In consequence they have been considered, by some persons, as a simple obstacle that only retarded the fatal issue of the Franco-Prussian war, and as a useless obstacle to the expansion of the great capital.

Was Bugeaud, in whom we have recognised a sort of prophetic gift of military foresight, mistaken on this most important question ?

No, but if he had foreseen the possibility of Reichshoffen and of Forbach, he had not foreseen our second army capitulating at Metz, and the third riddled with grape surrendering in the funnel of Sedan, instead of coming to interpose between the conquerors and the capital, its natural position. He had not foreseen Strasbourg burnt, and Metz starved out. He had not foreseen the speedy and easy transport of the immense siege material, destined for the reduction of Paris, over a continuous line of railway from Magdeburg to Châtillon.

Bugeaud, with prophetic foresight, speaking in May, 1839, said, that in order to overcome a future invasion, the French would not only have to show courage, but, more than anything else, union.

The only persons who responded in 1871 to this appeal for union were the royalist Zouaves killed at Patay. But how badly did the republicans of the 4th of September understand it, when their only care was to endeavour to terrorise the provinces, and disperse the councils and municipalities, while the irreconcilables of the risings of the 31st of October, and the 22nd of January, unintentionally played the game of our Prussian foes.

Bugeaud saw truly. In 1814 and 1815 Paris surrendered a month after Montmirail, a fortnight after Waterloo. In 1870-71 Paris did not surrender till six months after Reichshoffen, because the city was fortified. The proof of the justice of Bugeaud's views, is that military opinion in France after the capitulation of 1871 was unanimous, not by any means to dismantle Paris, but to perfect her fortifications by the construction of exterior redoubts. Bugeaud himself would certainly have desired them if he had seen the perfection of long-range artillery. So the construction of fresh forts at Paris is nothing but the reproduction of Marshal Bugeaud's views, adapted to circumstances, after the events of 1871.

Bugeaud did not believe alone in the necessity of the substitution of two or three vast entrenched camps for the system of numerous small fortresses, as the national defence. He especially believed in the necessity for a powerful army. He speaks of a strength of effectives that the ideas of his time were hardly used to, 200,000 men first, then 500,000.

Before the interesting revelations of M. Camille Rousset were made, General Bugeaud had reduced the story of the volunteers of 1792 to its proper proportions.

The other day (said he, in the sitting of the 17th of February, 1834), M. de Ludre asserted that I said that a Republican government was as favourable to discipline as any other.

I am very far from thinking so. A Republic, on the contrary, is inimical to any kind of discipline. The more liberty there is, the more clubs there are, the more popular societies, and liberty of the press; and the less discipline. (Murmurs from the extreme parties.)

I have said that the governing bodies under the Republic, feeling how the bonds of discipline were growing slacker every day, demanded excessively severe laws, and obtained them.

It was not till the severe laws were passed that discipline was restored to the army, after the clubs had banished it.

Regarding the heroes of July and the volunteers of 1792, he said on the 6th of January, 1834 :

The fighting of July, 1830, has turned the heads of several people. They have supposed that because they beat 7000 or 8000 men of the Guards and Swiss in Paris, they could beat all the armies of Europe. I wish to point out that there are no manœuvres to make in the streets of Paris, none of those movements that, as at Waterloo, taking the army in flank and reverse, decide the victory, although every soldier be an Achilles or an Ajax.

*   *   *   *   *   *   *

A battery of forty guns playing grape upon the enthusiasts soon stops the shouts of enthusiasm. We have been nauseated with tales that the battalions of volunteers at the beginning of the Revolution conquered Europe, thanks to enthusiasm. It is false, you have only to consult history. In the two first campaigns the volunteers were almost incapable of discipline, because there were men among them who had imported the spirit of the clubs into the army, incompatible with discipline and military power. They were beaten in almost every instance. It was only at the battle of Fleurus that they began to do service. (Interruption.) Gentlemen, it was only at Fleurus! At Jemmapes and Valmy, the greater part of the force was composed of the old army.

After boasting of the success of the army of Italy, he says that the camp at Boulogne was a still better school :—

Remember the famous campaign of 1805 ; an Austrian army destroyed in a week : our arrival at Vienna, at full gallop in a kind of way ; and then Austerlitz. Till then the revolutionary battles had been but child's play, compared to the war of 1805. No doubt the battles in Italy were very fine : but compared to the battles of Wagram, Jena, and all the other battles of the Empire, I repeat they were but child's play! I do not want to undervalue the revolutionary battles, but I know how to appraise them justly.

On the 11th of March, 1840, he made a humorous attack upon the preponderance of the civil element in the councils of revision :—

There is nothing more illogical than having the soldiers, who are to compose the army, chiefly selected by civilians. (Dissent.)

The selection of men by civilians is as illogical, quite as bad, as if the magistrates were chosen by the soldiers. (Laughter.)

I shall be told that civilians can judge of the cases of exemption as well as soldiers ; but I say that a man may not be in any of the classes of exemption that have been foreseen, and yet not fit to go on service. This is what civilians can never understand as well as soldiers.

When a council of revision finds a man who presents no defect of formation, it declares him fit, while we soldiers might declare him unfit. Why? Because we know the strength necessary to endure the fatigues of war. We know that there must be a deep chest and strong thighs, to carry a pack, eight or ten days' provisions, sixty rounds in the pouch, a sabre, and a musket. For that a man must be strongly built.

It is well known that in 1840 the Eastern question nearly induced France to declare war against all Europe. Mighty man of war as he was, Bugeaud was an energetic opponent of this madness.

In a remarkable speech which he made on the 30th of November, 1840, he was induced to notice again the invasion of 1792 :—

'With war it is allowable to fear an internal revolution. I know we should overcome the factions. But that would oblige us to raise fifty or sixty thousand men more : you will allow that to be an inconvenience, when such great efforts are necessary.

This is not a reason against making a war of interest, a war of honour, but it is a consideration against making it lightly, for weighing the motives well, and not showing too much touchiness.

The real danger is in the divisions of the country ; it is in the language of the factions.

M. Dupin.—In case of war we should unite!

M. Bugeaud.—Yes, I should have been more warlike, but for the horrible maxim, that a great invasion cannot be resisted but through the means of revolution. This fatal and barbarous error is unhappily shared by some of the youth of the schools! And how should they not share it? They have drawn it from the historians of the Revolution. It is treating our country with contempt to tell it that it is powerless to resist without the Terror behind it. (The left,—Hear! Long interruption.)

M. Manuel.—You calumniate the country!

M. Bugeaud.—The Terror, they say, saved France. Has it the prerogative of suddenly creating armies, training them, using them to war, and perchance can it call up spontaneously from the earth grenadiers like those of the Imperial Guard? (Laughter.) No, gentlemen : it can provide something, it can drive out a few more who do not like to go and fight, it can extract a few crowns out of the pockets of people who would not be inclined to give them. (Laughs and murmurs.) But that is all.'

It is time, gentlemen, to do justice upon these dangerous sophisms. If I insist upon it, the reason is that the error is excessively dangerous for my country. It will be said that, being unable to save ourselves but by the Terror, we must make a Terror. (No. no.) I have heard it said a hundred times to a crowd of young people. (Interruption.)

Should you like me to tell you what did save France? I shall teach you perhaps, for I venture to say that the history of the Revolution is less known than the history of the Medes and Persians. (General and prolonged hilarity.)

First, the armies of the Coalition were but weak in numbers : the military condition of Europe was not what it is at the present day.

The men who fought at that time have often told me that there were not more than a hundred and fifty thousand men in line against us.

A Member.—Such language is anti-national.

General Bugeaud.—The chief cause of our success lay not in the limited numbers, but in the system of war then in existence.

An Austrian Field-marshal, M. de Lassy, had published a specious work which he called *Methodical War*. And this method, or rather this absence of method, had led all Europe astray. This was the origin of war of details, of cordons, and tentatives, that gave the French Republic time to organize its armies.

It was natural that when a million of men were put in motion, a powerful army should come out of them. We were not fortunate in the first campaigns, with their little combats. Sometimes victors, oftener vanquished. (Great interruption from the Left.) Let the facts speak. Gentlemen, they must be recalled for you, at least for the public without; for there are many people in France quite convinced that singing the ' Marseillaise ' alone is enough to overthrow the armies of Europe. (Laughter in the Centre, murmurs on the Left.)

Gentlemen, it is necessary to learn that as long as our armies were not well organized, as long as there were no tactics, you had no decided successes, and you had reverses.

M. Taschereau.—The people of Paris in 1830 proved that it could overthrow an army.

M. Odilon Barrot.—Enthusiasm and exaltation are a power!

General Bugeaud.—I highly appreciate the singing of the ' Marseillaise ' (laughter), but I do not believe that it alone wins a victory. I think it a good thing, gentlemen, for the combatants to sing the ' Marseillaise ' before going into action, but not during the action ; what is wanted then is silence and self-possession. Silent troops must be respected, not those who shout and sing. (Murmurs.)

If you had been pursued, if the enemy had concentrated only 100,000 men in that first campaign, he certainly would have come to Paris. (Outburst of murmurs on the Left and some other benches, shouts of ' Order, order.')

Without this war of tentative operations, without the sieges of all our little places in the North, it is most likely the Republic would have succumbed in spite of Danton's fury. (Violent denials.)

The second campaign presented another appearance. Your armies had acquired experience and knowledge, and gained great victories. They did great things that I admired under the Revolution and took my share of under the Empire.

In this remarkable speech, directed against an

inconsiderate declaration of war with more numerous and more powerful enemies, it will be observed that, though the wise and politic general was animated by the same patriotic ardour, he remained faithful to the principles he had already supported from the tribune in 1831 and 1832 on the Polish question.

' I joined the commission full of warlike ideas.' said he, at another point of this same discussion ; 'and you may trust me that our national honour was not in bad hands with that commission, for four members out of nine had shed their blood for their country.'

If Marshal Bugeaud had lived to 1870, it may be supposed from his speech in 1840 that he would have used the whole weight of his authority against the declaration of war with Prussia, and would have exerted himself to reduce to its just proportions the famous insult inflicted by King William on our ambassador, M. Benedetti, at Ems.

CHAPTER XXVI.

BUGEAUD, GOVERNOR-GENERAL (1841).

WHEN the Government recalled Marshal Valée* from Algiers, in December, 1840, the chief command of the army in Africa was placed in the hands of General Schramm. Count Schramm, born in 1789, was already one of the oldest soldiers of the Empire. He was a man of the greatest probity, whose military

---

* Valée, Sylvain-Charles, Count, Marshal of France, 1773-1846, born at Brienne-le-Château, left the Artillery School at Chalons in 1792, to join the Army of the North. Captain in 1795, Lieutenant-Colonel in 1804, he made the Austerlitz campaign as Inspector-General of the artillery train. Colonel in 1807, he was summoned to the grand head-quarters as second of the artillery staff. After Eylau and Friedland, Napoleon gave him the command of the artillery of the Third Corps in Spain. General (of Brigade) in 1810, and in 1812 Lieutenant-General, he succeeded in bringing back a large proportion of our stores to France after the evacuation of Spain by our troops. Made Count by the Empire, the Royal Government appointed him in June, 1814, to the duties of Inspector-General of artillery. Though he had been commander of the artillery of the Fifth Corps during the hundred days, King Louis XVIII. reappointed him to the post of Inspector-General of his army. During the last years of the Restoration and the first of Louis-Philippe's reign, he remained unemployed.

In 1835 he was made a Peer of France; in 1837 he accompanied General de Damrémont to Algeria, and took the command of the artillery on the expedition to Constantine. When Damrémont was killed under the walls of that fortress the chief command of the expeditionary army devolved upon him, and next day he took Constantine by assault. When he returned to Algiers he found his Marshal's baton there, and in a few days' time was appointed Governor-General of Algeria. In October, 1839, in company with the Duke of Orleans, the Marshal undertook a military promenade from Constantine to the defile of the Iron Gates, Bibans. While this expedition was in progress, and in reprisal for this manifestation, a

talents were appreciated. However, the state of the colony required a more active and enterprising man.*

---

number of armed tribes invaded the plain of the Mitidjah, massacring the isolated detachments, destroying the agricultural establishments and harvests, and spreading terror over all that part of our possessions. In November Abdel-Kader himself appeared in the Mitidjah, while one of his lieutenants threw himself into the province of Oran. Not till this moment did Marshal Valée make serious preparations for defence. The winter passed in continual skirmishes ; and the struggle did not really commence till the following spring. In the month of March, 1840, a corps of 12,000 men advanced upon Cherchell and took possession of it, while 20,000 men were employed in chastising the Haractas. On the 27th of April the Marshal, accompanied by the Dukes d'Aumale and d'Orleans, left Blidah with 15,000 men crossed the Atlas on the 12th of May and occupied Medeah. On the 20th he repassed the Atlas, and by the end of the month had returned to Algiers. The forces placed at the Marshal's disposition were insufficient. He had made the mistake of scattering his troops too much, and was accused of sometimes sacrificing them through his obstinacy. The invasion of the Mitijdah by innumerable bands of Kabyles and Arabs spread terror as far as Algiers, and the warriors almost reached the walls of the city. He reopened the campaign in the first days of June, and occupied Milianah which Abdel-Kader had just devastated.

After the formation of the Cabinet of the 29th of October, 1840, Marshal Valée was replaced by General Bugeaud. His cultivated mind was unfortunately more lofty than extended. Firm enough in his resolutions, he was sometimes slow in coming to a decision, because he considered all the difficulties in an enterprise. But when he had come to a determination, and facts were so unkind as to turn out in disagreement with his previsions, he would refuse to recognise them, as if his infallible judgment ought to have ruled the course of events. His character was rough and positive, while he had natural ability, and his freaks were original.

Marshal Valée died in 1846.

* General Jean-Paul-Adam, Baron, and afterwards Count de Schramm, was born in 1789 at Arras, in Pas de Calais, and when but ten years of age entered the army. During his first year of service he rose from the ranks and became a sublieutenant in the year 1800. In 1805, on the field of Austerlitz, he was decorated and promoted to a lieutenancy of infantry, and by a daring act performed during the siege of Dantzic, in 1807, he won his commission as captain in the Imperial Guard. In the succeeding year he was wounded by a musket-shot at Heilsburg, from which he had barely recovered when he was sent to Spain, whence he was recalled in a few months to take part in the battles of Wagram and Essling. Returning to Spain, his gallantry there was soon after rewarded by promotion to the rank of commander of a battalion of the 2nd Voltigeurs. He served in the Russian campaign, and in that of Saxony, and at Lützen captured the entrenched camp of the Prussians at the point of the bayonet, a success which gave the victory in the battle to the French, and obtained for De Schramm the title of baron. He received two wounds in this affair, and for a time his life was thought to be in danger; but he rejoined the army before Dresden, and, being in the advanced guard, routed the enemy in front of him, and captured some of the guns. He afterwards led his regiment to Pirna to cut off the retreat of the Austrians. In

In October, 1840, the President of the Council of
Ministers was Marshal Soult, Duke of Dalmatia,*

this town Napoleon gave him the rank of general of brigade. This was the 26th
of September, 1813, and he was not then twenty-four years of age. He was sub-
sequently taken prisoner, and carried to Hungary, whence he returned to France
in 1814. During the Hundred Days he commanded in Maine et Loire, and was
energetic in contributing to the defence of Paris. After the fall of the Empire he
lived apart from public life till 1830, but in 1831 took part in the expedition to
Antwerp, and during the siege was raised to the rank of lieutenant-general, and
placed in command of a division of the infantry of the reserve. In 1840 he was
commander-in-chief of the army in Algeria, where he had been serving for a year
as chief of the staff, and in 1841 he was created a count. He was a Councillor of
State from the year 1830, and in 1834 had a seat in the Chamber of Deputies. In
1839 he became a peer of France, and in this, as well as the Lower Chamber, was
a supporter of Conservative principles. In 1850 he accepted the portfolio of
Minister-of-War, but resigned it a few months later, not wishing to countersign
the dismissal of General Changarnier. After the *coup d'état* he was appointed a
Senator, and though he was the senior general of the French army, his name was
always borne on the effective list as having commanded in chief in the face of the
enemy. He obtained the Grand Cross of the Legion of Honour in 1840.—*Morning
Post*, February 27, 1884, *notice of the Count's death.*

* It may be interesting to give the succession of Ministers-of-War from the year
1830 to 1848.

1st August, 1830, Gérard, Maurice-Etienne, Count, Lieutenant-General,
Deputy.

17th November, 1830, Soult, of Dalmatia, Jean-de-Dieu, Marshal Duke (for the
second time), he had been in the Ministry as President of Council from the 3rd of
December, 1814, to the 11th of March, 1815.

18th July, 1834, Gérard, Marshal Count, Peer of France.

10th November, 1834, Bernard, Simon, Baron, Lieutenant-General.

18th November, 1834, De Tréviso, Adolphe-Edouard-Casimir-Joseph Mortier,
Duke, Marshal, and Peer of France, President of Council.

30th of April 1835, Maison, Nicholas-Joseph, Marquis, Marshal, and Peer of
France.

19th of September, 1836, Bernard, Baron, Lieutenant-General, Peer of France,
for the second time.

31st March, 1839, Cubières, Amédée-Louis Despans, Lieutenant-General.

12th May, 1839, Schneider, Antoine-Virgile, Lieutenant-General, Deputy.

1st March, 1840, Cubières Despans, for the second time.

29th October, 1840, Soult, of Dalmatia, Marshal Duke, for the third time ;
President of Council to the 15th of September, 1845.

10th November, 1845, de Saint-Yon, Alexandre-Pierre Moline, Lieutenant-
General, Peer of France.

9th May, 1847, Trezel, Camille-Alphonse, Lieutenant-General, Peer of France.

25th February, 1848, Subervie, Jacques-Gervais, Baron, Lieutenant-General.

5th April, 1848, Arago François, Member of the Provisional Government.

17th May, 1848, Cavaignac, Louis-Eugene, General of Division, Member of the
Constituent Assembly.

assisted by M. Guizot for Foreign Affairs ; Martin du Nord, Keeper of the Seals ; the Comte Duchatel, for the Interior ; Admiral Duperré, for the Navy ; and M. Villemain, for Public Instruction. The frequent and severe criticisms directed against Marshal Valée's administration and management of military matters had determined the Government to replace him by General Bugeaud.

King Louis-Philippe must have had some courage and an absolute confidence in General Bugeaud to make such a choice. Indeed, no politician could count up so many personal enemies as the new governor. The Republicans, the Legitimists, even several Conservatives, were openly hostile to him, and the press was far from sparing him. His appointment stirred up the warmth of the journalists, and gave occasion for the sharpest criticisms. They said it was an actual challenge to select for governor of our African possessions the man who had so often declared from the tribune the necessity for renouncing our conquest, and had even gone so far as to advise its abandonment. In fact, in 1837, after Bugeaud's return from his first voyage to Africa, after the expedition to the Sickack, he had not hesitated, as we have seen, to show himself opposed to the colonisation of Algeria. He said that the most part of Algeria was only a great rock surrounded with thickets of brushwood, unfit for cultivation, that the olive could only grow, in these arid plains, by the

---

28th June, 1848, De Lamoricière, Christophe-Louis-Leon-Juchault, General of Division, Member of the Constituent Assembly.

20th December, 1848, Bullière, Joseph-Marcellin, General of Division, Member of the Constituent Assembly.

help of irrigation, and that it was pure madness to continue the war.

When General Bugeaud went to take leave of the Duke of Orleans, on his appointment as successor to Marshal Valée, the Prince rallied him on his determination to conquer and colonise a country which he did not like, and had spoken so ill of. The General replied, 'Sir, it is very agreeable and very pleasant for a man to marry a woman, young, rich, attractive, with whom he is desperately in love. Where is the wonder if he behaves well to her? But what would you say of a man compelled to marry an ugly woman, poor, and uncomely, whom he could not abide: what would you say of that man if he, notwithstanding, was never forgetful of any duty or any respect towards her? Well, sir! I will be that husband to Algeria, this new kind of gallant, and I will treat her so well, surround her with so much attention and love, that she shall be compelled to become young, attractive, and beautiful.'

The Government were not ignorant of the effect this nomination was likely to produce in Algeria; and thus the War Minister took care to preface the new chief's arrival with the following notice, and had it posted up everywhere :—

General Bugeaud will soon be on his way to Algiers. There is no reason to infer from his appointment that the occupation will be limited ; the campaign to be commenced in the spring will prove the contrary.

M. Guizot, in his *Memoirs*, thus draws the portrait of General Bugeaud at his departure. We cannot convey a better idea of the man of war than by re-

producing the magisterial judgment of the great writer
and statesman :—

When the King, on the 29th of December, at the request of his
cabinet, appointed General Bugeaud to be Governor-general of
Algeria, I did not conceal from myself the consequences of this selection, and the obligations, I will add the difficulties, that it imposed
upon us. General Bugeaud was not an officer to whom it was possible to give such or such instructions, with the certainty that he
would limit his ambition to executing them as best he could, and
making his way in his career by pleasing his chiefs. He was a man
of an original and independent mind, a fruitful and fervid imagination,
an ardent will that thought for itself, and took a great deal of room
for its own thoughts, while serving the power from whom he held
his mission. Neither education nor study had tamed his powerful
character, while they developed it. Early thrown among the stern
trials of military life, and too late into the complicated scenes of
political life, he had formed himself by his observations alone and his
own experience, according to the instincts of a strong good-sense,
that was sometimes deficient in proportion and tact, never in justice
or power. In everything, in especial the war and affairs in Algeria,
he had his own special views, his plans, his resolutions; and
not only did he pursue them indeed, but proclaimed them beforehand on every occasion, to all comers, in his conversations and his
correspondence with a force of conviction and a warmth of speech
that increased more and more in proportion to the contradiction and
doubt he encountered. He thus committed himself in his eagerness, both as regards himself and those who did not entirely accept
his views, was so full of his own decided judgment and his patriotic
intentions, that he did not perceive the prejudices aroused by the
intemperance of language, or foresee the difficulties that these preten-
sions would sow around his steps when he had to act, after so much
talk.

General Bugeaud reached Algiers on the 23rd of
February, 1841, and the same day the two following
proclamations were posted on the walls :—

Inhabitants of Algeria,—On the tribune, as well as during
my command in Africa, have I endeavoured to dissuade my country
from attempting the entire conquest of Algeria. I considered that a
numerous army and great sacrifices would be necessary for the attain-

ment of this object : that her policy might be embarrassed and her internal prosperity retarded during the prosecution of this vast enterprise.

My voice was not sufficiently powerful to stop an impulse that is perhaps the work of destiny. The country has committed itself; I must follow it. I have accepted the grand and beautiful mission of assisting in the accomplishment of its work, and I consecrate to it for the future all the activity, devotion, and resolution that nature has given me.

The Arabs must be conquered ; the standard of France must be the only one raised on this African land.

But the war now indispensable is not the object. The conquest will be barren without colonisation.

I shall therefore be an ardent coloniser, for I think there is less glory in gaining battles than in founding something of permanent utility for France.

The experience gained in the Mitidjah has only too clearly proved the impossibility of protecting colonisation by isolated farms ; and that is almost the only method hitherto tried : it has vanished at the first breath of war. Let us not recommence this attempt before the time is come ; the fighting strength would be weakened by being broken up into fractions, and the army perish by sickness without giving the farmers security for their crops.

Let us begin the colonisation by assemblies in defensible villages, convenient for agriculture, and, at the same time so tactically constituted, and combined with one another, as to give time for a central force to come up to their assistance ; and I devote myself to this work.

Agriculture and colonisation are one. It is useful and good no doubt to increase the population of towns, and to build edifices there; but that is not colonisation. First the subsistence of the new people must be assured, and of their defenders, parted by the sea from France ; so what the earth can give must be demanded from it.

The cultivation of the open country is in the forefront of colonial necessity. The towns will be no less the subject of my care ; but I shall induce them as much as is in my power to turn their industry and capital towards the fields ; for with the towns alone we should have only the head of colonisation, and not the body ; our situation would be precarious, and at length intolerable to the mother country.

Let us therefore endeavour to found something life-like, something productive : call, incite capital from without to join yours. We will build villages ; and when we can tell our countrymen and neighbours that we have to offer establishments ready-built, in healthy spots, surrounded by fertile fields, and effectually protected against sudden attacks from the enemy, be sure that colonists will come to fill them.*

Then France will really have founded a colony, and will reap a reward for the sacrifices she has made.

GOVERNOR-GENERAL BUGEAUD.

The second proclamation was addressed to the army :—

SOLDIERS OF THE ARMY OF AFRICA,—The King has called me to be your leader.

No man solicits such an honour, but if he accepts it with enthusiasm for the glory that is promised by men like you, the fear of being unequal to this immense task moderates the pride felt in commanding you.

You have often conquered the Arabs; you will conquer them again: but it is a trifle to make them fly: they must be made to submit.

Generally you are accustomed to severe marches and privations inseparable to war. You have endured them with courage and constancy in a country of nomades, who, when they fly, leave nothing to the conqueror.

The coming campaign again summons you to display to France the soldierly virtues she is so proud of. I shall call upon your ardour, your devotion to the country and the King, for all that is

---

* General Daumas tells us that Algeria, starting from the sea on the north to a variable depth of 450 or 500 kilomètres (300 to 340 miles), is divided into two principal zones, the Tell and the Sahara. The Tell is the portion nearest the sea; it is the country of mountains and valleys, of cereals and water-courses. Its population is made up of Kabyles and Arabs. Both of them follow the Mahometan religion; but their manners, the constitution of their society, as well as their origin and their language, make them like two distinct nations. The Sahara is the country of plains; it is the privileged resort of the herdsmen Arabs who find valuable resources and a vast amount of pasture in these immense distances. The want of water makes this country almost impossible for cultivation. This difference in the constitution of the soil produces notable differences in the manners and wealth of the respective populations as a natural consequence. The one gather the produce of a fertile land, raise cattle, but live a more sedentary life owing to the necessity of only moving within a restricted circle. Thus they are given the name of Hal el Gueraba, cottage people, Hal el Haomach, farm people, or Hal bit-ech-châar, people of the houses of hair, as they live in villages, farms, or tents. The others easily become owners of numerous herds, horses, camels, and sheep. They come and go over larger spaces, and therefore are called Rahhala Arabs, that is to say, who often shift their camp.

requisite to attain the object, and no more. I shall be careful to spare your strength and health. I am sure the officers of every rank and the sub-officers will support me. They never will neglect an opportunity of relieving the troop from some moments of fatigue, or of giving such moral encouragements as the circumstances may require.

It is by this constant care that we preserve our soldiers. Our duty, our humanity, the interest of our glory, alike enjoin them on us.

I shall always be glad to be able to report to the King not only courageous actions, but also in the same way the chiefs who distinguish themselves by their paternal care of their troops, under a climate where precautions must be multiplied.

Soldiers! on other occasions I have been able to gain the confidence of several corps of the African army; I am proud to believe that this feeling will soon be general, because I am resolved to do everything to deserve it. Without confidence in the chief, moral force, the first condition of success, cannot exist. Have confidence, therefore, in me, as France and your general have confidence in you.

The Lieutenant-General,

BUGEAUD.

The proclamation to the inhabitants of Algeria had not the effect in France that the Governor expected. It was far from satisfying the numerous partisans of restricted occupation. These persons, who thought they saw a victory in Marshal Valée's recall, were powerful enough to compel the Minister to give orders for the completion of works that were both ridiculous and useless. General de Berthois received from Marshal Soult orders to superintend the construction of a continuous obstacle in the Mitidjah. This work has left traces that we have actually seen in existence, in the neighbourhood of Algiers. It was the digging of a deep ditch, which, uniting Koleah, Blidah, and the 'Square House,' was to embrace a territory of sixty leagues round Algiers. The Engineers claimed that they could provide complete security by this blockading ditch, which they had staked out at every five hundred mètres, and a certain number of camps behind it. The idea of this singular defence came from General Rogniat,* of the Engineers, and was developed by him in a work on colonisation in Algeria, and the fortifications to secure it against the African tribes; in which he says he desired to make a continuous defensive line after the pattern of the great wall of China.

The new Governor's language was to the taste of the army and colonists in Algeria. The blunt, frank tone, the disdain of oratorical contrivances, this mixture of original thought, of advice and practical ideas, appears in General Bugeaud's proclamations, as it had in the speeches of the Excideuil deputy.

To-day, in the month of March, 1841 (wrote Louis Veuillot in his book *The French in Algeria*), after ten years of occupation it is a very melancholy thing to contemplate our possessions in Africa. No doubt the tint by which it pleases our map-makers to distinguish them is spread over a fine extent of coast, and the Parisians have nothing to do but to wander over it with eye and finger. Look closer. Let us mark with ink what really belongs to us, and let us make these points very small; they will not be numerous. Place the pen upon Algiers; Algiers is yours, and even, provided the night is still far distant, you may walk out a league around it. Two or three other points in a circle of three or four leagues;

---

* Vicomte Joseph Rogniat, 1767 to 1840, general of division in the Engineers, was born at Vienne, in Dauphiné. He served under Moreau in 1800, and made the campaigns of 1805 and 1807. Chef-de-bataillon at the siege of Dantzig, he distinguished himself there. Colonel in Spain, he assisted in the sieges of Saragossa, Tortosa, Tarragona, and Valencia, and came back to France as general of division. In 1813 he was transferred to the Grand Army, and fortified Dresden. In 1814 he commanded the Engineers at Metz; in 1830 he was inspector-general of Engineers, a peer of France. We are indebted to him for several works, among them the sieges of Saragossa and Tortosa, and some considerations on the art of war. But we do not suppose that General Rogniat, the Engineer-general, will ever go down to posterity as having invented the ingenious conception of the little Algerian ditch.

these are your posts or camps of the Square House, Fondouk, Habra, &c. You own the surface they cover, and the surroundings just as far as a musket will carry, but on condition of sowing and building nothing there, and on condition of having within your ditch ammunition and food enough to last till the column comes with a fresh supply. When there is no water within the camp, the soldiers can only go to the well in sufficient numbers; they are eaten up with vermin, worn out with weariness and disgust, decimated by fever, by the sun, and the pestilential exhalations of the marshes. Happy are they who have a few sheets of old newspaper to read. I have heard officers shut up in these burning prisons say that the most vigorous mind could not bear three or four months of such a punishment. Many give themselves up to strong liquors, turning to brutishness to save them from madness.

But to continue. A spot at Douera, a spot at Bouffarik, another at Blidah, two specks for Coleah and Cherchell. You maintain a certain number of troops in each of these spots, and drink-shop keepers, who poison those that the fever and the Arabs have left alive. This is your province of Algiers. As for what you have not marked, no doubt it belongs no more to the Arabs than it does to you. And yet the Hadjoutes get harvests there, now of cattle, now of heads and weapons of men who risk themselves in it : you get nothing but harvests of gunshots. I forgot your towns of Medeah and Milianah, two great tombs at the end of a road, where you might build twenty triumphal pyramids of the bones of your soldiers. Between Oran and Bona you have besides Algiers five maritime towns : Mostaganem, Cherchell, Bougie, Djijilly, and the nascent Philippeville. Be careful that your ships do not get wrecked beyond gunshot of these fortresses ; the sea is yours, the coast belongs to the Kabyles ; and if a vessel stops a moment, there is always a party of Arabs ready to fire on the Christian flag.

To go on to the province of Constantine, where peace is said to reign. Here is Bona and its quiet neighbourhood, and the marshes of the Seybouse, which have killed more Frenchmen than the two sieges of Constantine. Here is Philippeville, a town of planks. No fighting there, only death. Ghelma is a camp, Bougie and Djijilly are two prisons insulted by the Kabyles every day. Constantine is a focus of conspiracies. Abdel-Kader and the old Bey Achmed have partisans there under the tent of our best friends. You are safe at the Calle : nevertheless between Bona and the Calle a captain and several men of his squad were attacked and murdered. It is true vengeance was taken.

Mostaganem is near Mazagran ; that is enough to say. Oran extends its dominion as far as Mers-el-Kebir and Arzew on the coast, as far as Misserghine inwards, two to three leagues! Razzias have been made upon tribes encamped much nearer. They departed; and after all these razzias, it was found that Oran was without food. But the province of Oran is officially in a state of war; it is quite natural for the capital to close its gates, and bread to be scarce. If at least this melancholy state of things was not known to the Arabs! But they quite appreciate it, and are emboldened by it in the war they make against us. Abdel-Kader makes use of it with unusual dexterity. It is the favourite theme of the most cruel railleries, while the bulletins boasted to us in France of the excellent results of the last campaign; a bantering letter written in the Emir's camp laid bare the spectacle of our weakness and misery. There are plenty of documents of this kind. They say that the Arabs are discouraged! It is much more certain that they are as much as ever inclined to fight.

This was the critical condition of Algeria when Bugeaud came there, unpopular, and almost made ridiculous by newspaper abuse; dreaded by the colonists because of his probity, by the generals and office-holders because of his determination; considered a tyrant with a coarse and visionary mind. In France all the opinion of the liberals was against him; in Algeria all the world, except the soldier, who counted for very little.

If there is anything to be admired here below, it is the spectacle of a great will engaged with great difficulties. Power in itself is nothing. There are mean minds that possess it, and hesitate to make use of it, or warp and break it by clumsy blows. No weapon is more delicate. It is the will that does everything. But will itself is nothing but obstinacy and violence, when not directed by good-sense. The sensible man adheres to his plans, because having in advance taken judicious measures, foreseen obstacles, and calculated their power of resistance, no difficulty surprises or deters him; he marches upon his object. But where is bred the good-sense necessary for these grand exertions of human will? Whence does it derive its stability against the passions that might surprise it, against the obstacles it must overcome, and the certain dangers it has to brave? Good-sense then is the love of truth, zeal for good, it is virtue!

Marshal Bugeaud's good sense immediately showed him what he had to do; his virtue did not recoil before the enormous task. I say his virtue, not his courage. There is a kind of courage that Marshal Bugeaud did not possess, or only by an effort of virtue.

He was afraid of public opinion, and he was afraid of it in the most wretched form. This man who would not have been afraid of all deaths in combination, feared the newspapers, and was uneasy about what they would say. In fact he had a cruel experience of their powerful blows. To them he owed a reputation of being a boor and madman, such as added a good deal to the difficulties of his position. Notwithstanding this he no doubt was in the wrong to fear it so much, but he did fear it. He encountered it, resolved to act as if it did not exist. And he forthwith developed all his power at once, without troubling himself what might be said in Algeria, or written in France.

Our brilliant generals had carried on the war in Africa without profit, but not without glory, and enjoyed a popularity that encouraged them to speak a little too freely of the new system of occupation and war that the Governor intended to adopt. He summoned them to his presence, and told them that he would have none of their bravery or talents, unless he could reckon upon their perfect obedience; otherwise he should know how to do without them.

However, in the month of November, 1840, nearly 7000 Mahometans, horse or foot, were ranged under our banners. Algiers, Oran, Bôna, were rising from their ruins and rapidly extending. The European population was increasing in a constant ratio; and on the 21st of December, 1840, amounted to the number of 28,000, of whom 13,000 were French, 9000 Spaniards, 6000 Italians, Maltese, or Germans.

The new Governor had under his orders 78,000 men; 13,500 of them being horse.* War on a large

---

* We give a table of the numbers of the French army in Africa, as stated in the sitting of the 14th of May, 1840, on the authority of M. Emmanuel Poulle, Deputy :—

1831 . . . 17,900	1836 . . . 31,400
1832 . . . 22,400	1837 . . . 42,600
1833 . . . 27,000	1838 . . . 48,000
1834 . . . 31,000	1839 . . . 54,000
1835 . . . 30,000	1840 . . . 63,000

On the 1st July, 1841, our troops in Algiers amounted to 78,900 men, French troops, auxiliaries, and natives :

On the 1st of July, 1842, they reached 83,281 men.
,, ,, 1843 ,, 85,664 ,,
,, ,, 1844 ,, 90,562 ,,
,, ,, 1845 ,, 89,099
,, ,, 1846 ,, 107,688 ,
,, ,, 1847 ,, 101,520 ,,

scale was not to be continued in Africa. General Bugeaud speedily gave up the ring of isolated posts that protected nothing. The towns were to be held, and the system put in practice of radiating around, starting from a fixed and permanent position. In this fashion the enemy being always kept on the alert, and thrust to a distance were compelled to remain on the defensive at great fatigue and expense; being impoverished every day.

The eternal glory of General Bugeaud will be his understanding that it was not actually an army that we had to meet, but the population itself; and that, consequently, in order to maintain themselves in such a country our troops must be almost as numerous in time of peace as in time of war. At the same time he discovered that the populations who repelled our domination were not *nomades*, as had long been believed, but only much more *moveable* than those of Europe. In fact each tribe had its defined territory, that it only left with difficulty to find pasture for its herds, and was always obliged to return to. If there was no seizing the inhabitants' houses, the harvest might be taken, the herds captured, the individuals arrested, and likewise the women and children.

Thereupon the new conditions of war in Africa became apparent to General Bugeaud. There was no occasion, as in Europe, to collect great armies destined to encounter similar masses: but the object was to cover the country with little light bodies that might catch the population on the run, or when placed near their territory, might overlook them and compel them to remain and live there in peace. The principles of war inaugurated by him on the Sickack, in 1836, were going to be put in practice. Everything that encumbers the march of troops in Europe was to be renounced, and cannon almost entirely given up. The camel and the mule were to be used instead of carriages. Magazine posts placed in various positions rendered it possible to carry but few or no provisions. The officers learnt Arabic, studied the country, and led their columns over it without hesitation. As speed was much more important than numbers, the columns were only composed of picked men already inured to fatigue. An almost incredible rapidity of movement was thus obtained. If our soldiers of to-day, equalling the speed of an Arab army, move faster than the tribe on a march, to Marshal Bugeaud do we owe it.

While at Paris, in the Chambers, and the press, there was passionate discussion on the different methods of holding the regency, and the faults of the Excideuil deputy's character,* the new Governor-general was making his preparations for war like a man who understands it. To strike the enemy in his basis of operations and points of political support, to reach the material interests of hostile populations, that is to say, to hunt Abdel-Kader to bay, and

---

* A curious work, entitled *The French and Arabs in Algeria*, written in 1860 by a retired officer, M. Hugonnet, contains these lines which attracted our attention. They show that the Marshal was not very wrong in detesting the press. 'We may believe that the malevolence of the press was very prejudicial to General Bugeaud, because it injured his reputation. He himself sometimes felt it very keenly, and entered upon polemics with a certain acrimony. He has even been blamed for having been too sensitive to the newspaper attacks, and yet the drift of them is enough to be a considerable impediment to Marshal Bugeaud's celebrity becoming popularly established. This is one of the injustices of opinion that are but too common. So, some marshal of the First Empire, because his name is mentioned in the Great Captain's bulletins of the grand battles at the beginning of the century, perhaps may have for ever more renown than the conqueror of Isly, although he be of much less worth. For myself, I remember, and I confess it with humility

operate against the tribes by frequent razzias ; this was his conception, and by putting it in practice he demolished the Emir's edifice, bit by bit.

From the very beginning, as we shall see in the following chapter, General Bugeaud inaugurated a new strategy, new tactics. Till his time, our soldiers, fixed in block-houses, redoubts, and entrenched camps, had been decimated by sickness and privation ; doing but little service in return. To secure the safety of the country, the Governor-general had a more simple and effectual plan of policy ; this was, first, to force any Arab tribes, as soon as conquered, to recognise chiefs selected from among themselves, who were answerable for the quiet of the territory. One of General Bugeaud's merits was having a fixed system, an arranged plan. In fact, as soon as he had shown the goodness of his method by success, his presence, in person, was less necessary. It was allowable for him to entrust his generals, and even officers of a less elevated rank, with operations over a more or less extensive portion of the African territory ; according to the examples and categorical instructions given them by him.

The movable, or expeditionary, columns usually comprised three or four battalions of infantry, two squadrons of cavalry, two mountain howitzers, and a train of beasts of burden. The horsemen, riding

---

that when I left Saint-Cyr to go to Algeria, I was very glad to join my battalion, excepting for the fact that our fine army in Africa was under the orders of such a chief as Bugeaud. I had taken the accusations of a certain press literally. As may be supposed, a complete revulsion was not long in coming over my opinion. Some talk with my new comrades had soon undeceived me, and the moment I saw the Marshal, and heard him speak of war, I was for ever convinced of his real superiority.'

native horses, had their equipment as much simplified as possible, clothing lightened, and carried nothing but what was absolutely necessary. The natives in our pay, the contingents of conquered Arabs, further furnished us with horsemen valuable for reconnoitring, getting information, escort duty, and the protection of convoys. These cavaliers then performed the part taken by the Uhlans, of melancholy memory, during the disastrous Prussian invasion of 1870 and 1871.

The infantry were most changed by General Bugeaud. The campaigning bag which the foot-soldier had carried was given to him unsewn, that is to say, in the shape of a plain bit of canvas. When the bivouac was reached, three or four comrades made a tent by joining their several portions by the help of cords and supporting sticks. On an expedition the soldier carried no spare clothes or shoes; only his food, ammunition, and weapons. The meat went with the column on its own legs. The baggage followed or remained in reserve. The soldiers were to have loose clothing; generally open over the chest, the stock was abolished and replaced by the cotton neckerchief.

The order of march of the columns was almost always thus arranged; the cavalry, the main body of the infantry, the artillery, the ambulance, the convoy, the cattle, and a strong rear-guard. The camp was a square; the infantry at the four sides, the cavalry, artillery, the staff, and all the baggage in the centre, inside the infantry. The start was made according to the season, at from three to six in the morning; every hour there was a twenty minutes' halt for the head of the column, and it did did not start again till the rear-guard had come up.

When half of the day's march was done, there was a grand halt of about an hour. This was called 'coffee,' because that was the only cookery the men had time to finish. On ordinary marching days the halt for the bivouac took place at two or three in the afternoon ; the meat was immediately killed, and the soldiers cooked their evening meal of soup and beef. In the morning, before starting, they had rice. When it was necessary to push rapidly upon a point during a march, the commander of a column would, sometimes, leave all his baggage and convoy in a good position protected by one or two battalions; and proceed with the cavalry and the rest of the infantry, leaving their packs with the baggage. The foot-soldier having nothing to carry but his musket, his pouch, and packets of cartridges wrapped in the rolled tent slung over his shoulder, went light and full of animation, singing camp songs.

All these details of the soldier's equipment, the multitude of cares required for a march into the country, as well as the innovations introduced into our fashion of fighting the Arabs, and holding the country, took up all the time of the new head of the colony. Hitherto, it must be said that, though the successive governors of Algeria had all been animated by excellent intentions, they were far from possessing the ardent patriotism, the absolute and complete devotion to their work—their task, that Bugeaud so rarely exemplified.

Certainly, if General Bugeaud's predecessors

were not possessed of the lofty qualities so necessary for the regulation and ruling of men, it is just to say that when the new Governor reached Africa in the month of February, 1841, he found himself surrounded by a collection of officers, and young chiefs of corps as his subordinates, who, every one in his sphere, with various aptitudes and different dispositions, were already distinguished soldiers ; and almost all destined to become generals. Changarnier, Lamoricière, Bedeau, Cavaignac. Pelissier,* St. Arnaud, Moriss, Yusuff. Tartas. and so many others, in secondary rank. formed the nucleus of the valiant army of Africa that will remain for ever the glory and honour of France and of the monarchy of 1830.

---

* Pelissier, Amable-Jean-Jacques, was born on the 6th of November, 1794, at Maromme, Seine Inférieure. He was educated at the Military Prytaneum, and the School of Saint-Cyr. Two days before the return from Elba, he received his commission as sub-lieutenant, and was posted to the regiment stationed in observation on the Rhine. In 1823 Pelissier made the campaign in Spain, and was decorated with the Legion of Honour and the Order of Saint Ferdinand. As a result of the expedition to Algiers, in which he was engaged, Pelissier was promoted to the rank of chef-d'Escadron ; then he became aide-de-camp to General Pelet at the attack upon Antwerp. In 1839 he again went to Algiers with the rank of Lieutenant-colonel, and for three years managed the staff of the Province of Oran. He was distinguished in the expedition to Tackdempt, 1841, at the combat of Oued-Melah, and after the expedition to the Chélif was made Colonel.

Pelissier was engaged in the war with Morocco, and distinguished at the battle of Isly, where he commanded the left wing. In 1845, having been ordered to pursue a number of Arabs, who had taken refuge in the caves of Ouled Rhia, and seeing the difficulty of dislodging them from their position, he caused fires to be lighted at the mouths of the caves, and the Arabs perished by suffocation. There was great excitement: the War-Minister, Soult, being questioned in the Chambers, blamed Colonel Pelissier, though he had only acted upon the orders of Marshal Bugeaud, who was energetic in his support of his subordinate. Next year Pelissier received the epaulettes of General of Brigade. At the time of the *coup-d'état*, he took the place of General d'Hautpoul as Governor-general, declared Algeria in a state of siege, and gave his complete adhesion to the new government. Relieved by Marshal Randon, he returned to Oran, arranged the first expedition to Kabylia, took Aaghouat, and in 1852 compelled the tribes to submit.

General Pelissier had just been promoted to the Grand Cross of the Legion of Honour when he received orders to assume the direction of the siege operations at

We have seen, above, the position filled by the crown-prince of France in the history of the first years of our conquest. At the time when General Bugeaud entered upon the chief command of the army, two of the King's sons proceeded to support him in his task, and while fighting under his orders gave, to all, splendid examples of regard to discipline, of courage, and of self-denial.

The Duke d'Aumale,* the third son of Louis-Philippe, though young, was already an old African, as he had been with his eldest brother in his last campaign in 1840.

Returning to France at the end of 1840, he soon

Sebastopol, General Canrobert, commanding-in-chief, having resigned. After several combats, conducted with uncommon vigour, General Pelissier reduced the fortress, having taken the Malakoff in 1855.

This conquest gained him a marshal's baton, and the title of Duke de Malakoff. Returning to France he was sent Ambassador to London. In the war of 1859 the Emperor entrusted him with the organization of an army at Nancy, to watch Germany and stop her, if necessary. After the peace of Villa Franca, 1859, he became Grand Chancellor of the Legion of Honour, then in 1860 was appointed Governor-General of Algeria. He died there in 1864. Marshal Pelissier, besides most uncommon courage and daring, showed very great military intelligence. His traditional churlishness and bluntness were allayed by a great feeling of equity and singular natural ability.

* Henri-Eugene-Philippe-Louis d'Orleans, Duke d'Aumale, born at Paris on the 16th of January, 1822, was the fourth child of King Louis-Philippe. Educated, like his brothers, at the College Henri IV., he was distinguished in his studies. At seventeen he entered the army, and made his debût at the camp of Fontainebleau. Having for some time been a teacher in the school at Vincennes, he was, in 1839, promoted to be captain in the 4th of the Line. In 1840 he went as orderly-officer with his brother, the Duke of Orleans, whom he was most tenderly attached to, and went bravely through his first fight at the actions of the Affroun, the Col of Mouzaia, and the Olive Wood. The same year he obtained the rank of chef-de-bataillon and lieutenant-colonel. At that time (March, 1841) he returned to Africa, and, with his brother, the Duke de Nemours, took part in the campaign of Medeah and Milianah. Having caught a fever, he returned to France in July, 1841, and crossed France with great ovations ; just when he made his triumphal entry into Paris, at the head of the 11th Light, he and his brother, the Duke of Orleans, had a narrow escape of falling victims to the attempt of the republican Queuisset, on the 13th of September.

went back to Africa, doing duty in his rank. Thus, in 1841, he found himself, for the first time, under the orders of General Bugeaud. The Duke d'Aumale was then nineteen years of age.

We subjoin a bright, cheerful letter from him full of eagerness, like a trumpet-sound; and General Bugeaud's reply in the same strain :—

GENERAL.—As the King has appointed me to the vacant post of my rank in the 24th regiment of the line, I shall go to Africa in a few days to join my regiment; and hope to stay there a long time. I was determined to tell you myself, and as soon as possible, how glad I am and proud to serve under the orders of such a distinguished leader as yourself: and I will do my best to deserve your regard and justify the honour done me. I shall beg of you, General, to spare me no fatigue nor anything of any sort. I am young, strong, and a real cadet of Gascony; I must win my spurs.

After completing his military education at Courbevoie, the Duke d'Aumale, just made a marechal-de-camp, in October, 1842, returned to Algeria. He commanded the sub-district of Medeah, when, having been sent by the Governor-general, Bugeaud, in pursuit of Abdel-Kader, he captured the Emir's smalah, with surprising intrepidity and coolness, 16th of March, 1843. Made a lieutenant-general in the October of the same year, he received the chief command of the province of Constantine. In 1844 he commanded the expedition to Biskra, and distinguished himself in the campaigns against the Ziban and Ouled-Sultan. On the 25th of November he married the daughter of the Prince of Salerno, Marie-Caroline de Bourbon. He commanded the camp in the Gironde, 1845; took part in the pacification of Ouarcusenis in 1846. In 1847 he relieved General Bugeaud in the government of the colony, exercising a kind of vice-royalty. Abdel-Kader's surrender was the last act of his government. When the revolution broke out in February, 1848, he made over the government to General Cavaignac, and went to Gibraltar amid general regret. He then resided at Claremont and Twickenham, in England. Being heir of the Prince de Condé, and so very rich, he made a very fine collection of pictures and books.

After the fatal year 1870, and the fall of the Emperor, the Duke d'Aumale was elected representative of the department of the Oise by 52,222 votes. In the month of March, 1872, he was placed on the active list as general of division.

In 1873 he was nominated president of the court-martial on Marshal Bazaine; obliged to undertake it, he performed it so well that the intended snare only showed his discretion, and made him more popular.

Marshal MacMahon appointed him to the command of the Seventh Corps in 1873, and he was relieved according to a decree of 1879. The Duke d'Aumale was chosen a member of the Academy in 1871, and now takes no part in politics. He has even left Paris, and lives at Chantilly, where he keeps his wonderful collections.

I only make you one request; and that is, not to forget the Duke d'Aumale's regiment when there are blows to give and take.

Receive, General, the assurance of my respect,

Your affectionate

HENRI D'ORLEANS.

General Bugeaud's reply to the Duke was:—

Algiers, 6th March, 1841.

MY PRINCE,—The King is really spoiling me this year! It was not enough to have given me a mission that is the more honourable from its difficulty. His majesty is also willing to entrust two of the sons of France to my care! It is too much honour at once. But if I am confused at it, I am not alarmed. I do not fear the responsibility that such great marks of confidence impose upon me. Besides, my task is lightened by the presence of two princes; as the emulation, already so remarkable, in the Algerian army will be thereby augmented: and that is a pledge of success.

You, my prince, do not wish to be spared! I never had a notion of it. I will give you your fair share of the fatigues and dangers; you will know how to take your share of the glory.

Receive, &c.

BUGEAUD,

General.

END OF VOL. I.